Advance Praise for Inheritance

"When I started reading *Inheritance*, my first reaction was one word—WOW! I kept reading, and I was blown away. Police procedural? Yeah. Horror novel? That, too. But most importantly—one helluva novel. Joe tells a roaring good tale, and when you finish it, you'll have a lot to say, but WOW will be the first word out of your mouth."
—**Rick Hautala**, author of *Glimpses* and *Indian Summer*

"An artful haunting with the gloomy quality of a Terrance Malick crime drama"
—**Weston Ochse**, author of *SEAL Team 666*

"With Inheritance, Joe McKinney delivers a first-rate supernatural thriller with edge-of-your-seat suspense, a high-octane plot, and pitch-black horror. Add to this mix strong characterization and an insider's knowledge of law enforcement, and you have one of the best novels I've read in ages. I loved it!"
—**Tim Waggoner**, author of *The Harmony Society* and *Like Death*

"Joe McKinney has proven, yet again, that he is a true literary genius. *Inheritance* is a breath-taking thrill ride masterfully crafted to grip the reader, pulling them deep into the nightmares of its characters with a level of suspense that steals the breath from your lungs. Brilliant!"
— **Gabrielle Faust**, author of *Revenge* and *Eternal Vigilance*

"Joe McKinney delivers. *Inheritance* is a brisk, wry and deliriously creepy tale of family secrets and black magic that is guaranteed to get your goat!"
—**Harry Shannon**, author of *Dead and Gone* and *The Hungry*

"Joe McKinney writes with a confidence and clarity rarely seen. With *Inheritance*, he sets the chill factor high and tells a story that wraps around your spine and refuses to let go."
—**Nate Southard**, author of *Scavengers* and *Just Like Hell*

"Dead parents. A tormented cop. Pure evil. And that's just the beginning. From the brilliant mind of Joe McKinney comes *Inheritance*. A gift you don't want...but a story you must read!"
—**John C. Farris** of *Dead, Buried and Back*

"A harrowing pre-apocalyptic gem that will leave you in awe. I couldn't put it down!"
—**David Bernstein**, author of *Amongst the Dead*

"McKinney never fails to deliver. With *Inheritance* he's crafted a tale and characters that will inhabit you long after the last page."
—**David Dunwoody**, author of *The Harvest Cycle*

"Joe McKinney's *Inheritance* immediately joins the upper echelon of classic ghost novels. It is perfectly paced, balancing between moments of beautifully tragic drama and blood-chilling terror and suspense. Billing this as a 'Police-Procedural Thriller' does not do this masterpiece justice...with themes of loss and strained relationships, the occult, and the supernatural battle between good and evil, *Inheritance* examines some of the darkest places of the human heart and soul. This is the work of an author at the top of his game. *Inheritance* is simply riveting. I loved it."
—**Peter N. Dudar**, author of *A Requiem for Dead Flies*

"Each new work by Joe McKinney is more masterful than the last, bringing you in contact with real, dynamic, flesh and blood characters as you join them on their journeys into madness, horror and (sometimes) redemption. If this is your first McKinney tale, I envy you—you are about to experience the thrill of discovering a new favorite."
—**Mark Onspaugh**, author *Christmas Ghost Stories: A Collection of Winter Tales*

"*Inheritance* is one creepy story. I'll be a lifelong fan of anything McKinney writes. You should be, too!"
—**Ty Schwamberger**, author of *The Fields* and *DININ'*

"McKinney gets better with every book and *Inheritance* proves he's at the top of his game. Creepy and scary in some parts; reserved and lyrical in others. *Inheritance* seems like a very personal work for McKinney and you can feel the emotion and passion in every word. Don't miss this one!"
—**Anythinghorror.com**

Inheritance

Joe McKinney

Inheritance

Joe McKinney

To Sherri —
All my best.

Joe McKinney

Evil Jester Press

New York

Inheritance
Copyright © 2012 by Joe McKinney

First Edition

Edited by Peter Giglio

ISBN: 978-0615690896
Printed in the United States and the United Kingdom
First Printing: November 2012

1 2 3 4 5 6 7 8 9 10

Other books by Joe McKinney

*To my Mom and Dad, who,
thankfully, are nothing at all
like the mom and dad you're
about to meet.*

Nothing is very simple.
You must remember that certain things die out for a while
So that they can be remembered with affection
Later on and become holy.

—John Ashbery

sometimes the moon
and I discern a woman
I loved, drowning in secrets, fear wound round her throat
and choking her like hair. And this is she
with whom I tried to speak, whose hurt, expressive head
turning aside from pain, is dragged down deeper
where it cannot hear me,
and soon I shall know I was talking to my own soul

—Adrienne Rich

Prologue

Paul Henninger was eighteen, a senior in high school, when he saw his mother's ghost for the first time.

It was early October, late in the afternoon, and he was sitting in the passenger seat of Steve Sullivan's pickup truck, a bucket of KFC chicken in his lap, watching his house. All the big, commercial ranches around these parts had names—Double Js; Spriggs; Casa Navarro—but Paul's house wasn't one of those. Though it had been in his family for four generations, and was ostensibly a working commercial farm and ranch, he had never thought of it as anything more than a tired old farm, his father's house, the place where he and his father lived and worked.

The house stood knee deep in cheatgrass, nestled far back from the road in the shade of enormous, two hundred year old Spanish oaks that hung thick with ball moss, and sometimes in the summer with gauzelike colonies of web worms the size of lamp shades. The front porch was obscured behind a tangled screen of guajillo and chinaberry, so that from the driveway the place looked tumbledown, a derelict rotting in the weeds. But neither Paul nor his father worried much about appearances. They didn't use the front porch, and because it served no purpose in their daily lives, it got no attention. As long as Paul could remember it had been a graveyard of rusted machine parts and tools. Things went to the front of the house and were forgotten, like his mother. It was the back of the house, where the long, sloping metal roof was streaked with rust and the wood paneling had turned gray from decades of exposure to the harsh extremes of South Texas weather, where he and his father lived their lives. Everything of significance happened back there, away from the road.

Steve Sullivan was saying something, but Paul's mind was elsewhere. He was looking beyond the house to the ruined shell of the barn where his mother had hanged herself six years before. The day he came home and found her there had been on his mind a lot lately, even though his memories of that time were cloudy.

"You okay?" Steve asked.

He waited.

"Paul?"

"I said I'm fine."

"No you didn't. You haven't said a word."

Paul grunted. He looked back toward the house, lost in a dusty golden haze settling down through the trees.

Steve drummed his fingers on top of the steering wheel. "Hey Paul, if you don't want to go home, we could go driving around the lake. It might be fun, you know? Cut loose a little. It's been a hell of a week."

"Not tonight."

Again, Steve waited.

Finally, he said, "But you're still sitting here. What's wrong with you? Your dad's pissed about you signing with UTSA, isn't he? Christ, I told you he would be."

Paul sighed. He didn't want to explain this. He didn't even think he could. The University of Texas at San Antonio had offered him a full ride to play football, and he'd accepted the offer, but what was going on here had nothing to do with that. Steve's life revolved around football. And, for the most part, Paul's did, too. Except lately. Lately, ever since he started having flashbacks to his mother's death, football had faded into the background. But he couldn't make Steve understand that. His decision to stay close to Smithson Valley, and his father's farm, was tied to his mother's death with a knot he didn't feel smart enough to untangle. The problem was just too big. He couldn't see it all. But he sensed a connection there. What had happened six years ago with his mother was affecting the decisions he was making now. He just didn't see how. And that left him frustrated and bored with all the things that used to bring him such joy.

"Paul?" Steve said. "Dude, you okay?"

"I haven't told him," Paul admitted.

"You haven't...?" Steve suddenly smiled. "Bullshit. You're kidding, right?"

"No joke."

The smile slid off Steve's face.

"Dude, you're serious?"

Paul nodded, then opened the door and got out.

Inside the truck, Steve looked stunned. "You passed up a chance to play for the Cornhuskers and you didn't even talk to him about it?" Steve looked completely baffled. "We kind of all just assumed you'd...that'd he was making you..."

"No. He's been pushing Nebraska for two years now."

"Well, yeah. Christ, Paul, what are you gonna do?"

"It's my problem," Paul said. "Don't worry about it."

Paul walked away.

"Hey," Steve called after him. "What about this weekend? You wanna get some beers and head up to the lake with the girls? I don't know if you've noticed it or not, but all you'd have to do is look cross eyed at Jolene Arnold and she'd spread faster than—"

"Yeah, sure," Paul said. He waved over his shoulder as he walked away. "I'll see you tomorrow, Steve."

***

Steve's pickup pulled away from the driveway. Limestone pebbles popped beneath the truck's oversized tires as he accelerated up to speed, leaving Paul in a cloud of settling white dust. Late season crickets jumped in the grass all around him. The metal roof of the house was a checkerboard of dappled light and shadows, and from somewhere behind the house, he could hear the goats bleating.

Paul headed around to the back, where a screen door opened into the kitchen. Through the door he could see his father sitting cross-legged on the living room floor, all the lights off and the shades drawn. Martin Henninger was rocking back and forth and murmuring to himself while he constructed another of his lattice-like stick structures. Clearly his dad had been at it for some time, for this particular stick structure was already huge, a good three feet tall.

Paul went into the kitchen and put the bucket of chicken on the table. He didn't bother to announce himself. There wouldn't be any point to it anyway. When his father got into one of his spells—that was what his mother had called his father's meditative blackouts, during which he could sit for hours on the living room floor building his sculptures of sticks and baling wire—he was lost to the world. A train could crash through the house and he wouldn't notice. Paul slipped out again and went to feed the goats.

A dirt road led down past the barn and out to the fallow land that they called the horse pasture, even though there hadn't been horses to put there since before Paul was born. A haze of white dust hung over the road, depthless and still. The goats, big, dusky white Angoras, were not hungry, he could see that now. They were huddled together in a corner of the yard nearest the house, buzzing with a sort of mute agitation.

Rattlesnake, he thought tiredly. They were common enough here in the scrub brush of the Texas Hill Country.

"I'm coming," he muttered to the goats, and took the lock blade knife from his back pocket. If the snake was a little one he'd carry it off to the horse pasture and dump it in the brush. They were good and aggressive, got rid of the rats. But if it was a big one, one of the six footers that sometimes made their way up this far, he'd cut off its head and hang its hide on the barn door, for luck. There were already five others there.

He hadn't gone but a few steps towards the goats before movement out of the corner of his eye made him stop. His mother was standing by the corner of the barn in a yellow cotton sun dress that fit her rail-thin body like a potato sack on a pole. Strands of her long gray hair moved in the breeze across a face that was drawn and gray with sadness. Her eyes were sunken into her face, giving her a hollow, empty look that sent chills through him.

He had very few memories of her smiling when she was alive, and she wasn't smiling now. From what his father told him, she'd battled with a double-barreled curse of depression and anorexia for most of her life, and most of Paul's memories were of her sitting on the edge of the bed in the front room, huddled under a blanket, her eyes unfocused and vague. She looked like that now, fogged over, sad.

Paul stared back at her from across the yard, and though his heart was beating against his ribs like a wild bird in a cage, he couldn't move. He couldn't speak. He tried to lift a hand to do...he didn't know what...maybe wave, maybe try to touch her. But he couldn't even do that. His fingers seemed to weigh a ton.

He knew she wanted him to speak to her. On some level, he sensed that she needed him to speak, that she couldn't do whatever it was she wanted on her own. But he was too stricken to open his mouth. He couldn't get the words out.

She lowered her eyes and turned away. Sparks of sunlight scattered off the side of the barn and seemed to shoot right through her. She took a few steps toward the corner that led to the front of the barn and he lost her there in the shadows.

Then his voice came to him all at once, and he blurted out: "Momma? Momma, wait."

But she was gone.

Numb, Paul stumbled after her.

He rounded the corner of the barn and saw the front doors were open. The front doors of the barn were never open. His father was very particular about that, and a younger version of Paul had taken plenty of whippings to make sure the lesson took. But they were open now. Blades of grass came loose from the few bales of hay he and his father had stored up in the loft and fluttered down on the warm breeze that blew through the barn's shadowy gloom. A large sheet of mud-stained plastic moved listlessly, like a drape in an open kitchen window, from a nail on the wall to his left. Watching it, he remembered the day he found her, his mother. He and Steve, two twelve year old boys walking up the driveway through a maze of Comal County Sheriff's cars, wondering what in the hell was going on. There had been deputies everywhere. And here, in the barn, they'd seen his mother hanging by her neck from the rafters, the corpse stripped of the flesh from the waist down by wild hogs. A group of startled deputies who had been telling grim jokes near the body had come rushing forward to shoo them back outside, away from his mother and the flies that filled the barn's darkened stillness with their murmuring, and as they pulled him from the barn he'd taken one last look over his shoulder at the horror his mother had become.

But the barn was empty now.

She was gone.

***

"What are you doing out here, boy?"

Paul turned and faced his father. Martin Henninger was in his mid-fifties, a lean and weathered man. His face was clean-shaven and severe, deeply lined around the mouth. His arms were knotted with muscle, toughened by a lifetime of farm labor. He dressed in black pants, a heavily starched white shirt that was always buttoned at the neck and at the cuffs, even in the hottest part of the summer, and an old black Stetson hat. His dark eyes glinted like motor oil in the sun. They were the black eyes of a man who looked on everything, whether it was another human being, or a cut on his finger, or a dead deer on the side of the road, or even a twenty dollar bill he'd found on the sidewalk, with equal indifference.

"Who were you talking to?" his father asked.

"I was thinking about Momma," Paul said. He wanted to be defiant, like saying her name, her name to him anyway, somehow went out as a challenge, but he knew it was a fantasy and nothing more. His father was too strong, too...too much more than he could ever be. Though Paul was bigger than his father, faster, maybe even stronger, his father was infinitely more than he knew himself to be. The man was a force, a source of power, and Paul was only himself, a boy, a child, a thing that needed tending by this man, who knew better.

But if his father recognized the challenge, he showed no reaction, except to drive his hands down into his pockets and stare off at the deepening shadows spreading over the horse pasture. Paul felt suddenly dizzy and nauseous as his father probed his mind, trying to get into his head. Out of instinct, Paul cleared his thoughts and focused instead on nothingness. But his father's mind was strong, disciplined, insistent.

"You miss her?" Martin Henninger said suddenly.

Reluctantly, Paul nodded again.

"Yeah, well, I'll tell you what. How about the next time you find yourself out here talking to her, you tell her I miss her, too, okay? And maybe, if we both miss her hard enough, she'll climb up out of the ground and make us a fucking pot roast. I'd like that. Maybe she could clean the house while she's at it."

"Daddy, I—"

"Don't say anything, Paul. If you do, you'll just piss me off."

His father looked away from him then, his eyes sweeping the yard, taking in the goats, the tidal motion of the yellow cheatgrass blowing in the breeze, the whole sweep of a land that was as lonely as it was vast.

Paul could feel his father's hold on his mind slackening, and he sagged inward, as though he were a marionette whose strings had just been cut.

"Go feed the goats," he said.

Paul did as he was told. He went back into the barn and filled two large plastic buckets with feed, and when he came back out, his father was gone.

Paul went to work, pouring out little piles of green feed pellets along the road, the herd following along a few feet behind him. Between the full grown goats and the new crop of kids born earlier that summer, they had ninety-six animals. But the king of the herd was a huge two hundred and fifty pound billy that Paul called Oscar. Oscar always had to have the first pile of food. None of the others were dumb enough to challenge him for it. If they tried, he'd piss on their heads, the typical way one goat asserts dominance over another. He'd probably piss on the food they were trying to eat, too. Then, likely as not, he'd ram them into the ground. He'd killed a young billy that way last February.

After that, Paul had developed a system for feeding time. The first pile was Oscar's. He'd drop a mound of the green feed pellets up near the barn, then he'd head down the road a ways and drop most of the rest of the feed farther off. By the time he made it back to Oscar's pile, the big billy was usually about done. He'd drop the last handful or so on Oscar's pile and that was usually enough to keep him away while the others finished eating.

He went through his chores in a drowsy haze, still thinking of his mother. When he was done he walked back to the barn and hung the feed buckets up on the wall. He looked around. A part of him was hoping his mother would be there, waiting for him. But when he peered into the darkness of the barn's hold, it was empty.

Confused, and still a little light-headed from his encounter with his father, Paul walked back to the house. His father was standing in the doorway, holding the screen door open, watching him, waiting for him.

* * *

They ate at a small wooden table in the kitchen, heavy cloth drapes over the windows. The living room beyond the kitchen was dark, the floor strewn with machine parts and tools and spools of baling wire. The latest stick sculpture his father had made was smashed to bits in the corner. Sometimes he did that, smashed them right after he made them.

Martin Henninger ate methodically, turning each piece of chicken over and over in his hands, working every last strip of meat off the bone before discarding it and going on to the next. It was the same way he did everything, one thing at a time, painstakingly deliberate in every detail, however long it took.

Paul fished through the box, looking for a thigh. His father only ate the breasts and the drumsticks and Paul knew to avoid those.

"How're those new kids doing?" his father asked.

Paul looked up. They hardly ever spoke at the dinner table.

"They're fine, sir. They're getting plenty to eat from what I can tell."

His father grunted.

"That big son of a bitch isn't muscling them out, is he?"

"No sir," Paul said. That big son of a bitch was Oscar, but "that big son of a bitch" was as close as he'd ever get to a name from Paul's father, who thought that people who gave names to animals were idiots.

Martin Henninger grunted again and chased a spoonful of mashed potatoes around his Dixie plate with a plastic Spork. Paul watched him furtively, trying to decide if this was the right time to bring up his decision about UTSA.

"You're thinking about college," his father said, and Paul felt like he shouldn't have been surprised, even though he was, to find his thoughts so neatly laid out on the table, waiting to be stripped clean, like the chicken. "You made a decision, haven't you?"

"That's right," Paul said. He was alarmed. He hadn't even been aware of his father reaching into his head. Ordinarily, he knew it was happening, and sometimes he could withhold at least some of his thoughts. But this time his father had reached into his head without Paul even knowing.

"You have bad news. You're afraid I'm going to be angry."

"It's not bad news," Paul said, a little too hurriedly. "It's good news. I got an offer to play for UTSA."

Martin Henninger grunted, then took another bite of mashed potatoes. "You got a lot of offers, from what I hear."

"Yes sir. That's true."

"UTSA is a brand new program. It'd be a waste of your time. You want to go to Nebraska. The Big Ten can get you the kind of exposure you need."

"Well, yeah, Nebraska's a great program, but..."

"But what? What are you trying to say?"

"I decided to take the offer. I'm going to UTSA."

Martin Henninger dabbed at the corner of his mouth with a paper napkin, pushed his chair back, and stared at him. "Come again?"

"Yes, sir. I'm gonna stay here. It's a full ride. Everything's paid for, same as Nebraska."

"It's not the same as Nebraska, Paul."

"Yeah, I know, but Daddy, I want to stay here. In San Antonio. I want to stay with you."

"Why in the hell would you want to do that?"

"The farm, Daddy. Our farm. I want to work this land. I feel connected to it. I've been feeling like that's what I'm supposed to do, you know? Have you ever had that feeling? I've been thinking about this a lot lately. You know, really trying to get at what it is I'm supposed to be doing, and I think this is it. I want to be here with you. I want to be on this land."

Paul stopped there and waited for his father to say something, anything. But it didn't happen. Martin Henninger simply leaned over his plate again and started eating.

But between bites Paul heard him mutter, "Idiot."

***

That night, up in his room, Paul's eyes fluttered open in the dark, and the next moment he was wide awake. It wasn't an unpleasant feeling, rising so suddenly from a deep, dreamless sleep. But still, something felt wrong.

He lay on his side in his metal-framed twin bed, his back against the wall, watching his desk and chair and a few posters on the wall slowly take shape as his eyes adjusted to the dark. The moon was a faint sliver just behind the roof of the barn, and its light gave the window glass a bluish glow. He took a slow breath and stared at the window—not through it, but *at* it, listening.

The house creaked in the wind like an old boat. It made noise all the time, but he usually only noticed it at times like this, when everything was quiet and he was deep in thought.

Paul got out of bed and walked to the window. The yard below was lost in shadows, the grass moving with the wind, the goats sleeping in clusters around the yard.

He watched the corner of the barn where he had seen his mother standing. She wasn't there now, but of course he hadn't expected her to be. Seeing her there, standing there, hugging herself like she was miserably cold, he'd felt like he had electricity moving through his skin. He wasn't feeling that now. Now, all he felt was a deep, abiding emptiness.

He heard footsteps on the stairs, the old wood there creaking. Turning his head sharply towards his closed bedroom door, he listened to the steps coming closer to his door.

Daddy?

He moved quickly. Paul slipped on a pair of jeans and his tennis shoes, and when his father opened the bedroom door, Paul was standing there in the middle of the room, in the dark, fully dressed and waiting for him.

Martin Henninger's eyes were overbright, lit with an almost fevered intensity. And there were three strange-looking markings on his forehead. They looked like they'd been written with a fingertip dipped in wet ash.

Paul pointed at the markings. "Daddy, what's—"

"Come down to the barn with me," he said. He seemed short of breath, excited. "You wanted to stay. It's time you learned what there is to learn."

He turned and walked down the stairs.

Paul followed him out the back door and across the lawn. Wind moved through the Spanish oaks above them and moonlight colored the dirt road leading down to the horse pasture a bluish-silver. Paul was trembling, but not from the cool night air. He wanted to ask what was happening, but knew it wouldn't do any good. His father wouldn't answer.

But the next instant, they rounded the corner of the barn and Paul found himself looking in on the cavernous space inside, and he couldn't help himself.

"Daddy, what is...?"

"This is what it means to stay with me."

They were standing side by side now, looking into the barn.

Paul glanced at his father, and then at the barn. A faint tinge of wood smoke filled the air. Oscar was tied to one of the barn's support beams. One of the smaller males was standing beside him. The goats looked at Paul with black, glassy eyes. They made no noise, but Paul could see they were scared.

Arranged around the goats, in a half circle, were five of the strange, lattice-like stick sculptures his father had made. Each was different, each of them complex in their own strange architecture. Paul's gaze moved from one to the next, too confused to ask questions.

It took him a moment longer to realize the walls were covered with writing. With his mouth agape he scanned the words, if that was even what they were. They weren't in any language he could understand.

"Daddy, what is all this?"

"You wanted to stay, Paul. I tried to keep you away. I tried to get you to go as far away from here as possible. But you wouldn't go. So this is what there is. This is the world I have to give you."

Paul looked at his father. If what the man had said was meant as an apology, there was no trace of it in his expression. The same fevered intensity lit his eyes, and his skin was glistening with sweat. He looked crazed, and without thinking, Paul took a step back.

"I never got to prepare you, Paul. I'm sorry. When I went through this, I was more prepared than you are now. But the time is now. This won't wait."

"What...?"

"This is gonna terrify you. I know that. But you don't need to be afraid. It won't hurt. I promise. It'll make you stronger."

"I don't understand."

"Paul, I'm about to show you how to do things you've never imagined before. I can teach you how to control your world. I mean *really* control it, bend it to your will."

Paul took another step back. The alarms in his head were screaming.

"Stop!" his father commanded.

And suddenly, he couldn't move. His body felt numb, his legs weak. Something was in the barn with them. Something dark, focused, getting stronger. Paul felt it swirling all around him, moving up his spine like a cold shiver. He wasn't sure how he knew it, but Paul was certain the presence was feeding off the lattice-like stick sculptures his father had arranged around the barn. Somehow, they were focusing whatever this was, helping it to take shape.

The presence wrapped itself around Paul's chest. It was hard to breathe. The air smelled rich, intensely fragrant, like cedar. Paul felt nauseous, light-headed, and only at that moment did he realize the presence was trying to enter his head, trying to find a way inside his mind, though its grip was delicate, subtle, not at all like his father's brutal assaults.

Paul gasped in fear, his eyes wide open and staring all about the barn for some way to escape.

"Don't be frightened," his father said. "You can feel it, can't you? That's power, Paul. Raw, primal power. I'm going to show you how to use it, how to channel it to do whatever you want."

Martin Henninger closed his eyes, his lips parting.

"Daddy, let me go. Please."

His father snapped his eyes open again.

"I tried this once before, Paul, but that was a mistake. You were only twelve. I made you forget because it was too much for you. You were too young to have so much power." He pointed toward the stick lattices. "I was supposed to. The lenses told me to. But I couldn't. I resisted. I told myself right then I'd drive you away before I gave you so much power, but now I see I was a fool. You're meant for great things, Paul." He spread his arms wide to include the stick lattices and the smoking bowl and the goats and the writing on the walls. "You were meant for this."

He grabbed Paul by the shirt and pulled him deeper into the barn.

"Stand there. Don't move."

He let go of Paul's shirt, but Paul was too stunned to notice. His father put a hand on each of the goats' head.

The animals flinched, at first, and then calmed as though they'd been drugged. The smaller of the two sank to its knees and turned its head to expose its neck, its mouth open in a silent bleat.

The presence was stronger than ever now. The air had filled with an almost audible vibration. Paul could feel it sliding over his skin, and wanted to scream, to cry out, but couldn't. He could barely breathe.

Martin Henninger reached behind his back and brought out a large hunting knife.

Paul's eyes went wide, and still he couldn't move.

His father grabbed the smaller billy by the throat and lifted him into the air one-handed. Then, without hesitation, he gutted the animal, creating a long, jagged gash from the top of the ribcage down to the rectum.

The goat's guts spilled out on the floor, and Paul felt vomit rise in his throat.

He forced it back down.

After making the cut, Martin Henninger put the carcass on the ground at Paul's feet. Then he reached inside and removed the heart. He carried it, blood dripping between his fingers, to a wide, shallow brass bowl in the middle of the barn. Wood shavings were still smoking inside it. He put the bleeding heart into the bowl, and Paul heard the hiss of liquid meeting heat.

He turned to Paul and pointed at the post where Oscar still stood.

"Stand there, next to that big son of a bitch."

Whatever it was that held him loosened its grip. Paul could feel the blood running through his legs and arms again. He sensed his father's mind pushing him toward the barn's center support column.

"No," Paul said.

His father squinted at him. "Stand there."

"No way," Paul said, shaking his head. He tried to run for the door, but his father was faster. He grabbed Paul by the back of his neck and spun him around.

"Get the hell off!" Paul said, and threw a punch at the same time. It landed solidly at the corner of his father's jaw. But his father didn't go down. Martin Henninger turned his head to one side and spit blood onto the floor, then squared his shoulders at Paul. Paul barely had time to think before his father balled his left hand into a fist and shot a jab into his face.

He felt like he'd been hit in the mouth with a cinder block. He staggered backwards, arms pin-wheeling for balance. His front tooth was loose. Martin Henninger grabbed him by the front of his shirt and threw him against the support post.

The whole barn shook with the impact, and Paul, unable to keep his feet, slid down onto his butt, eyes blinking stupidly up at his father.

Martin Henninger took off his belt.

Paul, his vision swimming, felt the belt tightening around his neck, and his head snapped back against the post. He groped at the leather, but couldn't get his fingers under it.

His father twined the belt around his fist like a rodeo cowboy getting ready his ride, then reached into the shadows and came back with the wide, brass bowl. He dipped his thumb into the bowl of blood and ashes, tossed the bowl aside, and ran his thumb across Paul's forehead, leaving three shapes there.

"This is the name of truth," he said. "*emet, emet, emet.* It is my gift to you, Paul, and it marks you." Martin Henninger touched the marks on his own forehead with his fingertips, then touched the marks on Paul's forehead. "Wherever you go, this mark will be with you. As will I."

"No," Paul said, trying to shake his head. The word came out as a strangled pant. His vision was fuzzy at the edges, his fight to breathe a losing battle. He began to kick, trying to get a foot or a knee or anything between himself and his father.

"Be still, boy."

Paul tightened the muscles in his neck and strained against the leather with every bit of strength he had. He arched his whole body up, looking like an epileptic in the midst of a seizure. His father moved to one side to better keep his hold on the belt, and suddenly Paul had enough room to kick. He brought his knee up sharply and caught Martin Henninger in the ribcage hard enough to knock the wind out of him.

His father's grip on the belt loosened for just a moment, and Paul kicked him square in the chest, sending him tumbling backwards. Martin Henninger landed on his ass in front of their tractor's aerating attachment, his eyes suddenly going wide with pain. A strangled sound escaped him as he looked down and saw the aerator's tines poking through his chest.

The two of them sat there, looking at each other, the one dying, the other numbed by what he had just done.

"You aren't gonna stop this from happening," Martin Henninger said, wheezing, blood-veined bubbles forming on his lips. "I've marked you."

"No."

Martin Henninger coughed. Blood was filling his lungs. "You don't choose this, Paul," he said. "It chooses you."

"I don't want it," Paul said.

"It's already done. You've got a charge to keep."

"Take it back. Daddy, please. I don't want this."

"This thing picks its own time and place. It's my job to give this to you, to channel it into you. Death can't stop me from doing that. You have a charge to keep, Paul, and so do I. Make sure you're ready."

And then he was dead, his chest sagging like a tire going flat, his sightless eyes still staring into Paul's.

Six years later...

Chapter 1

Paul Henninger sat in the roll call room of the San Antonio Police Department's Eastside Service Area Substation with eighty other cops, nervously waiting out the final minutes before the lieutenant in charge of the shift came out of his office to deliver his briefing.

Paul had just completed nearly a year of training to become a cop. First, the standard seven month course of study at the San Antonio Police Department's Training Academy, where his instructors had taught him the legal stuff he needed to know to be a street cop in Texas, and then a seventeen week on-the-job training program where he'd been assigned to a Field Training Officer, an FTO, who was supposed to have taught him everything he needed to know to survive as a San Antonio street cop. Tonight was his first night without an FTO, the umbilical cord cut. Now he was in that phase of his career known throughout the Department as "breaking out," time to prove he had what it took to be one of San Antonio's finest.

He remembered what his instructors at the Academy had said. You build your reputation early. Make sure it's a good one, because it'll follow you the rest of your career.

Good to know there isn't any pressure to perform, he thought.

That night's worksheet was posted on a bulletin board on the front wall next to the lieutenant's office. Paul had read it on the way in, while he was milling about, waiting for the shift to start, trying to look like he belonged there. From the worksheet he learned that his new partner was a guy named Mike Garcia, and watching from his little corner of the room, he tried to sneak a look at the nametags of the other officers as they entered the room.

So far, he hadn't seen anybody named Garcia.

About the only thing he *had* noticed was an occasional officer glancing over at him, smiling wickedly as they crumpled up sheets of paper into hard little balls. It made him feel like somebody had tied a raw steak around his neck and tossed him into a bear cave.

His hands were moving in his lap, and for a moment, he could almost feel the cool greasy slide of baling wire in his fingers.

He stopped, arrested by the thought. *Why did I think that? Baling wire? I haven't touched that since...*

Chilled by the sudden memory of his father and the stick lattice sculptures he used to make, Paul reached into his pocket and took out the Barber fifty cent piece his wife Rachel had given him back in college, when they were dating. He rolled it back and forth over his knuckles, dropped it into his palm, and made a few passes over the coin with the other hand, making it disappear and then reappear again. It was a nervous habit, something to do with his hands. Something to take his mind away from unpleasant memories.

The lieutenant, a lean, balding man named Richard Green, emerged from his office and limped to the podium at the front of the room.

The laughing and paper crumpling stopped.

Green went over a couple of points from the Daily Bulletin as a few stragglers hustled in and took their seats, then he started reading the roll.

Paul kept an eye on the officers around him, waiting to see who would answer up when Green called Mike Garcia's name.

"Barris," Green said.

"Here, sir."

"Seles."

"Here, sir."

"Stokes."

"Here, sir." Laughing from the other side of the room.

"Collins."

"Present." More laughing.

"Garcia."

The laughing stopped and the entire opposite side of the room answered "Here, sir" all at once.

Lieutenant Green just shook his head and smiled. Next he called Paul's name and said, "You're riding with Mike Garcia. That's him over there." He pointed at the jokers along the opposite wall.

"Right here," said a big white guy, and raised his hand.

"Shut up, man," said a black female officer. "You ain't even Mexican. Right here, dude. I'm Mike."

Soon the whole room was at it.

Paul tried hard to smile.

The lieutenant cleared his throat and said, "Henninger, it's customary for the new guys to come up here and introduce themselves." Green stepped away from the podium, gesturing for Paul to take his place.

Paul hesitated. He looked around the room, uncertain what to do.

"Just tell us what you did before you became a policeman," Green said.

Feeling dizzy and embarrassed, Paul got up from his chair and went to the podium. He looked out at the sea of faces before him, all those hard-faced cops who weren't smiling anymore, and blurted out the first thing that came to mind. "My name is Paul—"

But he never got the chance to finish. As soon as he opened his mouth the entire room erupted with waded up paper balls, all of them flying at his head. Cat calls of "Shut up, boot!" and "Sit down!" came from every direction.

When the pelting was done, Green put a hand on his shoulder and silenced the room with a wave of his hand.

"All right," he said. "You guys get to work."

The room turned into an exodus as all eighty officers stood up at once and made their way towards the back door that led out to the parking lot. Paul nodded and smiled like an idiot as a long line of officers paraded by him. He shook hands with most of them and forgot their names as soon as they said them.

And at last an officer stopped in front of him and said, "Hi, I'm Mike."

Paul searched the man's plump, smiling face, half expecting another round of jokes. But when that didn't happen he nodded and shook the man's hand.

"Paul Henninger," he said.

"Damn," Mike said, "you're a big one, ain't ya? What are you, about six-four, two-thirty, two-forty?"

"Two-thirty," Paul said.

Mike whistled.

"Yeah, well, if we get into any fights, I'm gonna let you take it."

But looking at Mike, Paul got the feeling he didn't need much help when it came to fighting. He was probably five inches shorter than Paul, and Paul probably had thirty pounds on him at least, but Mike carried himself like a brawler, the Hispanic version of a tough Irish beat cop. All it took was one look into Mike Garcia's eyes and Paul knew there was grit there that he himself didn't possess. And though Mike's smile was friendly, Paul could still tell he was being summed up by an experienced street cop, that his measure had been taken.

He knows I'm scared shitless, Paul thought.

Lt. Green said, "Paul, when you're done getting my roll call room cleaned up, you and Mike need to see your sergeant."

"Yes, sir."

Mike handed him the trash can. "I'll see you in there," he said, and pointed to a room next to the Lieutenant's Office.

"Okay," he said. "Thanks."

"Hurry it up, though. I wanna go eat before it gets busy. Friday nights, we don't eat early, we won't get to eat at all."

After picking up the paper balls, Paul made his way to the Sergeants' Office. Mike was sitting across from a heavyset, ruddy-faced man in his early fifties. Two other sergeants shared the office, but they didn't bother to look at Paul. All of them were focused on an angry, gray haired man who was glowering at the sergeant next to Mike.

"I don't care if they are good workers," the man said. He was a detective. Paul could see that now. He wore a blue golf shirt tucked into neatly pressed jeans. A silver detective's badge, with its distinctive black stripe across the front, just above the badge number, was hooked over his brown leather belt. He didn't seem to be wearing a gun, though. Not even the little short-barreled Glock 27 favored by so many of the detectives Paul had seen.

The man was definitely angry.

"They screwed up a murder investigation," he was saying.

"No, come on, Keith," the sergeant next to Mike said, and Paul figured the uniformed sergeant must be Stephen Garwin, who was listed on the worksheets as Paul's section supervisor, his new boss. "That's a little harsh, don't you think, Keith? Collins and Stokes are good cops. Maybe they made a mistake, but I hardly think that's—"

"A mistake?" the detective blurted out. "A *mistake?* Sarge, you gotta be kidding me. You've read the same reports I have, right? Those two idiots charged into that house without a warrant, without anything even remotely close to probable cause, pulled my suspect out of his own house, and proceeded to kick his ass on the front lawn. His entire neighborhood saw it. You say they're good cops, but from where I'm standing, it looks like some staggeringly sloppy police work. His lawyer is already pressuring the DA to drop the charges. And you know what? It's starting to look like that's gonna happen."

"My men did get a warrant, Detective Anderson."

"Yeah, after they searched the place. *After.*" The detective stared about the room, a look of righteous incredulity on his face. He looked like he was begging someone else to acknowledge how wrong all of this was.

Sergeant Garwin crossed his arms over his chest. "I'm gonna stand behind my men, Detective Anderson."

The detective scoffed at him. "That's great," he said. "That's really great, Sarge. I'm sure the jury that acquits this slime ball is gonna be thrilled to know you stand behind your men."

"Now just a minute, Detective." Garwin looked offended. Not angry, Paul thought, offended. That seemed strange to him. He was trying to sound angry. But Paul could sense that his ire wasn't really up. The detective waited for Garwin to go on, a challenging sneer on his face, but Garwin only blinked at him.

He's backing down, Paul thought, not believing what he was seeing. Sergeant Garwin looked almost impotent, like he knew he was arguing on the wrong side of the issue but was too proud or too committed to back down now.

The detective must have sensed the same thing, for he huffed impatiently and turned away from Garwin.

Paul was amazed. He had never seen anyone, even a seasoned detective, as this Keith Anderson no doubt was, take such an attitude with a uniformed sergeant. In the SAPD, the sergeant was the front line supervisor, and Paul had learned to hold them in fear and awe in the short time he'd been on the Department. Anything a Patrolman or a Detective needed, as an employee of the City, had to go through a sergeant for approval. They were the ones who disciplined you when you screwed up. They were the ones who wrote your merits when you did a good job. They approved your vacation, investigated your car crashes, did your performance evaluations, and sometimes showed up at the major scenes you were involved in to fix a situation that had gone completely wrong. They were the brass gods of the street, the Department's guiding hand, and Paul would no sooner take a disrespectful tone with one than he would slap a tiger across the snout.

"Frankly," the detective said, waving his hand in the air like all of this was pointless now, "I don't know how I'm gonna do damage control on this one. I had Hector Avalos on four murder counts." He held up the appropriate number of fingers. "Four. But your men screwed it up, Sarge. Thanks to them, this case has just taken a major nose dive, and I want to know what you're gonna do about it."

"I told you," Garwin said. "I'm gonna—"

"Yeah, yeah," Anderson said with another dismissive wave of his hand. "You're gonna stand by your men. I heard you."

Why wasn't anybody doing anything about this? Paul wondered. There were three sergeants in the room. One of them should have been chewing this detective's ass by now. But it wasn't happening. They were all just sitting there, taking it.

And then Mike spoke up. "Detective Anderson, I hate to say it, but I think you're full of crap."

The detective wheeled on him. "Excuse me?"

"You heard me. You don't have half the case on Avalos you claim you do. You're just pissed that a bunch of patrolmen got the probable cause you couldn't find."

"You mean the probable cause they found doing an illegal search?"

"There was no illegal search."

"Like hell—"

"Yeah, like hell. I know. I was there."

Anderson's eyebrows shot up. "Oh yeah? You were there, were you? So I have you to thank for this mess as well, huh?"

"It was a legal search."

"You call kicking down a man's door without a warrant, tearing his home apart, then beating him to a pulp in front of his neighbors a legal search? Please, explain that to me, Officer Garcia. I'm dying to know."

"They heard a girl screaming. That's why they made entry."

"A girl?"

"You read the reports. Cynthia Avalos, Hector's daughter. The one he was beating the shit out of when Wes and Collins showed up. She had a black eye, a busted lip. You saw that right?"

"Yeah, I read that in the report." Suddenly Anderson's tone had softened. He was looking at Mike now, interested despite his anger.

"They thought someone was being assaulted. So, they entered."

"The girl denied anything was going on."

"Of course she did," Mike said. "She's fourteen. What do you expect her to say, especially when we took her daddy away from her?"

"So what are you saying?"

"I'm saying Wes and Collins went inside to prevent the imminent consequences of family violence. Once inside, they saw the guns, they saw the stuff Hector Avalos had stolen from the Best Value Pawn robbery. It still had the tags on it. It was a no brainer. Wes and Collins knew right away what they were looking at."

Anderson was nodding, as though pieces were falling into place in his mind, connections were being made.

"Okay," he said, waiting for Mike to go on.

"They did a protective sweep," Mike said. "They searched the house for other people who might be present to destroy evidence, and then they got out of there. When I arrived, I instructed them to get a warrant based on the things they saw during their initial entry, which was made under exigent circumstances. Everything's above board. It's a legal search."

Anderson worked his jaw around like he was chewing gum. "Yeah, but that's not in any of the reports," he said.

"I don't know why," Mike countered. "I turned in my report. It was all there, just as I told it to you."

"Well, I don't have it."

"Reports get lost," Mike said. "Those folks from the Records Unit are notoriously sloppy."

Slowly, a smile spread across Anderson's face. "You think maybe you could make sure that lost report gets to Records? That could, uh, potentially salvage this case."

"Yeah," Mike said. "Sure. I bet I have a copy somewhere."

"Alright." And with that, Anderson spun around and nearly ran into Paul's chest. He looked up at Paul, who was easily a head taller than the detective, and scowled. "Excuse me," he said, his tone implying that it was Paul who had done something wrong.

Paul stepped out of the way and let the detective pass.

He looked back at Mike, a *What did I do?* look on his face.

Mike gestured toward the chair opposite Sergeant Garwin with a quick nod of his chin. He turned to Garwin and said, "Well, that sucked."

The female sergeant behind him laughed.

Garwin didn't say anything, but it was obvious that Mike's joke had broken the tension in the room.

"Paul," Mike said, "this is Sergeant Stephen Garwin. He's in charge of the Forty-four Section, so he's our direct supervisor. Over there is Sergeant George Catton—he runs the Forty-two Section. And that's Sergeant Gloria Naylor. She runs the Forty-three Section."

The other two sergeants nodded to him and Paul nodded back. Then he shook hands with Garwin, who seemed to have already recovered his wits. His back looked straighter, his shoulders squared, and suddenly, he looked like one accustomed to command. He was a different man, definitely, than the one who had just stalled out in front of Detective Anderson.

"Good to meet you, sir," Paul said.

"You too, bud. Welcome to East Patrol."

"Thank you."

"You married, Paul?" Garwin asked.

Paul hesitated. His mind was still on the scene he had just witnessed, but it seemed like Sergeant Garwin had forgotten it and was now intent on interviewing him.

Paul forced himself to readjust. "Yes, sir," he said. "For about a year and a half now. My wife's name is Rachel."

"Outstanding," Garwin said. "Marriage is a wonderful thing. I liked it so much I did it four times."

Paul blinked at him, and both Garwin and Mike laughed.

"I'm trying to catch up with Mike here," Garwin said.

Paul looked at Mike, who shrugged.

"How about kids?" Garwin asked.

"None."

"That's okay. Where'd you come from, college or the military?"

"College," Paul said. "UTSA."

"Major?"

"Criminal Justice."

"That figures. You play ball?"

"Yes, sir," Paul said.

"What'd you play?"

"Linebacker."

"You any good?"

"I was okay, sir. Not good enough to go pro, but pretty good."

"Well, the fact that you played college ball is still pretty impressive. I like it when my officers can take care of themselves."

Paul nodded. "I hope to do just that, sir."

"I'm sure you will, bud. There's only a couple things I ask."

Paul waited.

"First off, don't be late to roll call. I hate that. Secondly, turn in good reports. Mike here will help you with what I want. And if you screw up, admit it. I really hate it when officers don't accept responsibility for their actions. That's big with me. I get enough of that stupidity from the public, so I definitely don't want it from my own officers. Besides, if you do screw up—and it's gonna happen, believe me—I can help you out of it as long as you tell me the truth up front. If you lie to me...well, don't do that, okay? If you lie to me, I'll hang you out to dry."

"Understood," Paul said.

"Outstanding. Now the two of you need to get out there."

Mike nodded.

Paul looked from his new partner to Garwin. It took him a moment to realize he was being dismissed.

Still feeling confused, he nodded, then rose to his feet.

Mike motioned to Paul to follow him and they both turned to go. They made it as far as the doorway before Garwin stopped them.

"Hey Mike..." he said.

"Yes sir?"

"Do me a favor, would you, bud?"

"What's that, sir?"

Garwin suddenly looked uncomfortable. He had the same slumped shoulder aspect he had just a few moments earlier with Detective Anderson.

Strong-willed subordinates scare him, Paul realized then. Detective Anderson, and Mike here, they scared Garwin.

"Yes sir?" Mike said.

Garwin wouldn't look at him. He fidgeted with a pen on his desk, glanced at his computer monitor. He seemed to be looking everywhere but at Mike, refusing to meet the officer's smiling face.

Finally he said, "Barris told me somebody put a passed out homeless guy in the backseat of their car while they were at lunch. Apparently, the guy vomited all over the car. You know anything about that?"

Mike looked shocked, but not convincingly so. "Who, me? No, sir."

"Uh huh. Listen, no more pranks on him, okay? I mean it. Some guys just can't take a joke."

Mike gave him a flyboy salute. "You got it, sir."

But when he turned back to Paul he winked.

***

They headed out the back door, towards the parking lot behind the substation where East Patrol's squad cars were parked.

"That's our car over there," Mike said. "You got your gear with you?"

"It's in my truck."

"Okay. We'll get it in a bit. For now, let's just wait."

"For what?"

"You'll see." Mike stood there for a moment, hands in his pockets, rocking back and forth on his heels. Then, abruptly, he turned to Paul and said, "Hey, what were you doing with that coin before roll call?"

Paul took the Barber out of his pocket. "Coin tricks," he said, and handed the Barber to Mike.

"It's heavier than it looks."

"It's a Barber fifty piece," Paul said.

"Why do they call it a Barber?"

"It's named after Charles E. Barber. He was the head engraver at the U.S. Mint for a while."

Mike held the coin up to the sodium vapor lights. "Nineteen-oh-one?" he said, reading the date at the bottom. "Damn. Is this thing valuable?"

"Not really. They made a bunch of them. That one's not even close to mint condition. And even if it was, it'd only be worth a few bucks."

"Yeah, well, something that old is still pretty cool."

He handed it back to Paul. "Hey, show me a trick. We got a minute."

Paul was used to this. People who saw the tricks he could do always asked for more. He flicked the coin into the air, caught it, then rolled it back and forth over the back of his knuckles and dropped it into his palm. He waved the other hand over it and the Barber disappeared. He waved the hand back again and the Barber reappeared.

"Bad ass," Mike said. "Do another one."

Paul made the coin disappear again. He held up his hands and showed Mike his palms, turned them over, showed him the backs of his hands. Then he reached into his shirt pocket and fished around.

His smile faded.

"Hmmm," he said.

"What's wrong? Didn't work?"

Paul took his hand out of his pocket. No coin.

"That's weird," Paul said.

Mike smiled patiently. "You wanna try it again?"

"No," Paul said, still frowning. He looked on the ground. "It's around here somewhere."

"I didn't hear it drop," Mike said. He started looking around on the ground, too.

"No. Me either. Hey, check your pocket. Maybe you got it."

Mike gave him an amused, *Yeah, right* look. He reached into his pocket and felt the coin. "Holy shit!" He pulled out the coin and looked at it, dumbfounded. "How'd you do that? I didn't even feel you put it in my pocket."

Paul smiled and took the coin.

"Seriously, that was amazing. How'd you do that?"

Paul shrugged.

"You gotta show me how to do that," Mike said.

"Okay." He was about to take it out again and show Mike the basic palm hide when Mike stopped him.

"Wait a sec. I want you to meet these guys."

They had drifted over to their car and were standing by the trunk, Mike nodding at two officers walking across the parking lot towards them.

"I hang out with these guys a lot," Mike said. "They're the regular 44-60."

"And we're 44-70, right?"

Mike nodded.

"Paul, meet Wes and Collins."

Wes was Wesley Stokes. He had to be six-eight, and was probably pushing three hundred pounds. He wore his sandy brown hair in a tight crew cut that made his head look small and bullet-shaped.

"Hey," he said to Paul. He shook Paul's hand, his hand swallowing Paul's, which was an odd feeling for somebody accustomed to being the biggest guy in the room, then turned away and started checking Facebook on his phone.

Paul turned to the other officer. His name was Chris Collins. He was squat and muscular, box-shaped, with an almost perfect helmet of black hair slicked back with what had to be a gallon of gel. He stood with his hands crossed over his chest, chewing on his lip, an expression on his face that suggested all of this was a big hassle he didn't need.

"How's it going?" Paul said, offering him his hand.

"Fucking crappy."

Paul blinked.

Collins didn't smile. "Every day I gotta come back to this hellhole fucking sucks."

Paul just stared at him.

Mike gave Paul a nudge. "Ignore him." He turned to Collins. "Tone it down for the new guy, would you?"

"Why? He's gonna find out how much this place fucking sucks soon enough."

"This guy, he makes a career out of bitching," Mike said. "I'm about to start calling him Monica, after my ex-wife. She was a little bitch, too."

"Yeah, I got your little bitch right here."

Mike laughed at him. "Wes, were they in there?"

Wes put his phone back in his shirt pocket and chuckled a little. "Yeah. They should be coming out here in a sec."

Even Collins cracked a smile.

These three guys, Paul sensed, were old friends. They were tight. He could tell it just by listening to them.

"What's going on?" Paul asked.

"First lesson of survival out here," Mike said. "What I do, whenever this job drives me so fucking nuts I can't stand myself, is pull a good prank on Barris and Seles. Keeping those two in misery boosts my morale."

The four of them stood in a huddle. From where he stood Paul had a view of Barris and Seles walking across the parking lot to their patrol car. Barris put his gear bag down on the ground next to the trunk and fished through his key chain for the right keys. Seles glanced down at his car and scratched his head.

And then he dropped his gear bag and said something to Barris, who stopped what he was doing and looked at what his partner was pointing at.

Paul didn't see what Mike had done until Seles rapped his knuckles on the back quarter panel. All the patrol cars were white Ford Crown Victorias with a thick blue stripe down the sides. Written in red decal letters above the top stripe was 1-800-CRIME STOPPERS. Every car had the logo, but on Barris and Seles' car the letters now read 1-800-PIMP STOMPERS.

"Holy crap," Paul said. He turned to Mike. "How did you do that?"

"I disavow all knowledge," Mike said. "But I would imagine all it would take is getting in good with the guys in the body shop. If someone were to do that, he could probably get hooked up with all the decals he wanted. Not like I would know, though."

"No," Paul said, "of course not. But didn't Garwin just tell you—"

"A little secret about Garwin. Whenever he tells you to do something just smile and nod and he'll go away happy. Then you go back to doing whatever it was you were doing in the first place."

Barris turned towards them. "That's real funny, Wes. Nice."

"What?" Wes said. He looked genuinely indignant. "I didn't do anything."

"You guys are the only ones who think this shit is funny, you know that? You behave like children."

"It wasn't..." he said to Barris, then turned to the others. "He thinks it was me. Why does he always think it's me?"

Barris and Seles got in their car and drove off in tire-smoking hurry, Barris with one hand out the window and his finger up in the air.

Mike, Wes, and Collins all laughed. Paul felt like he'd fallen into a good thing with these guys. They were cool, and they were making him feel welcome.

"We're going to the Cave, right?" Collins asked. "My blood sugar's gonna crash if we don't eat soon."

Just then, an emergency tone sounded on their radios. Instantly, the other three officers stopped talking and focused on the radio. Paul watched them. It still intrigued him, even after nearly a year on the Department, how an emergency tone could instantly silence any conversation.

"In Fifty-two Seventy's," a dispatcher said. "High Street and Garden Ridge, I have a shooting with a hit, clearing all but West."

All the way across the city, Paul thought. Not our service area.

"We'll meet you there," Mike said, picking up the conversation as though the tone had never sounded. To Paul he said, "We better eat quick. When they start killing each other early like this, it means we're in for a hell of a night."

Chapter 2

Detective Bobby Cantrell turned off the Chevy's headlights as they left the main road and pulled into the south entrance of the old Morgan Rollins Iron Works factory. He parked just inside the gate, which was little more than a remnant now, a rusted ribbon of metal hanging from a leaning post, and told his partner, "We're gonna walk from here."

As they got out of the car, his partner, Detective Raul Herrera, looked up at the silhouetted ruins of the old factory and whistled. The place looked like the skyline of some war-torn, bombed-out city, backlit by the hazy orange glow of the San Antonio skyline many miles to the west. He frowned. This place felt weird. Wrong somehow. Off to their right was a train yard. He could see the tops of old trains rusting on the tracks. Beyond that he had a view of the sprawling slums of San Antonio's East Side. There was urban desolation everywhere he turned. There was misery everywhere he looked, but at least it was a living, breathing place. Not here, though. Not this factory. This place felt dead. He shivered, despite the heat.

Which was something else altogether. It'd been dark for hours, but it was still miserably hot, and he could feel the baked-in smell of rot and corruption that emanated from the old factory.

"You didn't want to get any closer?" Herrera asked, rubbing a hand over the back of his neck. It was damp with sweat and gritty from all the dust in the air.

"This is fine," Cantrell said. "They may be just a bunch of junkies, but if they see us coming they'll take off for sure."

As he spoke, Cantrell studied the outline of the old factory, looking for the best place to enter. The problem wasn't the junkies. Most of them were so browned out they wouldn't know what hit them until the handcuffs bit down on their wrists. The real problem was the structure itself. It had been falling apart for twenty years, since the company closed it down. There were catwalks up there that looked sound, but would collapse under a man's weight without warning. He and the other detectives on the San Antonio Police Department's Narcotics Unit had been lucky so far. No accidents. He wanted to keep it that way.

"What did you call this place again?"

"The Shooter's Gallery," Cantrell said, still watching the structure.

"And we can make our cases here?"

Cantrell glanced over the roof of the car at his new partner. It suddenly occurred to him that he might have a lot of ground to cover with Herrera.

"Didn't you grow up in San Antonio?" Cantrell asked.

"Houston."

"And you never worked the East Side when you were on Patrol?"

"Two years on South, five on Central."

"Never heard this place come out on the radio?"

Herrera shook his head. "Not that I can remember."

Cantrell closed his door and walked up to the front of the car. "Well, welcome to The Shooter's Gallery. We got junkies by the dozens here. And enough brown tar heroin to make the Mexican Mafia blush."

"Really?" Herrera said, wide-eyed.

"Oh, yeah. It's a gold mine in there."

Herrera glanced up at the factory, then back to Cantrell. "If it's that good, how come we don't sweep the place? Get them all in one shot."

Cantrell just laughed.

"What's so funny?"

"Raul, when you were working a district on Patrol, didn't you have a favorite honey hole where you'd go to write a few quick tickets to keep the sergeant off your ass?"

"Yeah."

"Okay, well, The Shooter's Gallery is ours. We knock out our small cases here and then go on to the bigger stuff later."

Herrera glanced over the factory in silence, but he was obviously disappointed. Cantrell knew the look. Most patrolmen who promoted directly into Narcotics had casino eyes. They were looking for the big busts, the eighteen wheelers full of cocaine, the sophisticated methamphetamine labs, the cornfields full of pot. When they learned that the little bullshit cases were the real meat and potatoes of the job, they looked a lot like Herrera looked now.

"Alright," Cantrell said, because he felt like he owed it to the new guys to set them straight, "you remember when Sarge told you he expects six felony cases every month?"

"Yeah."

"Well, I'll let you in on a little secret. There's nobody big in there—just a bunch of burned-out bottom-feeders who live for their next high. The name of the game is quantity, not quality. What we do is come in here and pop six small time cases every month for one or two balloons a piece. That covers our six felonies with the Sarge. After that, you can focus on making your real cases, your big ones. You just got to learn the game. Give them the numbers *they* want, and then you can spend the rest of the month doing whatever *you* want."

"And it's just that simple?"

"Just that simple," Cantrell said. "Come on. Let's go make some numbers."

***

Cantrell led the way up to the main part of the factory and pointed out the rough spots for Herrera to avoid. By the time they'd made it to the hive-like series of corridors in the superstructure, where most of the junkies shot up, they'd already spotted a few who were passed out and riding their highs in quiet little corners.

"You don't want any of them?" Herrera asked.

"No."

"Why not?"

Cantrell looked around before he answered. When he spoke again, it was in a whisper. "The ones out here have already shot up. We want the ones closer in to the courtyard. They shoot up there and stumble out here to sleep. You're only gonna find dope on the ones still inside the Gallery."

Herrera nodded. Cantrell watched his trainee's gaze shift down to the ground. Cantrell didn't like knocking the new guys down like that, but sometimes it had to be done. Patrolmen came to Narcotics with a skewed sense of tactics. They approached everything with the beat cop's mindset of visible authority and control. The bodies folded up in the shadows of the superstructure were a good example. Herrera was having obvious trouble passing them by. He clearly wanted to go over and check out every one. Teaching the new guys to blend in to a bad situation, to accept the kinds of tactical risks no beat cop would ever take, was one of the hardest lessons to pass on.

They passed a man sitting in the dust, his back against a wall of corrugated tin, head slumped down between his knees, the ground dark and wet between his legs. His hands were open on the ground next to his feet. Cantrell glanced at him, then moved deeper into the ruins of the factory.

But Herrera hung back. He took his Stinger MiniLight from his back pocket and lit the guy up with a quick flash.

Cantrell spun around on him and hissed, "What are you doing? Kill that light."

"I think he's dead," Herrera said.

"What?" Cantrell paused for a second, then walked closer. "No."

"Yeah, I think so."

Cantrell lit the man up with his own flashlight. He saw the puddle between the man's legs, a red rope of something that looked like fish guts hanging from his lips. He knelt down in front of the man and turned his light up into the man's face. The eyes were wide open and the corneas were already clouding over.

"Fuck."

"What is it?" Herrera asked. "Overdose?"

"No. Look at his face."

Herrera knelt down next to him and his eyes went wide. The left side of the dead guy's face looked like somebody had beat on it with a hammer.

"What's that written on his face?" Herrera asked. "You see that, there on his forehead?"

Cantrell shook his head in disgust. "This is fucking perfect. This place is a bust now. Homicide's gonna want to shut it down for sure."

"Seriously, Bobby, what is that stuff written on his face? Gang graffiti?"

Cantrell studied the body without answering.

"We need to canvass the area, right?" Herrera asked. "See if anybody saw anything."

"Yeah, right. You're gonna get some great witnesses out of these oxygen thieves. I'll tell you what this is. This here is misdemeanor homicide. Ain't nobody gonna be broken up this piece of shit's dead."

"Still, we ought to—"

"Fine," said Cantrell. "We'll sweep the area."

There was another man sitting in the shadows just a few yards away from the body, and Herrera walked over to him carefully, his gun snug against his thigh. He kicked the man's foot, hard.

"Get up," he said.

The man didn't move.

Herrera kicked him again, even harder. "Come on, asshole. Get up. I want to talk to you." The man fell over onto his side, landing face up. His face was smashed, just like the other junkie, the same strange symbols scrawled across his forehead. "Holy shit!" Herrera backed away from him. "Cantrell! Hey Cantrell, I got another one over here."

Cantrell was standing next to him a moment later with his gun in his hand.

Herrera lit up the body with his flashlight. "Look at his face," Herrera said.

Cantrell shook his head.

Herrera moved his flashlight over the rest of the scene. They were standing in what amounted to a long corridor. The walls on either side of them were rusted sheets of corrugated metal that the resident dopers had covered with blankets and piled high with trash. There were three more bodies further down the corridor, all of them dead, and it looked like parts of the walls were spattered with blood. Somebody had gone through here and torn everything to pieces. Walls, clothing, blankets, trash, bodies—everything was destroyed. Herrera thought, *Run a tornado through a homeless shelter and this is what you'd have left over.*

He started to speak, but Cantrell put up his hand to silence him.

"Shhh," he hissed. "Listen."

Herrera stood perfectly still. Somewhere in the darkened gloom ahead of them, a goat was bleating quietly. He looked at Cantrell for guidance, but Cantrell's eyes were focused on the dark.

***

Both men had their weapons ready. They covered each other as they moved out, leap-frogging past each other, taking the hallway in stages all the way to the far end, where the hallway opened up on an immense circular chamber with no ceiling. The walls around it were twenty feet high at least. Three gray, crumbling smokestacks jutted up against the ash gray sky beyond the rim of the far wall. The air smelled like blood and the horrible gut-wrenching stench of decay.

There were bodies everywhere.

Most looked like they'd been beat to death with a bat.

A weird-looking white goat was standing in the middle of the chamber, looking at them with black, glassy eyes. Another just like it, white and shaggy like a sheepdog, was nearby. It had been carved, neck to belly, so that now the carcass was open on the ground like a canoe.

Something glinted off to their left, and both men immediately turned to the man seated cross-legged in the shadows. He wore a white, long-sleeved shirt, black pants, and a black Stetson cowboy hat. His hands were working furiously on a three foot high pile of sticks that he was tying together with baling wire while he rocked back and forth, murmuring in a language they couldn't understand.

Cantrell tried to tell the man to show his hands, but couldn't quite get the words out. He was stammering, choking, like he had a walnut crammed down his throat. He tried to raise his gun, but it felt heavy in his hand. Part of his mind was screaming at him to get his gun up, front sight on target, scan the area for additional threats, but that was a small part, a distant far away part.

He glanced at Herrera. The detective was standing too close to the man, his hands hanging limply at his side. To Cantrell he looked like a deer caught in headlights, frozen with fear.

"Get back!" Cantrell tried to scream. But the words still wouldn't come.

The man on the floor glanced up at Herrera, though his hands never stopped lashing the sticks together. His forehead was marked with the same three symbols they'd seen on the bodies out in the corridor. His eyes were solid white, like they'd turned up into his head, and his mouth was hanging open, no teeth showing behind the man's razor thin lips.

The man's hands stopped moving. The next instant, he rose to his feet in a series of jerks and starts, like a drunk moving through a darkened club under a strobe light.

The strike was so fast and vicious that Herrera never even had a chance to react. The man punched out at him with one hand, locking an iron grip around his throat with a force that bent him over backwards like his spine was made from a rope of licorice.

Cantrell fell backwards with a whimper. He felt a horrible nausea wash over him, the bile rising in his throat, his strength slipping away.

Somehow, he made himself move. He brought his pistol up and fired twice into the looming figure, but the man in the starched white shirt and black Stetson didn't seem to notice the bullets pounding into his chest.

Cantrell turned and ran down the corridor, hitting his radio's emergency tone the whole way.

He ran past the bodies they had seen on the way in without really seeing them. Panic blinded him. He rounded the first corner he came to, and found himself facing a wall. He turned left, then right, and as his panic mounted he felt the fetid stench of decay crashing down around him, suffocating him.

He sensed the man in the black Stetson behind him and turned to face him.

He raised his pistol but couldn't make himself shoot. It was as if the man's very presence was sucking away his will to fight. He could feel himself weakening as the man drew nearer.

He fell to his knees and sobbed. "Please dear God don't," he said, the word's coming out all at once, slurred together.

A white, shaggy goat emerged from the circular chamber behind the man.

Cantrell looked up again into the man's face, but couldn't make out his features. He was veiled in heat shimmers. The man reached out a dried, mummified hand, the skin cracked and discolored, like old parchment, and as the fingers sought out his throat, pushing his chin out of the way, Cantrell knew that this was the end.

Chapter 3

Mike gunned the Ford onto Houston Street, the main road that ran in front of the Eastside Substation, the big V8 winding up under his expert touch, the car's back end sliding into oversteer. All Paul could do was hold onto the dashboard, his stomach rising into his throat as Mike shot around a slow-moving Coca Cola truck and into traffic.

"Jesus," Paul said. His mouth had gone dry. He looked at Mike. "What's the rush?"

Smiling to himself, Mike slid around a turn and accelerated hard onto a straightaway. He's trying to impress me, Paul thought. He's the alpha dog, that's what this is.

Beside him, Mike chuckled.

This is pointless, Paul thought. He leaned back into his seat and tried to keep from getting car sick.

"Listen," Mike said, after they'd gone a couple of blocks, "don't take that shit that Collins says personally, okay? He's just pleasantly disgruntled."

"What does that mean?" Paul had to speak up to hear himself over the Metallica Mike liked to listen to while he drove.

"He's a good guy," Mike said. "He's just a little—aw, fuck!"

Mike jogged the wheel slightly to the right, then turned a U-turn so hard it threw Paul against the passenger door.

"What's going on?" Paul managed. He was holding onto the dashboard like it was the edge of a cliff. Before he had been irritated with Mike for showing off like this, but now, with the tires shrieking on the pavement, he was starting to get scared.

"Drug buy," Mike said. The smile was gone from his face now. His lips had pulled inward, his gaze lasered in on a small section of parking lot across the street.

They drove into the lot at high speed. The tiny stretch of cement was lit with weak, yellowish lights on leaning wooden poles. Paul saw a pair of men framed in the patrol car's takedown lights—one old, leaning on a cane, the other young, wearing a wife beater t-shirt and jeans sagging off his ass. They were looking into the lights with wide open, terrified eyes.

The young one took off running instantly, making for the darkened, overgrown alley behind the convenience store. Paul threw off his seatbelt and made ready to chase after him before the car even stopped rolling.

"No!" Mike said. "He's the buyer. The old man's the one we want."

Mike slid the car to a stop and got out. And just like that his demeanor changed. He had the same calm, affable swagger Paul had seen back at the East Side Substation, when they were hanging out with the guys, though now there was a predatory glint in his eyes. He would have made a good linebacker, Paul thought.

Mike walked up to the old man casually. To someone who didn't know better, he might have looked bored, but Paul recognized it was just part of an act. This was some kind of ritual display of dominance he was witnessing, the time-honored dance of cop confronting crook.

"Hey there, Wilson," Mike said. "Whatcha doing?"

Paul glanced at Mike. *You know him?*

"I ain't doin' nothin'," the old man said petulantly.

"Sellin' rock ain't exactly doin' nothin'," Mike said.

"I ain't sellin' no rock," the old man snapped back.

"Why don't you save me the effort of searching you Wilson and just put your shit there on the hood of my car?"

"Fuck you," the man said. "I don't have to talk to you. My lawyer said so." He turned around and started to walk off.

Mike shook his head. He glanced at Paul and smiled a winning, self-assured smile. "He always wants to do it this way," he said. He walked after Wilson, caught up with him, and grabbed the man's arm by the wrist and spun him around.

The move startled Wilson, who turned and swung his cane high in the air, trying to get himself loose. Paul had closed in when he saw Mike making his move, and he was standing in the wrong spot when the old man swung. The cane caught Paul square in the forehead with a loud *thwapp!*

Paul recoiled. He wasn't hurt, but the blow had surprised him.

Mike tossed Wilson unceremoniously onto the hood of the car, kicked his cane aside, and handcuffed him.

"You okay?" he said to Paul.

Paul held his forehead. He looked at his fingers, as though he expected to see something there. His fingers were dry, though.

"Yeah," he said. "Nothing to it."

Mike went through the man's pockets and came up with twenty-four little blue Ziploc baggies and a big rolled up wad of money. Inside each baggie was a chunk of white crack cocaine about the size of Paul's pinkie fingernail.

Holy shit, Paul thought, staring at the load. *Holy shit!*

Mike stood Wilson up near the front of the car and read him his rights. When he was finished he said, "I thought you told me you weren't selling no rock."

"You fuckin' put it there, man. I done tol' you, I ain't sellin' no rock."

"My partner's the one makes things magically appear in people's pockets," Mike said, smiling at Paul. "Not me. Paul, call this in, will you? You know what I want?"

"Yeah," Paul said, running through the narcotics arrest procedures in his head. "Case for narcotics, uniformed detective with a test kit for the crack, and a drug dog to sniff out the area in case he or the buyer tossed anything."

"Don't worry about the dog."

"But the General Manual says—"

"Haven't you been listening to the radio?"

Paul swallowed, mentally kicking himself. Between the excitement of the arrest and Mike's crazy driving, he hadn't heard anything. He shook his head.

"Carlson and Jeffers just got a stolen truck down in 230's district. You heard them calling for the drug dogs?"

Paul hadn't. He shook his head.

"They'll be searching that thing for meth for sure. There's a lot of it around there. The drug dogs'll be tied up for hours."

Paul nodded.

Then he saw the video camera on the corner of the convenience store's roof and said, "What about that? They might have caught the arrest on video."

Mike shook his head. "Good instincts, but no. That camera hasn't worked in months. That's why old Wilson does his business in this lot. Ain't that right, Wilson?"

"Fuck you, man."

Mike chuckled. To Paul, he said, "Just get us a case and call for a DI."

"Okay," Paul said, and got on the radio. When he was done he went back to where Mike and Wilson were talking. Wilson was trying to tell Mike he had to take him to the hospital.

Paul's spirits fell. When a prisoner complained of injury there was always paperwork, endless paperwork. Then there was the trip to the hospital, the tedious, depressing, boring-as-all-hell hospital. Babysitting duty, the guys called it. It was a detestable assignment, sitting in some industrial-lit teaching hospital for hours on end for some tired old doctor to make a seven second diagnosis. If they had to take Wilson to the hospital, the rest of the night would be a wash.

Mike caught the look in Paul's eye, and it was like he could read the thoughts in his head. "Wilson here says he's sick," Mike said. "He says we got to take him to the hospital. What was it you said you've got, Wilson, Dutch Elm Disease?"

"I'm sick, man. You can't refuse to take me to a hospital. I know my fuckin' rights."

Mike smiled.

"Look, Wilson, how many times have I arrested you now? Four, five times?"

"Fuck you, man."

"Yeah, I think you're right. It is six times, isn't it?" He said, "Look, you know how this goes, Wilson. The hospital's got better things to do than babysit an old crackhead. I'll tell you what. How about I go inside that store there and buy you a cinnamon roll and a Slim Jim? If I do that, will you stop being such an asshole?"

"Say what?" Wilson tried to wheel around on Mike. From his tone, from the defiance in his stance, even with the handcuffs locking his hands behind his back, it was obvious all he had heard was a Hispanic cop calling him an asshole.

"A cinnamon roll," Mike said patiently. "And a Slim Jim. When was the last time you ate, Wilson?"

Wilson hesitated. "I don't know."

"Yesterday?"

"Yeah, maybe. I ain't sure. Maybe yesterday."

"That's a long time," Mike said. "I mean, if you can't remember, that's a long time, right?"

Wilson thought about that. He said, "I want a coffee, too."

"With cream?" Mike asked.

"Yeah. And sugar."

***

Later, after they'd dropped Wilson off at the Magistrate's Office and turned in all the paperwork and secured the drugs and the cash in the property room, they were on the road back to the East Side, back to their district.

Mike was driving. Mike insisted on driving. He said, "I was telling you about Wes and Collins."

"Yeah," Paul said, "I remember."

"Those guys are my friends. I mean, you know, they're good guys."

"Sure," Paul said. "I get it."

"I don't want you to think wrong of Collins. I know he comes across like he'd rather piss on your toes than shake your hand, but he's a good friend. He'll have your back when it counts. He may not seem like it, but he's a good cop."

"Does he always act that pissed off?"

Mike chuckled. It was a warm sound that made the interior of the police car seem warm, welcoming. Paul liked this guy. He could tell that already. Something about Mike put him at ease. New as he was to police work, Paul went around most of the time feeling exposed, unprepared, like he was up in front of an angry crowd and had forgotten his lines. Every encounter with the public threatened disaster, every decision he was forced to make haunted by self-doubt. But Mike, Paul sensed, had his back. He was a joker, and could be cruel as pranksters often were, but he wasn't going to let Paul fail. Of that Paul was certain.

"It was the bit with that detective that did it to him tonight," Mike said.

"Yeah, what was that about?"

"How much did you hear?"

"Just that last part about Wes and Collins doing an illegal search. You kind of saved their ass, from what it sounds like."

Mike shrugged, as though to say: *Yeah, maybe.* "Their heart was in the right place," he said. "Those two, Wes and Collins, sometimes they get a little overeager."

Paul laughed. When they taught the rules of Arrest, Search, and Seizure at the Academy, overeager wasn't exactly the kind of virtue they praised.

"No really," Mike said, as though picking up the train of Paul's thought. Mike could do that. He had a facile ease when it came to reading people. "That bit about the young girl screaming?" Mike went on. "That was all for real. They really did kick down that guy's door because they heard a young girl screaming. They were there for a family disturbance. The girl was even the one who called it in."

"Sounds straightforward enough," Paul said.

"It was. At least until they knocked the front door down. Then, when they got inside, they saw all that jewelry. I mean, it was laid out everywhere. All over the couches and the beds and the floor. Most of it still had the price tags on it. It was like the guy was taking inventory, you know? He meant business, too. He had police scanners and bulletproof vests and Chinese-made SKSs. He was the real deal. Then they saw all that stuff from the robbery, and they froze."

"I thought that detective said they beat the guy up."

"Oh, they did. You got to remember, that guy killed four people in that robbery. He's looking at the death penalty easy. Wes and Collins knew that. They knew the guy would do anything to stay out of jail. So when he tried to push them back out the front door they ended up in a massive fight. They managed to get him out onto the front lawn, and that's where the fight got really bad."

"That detective said the neighbors complained to Internal Affairs."

"Yeah, of course they did. Hector Avalos is a lieutenant in the Mexican Mafia. He owns that block. He and all his buddies. Every neighbor who didn't want their house lit up like a rifle range was out there shooting video on their iPhone. IA's probably got forty different videos from that night, and I bet every one of them shows Wes and Collins kicking the snot out of that guy."

"You don't sound worried, though."

"No need, really. They were kicking his ass, sure, but it wasn't like he was just sitting there taking it, you know? I mean, this guy's a mean motherfucker. The guy learned to kill people in the state prison at Beeville. By the end of the fight Collins' uniform shirt was hanging around his waist like a hula skirt."

Paul nodded. He'd heard of fights like that before, but hadn't been in one himself. His instructors at the Academy had told him they didn't happen all that often.

"You said they froze, though?"

"Yeah," Mike said. "They did. They had everything they needed for a search warrant. The girl screaming would have been great probable cause in and of itself. They could have established everything they needed right there."

Paul saw the problem immediately. "They went back in, didn't they?"

Mike nodded. "Collins did. Wes still had Hector Avalos face down in the grass. But Collins went in and started checking out the stolen property. Collins, he was looking at all that jewelry and thinking he'd just caught a capital murder suspect. It doesn't get that much bigger than that. He had casino eyes, you know?"

Not really, Paul thought. It seemed absolutely stupid to him that Collins would risk a good arrest by doing what was, at best, a questionable search.

But Mike turned to Paul and his smile leveled out. "It wasn't as bad as it sounds," he said.

Once again, Paul got the feeling that Mike had read his mind.

It's going to be interesting, Paul thought, partnering with somebody who could read him so well.

"Really," Mike said. "It wasn't. They had all the elements of a good arrest. They just needed somebody to articulate it for them. You know, make it fly?"

Paul was about ready to agree, just out of politeness, when the radio's emergency tone went off.

Instantly, he and Mike broke off their conversation and listened in. The dispatcher said, "Three-zero-zero-three Morgan Rollins Road at the Morgan Rollins Iron Works." She sounded implacably calm. "I have Eighty-five Fourteen hitting his e-tone, not answering his radio. Possible officer-in-trouble. Clearing all but East."

The dispatcher cleared from the all-routes channel and was speaking only to her guys on East again.

"I've got everybody assigned to a call right now, guys," she said. "I need somebody to go ten-eight. I'll take any unit."

"Shit," Mike muttered.

"That's us, isn't it?" Paul said. "That's our district."

"Yeah," Mike said, gripping the steering wheel. "We're not even halfway back yet." He mashed the throttle down to the floor and within seconds the Crown Victoria was up to its top speed, the car heaving up and down over the uneven pavement like a speed boat skipping over waves. Again Paul felt his stomach rising into in throat. His fingers clutched at the edge of the seat, at the door handle, anything to steady himself.

Mike keyed the radio. "44-70, show us on the way."

"10-4," the dispatcher responded.

Everybody was so calm, Paul thought. Their voices never cracked. He, on the other hand, could barely focus. He tried to picture a map of their district in his mind, but couldn't locate the Morgan Rollins Iron Works in it.

Paul looked over at Mike. His face was suffused with a sort suppressed tension, but there was no weakness, no self-doubt.

"Who's Eight-five Fourteen?" he said.

"Narcotics," Mike answered. "Hold on, okay?"

Mike banked the car toward an exit ramp so sharply that Paul came dangerously close to vomiting. He held on to the edge of the seat, willing himself not to close his eyes, because he knew if he did he'd throw up all over himself. The engine whined loudly and Paul gripped the seat even tighter.

Paul's head rolled to one side and he made the mistake of looking out at the ruined buildings and clapboard houses they passed. He was only dimly aware of the radio chatter. The voices merged with the wailing sirens so that, to Paul at least, it sounded like a blur of noise. He was too frightened by their speed to untangle anything he heard.

And then they left the street lights behind them, and all that remained was the empty black of vacant lots and a ribbon of a dark uneven road ahead. Toward the end of that road, beyond a line of trees, Paul thought he could make out three crumbling smokestacks rising up into the air.

"That's it there," Mike said. He grabbed the radio again. "44-70, we're coming up on it now. We should be ten-six in just a moment."

"Acknowledged, 44-70," the dispatcher answered.

A voice Paul didn't recognize came on the radio. "Hawkeye Bravo, we're ten-six over the location. We've got a visual on 44-70's approach."

"That's the helicopter," Mike said.

Paul nodded. He craned his neck forward to try to look up through the windshield into the night sky, but he couldn't see the helicopter.

"10-4, Hawkeye Bravo," the dispatcher said. "Can you see Eighty-five Fourteen?"

"Negative," the helicopter pilot answered. "We're searching with the

FLIR cameras now."

"10-4," the dispatcher answered. "Let us know. All officers, be advised, Hawkeye Bravo is ten-six."

And then the ruins of the Morgan Rollins Iron Works rose up before them, and had Paul been driving, he thought for sure he would have slammed on the brakes, officer in trouble or not. The ruins were—his mind groped for the right word—vile. Yes, that was it, vile. That is a bad place, he thought, a diseased, insane, wretched place. Don't go any further, his mind insisted. Don't, for the love of God, don't.

But they were already skidding through the remnants of the old iron gate at the entrance, passing a parked Malibu—the detective's car, Paul thought—and climbing a cracked and winding road bordered by overgrown shrubs. They slid to a stop near a twisted pile of metal blocking a rickety staircase that led up into a black confusion of catwalks and loose cables and rusted pipes.

Mike didn't bother to shut off the car. He pushed his door open and was running before Paul even had his seatbelt off. Paul groped at the release for a moment before freeing himself, then ran after Mike. For a moment, Paul thought they were going up the staircase, though he didn't see how. It was far too packed in with debris. Then he froze again, something lurching in the pit of his stomach like a hand had reached inside him and squeezed. This place, this old moldering pile of scrap iron, had caught him. His gaze wandered upwards, searching the darkened upper reaches of the superstructure, trying to isolate exactly what it was that frightened him so about this place. He felt his lips tingle and grow cold. An undeniable dread was worming its way through him, and it occurred to him that worming was the perfect word for it, for that dread was a living thing. He was sure of that. It was as real and as alive as the voice in his head, the one pleading with him to turn back, to get far away from there.

"Move it!" Mike shouted.

Paul shook himself. Mike was slipping into a narrow gap in the twisted metal at the base of the stairs. He's not going up them, Paul told himself. He's going around them. He knows this place.

"Come on," Mike said to him. "You have to stay close. You can get lost in here." Then he keyed up his radio. "44-70, be advised, we're entering the structure. Ask Hawkeye Bravo if he can give me a visual on something in here."

"10-4," the dispatcher said. "Everybody hold the air. I got 44-70 out on officers in trouble. Hawkeye Bravo, you copy on that visual?"

A short pause.

"Hawkeye Bravo, 10-4, Ma'am. We've got 44-70 and his partner on the FLIR. I've got faint heat signatures up near the round room, but nothing moving—Wait! Hold that. I got movement just south of the round room. Can't tell if it's a person or a..."

The helicopter pilot trailed off. Paul stared at his radio, waiting for more, but nothing came.

"Or a what?" he said. "What's the round room?"

"This way," Mike said. He had his gun in his right hand, his flashlight in his left, hands back to back in the classical style Paul remembered from tactics training back at the Academy. He drew his own weapon, clicked on his flashlight, and followed after him.

"Middle of this place," Mike said, glancing back over his shoulder, "is a round room. Big place, walls are twenty feet high at least. That's what he was talking about."

Not the round room, Paul thought. *That's not right. It's the diesel generator access station.*

He stopped again, wondering where that knowledge had come from. He had never been here. He'd never worked in an iron works. None of what he saw looked familiar in the slightest, and yet he knew beyond a shadow of a doubt that this place was a bad place, and that the round room Mike and the helicopter pilot spoke of was actually a place the men who worked here so long ago had come to repair the diesel generators that operated the slider belts and the electricity and a hundred other things that made this place run. Why was that, he thought. How did he know that?

"Let's go! Look sharp," Mike said.

Paul tried not to look up at the superstructure. He focused instead on the dark tunnel before them, on the small, moving circles of dusty metal walkway lit by their flashlights.

I am doing a very stupid thing, he realized. *I know this place is bad, and yet I'm allowing myself to be led like a lamb to the slaughter. No*, he thought, correcting himself almost angrily. He was very sure of himself now. He was not going like a lamb to the slaughter. Not like a lamb.

Like a goat.

"Paul," Mike said in a brutal stage whisper. At the same time he motioned with his gun. "Get your gun up. Be ready."

Paul nodded slowly, not wanting to show any weakness but at the same time unable to keep his fear down. *God*, he thought, *I'm doing this badly. He's not going to trust me after this. How could he? I wouldn't, if I were him.*

But then Mike was pushing a blanket aside and stepping through, and for a moment, Paul stood alone. The crumbling metal walls suddenly seemed very close. The totality of this place, its immense wrongness, was leaning in on him, covering him.

No, he thought. *Not covering me. Pulling me in. This place, it wants to hold me, own me, devour me whole. It wants to consume me.*

On his hip, the radio sizzled.

He looked down at it, surprised. He couldn't make out the voices, the words used, but he could sense the urgency, and that urgency snapped him loose from whatever this was, the hold this factory had on him.

Paul pushed his way through the blanket and emerged into another metal tunnel, this one lined with broken bodies and trash and used needles in the dust. Mike was standing there, his gun lowered to his waist. Beyond him was a large circular chamber formed by immense walls. The body of a mutilated detective lay there, a crumpled, broken thing.

But Paul noticed none of that. His eye was drawn immediately to the large white Angora goat milling around in confused circles inside the chamber. Its large, black, vacant eyes caught Paul's, and then it looked away.

"No," he said, taking an involuntary step back.

"Do you see it?" the helicopter pilot shouted over the radio. Paul could hear him clearly now. The calm veneer had slipped from his voice. He was absolutely frantic. "You should be right on top of it?"

Paul could only stare. The goat ducked its head and made a low, moaning noise that Paul remembered from his days on his father's farm. The animal was confused, frightened.

Or is that me, Paul thought, *projecting my fears onto it?*

He wasn't sure.

"Do you see it?" the helicopter pilot said again.

"44-70," Mike said, and dimly, absently, Paul was aware of the crack in Mike's normally calm exterior. His words broke off there as he stared at the dead detective, the staggering white goat, the blood spattered over everything.

He's frightened, too, Paul thought. *But not as frightened as me.*

"44-70, are you okay?" the dispatcher said. "Mike, answer me. Are you okay?"

"10-4," Mike said, sounding for a moment like his response was automatic. "10-4," he said. "We see it." His voice cracked. "Oh Jesus, we see it. 44-70, start us EMS. The shooting team. I need more officers to contain this scene. Start me a supervisor, too. Jesus, start everybody. You're not gonna believe what we got here."

Chapter 4

After twenty-six years on the job, and sixteen of those in Homicide, Keith Anderson was used to nights like this. When they went to parties with their non-cop friends, and somebody would say they bet he had to work some weird hours, Keith would joke he was so used to it he could do it on autopilot. But it really wasn't a joke. Truth be told, he could have done it on autopilot, though he never did. He loved it too much.

But he had been just about to get into bed. He was standing there in a white t-shirt and boxer shorts, looking at his Blackberry on the nightstand, studying the caller ID display. Margie, his wife, was still asleep, but groaning irritably at the buzzing phone. It would have been nice, Anderson thought, to spend at least one uninterrupted night in bed with his wife.

He accepted the call.

"What's going on, Chuck?"

"Keith? You awake?"

"That's kind of a stupid question."

"Keith, listen, we've got some real trouble."

Chuck was Charles Levy. He'd been Keith's sergeant in Homicide for the last six years now, and he was one of Anderson's oldest friends.

Anderson was only forty-eight, but there were times, like this, as he looked down on his pasty white legs and felt every muscle in his back aching, that he felt positively ancient. He mopped a hand across his face and sighed. "What's going on, Chuck?"

Beside him, Margie stirred. She sat up and turned on her light, then leaned against the headboard of their bed.

Anderson glanced over at her and nodded as Chuck Levy spoke into his ear.

"East Patrol's got a huge fucking mess on their hands," he said. "Real bad." His voice sounded like it was about to break. "Keith, it's Ram. He's been killed. His partner, too. Raul Herrera, if you know him. I...I don't know Herrera."

Anderson was certain he hadn't heard that right. "Wait, say that again. What do you mean Ram's been...you mean our Ram? You mean Bobby Cantrell?"

"Yeah," Levy said.

This isn't happening, Anderson thought. *I'm about to wake up. Come on, Keith, wake up.*

"What's wrong?" Margie asked. "Is Ram okay?"

He put his hand on her stomach. He tried to tell her no, that somehow Ram had just been killed, but the words wouldn't come. Instead all he could do was shake his head.

"Keith," she asked, more urgently now, "what's going on? Tell me what happened."

"Killed," was all he could say.

Margie clapped her hands over her mouth, and as Anderson watched she drew her knees up to her chest and started breathing in short, noisy sobs. She shook her head violently back and forth. She watched him without blinking.

"How did it happen?" Anderson asked.

"I have no idea. Like I said, East Patrol's got a mess out there. They've got Ram and Herrera down and about forty others, too. A bunch of junkies apparently."

"Forty?" Keith said disbelieving. "Did you say forty people dead?"

"At least that many."

"What did they tell you? They must have told you something."

"They don't know anything yet. I'm still on the way there. Garwin is the sergeant on the scene right now. I talked to him for about thirty seconds on the phone, but he's swamped. All I know is that Ram's chest was ripped open. Garwin thinks somebody used a rib spreader to open him up, but that hasn't been confirmed."

Anderson shook his head. He and Chuck and Bobby Cantrell had been friends since the Academy. Back then, Keith and Chuck had just been kids. No life experience whatsoever. But Bobby, he'd been in the Marines for five years. He was tough. He was the guy you didn't fuck with. Keith had been on more than a few calls where everything went wrong and there had been times when he wondered if he was going to make it out alive. And then he'd seen Bobby "Ram" Cantrell come running through the door and it was like a calm radiant confidence had suddenly flooded into the room. Bobby was like that, the rock, the one you wanted at your back. He couldn't be dead.

"Where am I going?" he asked Levy.

"The Morgan Rollins Iron Works. You know it?"

"Yeah," Anderson said, still feeling like he was floating, like his head was in a haze he couldn't shake loose. "I know it."

"I'm just now getting on the road," Levy said. "I've got, I don't know, about an hour or so before I get there from out here."

Levy lived on ten acres way out in Fredericksburg, an hour's drive north of San Antonio, out in the Hill Country. An hour to get from there to the far East Side of San Antonio sounded optimistic.

"Okay," Anderson said. He took a moment to steady himself. "All right. I'll meet you there."

Anderson hung up the phone and sat there on the side of the bed, one hand touching his wife's arm, his mind a confused jumble of grief and confusion and anger. He ran a hand through his thinning gray hair and tried to clear his head. An awful lot was going to depend on his ability to focus here in the next few hours. He had to be sharp.

But his thoughts just wouldn't fall in line.

He was too numb for that.

Margie put her arms around him and he put his around her. They stayed that way for nearly a minute, neither of them speaking.

She finally broke the silence.

"I need to call Jenny. I've got to talk to her. Tell her we're here for her. She'll need someone there with her."

He started to object and thought better of it. The Department had very set procedures for handling next of kin notifications when officers were involved. It would start with two uniformed sergeants from the Crisis Response Unit delivering the initial bad news. Then, over the next few hours, the wife—it was almost always the wife—would get visits from counselors and the Police Officers Association president and even members of the Command Staff. His first instinct was to tell Margie that Jenny Cantrell would have enough people there with her, but a voice in his head silenced that. Margie and Jenny Cantrell were best friends. It had been Jenny, after all, who introduced them. He could no more keep his wife from Jenny's side now than he could turn back time to before this call landed in his lap. And with all the administrative visits that Jenny Cantrell was going to have to endure over the next few hours, maybe Margie could help.

Anderson simply nodded.

She sniffled and rubbed her nose with the back of her hand. "I'll go make us some coffee," she said.

He went into the bathroom and wet his face and hair at the sink. He dressed quickly, then slipped back into the blue golf shirt and jeans he had just put in the dirty clothes hamper

Keith stared at himself in the mirror for a moment, then went to work.

***

A fleet of marked Patrol units and Evidence units and unmarked supervisor cars were parked inside the gate. Beyond them, closer to the main part of the factory, Anderson could see eight EMS wagons and more Patrol vehicles parked in the grass. The factory itself looked like Dresden at the end of World War II, rubble everywhere, the moon-silvered ruins of walls and smokestacks thrown up against greasy-looking clouds.

And the night was hot.

Anderson felt the heat on his face almost as soon as he stepped out of his car. He took off his favorite gray sweater—his Mr. Rogers sweater, as the younger detectives in Homicide called it—and tossed it on the passenger seat. From the south entrance he had a view of the superstructure straight ahead and the other part of the factory to his left. He had no idea what that part was called, but to Anderson it looked like a bowl of spaghetti, catwalks and ramps and pipes leading every which way. Most of the police and EMS personnel were there, so he went that way, too.

A uniformed officer gave him a tired, almost bored look, but when he saw the gold emblem on Anderson's shirt he straightened up and pointed and said, "Over there, sir."

Anderson gave him a nod and walked into the thick of things.

There were people everywhere, spotlights shining into the superstructure and the adjacent catwalks. Anderson stared at the wreckage of the factory with all its twisted metal and the skeins of orange dust streaking across the broken asphalt that had once been a parking lot. *It's not real*, he tried to tell himself, though he had no illusions about that. It was all too real. So damn real it made his head spin.

A camera flash went off on the second level and Anderson glanced up at it. Another flash went off and in the moment that the flash lit the scene, Anderson could see the body of a junkie on his back on the catwalk, one knee bent, pointed up in the air, one hand sagged over the belly, the head craned back, the mouth open, and a gory hole in the chest area.

Jesus, he thought. *What am I gonna tell Jenny Cantrell about this?*

***

There were still a few EMS technicians coming and going from the maze of catwalks at the edge of the scene. Special lanes had been marked off for them in order to minimize contamination with the crime scene, but Anderson was pretty sure plenty of valuable evidence had been trampled underfoot nonetheless. Despite all the training, all the reminders, it happened at every crime scene.

He watched the EMS guys lugging their orange and white tackle boxes out of the structure, most of them looking down at the ground in front of them with weary, haunted eyes, and he thought, *When you see those guys looking like that, you know it's bad.*

"Hey Keith!"

Anderson turned toward the voice. It belonged to Deputy Chief

Robert Allen. If he'd been awakened in the middle of a sound sleep by an urgent phone call, as Anderson suspected he had, it didn't show on him. His iron gray hair was perfect, and his suit hung on his still athletic frame with sartorial precision.

Anderson walked over to him and shook hands. "How are you, sir?" he said to Allen.

"I'm all right, Keith. I'm sorry about Ram."

"Thank you, sir."

"Have you gotten a chance to see inside yet?" Allen asked.

"No sir."

"It's..." he trailed off, shaking his head. "So far EMS has pronounced forty-five dead. That includes Ram and Herrera. They tell me they found three shell casings from Ram's gun. At least he got to fight back. I have a bad feeling this one's going to be hanging over our heads for a long time to come."

Anderson had been thinking the same thing. Later, when all the patrol officers were gone and their reports filed, and the evidence technicians had processed the scene and submitted their evidence for testing, and the junkies were all interviewed, it would be Anderson's job to go through the mountain of paperwork and forensic testing reports and autopsies and photographs and videos and statements and try to find the through line that connected them—the one cohesive answer, the thread, explaining how and why something like this could possibly happen. He would have help, of course, because every member of the Homicide Unit's Murder Squad worked on each and every case, doing whatever was needed to move the case along towards a successful resolution. But in the end, the weight of coming up with that explanation was squarely on his shoulders, and no one else's. And, of course, he still had thirty other murder cases open. He'd have to work those at the same time.

Anderson chewed on his bottom lip, a nervous habit. When he looked back at Allen, Allen curled one corner of his mouth into a sort of smile. "You know," Allen said, "if you hadn't drawn this case, I think I would have ordered Levy to assign it to you."

That surprised Anderson. He had half-expected to have the case taken from him and assigned to somebody else, simply because of his personal involvement with the victim. "Why's that, sir?"

"There's a lot riding on this, Keith. An awful lot. You know that, of course, but I want you to know that I would have ordered you back here from a European vacation if I'd had to. You're the one I want on this. You're the one I *need* on this. Do you understand?"

"Yes sir," he said. "I understand you loud and clear."

***

The last of the EMS crews were walking back across the barricades, and Anderson happened to overhear a technician who had been inside saying that the whole place was crawling with fleas.

"Fucking gross is what it was," the man's partner said. "I looked down and saw those little bastards all over my pants."

Fleas? Anderson thought. *Oh great.*

As a boot patrolman, he'd made a burglary call where a woman told him somebody had broken into the shed behind her house. Anderson went into the yard to investigate. He walked around the shed in knee high grass, examining the busted lock on the door, when he felt an itch in his crotch. He looked down to scratch himself, and saw fleas all over his pant legs. They made it look like he had spilled pepper on himself. Fleas gave him the shivers ever since.

Someone from inside the building started screaming. It was a horrible sound, less that of a man than of a trapped animal, whimpering and afraid and screaming all at the same time.

Anderson backed up so he could see the catwalks directly above him, trying to find where the sound was coming from. Soon there was more yelling. Anderson had to fight the urge to charge inside. There was enough going on in there without him becoming part of the problem, and as he looked up and down the line of barricades he saw others watching the superstructure with the same look of confused irritation he wore, all of them fighting the urge to rush inside.

And then, just as suddenly as it started, the yelling stopped. Anderson listened expectantly for a moment, and then, from somewhere off to his right, he heard Deputy Chief Allen yelling at somebody for an explanation.

The radio was silent.

Whoever had run up there to investigate the noise hadn't reported anything over the air yet. Anderson checked his radio instinctively, just to make sure it was still on, and waited.

From where he stood, he could see a long, rickety section of the catwalk that wound around the old rusted supervisor's station. A very terrified, very mangy-looking man ran onto that catwalk, screaming the whole way at the policemen who were trying to grab him. Uniformed officers closed in on both sides.

From three stories down, Anderson watched the fear play out on the man's face and thought, *Oh my God, he's gonna jump.*

The man grabbed onto the railing like he believed it was the only thing in the world that wasn't trying to kill him. He glanced wide-eyed at the officers closing in on him, his lips white with spit, his mouth a grimace of terror, and then, for no reason Anderson could see, he just gave up. He slumped down into a pile on the catwalk and sobbed helplessly as uniformed officers closed in on him.

"What in the hell?" Anderson said.

But he was thinking: *Hot damn, maybe we got us a witness.*

Chapter 5

Interview Room Two.

Everything in here was videotaped by a camera hidden in a light switch on the back wall. *Burned to CD now, actually,* Anderson reminded himself. Everything is on CD these days. Technically speaking, they hadn't videotaped anybody in four or five years at least.

There were signs in English and Spanish on every door leading into SAPD Headquarters that said:

**WARNING: ALL PERSONS
ENTERING THIS FACILITY
ARE SUBJECT TO VIDEO
SURVEILLANCE AT ALL
TIMES.**

The same sign was repeated on the doors to the Homicide Office, and this, as far as the courts were concerned, was sufficient notice to witnesses and suspects alike that anything they said to a detective in here was likely to end up on video.

But Anderson doubted that the nearly comatose junkie sitting across from him had read the signs, or seen them, or if he could even read at all. *And if he can read, and if he did see the signs, he probably doesn't care,* Anderson thought. *Guys like him, with their slushed brains, their minds charred to cinders, don't give a shit about anything except their next dose. Where's it coming from? Who can get it for me? What can I steal to pay for it?*

The room they were in was drab in the extreme. Anderson had been in here a thousand times over the years, interviewing suspects beyond number. It was little more than a closet, not anywhere near what they showed in those TV detective shows where there's plenty of space to pace around and slap files down on the desk and a one way mirror so the lieutenant and the DA can look on eagerly. There was none of that. What he had was a desk with a busted top drawer that hung down and barked you in the knees if you tried to take notes, two old chairs, a phone, a trashcan in the corner that somebody had spit tobacco juice into, and black dirt thick as tree moss in the space where the walls met the floor.

Over the years, Anderson had come to know every stray ink mark on the white plaster walls, every stain on the carpet; and now, having spent the last hour trying to get something, *anything*, out of what he saw as the worthless piece of human garbage sitting next to him, he felt like he knew every stain on this man's face as well. He certainly knew his smell. He stank like a corpse.

Earlier, when the officers pulled him down from the catwalks at the Morgan Rollins Iron Works, they'd managed to get him to say his name, but that had pretty much been the one and only boxcar in the information train. But it was enough for them to look him up in the Master Name File. A few minutes of poking around, and the other Murder Squad detectives assisting Anderson on the case had been able to come up with nearly two hundred pages of history on the man—basically his whole adult life, reduced to a list of arrests and mentions in various official reports from one agency or another.

He was David Everett, thirty-eight years old. Everett stood five foot ten and a hundred and twenty pounds. He wore blue, mud-stained pants, tennis shoes with holes in the sides and jerry rigged shoelaces tied in places other than the ends, and a nasty t-shirt that may once have been white under all that dirt and grime and dried sweat but certainly wasn't now. His face was a disgusting mess of sores and blisters, his lips scorched. His teeth were black, what few of them he still had, and his eyes were sunken pits, the light all but gone from them. The veins on the inside of his elbows had collapsed beneath a ladder of track marks.

He was a non-functioning heroin addict, which meant, in practical terms, no job, no home, no family, no future. Not much more than what was necessary in the way of biography to tell Anderson what kind of man he was dealing with. Here was a junkie, plain and simple.

There was a report in his file written by an investigator with Adult Protective Services describing his last known physical address. David Everett had once lived with his invalid grandmother in a house in the 1200 block of Berryhill Street, which was where you'd stick the applicator if you needed to give the City of San Antonio an enema. The investigator from APS described the house as a crumbling shack with a weedpatch yard swarming with fleas, rubble strewn all over the floors, a cat box in the center of the living room that looked like it had never been emptied, cats everywhere, walking on the table, nosing through the endless piles of garbage on the floor, and Mrs. Thompson, David Everett's grandmother, blind, diabetic, delirious with Alzheimer's, abandoned in her bed, stuck to filthy sheets by oozing bed sores all over her back and the places around her hips where she'd soiled herself.

Mrs. Thompson was removed from the home and charges were filed against David Everett for Neglect and Injury to the Elderly, for which he spent eight months in the Bexar County Jail while he awaited trial. Mrs.

Thompson died while David Everett was in jail and the charges just seemed to have simply evaporated. They should have been refiled as Criminally Negligent Homicide, but for whatever reason they weren't, and David Everett left the jail with no home to go back to and an aching in his belly for the numbing glow of heroin.

You gotta love it when the system fucks up, Anderson thought. *Nothing else can equal this kind of inhuman tragedy.*

David Everett had been arrested nearly forty other times for crimes ranging from burglary of a habitation to heroin possession to inhalant abuse. Several of his heroin arrests had been made by Bobby Cantrell, and that little bit of information had caused a flurry of excitement around the office when it first came up. But the idea of a junkie seeking revenge against a Narcotics detective was shot down almost immediately. Between huffing paint and shooting heroin, David Everett's mind had become a desert and his body a walking Petri dish of disease. He was little more than a shell of a man, and everyone agreed he just wasn't capable of the kind of systematic carnage that they had seen at the crime scene—not against forty something other junkies, and certainly not against two armed Narcotics detectives.

And certainly not against Bobby Cantrell. Ram would have snapped the man in half like a twig if he'd so much as raised a finger against him.

So the question remained. How come so many people died, including two very well-trained and well-armed detectives, and this worthless piece of shit lived? How does something like that happen?

Anderson felt a migraine coming on. For him, they always started right between his eyes, and he pinched the bridge of his nose, trying to head off the pressure. He stared at David Everett for maybe a minute, asking himself the same set of questions over and over again—*Why? How?*—but he was unable to work around the thought that the migraine was about to explode like a hydrogen bomb, no matter what he did at this point.

It was cold inside the room. He said, "I'm going to get a cup of coffee. You want something? A soda maybe?"

David Everett said nothing, just looked vacantly off into space.

"Right," Anderson said, and left the room.

***

He stepped into the main part of the Homicide Office and looked over a sea of cubicles. Detectives and uniformed patrol officers were everywhere. The noise was tremendous. The phones wouldn't stop ringing. Levy had authorized emergency call-in overtime for most of the Homicide Unit, even those not assigned to the Murder Squad, and even though regular office hours didn't start for another thirty minutes or so, most of the cubicles were occupied. The noise hit Anderson like a wave and he groaned as the migraine that had been threatening to explode for the past hour or so finally blew up.

He took a few deep breaths and tried to control the pain. It was like some little bastard was standing on the bridge of his nose and pounding on his forehead with a sledgehammer.

And the office was freezing cold.

He put on his Mr. Rogers sweater. Then he went to the little kitchenette up by the secretary's desk and poured himself a cup of coffee. He liked it straight up black, no cream, no sugar. He put the cup to his lips, sniffed the steam, and took a sip. Then he went to the video room and stood next to Levy, watching David Everett on a monitor.

"Not going so well," Levy said.

"Nope."

Levy was short and nearly round. He wore comfort fit black Walmart slacks and a white shirt with a green and gold colored tie. The shirt was wrinkled, with a coffee stain on the left elbow, and the neck was too tight for him. It pinched him there, and his skin rolled over the top of the collar. Anderson wondered if the man could breathe with it that tight. He listened, and he could hear him wheezing.

"I've never seen anybody go comatose with fear," Levy said. "I've seen men lock up, sure, but never like this." He chewed on the skin at the corner of the fingernail of his right thumb and then spit it into a trashcan below the TV. "I don't get it."

"Me either."

"What do you think? Are we wasting our time with this guy?"

"Probably."

Levy shook his head. "I don't get it. Why is he like that? What did he see in there? I mean, he obviously saw something."

"I'm sure he did," Anderson said.

There were six interview rooms, and all of them were in use, all of them with a video feed to the TV screens in front of them. One of the screens showed a junkie named Gustavo Guerrero, who'd been found sleeping in the tall grass near the south entrance to the plant. He'd told them he'd shot up inside the plant earlier in the day and then wandered out to the gate to sit and watch the sunset, but had fallen asleep instead. He said he woke up a few hours later and thought he heard people screaming inside, but it was hazy in his mind, and anyway he hadn't paid it any attention when it happened. He'd just rolled over and went back to sleep.

Anderson wondered who he'd heard screaming. There were bodies everywhere inside the plant, and yet only a few of the victims seemed to have put up any struggle at all. Whoever had done the murders had evidently gone systematically through the tangle of rusted catwalks and pipes and machinery and rooted out everybody he could find, almost as if he—*Or they,* Anderson reminded himself—were clearing the building, exterminating it. He didn't know if exterminating was the right word to describe what he had seen on the inside, but it sure seemed like it.

"But what did *you* see?" Anderson said to the man centered in Screen Two. "How did you make it out alive?"

And then, almost as if he were responding to a movie director's call of *Action!* David Everett reacted. His eyes had been open the whole time, but suddenly they *shot* open. They changed in a flash from lifeless black coals to a terrorized, rolling stare. He exploded out of his chair and crashed into the desk, into the wall, into the door. He knocked his chair over and fell over the side of the desk, and as his face splashed across the camera's view Anderson could see the man's eyes bulging from his face, like a horse that's fallen into a bolus of denning rattlesnakes, white flecks of spittle bubbling on his scorched lips.

The man screamed—an unnatural, primal sound so shamelessly naked in its pain that it sent goosebumps down Anderson's spine.

"What the...?" Levy said.

Anderson ran to Interview Room #2, Levy close on his heels. Three detectives got there ahead of them and charged into the room. David Everett spun around on them right as they entered, grabbed the chair next to him, and smashed it into the chest of the first man through the door. He ran at them, screaming and kicking, not to fight, but to get away from something that seemed to close in on him from all sides at once.

He punched a detective in the jaw. The man grabbed Everett by the hair at the back of his head and spun him around, slamming his face into the wall and then spinning him around again as he forced him down to the carpet. Two other detectives grabbed Everett by his wrists and forced his hands behind his back.

Anderson looked over his shoulder and saw detectives and uniformed officers running their way. He pointed at the closest uniformed officer and said, "Gimme your cuffs! Now!"

The officer slapped the cuffs into Anderson's palm and Anderson pushed his way between the detectives holding Everett down. He worked one cuff onto the junkie's left hand, but Everett was fighting hard, and he'd pulled his right hand loose and stuffed it under his body. Two officers were trying to extract it, but he was slippery, and they couldn't get it.

"Stop fighting!" Anderson yelled at him. "Gimme your hand. Now!"

A uniformed officer knelt down next to Everett's head and dug his thumb into the mandibular angle where Everett's bottom jaw hinged with his skull.

"Put your hand behind your back!" he said.

The officer's hand was turning white from the force he was applying to Everett's pressure point. It was an old school pain compliance technique they taught at the Academy. Anderson had had it done to him many times during training exercises, but never with the kind of force this officer was applying. Even a little pressure should have been enough to make most people comply, but Everett was clearly in another world, because the pain didn't seem to touch him.

"No," Everett said. "No no no no no!"

"Just put your hands behind your back and the pain'll stop," Anderson said.

"No," he said. He was panting, the words barely audible. "No don't no don't no don't. He'll find me. No...can't...stop! Stop him...he hurts." And then he stopped saying words altogether and sank into screaming. Horrible, horrible screaming.

Somebody got leverage and forced Everett's hand out from under his body. Anderson grabbed it and slapped the cuff on it, then stepped back and threw his hands up, like a calf roper at a rodeo.

Everett went on screaming. It wasn't the sound of pain though. Not pain of the body anyway. The man's soul was being shredded like a piece of paper. He screamed and screamed and screamed until there was nothing left inside him but the pain, and then he let his face fall to the carpet and he began to sob.

Some of the officers stepped back, leaving a uniformed officer holding him at each shoulder.

"Sit him there," Anderson said.

The officers picked him up and sat him in the chair he'd thrown at the first detective to bust through the door.

"What's your fucking problem?" Levy barked at the man, but Everett had sunk into his comatose state again.

"He wants more dope," one of the officers said.

"Meth freak," another said.

Anderson ignored that. Everett wasn't a meth freak. This was something else. Not the ravings of a drug addict. Not meth. Not heroin. Not cocaine or horse tranquilizers or anything else. *That man's just looked into hell*, he thought. *Not a hell of his own making, either. Somebody opened the gates and showed it to him. Held his face down into the stink of it and rubbed his nose in it.*

Everett's head lolled on his shoulders, and for a moment, there was something in his eyes, something like a cry for help. Anderson was sure he'd seen it. There was a man inside there, a person, however despicable, but a person nonetheless, being tortured beyond the limits any flesh could endure.

But if the man had been there, he was gone now. All that was left was a burned out shell, breathing raggedly.

"He's got something on him," one of the detectives said.

The detective was looking at the palms of his hand with his nose scrunched up in disgust. Anderson looked at his own hands and saw a fine coating of black oily soot there. He ran a finger along his palm and it felt gritty, oily and...nasty.

The two officers holding Everett to the chair recoiled, but kept him at fingertip range, just in case.

"Somebody get a box of gloves," Levy said.

An evidence technician came forward a moment later with a box of blue latex surgical gloves and passed them out. Levy directed two uniformed officers who had just put on gloves to watch Everett, then directed everybody else to go wash up.

"No telling what he's got," he said.

***

Anderson washed his hands in the bathroom sink down the hall. He turned the water on as hot as it could go and scrubbed his hands with soap, but the gritty stuff was slow to come off. It stuck to his skin like grease.

Levy walked in and stood beside him. "You okay?"

"Yeah. It's coming off."

"What are your thoughts?"

"We can't let him go," Anderson said. "As soon as he walks out that door, we lose him."

"You think he'll talk?"

"I don't know. Maybe. Eventually."

"What was that nonsense he was talking about?"

Anderson looked at him in the mirror and shrugged.

"You heard that, right? He sounded deranged."

"Yeah."

"There's no way the DA will sign an order to hold him as a material witness based on that. He's delusional."

Anderson shut off the water and shook the excess from his hands. Then he pulled a few paper towels down from the dispenser and dried off. He sighed deeply and said, "I don't know what to tell you, Chuck. But there's something there. I saw something."

Levy cocked his head at him. "What?"

"I don't know," Anderson said honestly. "I don't know. Something."

Levy looked at himself in the mirror and adjusted his collar. Then he said, "I can't justify holding him."

"We have to, Chuck."

"Well, I'm open to suggestions. Give me a reason."

"What about taking him to a psych hospital? Have him held there for observation?"

"You mean an emergency detention?" Levy considered that for a moment and nodded. "That might work."

"It'd be good for seventy-two hours at least."

"Yeah. Okay. Let's do that. I'll have a patrolman write up the order. Here's hoping we'll get something for our trouble."

Anderson loo
ked at his hands and frowned.

"What?" Levy asked. "You okay?"

"Yeah. This stuff won't come off." He turned the hot water up all the way and got more soap. "Damn it. What is this stuff?"

Chapter 6

Paul awoke from a restless dream he couldn't quite remember. All that remained of the dream were a few random images. They were vague and disjointed and unsettling. He'd stood on a sun-baked, dusty plain in...had it been Mexico? In the dream he'd been certain, but now all he could remember was the heat of a white sun, bone-colored dust blowing in his eyes. He remembered black, rock-strewn mountains in the distance. A goat stood under a blue sky streaked with fast-moving cirrus clouds. There was an old, leather-skinned Indio woman holding out a live rattlesnake for him to take.

He rolled over onto his side and looked across the open space of the apartment. The dream slipped away and he didn't bother to pursue it. Shafts of sunlight pierced the yellowed windows on the west wall, filling the room with light. The room felt hot, and his skin was damp.

Rachel was unpacking a box of paperbacks and sorting them onto a bookshelf. He watched her without moving. She wore pajama pants low on her hips and a white camisole top with no bra underneath. He breathed slowly, tracing her curves with his gaze.

He could smell coffee and something cooking, a strong spicy smell of cumin and garlic and chili powder, and it got him out of bed. Rachel's chili was his favorite. He came up behind her and put his hands on her hips. She eased into him as the tips of his fingers ran lightly along the inside of the waistband of her pajama pants. He felt the warmth of her skin, the smoothness of her belly. He let his hand sink lower.

"Paul," she said, like she was annoyed, but also amused. She put her hands on top of his, but didn't push him away.

"Good morning," he said.

"It's not morning."

"Feels like morning," he said.

"Yeah," she said, and giggled. "I can feel that, too."

Her breasts rose and fell against his arms. He kissed her neck, tasted the light sheen of sweat on her skin with the tip of his tongue, and she yielded to him with a breathy sigh. Her hair brushed against his cheek and the smell of it, clean and light, pulled him in.

Rachel turned into his arms and kissed him. His arms and his shoulders were massive in her small hands. She touched his chin with her lips, and then his shoulders, and his chest, and then stared up into his eyes, taking in his face.

She frowned gently, backing away without stepping out of his arms. "Are you okay?" she asked.

"What?"

"Your forehead?"

"Does it look bad?"

"It looks gray, almost like ash or something."

"Ash?"

"Yeah. Does it hurt?"

"No," he said.

"It's darker than it was this morning." She squinted at it. "It's weird. It almost looks like letters. Are you sure it doesn't hurt?"

"I don't feel it at all." He touched it, pressed it with his fingers. "Don't feel a thing."

From the street, brakes squealed. A horn went off. Their rented house was on a main road, and traffic noises were common throughout the day. Paul had already gotten to the point where he could pretty much block it out.

She touched his cheek.

"We'll keep an eye on it," she said. "Are you hungry?"

He moved his hands down to her hips. He picked her up so suddenly, so effortlessly, that she gasped. Then he lowered her back onto the bed with exaggerated ease.

"You bet I am," he said, and nibbled at her ear as she giggled and writhed in his arms.

***

When Paul went into work later that night he realized he was the only cop in the place without black tape over his badge. He'd seen pictures of officers with their badges blacked out when he was a cadet. Paul knew the officers in the field did this kind of thing, but it never occurred to him to ask where the black tape came from. He'd just assumed…well, he didn't know what he'd assumed. That someone would just give it to him and tell him how to wear it maybe.

He tried to get Mike's attention so he could ask where to get some, but Mike was standing with a bunch of other officers, deep in conversation. And then roll call started and Paul found himself sitting through the lieutenant's briefing feeling conspicuous and stupid. No one said anything to him, no one got on his case about it, but he still felt like people were staring at him, judging him somehow.

There wasn't time to talk to Mike after roll call either. Sergeant Garwin called the entire Forty-Four Section into the conference room for a meeting. When Garwin entered the room he patted Paul on the shoulder and took up his spot at the head of the table.

"Okay, buds, you guys gather around." He waited for the stragglers to filter in from the roll call room, and then for the chatter to die down. "Okay, you guys all in?"

They all mumbled "Yes sirs" back at him.

"Okay, buds, you know what happened last night. The Lieutenant wants us to find witnesses. He thinks if that guy we pulled down off the catwalk made it, then maybe somebody else did too and we just don't know about them yet. What I want you to do is spend all your downtime asking questions. Find the junkies in your districts and ask them if they were there or if somebody they know was there. Okay?"

Collins leaned over to Wes and said, "Yeah, I see that going nowhere fast."

"That's the wrong attitude, bud," Garwin said, looking straight at Collins. "We all got to do what we can in this, and I think we got a good game plan to work with. All we've got to do is find that one person who saw something. We're not gonna do that if we don't look."

"Sarge," Collins said, "I agree we gotta do something. But you know as well as I do that a junkie's a completely worthless piece of crap. He'll tell you anything or nothing, whatever he thinks is gonna get rid of you faster. You can't believe anything they say."

"We just want you to talk to them, bud. That's all. We're not arresting them. If we make that plain to them, then they'll talk to us."

"Yeah, but Sarge, that's my point. They're not gonna talk to us. Or if they do, whatever they say is gonna be a lie. All we're gonna end up doing is gathering a bunch of gossip together. And once they figure out what we're doing, they're just gonna start having fun with us. We're gonna end up chasing down a bunch of dead-end leads, and meanwhile the guy who did this is gonna be running straight to Mexico."

Several of the guys grumbled at this, but Paul couldn't tell if they were angry at Collins or if they agreed with him. He suspected it was probably a little of both.

Seles said, "Would you let him finish, please? Christ, what an idiot."

Collins wheeled on him. "What'd you say? Come down here and say that."

"Knock it off," Mike said.

"You heard what he called me."

"I said, 'Knock it off.'"

Collins backed off. He didn't say anything else. No one did.

Mike turned to Garwin and said, "So, Sarge, you want us to talk to every junkie we can find?"

Garwin looked at him, and he seemed uncertain. Paul could see that Mike was giving Garwin a clue to move on, just get the briefing done with, and he was stunned that a patrolman could have so much unofficial influence over the way a unit worked together. There were leaders, he realized, whose power didn't come with chevrons and brass badges.

Garwin said, "Yeah, that's right, Mike. Even if you don't like it, I want you to start talking to your junkies anyway. Don't make any arrests if you don't have to. Make it plain we're just talking to them. Try to get some cooperation."

He looked around. Nobody spoke.

Garwin dismissed them, and as they were filing out, he stopped Paul and said, "Hey bud, where's your tape?"

Paul put a hand over his badge.

"I didn't know where to get it," he said, which wasn't really a lie. There hadn't been a line-of-duty death since he'd joined the Department, and this was all new to him. It was one of those things they don't really teach at the Academy, the etiquette of death.

Garwin nodded.

"Here," he said, reaching into his shirt pocket and taking out a black felt ribbon with purple at the top and bottom edge. There was phrase stitched into the ribbon with gold thread: NEMO ME IMPUNE LACESSIT. Paul had no idea what it meant, but he fumbled to put it on his badge anyway.

Garwin watched him struggle with it, then said to Mike, "Help him with that, bud. Will you please?"

"Come here, genius," Mike said, and took the tape from Paul and worked it onto his badge for him.

"And Paul..."

"Yes sir."

Garwin made a vague gesture towards his own forehead. "Does that, uh, hurt?"

"No sir. I'm fine."

Garwin looked doubtful.

"It looks bad. You're off tomorrow and Monday, right?"

"Yes sir."

"Okay. If it's still like that on Tuesday, I'm gonna fill out an I9 Form on you, okay? An injured officer report. That means you're gonna have to go to a doctor and get it checked out. Understand?"

"Yes, sir. I'll be fine."

"I'm sure you will. Just take care of yourself, bud."

***

Mike already had his gear stowed in their patrol car. He drove them over to Paul's truck and leaned against the patrol car and smoked a cigarette while Paul got his gear.

"Hey, that stuff in there with Collins. What was that all about?"

Mike exhaled a long thin stream of smoke. "I think he thinks he's in the wrong career field."

"How's that?"

Mike shrugged. "Some people, you know, they don't really see themselves doing this job forever. Collins, he's about one of the smartest guys I've ever met. You should see him with anything electronic. Doesn't matter what it is, he can figure it out. Locks too. You ever need to pick a lock, he can do it."

"Does that come up a lot?"

Mike shrugged again.

"I hope I don't ever get that way," Paul said. "To the point I hate coming to work."

"He's harmless. Plus, he's not as bad as he used to be."

"You're kidding? He used to be worse?"

"There was a while, about two years ago I guess, he was fucking miserable. He was calling in sick all the time, bitching about every call he made. Getting in trouble over stupid shit. It was a pretty spectacular case of burnout. You'll see guys go through it every once in a while. It comes with the job."

"Why?"

"You mean, why does it come with the job?"

"No, I mean about Collins. Why was he so miserable?"

"He was bitter." Mike laughed. "I mean bitterer than he is now. Bitterer...is that a word? Fuck, who cares? Anyway, he got sued a few years ago. I think that's what did it."

"What'd he get sued for?"

"He and Wes pulled up on a guy who was trying to break into a car and they chased him into somebody's backyard tool shed. Inside there were all these paint cans all over the place. The car burglar pulled a screwdriver on them. After that, the fight was on. They were bumping into the walls and knocking shit over and the paint got everywhere. They were all covered with it. The car burglar, he got some of it in his eyes and ended up suing them for like fifty thousand each."

"They had to pay fifty thousand each to the guy?"

"No," Mike said. "Suits like that, they almost never go to trial. Most of the time, the guy just wants to get his hands in some deep pockets. Of course, the City doesn't help matters much. They usually settle out of court in suits like that. They paid the car burglar something like two thousand bucks and that shut him up. It's cheaper than paying the lawyers to take it to court. But what really pissed Collins off was that the DA's Office dismissed the resisting arrest charges against the car burglar, so it was like the guy got paid for fighting with the police. Ever since then, Collins feels like the job's got it in for him. He started calling in sick all the time, and Garwin ended up having to jump his shit about it."

"Garwin did?"

Mike took one last pull on his smoke and crushed it out on the pavement with the toe of his boot, nodding.

"I can't picture Garwin jumping anybody's shit," Paul said. "He seems kind of, well, meek, you know? I mean, inside, Collins and Seles looked like they were going to fight, and he didn't do anything."

"Garwin's a good guy," Mike said. "You may not have got a sense of it yet, but he's about the best supervisor you'll ever work for. I mean that, and not just because he lets me get away with fucking off on duty. It's easy to start despising the public, seeing the kind of crap we see every day. But Garwin's not that way. He really cares about people. I handled an accident one time where this six year old little boy got killed. The next day, I got called out to the pound to meet the family. They wanted to bury him in his favorite tennis shoes, those ones that light up with every step, you know? Thing was though, the car was all fucked up. His shoes were stuck inside all that twisted metal, and I looked at it and I was like, 'There ain't no way in hell I'm gonna be able to get those shoes out of there. I mean...I feel for you folks and all, but there's just no way.'"

He took his keys from his belt and motioned Paul towards the passenger seat.

Mike said, "At least, that's what I thought. Garwin came out and he talked to the family and then he told me to go back to my district. I thought that was the end of it. I didn't find out until later that he ended up spending the rest of the night prying those shoes out of that car with a tire iron. All by himself, you know? There was blood everywhere. Big bloody clumps of the kid's hair were stuck to the A pillar. The mom was crying her eyes out the whole time. It was the kind of thing that just sort of humbles you emotionally, you know? But Garwin just kept at it until he got those shoes out of there. He's good people, no matter what you may have seen tonight. I can't think of many people who'd do that."

"You know a story about everybody, don't you?"

Mike smiled. "Seems like it."

They got in the car, plugged their radios into the chargers, and Mike started going over the pre-trip vehicle inspection. He went down the list, putting check marks on a five-by-eight sheet of paper, then secured it to the sun visor with a rubber band.

"You ready?" Mike said.

"Let's do it."

But they hadn't even put the car in gear yet when Barris' voice broke the calm on the radio. He sounded panicked, urgent.

"44-50, we got a major accident here at East Houston and I-10, on the access road. I got a car just ran the light and hit an eighteen wheeler. He's jammed up under it. I'm gonna need EMS and two wreckers for sure. Start us some cover for traffic control, too, if you got it. We're gonna have to shut down the intersection."

"10-4," the dispatcher answered. "I got anybody leavin' the Sub can help him out?"

Mike keyed up their radio. "10-4, 44-70. Show us on the way."

"10-4," the dispatcher said.

She almost sounded bored.

Mike put the gas pedal all the way to floor. He had the car sliding sideways as they shot out of the parking lot, tires smoking, lights and sirens going full blast as he threaded through the sparse traffic.

Paul just held on to the dashboard and groaned.

Less than two minutes later they pulled up on Barris and Seles' call. The whole intersection was blocked. An eighteen wheeler hauling a load of hay had been turning from East Houston Street onto the access road of 10. A guy in a Ford pickup had been going too fast, tried to beat a yellow light, and ended up smashed underneath the flatbed trailer. The air was swirling with hay. Fluid was all over the road. Cars were driving up onto the curb to go around the scene, honking at each other. Barris was standing near the driver's side door of the Ford, trying to talk to the guy wedged inside. Seles was in the intersection, directing traffic.

"Oh Christ," Mike said. "What a clusterfuck."

He turned the car at an angle in front of Seles, blocking off the traffic lanes. The cars stuck behind him honked, but he ignored them. He strolled up to Seles, pointed him towards the wreck, and Seles turned and ran off to do whatever Mike had told him to do.

As Paul approached, Mike said, "Get some flares out of the trunk. Set up a flare line across here and force everybody to go that way."

He pointed towards the access road.

"Okay," Paul said.

Paul made it happen. Drivers started honking at him. He tried waving them on, but they stopped anyway and yelled at him out their open windows.

"I gotta go that way," one guy said.

"Nobody goes through," Paul answered back.

"My house is right there."

"Go down to MLK and turn around," Paul answered. He turned on his flashlight and pointed the beam down the road. "Come on. Move it."

The man shot him the bird with his finger. "Asshole," he shouted, and drove off.

Two more cars followed after him, but the third one stopped and yelled at Paul that he had to get through. A fire truck showed up while Paul was arguing with the guy and squeezed in between the front of Paul and Mike's patrol car and the wreck. Fire fighters got out and started trying to get the driver in the wrecked pickup out of his vehicle.

"You let him go through," the guy said, pointing at the fire truck.

What are you, a fucking idiot? Paul thought. But what he said was, "They're the fire department," and he couldn't believe he was even having to explain himself.

The man cursed, and Paul thought he saw the words *Fuck it* on the man's lips. The next moment he was driving around Paul, up on the curb, and around the accident scene. Paul trotted after him, then stopped, knowing that he couldn't stop him.

"Holy shit," Paul said. "Hey..."

Another car slipped behind him and drove up on the curb. Three more followed him.

"What the hell are you doing?" Paul yelled. He waved his flashlight at the cars, but the drivers just drove on by him.

All but the last car made it through. Before that one could get up on the curb, Mike appeared in front of it and hit the driver's side window with his fist so hard that Paul thought for a moment that the glass was going to break.

The driver slammed on the brakes and Mike yelled at him. A moment later, the car was headed down the access road, the driver scared near to death.

"What in the hell are you doing?" Mike asked him.

"I'm trying to turn them," Paul said, "but that first guy just drove around me."

"You can't let them through," Mike said. "They're trying to pull that guy out of the car. They need room to work."

"I know. They're not doing what I tell them."

Mike stepped around Paul and waved some cars towards the access road. Once he got the first few going, the line behind them followed.

Mike came back to Paul and said, "They try that shit again, put your gas mask on."

"My what?" Paul looked at him, not believing what he'd just heard. "You're kidding?"

Mike pointed to the flare line. "Stand out there with your gas mask on. If people think going straight is gonna kill them, they'll do what you say."

Paul wasn't sure if Mike was serious or not. He searched his face, looking for a hint of a smile or something, but he just couldn't tell. He actually looked serious.

"I'm kidding you," Mike said, smiling slightly. "You're doing okay. Just keep pushing them down the access road. Don't talk to them. Don't explain why. Just keep pushing them that way."

Paul looked relieved. "Okay," he said.

Mike's gaze shifted over Paul's shoulder and his eyes went wide.

"Ah shit!" Mike said.

Paul followed his gaze and saw a pair of headlights coming at them way too fast. Mike scrambled towards a lady who had stopped her car at the flare line. She had cracked her window a little and was trying to ask him what she was supposed to do. Mike yelled at her to move out of the way. She stared up at him blankly, too startled by his urgency to do what he said.

"Go!" he yelled. "Go go go go!"

He pounded on her door as the headlights closed on them. Paul could see it was an SUV. The driver was going so fast he could barely hold the road, the SUV's engine whining at full throttle.

"Mike!" Paul said.

"Move your fucking car!" Mike yelled at the woman. He looked over his shoulder at the SUV barreling down on him. For a horrible moment Paul saw his partner lit up by the approaching headlights, and it seemed that every passing second became elastic, stretched out in slow motion.

He saw Mike yell at the headlights, the SUV swerving blindly in response.

He saw the lady start to move her car, creeping, creeping.

Damn it, lady. Move!

He saw Mike jump on the hood of the lady's car. He heard the SUV's brakes lock. Saw it slide through the flare line, standing on its front wheels, passing right through the spot where the lady's car had just been and within inches of Mike rolling across her hood.

And then Paul heard the loudest crash he'd ever heard.

***

When the smoke cleared, Paul was standing in the middle of the intersection with ash and hay and dust swirling all around him, the lone, continuous drone of a car horn playing the same, ear-splitting note without ceasing.

The SUV, a candy blue Cadillac Escalade, had crashed into and under the back of the fire truck. The Escalade was smashed beyond recognition, the front end compressed into ruin, the back end sticking up at an angle into the air. The back tires were a good eight inches off the ground, still spinning. The passenger cab of the fire truck was undamaged, but the back end was completely destroyed, and the nine hundred feet of hoses it carried were spilled out on the roadway like intestines.

"Holy shit," Paul muttered. "Holy, holy shit."

The driver of the Escalade stank of beer and was acting wild, like he was high on methamphetamines. He had a bloody nose from the airbag, but otherwise, miraculously, he was fine. They pulled him out of the vehicle, and when the firefighters tried to check him out, he just stared at them and said, "Get off me, fool. What the fuck you doing in my house?"

"He's fine," one of the firefighters said.

"Really?" Paul asked.

"Yeah," the firefighter said. "He's an asshole, but he ain't injured."

When the firefighters were done with the guy, Paul cuffed him and put him in the back of their patrol car. He came back to the scene in time to witness a paramedic turn from the passenger side door and shake his head at Mike.

He and Mike made eye contact.

Mike said, "She's 10-60."

Dead, Paul thought. *10-60 is a D-O-A.*

"Go ask that guy her name," Mike said.

Paul leaned into the car. The man was enormous, even compared to Paul. He was platinum blond and dressed in a skin tight blue silk shirt and white linen pants. His eyeballs jerked in his sockets with a methamphetamine-induced nystagmus. He smelled like beer and cigars. The air around him was liquid with the stink of it.

Paul said, "That girl with you, what's her name?"

"Huh?"

"The girl you just killed. What's her name?"

"What fucking dead girl, man? I didn't kill no dead girl. You come in my house and hook me the fuck up? Bullshit's what that is, man." He leaned back into the seat and stared straight ahead. "Ain't no fucking dead girl in my house. *Sheeet.*"

Paul slammed the door on him.

"He doesn't even know what planet he's on," Paul said when he rejoined Mike. "He thinks we just pulled him off his couch."

"Nice. Listen, I gotta go talk to that woman over there, the one I was trying to get out of the way. She's pretty shaken up, but we're gonna need her as a witness. Can you go check his car? See if you can find that girl's purse or something. Something with her name on it for the report."

"Okay," Paul said. He looked towards the wrecked Escalade and swallowed. He mentally steadied himself for what he knew he was about to see and said, "All right."

The inside of the Escalade smelled like ash from the exploded airbags. Everything that had been in the rear of the vehicle had shifted forward—seats, clothes, CDs, speakers, hundreds of red pills that Paul guessed were probably ecstasy, maybe something else, bottles of beer—everything.

The dead girl in the passenger seat looked to be around seventeen, her little white halter top soaked with blood. More blood had pooled in the bowl her skirt made of her lap. When the Escalade had folded forward into a V shape, the roof had pushed down on the back of her head, slicing part of it away. Her eyes were open. So was her mouth. Her body was wedged up under the dashboard, her bare arms and shoulders laced with a thousand cuts from all the broken glass. From the way she was twisted up, Paul guessed every bone in her body was broken.

His eyes kept returning the tips of her blonde hair. They were clumped together, saturated with blood. They looked like wet paint brushes.

The Escalade's horn droned on.

Paul swallowed again, forcing his eyes away from her broken body. There was a strap of something that might have been her purse wedged up by her feet. He glanced at the girl's face, feeling almost like he needed to ask her permission, and then reached inside, cringing as his hand groped between her ankles, touching her bare legs, her gummy skin.

He couldn't pull the purse loose and he quickly took his hand away. He felt corrupted, like touching her had made his hand dirty somehow. His lips curled up in disgust. He wanted to wash himself. Then go somewhere and throw up.

He closed his eyes to steady himself, and when he opened them, the dead girl was looking at him, her eyes white as a bed sheet. She was trying to speak to him.

Paul suddenly had a flash of recognition. He saw through the blood and the shattered body and the horror of it all. He saw down to the depths, where another presence was rising up towards him.

"Momma?" he said.

Her mouth moved. He thought he saw his name form on her lips.

She reached a hand out towards his cheek.

Paul.

He shook his head, gently at first, then harder. "No," he said. "No, go away."

"Paul."

He felt confused, not knowing where the voices were coming from. The girl's lips were moving, but the sound was a man's voice. Mike's voice, distant, a world away.

Paul.

"Please don't touch me," Paul muttered, staring into the dead girl's white eyes—the eyes that weren't just hers any longer. "Please don't."

"Hey, Paul!"

All at once, Paul's attention was pulled away from the dead girl's face. He glanced up at Mike, their eyes meeting over the wreckage. Red and blue lights licked across the twisted metal and the fluid on the pavement.

"You have any luck with her ID?"

Paul looked down at the girl. She was dead again, empty brown eyes staring up into nothing.

He looked back at Mike and shook his head.

***

Several hours later, after they had written page after page of reports and the driver had been booked for Intoxication Manslaughter and Possession with Intent to Deliver on the ecstasy, Paul and Mike were back in their district.

They sat in their car, watching a group of three black men who were standing near a pay phone in the parking lot of a convenience store on the edge of the Witherby Courts Housing Project. Mike had the car blacked out, no lights, the radio turned down low. He had backed it into an alleyway choked with mesquite shrubs and scraggly hackberry and straw colored alkali grass. From where they sat they had a clear view of the intersection of Wedding and Hall Streets, the entire parking lot and two sides of the store, and a good part of the Courts, which was basically a sprawling complex of battered white concrete buildings splashed with graffiti and riddled with cracks and pocked by bullet holes.

Mike had leaned the driver's seat back as far as the plexiglass prisoner cage would let it go and was slouched down, his arms crossed over his chest, eyes nearly closed. Paul sat in the passenger seat, trying desperately to push the image of the dead girl in the Escalade from his mind while he fingered his badge and thought about what the Latin on the ribbon over his badge number meant.

I bet Rachel would know.

Mike coughed quietly to himself, but never took his eyes off the three men. So far, they hadn't seen the patrol car and Paul hadn't seen them do anything strange.

"What does this mean?" Paul said.

"What does what mean?"

"This ribbon Sarge gave me." He tried to pronounce the words, but couldn't get the last one out.

Mike glanced at him out of the corner of his eye and said, "It means, 'Nobody provokes me with impunity.'" Then he went back to watching the three men.

Paul thought about that, wondering why the translation made even less sense to him than the original Latin did.

"Why are you so interested in those guys?" he said.

"Garwin told us to shake down the junkies in our district for information. Those guys are junkies."

"Those guys?"

"Yeah."

At the Academy, one of Paul's instructors, a former Narcotics detective, told his class that while there was no place for racial stereotyping in police work, there was some truth to it when it came to racial preferences for certain kinds of drugs. Everybody smokes pot, he'd said. But beyond that, blacks usually go for cocaine. Mexican guys like heroin, and the white guys are the sluts of the drug world. They'll do just about anything they can get their hands on.

Paul studied the three black guys and felt like he was missing something. Why would they be messing around with heroin? If he'd been by himself, he'd have driven right by them and not given them a second thought.

Unable to figure it out, he said "How do you know they're junkies?"

"Because this is the Witherby Courts, the flea market of heroin sales."

Paul laughed, but Mike didn't even smile. Evidently, he was serious. And, evidently, he thought that was explanation enough.

Paul watched the men. He saw three dirty looking guys drinking oversized beers, but nothing like what he'd expected a heroin junkie to look like. Weren't junkies supposed to be famine refugee skinny with stringy hair and tattoos all over the place? He had expected to see a listless, comfortably numb sort of haze in their eyes. That was his picture of a heroin addict. But these guys, none of them were skinny, and one of the guys looked to be pushing three hundred pounds easy. They laughed and joked with each other and seemed fairly animated. All three watched the streets and the buildings around them carefully, constantly scanning every vehicle in the sparse parade of beat up cars that rolled by.

He was about to ask Mike what he was missing when Mike suddenly spoke up. "That guy in the green shirt—the fat one—I've hooked him up before. It was about eight months ago, on the other side of the Courts. The other two I don't know, but I doubt seriously they're hanging around with fat boy there for the pleasure of his company."

"Are they selling or trying to score?"

"Selling."

"Oh."

They had the windows down. It was hot, the air dusty. The alleyway smelled liked scorched vegetation. Paul could hear cicadas close by.

Mike said, "You see them with those beers, right?"

"Yeah."

"Have you seen them drink any since we've been here?"

Paul thought about that. "No," he said slowly.

"Most of the time they package heroin in little colored balloons. They keep the balloons in their mouths. The beers are in case we show up. If we get too close, they swig the beer and swallow the dope."

"Oh," Paul said. After a moment, he said, "Then what?"

"What do you think? They wait for us to leave, then they go behind the store there and get their dope back."

"They..."

Mike smiled. "It comes out one end or the other."

"Oh God."

"Heroin's a nasty business," Mike said, and shrugged.

"You ain't kidding."

"I'm waiting for them to make a sale. When they do, we'll take them down."

"We're gonna arrest them? Didn't Garwin say—"

"Paul, we're not gonna waste time talking to these clowns without anything to hold over their heads. Collins was right about that. Look at those guys. Do you really believe they'd tell us all about life as a heroin dealer if we just walked up there and started shooting the shit?"

"No, I guess not."

"You're damn right. These guys, they're not gonna talk to you unless they think they can get something out of the deal. As it is, we've got nothing to bargain with. But if we've got them in handcuffs, well, that changes things, doesn't it?"

Paul thought about that. "Yeah," he said, "I guess it does."

Out on the street, a dark blue Chevy Monte Carlo rolled up to the three heroin dealers. One of the dealers walked up to the passenger window and leaned in. A few seconds later, the man walked back to the other two men and the car drove off.

"That's it," Mike said.

"What?" Paul said. "What happened?"

"The guys in the Monte Carlo just scored. That's what I've been waiting for."

"Okay," Paul said. "Now what?"

"Now we go take them down." Mike was sitting up in his seat now, his eyes sparkling with anticipation. "This is what I want you to do. We're gonna roll up on them as fast as possible. When we do, you jump out, knock down the closest one to you, and grab him by the throat and squeeze. Don't let go until he spits out the dope, you hear?"

Paul looked at Mike like he'd just grown four heads. "You're kidding?"

"Do I look like I'm kidding?"

Paul decided that he didn't. Of course, with Mike that didn't necessarily mean anything one way or the other.

"Can we do that?" Paul said. "I mean, just start choking people."

Mike grew very serious, and suddenly there was no doubt that he meant exactly what he was saying.

"Look," he said, "we play dumb jokes on each other all the time, but when it comes to dealing with the dope dealers, the fun and games stop. Those guys over there don't give a rat's ass about you, and they don't care whether you go home in the morning or not. If they can kill you and get away with it, they will. Do not let your guard down for a second. I mean that. You keep choking that motherfucker until he gives up. If you don't, he'll know you're weak, and not only will he swallow the dope, but he will proceed to fuck your world. We clear on that?"

"Yeah," Paul said. "We're clear."

"Don't think it's like the Academy, where you let the other person tap out because you think they might get hurt. Out here, you go full tilt. You hear?"

"I hear you."

"Okay. You ready?"

No, Paul wanted to say. Suddenly things were going way too fast for him. But he nodded. "Yeah, I'm ready."

That was good enough for Mike. He dropped the Crown Victoria into gear and charged out of the alleyway under full acceleration, closing the distance to the dealers in a matter of seconds.

The three men scattered. They were already running by the time Paul and Mike jumped out of their car, but they were hardly a match for Paul. Paul had played college football for a Division II school, and you don't make it to that level without being graced by a few rare gifts. He had size and raw physical strength and agility and above all speed. Plus, he was still close to his physical peak. The heroin dealer was not. One of them tried to feint left, then veered right, cutting a diagonal across Paul's track. Paul wasn't fooled for a second. He moved quickly and overtook the man within a few steps. Paul grabbed him around the neck and slung him face first into the asphalt.

He rolled the dealer over and dropped down on top of him so that he was straddling his chest. Paul pushed his hand under the man's chin and found the windpipe. His fingers closed down around it and he squeezed. He squeezed as hard as he could.

The man grabbed his wrist with both hands and tried to pull his hand away, but Paul kept up the pressure. He could feel the resistance in the muscles and the tendons beneath the man's skin. The man's jaw was clenched so tightly it seemed like his teeth might shatter in his mouth.

"Spit it out!" Paul yelled at him. "Mother fucker, spit it out."

Paul didn't even realize he was banging the back of the man's head on the asphalt with every word. There was too much adrenaline coursing through him for him to do anything else but squeeze.

The man was trying to speak, but no sound came out. Finally, after what seemed to be forever, the man rolled his head to one side and spit out four small, brightly colored balloons. They looked like gumballs.

"All of them!" Paul said, and squeezed harder.

Two more balloons came out.

The man wasn't breathing. His eyes looked as if they might turn up into his skull. Paul let go, and the man sucked in a huge lungful of air. His eyes regained their focus. But before the man could completely regroup, Paul flipped him over and forced one arm behind his back.

"Put your other hand behind your back," he shouted. "Sir, put your hand behind your back."

"Fuck you," the man wheezed.

Paul dug his knee into the man's back. "Put your hands behind your back. Now!"

The man kept his left arm tucked under his body, using his weight to keep it from Paul. There was no way he could get up, because Paul had him pinned, but he was still fighting to stay out of the cuffs. Paul rose up a little and then rammed his knee down into the man's spine.

"Give me your hand. Now!"

The man just grunted. He kept his left arm hidden under his body. Paul twisted the man's right arm further up behind his back, wrenching it so hard the man had to arch his back to fight against the pain.

"I'll break it," Paul said. "I swear I will. Now get your other hand—"

The high-pitched, metallic-sounding *pop pop pop pop pop pop* of a small caliber semiautomatic pistol erupted somewhere to his left. It was like a car backfiring, only faster, more purposeful.

Paul looked in the direction of the shots. His grip on the dealer slackened. The man jumped at the opportunity and started fighting. By the time Paul could regain his hold, the man had already squirmed out from beneath him and was up on his feet. He took off running, the cuffs still dangling from his right wrist, and didn't look back.

Paul started after him, but stopped after only a few steps. Even as the man was breaking away from him, Paul heard the sound of an engine revving up, and a moment later a beige Cadillac Deville skidded around the corner. It turned toward them, but the driver slammed on the brakes at the sight of the police car. The driver put the car in reverse and burned out backwards down the street. As Paul stood there watching, too startled to move, the car spun around and took off the other way.

"Come on, dammit!" Mike yelled at him.

He had already let his guy go and was running to the car.

***

Paul followed him. He jumped into the passenger seat as Mike threw the car into gear. They crashed down over the curb and fishtailed onto the street, the Cadillac's taillights disappearing around a corner two blocks down.

Mike keyed up the car's radio.

"44-70," he said.

Mike sounded perfectly calm, like he was ordering a cheeseburger at the drive-thru. Paul was shaking like an epileptic.

"44-70," Mike said again.

"Go ahead, 44-70," the dispatcher answered.

"44-70, we got one running. Westbound on Wedding from Hall Street. Approaching Ash Street now. Still westbound."

"10-4, vehicle description?"

"Beige four door Cadillac. Late model, rear end damage. Texas plate four-whiskey-golf-hotel-three-nine."

"Copy that, 44-70. What's he running for?"

"On Ash Street now, going southbound."

"10-4," the dispatcher answered. "Southbound on Ash Street from Wedding. 44-50, 44-60, start that way. What's he running for, 44-70?"

"We're westbound again. On Clarke Street now."

Paul noticed the way Mike's voice got much quieter when he was excited. As he worked the car through the neighborhood, all the way on the gas, then all the way on the brakes, then back on the gas again, shuffle-steering around the corners, hitting the apex of every curve with surgical precision, he still managed to call out their position with perfect clarity. And then, somewhere between watching Mike work the Crown Victoria like a race car and holding onto the dashboard for dear life, it dawned on him that he was in the middle of his first bona fide car chase.

At the Academy, Paul had taken eighty hours of performance driving training. The cadets learned how to take corners at high speed, how to shuffle steer so the radio cord doesn't get tangled around your hands, how to use the car's weight and power to your advantage. There was even a twenty-four hour long segment on how to do the Pursuit Interdiction Technique, or PIT maneuver.

But the most important lesson the instructors had tried to convey was the need to stay calm. Think about fist fights you've been in, the instructors had said. It doesn't matter how good you are, everybody gets scared. Everybody. We all feel the same sense of nausea, the same tightening of the muscles, the same tunnel vision. It's completely natural, even when you've done it before. The same thing happens in vehicle pursuits. No matter how much training you have, or how many times you've done it, you still feel that giant fist squeezing around your belly, taking your breath away.

The trick is to use that feeling, channel it, focus it, make it work for you and against the bad guy. You start by breathing slowly and regularly. You keep your head moving, your eyes scanning the road in front of you and beside you. That way, you avoid tunnel vision, and you decrease the chances of running headlong into an accident.

Paul was dimly aware of all that somewhere in the back of his head, but he was a long ways from applying it. He kept his eyes on the Cadillac's taillights, oblivious to almost everything else that was going on.

They chased the Cadillac through a maze of smaller streets, but Mike stayed with them, calling out street names and directions of travel without ever having to look at the signs. Paul wasn't able to keep up with the course they had taken. He occupied himself with holding onto the dashboard, ready to bail out when the foot chase started.

When they turned onto Wintertime Avenue from Vance Alley, Mike said, "He screwed up. If he doesn't turn off before the bridge, he'll end up in the train yard."

The driver of the Cadillac seemed to realize it, too, though he couldn't stop in time to make the turn. He rocked the car to the left and then tried to make the right turn, but he was going way too fast for that. The back end kicked out and he started to fishtail. He locked up the brakes, which was the wrong thing to do, and the car spun up over a curb, landing in the grass about twenty feet to the left of the street where he had planned to turn.

Mike brought the patrol car up to the curb near the turn off, blocking the Cadillac from cutting through the grass and getting to the street that would have taken them out of the area. But the Cadillac wasn't done. The driver put it in reverse and backed up, grinding the tailpipes on the pavement as his back end went over the curb.

"Continuing eastbound on Wintertime," Mike said into the radio. "Looks like he's gonna go into the train yard."

"10-4, 44-70, still eastbound. What's he running for?"

"He did a drive-by at the Witherby Courts. Somewhere around Wedding and Hall."

"10-4," the dispatcher said. "I'm getting that call now. 44-100, are you monitoring, sir?"

Garwin's voice came over the radio.

"10-4, 44-100. Speed and traffic conditions?"

"Speed and traffic, 44-70?" the dispatcher asked.

"We're going over the bridge now," Mike said. "Speed's about eighty miles per hour. No traffic."

"Copy that, 44-100?" the dispatcher asked.

"I copy," said Garwin. "See if we can get Hawkeye Bravo overhead. Pursuit is authorized."

Mike laughed. "Way to go, Garwin."

"Copy that, 44-70?" the dispatcher asked. "You are authorized to pursue."

"We copy," Mike said. "We're over the bridge now. Looks like he's gonna be entering the train yard."

The road ahead of them was completely dark, save for the Cadillac's red taillights bouncing all over the place. They were leaving the regularly traveled part of the road behind and entering the service drive to the train yard. Paul had only the vaguest idea of what that meant and what the train yard was, but from the way Mike was acting, Paul expected the chase to be over real soon.

They hit a bump and the car bottomed out. Paul's soda went flying out of the cup holder and rolled under the cage and into the backseat foot wells. Mike cursed under his breath as he struggled to maintain control of the car over the rutted road.

"44-70," Mike said. "Advise our cover they're entering the train yard. They're probably gonna try and bail on us here real soon."

"10-4, 44-70. 44-50, 44-60, you copy that?"

The others acknowledged the dispatcher.

"Get ready," Mike said. "They won't be able to get very far inside with the car."

Paul was watching the taillights eagerly. Once they got inside the train yard, his view widened to include a little more of their surroundings. The train yard was exactly what it sounded like. As far as he could see in both directions were rusted-out boxcars on rust-colored tracks crisscrossing the yard. The road they were on went straight into the center of the yard, up a fairly steep, but not very high, embankment, and disappeared on the other side of an engineless line of boxcars.

"Hawkeye Bravo to East Patrol Dispatch, be advised we are overhead and the cameras are rolling."

"10-4," the dispatcher said. "All units, be advised, Hawkeye Bravo is ten-six over the location. Hawkeye Bravo, you will be calling the pursuit."

"10-4, Hawkeye Bravo, we have the ball."

Paul tried to hold onto the dashboard, but Mike's driving was throwing him all over the car, even with his seatbelt on.

Mike steered the car around a curve, turning into the skid to hold the road.

He said, "When they run for it, if your guy gets too far away from you, just backtrack to the car and let Hawkeye use the FLIR to find him. That way we can get some cover out here. Remember, they're armed."

Paul nodded, then held on tight and waited for the end.

***

Just ahead, a line of boxcars was blocking the road. The flutter in Paul's stomach started up again. The end was almost here.

But instead of stopping, the Cadillac veered to the right, off the roadway, and drove down a dirt path parallel to the tracks. Mike followed, bottoming out the police car as he dropped them into the ruts in the road. He backed off on his speed and let the Cadillac pull ahead. Paul knew what he was doing. He'd heard it plenty of times in the Academy's driving course. Whenever possible, let the bad guy screw himself up. You don't have to drive up their tailpipe to be effective in a pursuit. Just back off and wait for them to lose control.

The Cadillac passed the last boxcar and then did something unexpected. The tracks were elevated above the road on a bed of white limestone rocks about the size of golf balls, and after passing the last boxcar in the line, the Cadillac turned into the embankment and tried to drive up and over the tracks. Its front wheels slid into the rocks and then got airborne for a moment, landing on top of the tracks and grinding to a stop, so that it was high-centered across both rails.

Mike guided the patrol car to a stop. Both front doors and the back door on the passenger side of the Cadillac flew open. Three teenagers jumped out and ran in different directions.

"Here we go," Mike said over the radio. "They're on foot now."

"Hawkeye Bravo, we've got a good visual on all three."

"10-4," the dispatcher said. "44-50, 44-60, let me know when you're out with them."

Mike took off after the driver. The two from the passenger side went in different directions. The guy in the front seat ran off into the tall weeds to Paul's right. The guy in the backseat still had the gun in his hand, and he ran into the train yard.

Paul went after him.

He chased the kid—for he could tell now that he was a kid, no more than sixteen or seventeen, at the most—across the tracks and down the other side. The kid was fast, and he had a pretty good lead on Paul, but Paul was faster. He closed the gap quickly, gaining on him as they rounded the back corner of another line of boxcars and jumped over a large cement block that must have been a loading ramp at one time.

The kid let out a startled whine when he saw Paul closing in, and he turned and pointed his pistol at Paul. Paul ducked between two boxcars and pulled his own pistol. He was breathing hard, but he wasn't winded. If anything, he felt wide awake, hyperaware of his surroundings. Hawkeye Bravo was overhead, its spotlight filling the gap between the two lines of boxcars with a flickering blue light. Paul could hear the rotors thumping against the air. He could see skeins of dust moving snakelike across the ground. He could smell his own breath, hot and dry. And though the rotors were making a huge noise, he could still hear the sound of the kid's sneakers slapping the ground as he ran. He was in the zone.

Paul ducked down and looked under the boxcar. He caught a glimpse of the kid jumping into another boxcar further up the row. He waited a second to see if the kid would stick his head back out.

Nothing happened.

Hawkeye Bravo's spotlight flooded the scene. Paul watched shadows dancing on the ground. He saw clouds of dust fill the air.

Where are you, you little shit? Come on, I know you're there. Show me.

And then a scream filled the air. He didn't so much hear it, as felt it. The sound was high-pitched, terrified, laced with pain. It was like an icepick jammed into his ear.

Paul ducked back behind the corner of the boxcar and waited and listened. He heard a dull thud, something heavy landing in the dirt up ahead. Peering under the bottom lip of the boxcar, he saw something white on the ground near the entrance where the kid had climbed inside. In the glow of the helicopter's spotlight, whatever it was had a blue cast to it.

Paul waited for it to move.

It didn't.

He swallowed, took a deep breath, then, with his gun up and ready, Paul charged into the gap between the two rows of boxcars.

And stopped.

There, next to the open door of the boxcar, was a dead Angora goat. "Oh my God," he said. The animal was on its side, but its chin was flat on the ground, the neck twisted at a horrible angle. Its eyes were open and glassy, its tongue hanging from its mouth. Even from three boxcars away, Paul could tell the animal's chest was torn wide open.

From the boxcar, he heard the sickening crunch of breaking bones, and beneath that, a wet, *shlopping* sound.

In his heart he knew what that sound was, though his mind refused to get around it. His hands dropped to his side, and he walked forward to the open doors of the boxcar, not even glancing at the dead goat on the ground at his feet.

Inside, he saw a man in a white, heavily starched long-sleeved shirt, black Stetson hat, and black pants. The man was kneeling over the supine body of the teenager Paul had been chasing, the boy's chest ripped open, his face warped by a look of profound terror.

An unfinished lattice sculpture of sticks and baling wire was propped up in the middle of the boxcar.

Martin Henninger painted three symbols across the boy's forehead, chanting, "*emet, emet, emet*." Then he rose to his feet and turned to look at Paul. The whole front of his shirt was stained with blood, the shirt sleeves red all the way up to his biceps. His face was exactly as Paul remembered it, lean and hard, his dark eyes completely devoid of emotion.

Paul sucked in a breath. His knees felt weak from fear, and he could almost feel the blood draining from his face.

"Come in here, boy," Martin Henninger said. "I've got something to tell you, and we don't have much time."

Paul just stood there.

"Now, boy."

Paul flinched. His body remembered the anger in that voice, even after all the years that had passed since the last beating he had taken at this man's hands. He put his hands on the ledge of the boxcar and pulled himself inside.

Then he stood there, facing his father.

Martin Henninger stepped forward.

"I told you you've been marked. Don't you remember that? I told you I'd be coming to finish this. You got a charge to keep, boy. I mean to pass it on to you."

Paul shook his head. His eyes were wide open.

"No," he said. "No, no, no."

"You remember what we talked about?" Martin Henninger touched his chest to where the aerator's spikes had pushed through his body. "You remember? The night you gave me this? Yeah, you remember. I can see it on your face. Paul, this thing I'm asking of you, this responsibility, you don't choose it. It chooses you."

Paul shook his head again.

His father pointed at Paul's forehead, blood dripping from his fingers onto the metal floor of the boxcar. "Paul, I got so much I've got to tell you. You still have so much to learn. And I ain't got much time to do it in."

"Daddy, no." Paul backed away. "Daddy, please, I don't want it."

"Don't cry around me, boy. It makes me furious to see you acting like a pussy. I'm gonna come for you, real soon. You hear me? You get yourself ready."

Paul took another step back and hit the wall. There was no place left to go.

The helicopter's spotlight flickered all around him. His hair whipped in the rotor wash. His father came closer.

"I'll see you again real soon, Paul. Mind that mark I put on you. Your time is coming."

Paul looked away from his father's face, and saw dust pouring out from under his father's shirt. It was coming out from under the sleeves at his wrist and pouring over the collar buttoned at his neck.

Martin Henninger's face was coming apart as more and more of his skin turned to dust.

Paul's lip curled at it in disgust.

"Make yourself ready, Paul," his father said. "What's coming is coming soon."

And then he came apart, dissolving and drifting out of the boxcar like smoke on the wind.

***

Paul still had his face turned away from where his father had been, his eyes tightly closed, his nerves raw. But gradually, his breath came back, and with it his other senses stirred to life again. The helicopter's spotlight danced all over him, and in the glow he could see the broken body of the kid from the Cadillac crumpled up in the far corner of the boxcar.

His radio was buzzing with panicked voices. Somewhere in the jumble of noise he heard his own name being called, and he responded mechanically.

"44-70 Bravo."

"Are you okay, 44-70?"

The dispatcher sounded frantic.

"10-4, ma'am," he said. He stared at the gore in front of him, then keyed up his radio again and said, "But I think the suspect is dead."

From outside the car he heard other officers running for his location, and he stood there in shock, his skin gritty with something soot-like, and he wondered what in the hell he was going to say to the others when they saw the mess at his feet.

Chapter 7

Paul sat in the doorway of an open boxcar about seventy feet from where he had just watched his father murder that poor black kid. He had his Barber fifty cent piece out and he was rolling it absently across the back of his hand. Evidence technicians were all over the scene, taking pictures of the boxcar and the dead body inside it. He saw one of them point at the dead goat. Paul could read the man's lips and the expression on his face. *What the hell am I supposed to do with this?*

Earlier, the evidence technicians had run a line of yellow crime scene tape in a wide circle around the boxcar, and now Paul watched it flutter in the breeze. He felt like he was overheated, muddleheaded. People moved all around him, and it seemed so unreal. Everyone was busy, focused on their jobs. They moved with such purpose, while Paul, who just sat there, waiting, felt like he was drifting aimlessly. Nothing made sense, and the fact that everyone around him seemed so composed only added to his unease.

There was black, sooty grime on his hands. It was gritty to the touch, yet oily too. Growing up, Paul spent most of his summers picking peaches from the orchard on their land. His father kept the orchard as a way of making a little extra cash during the summer months. He and Paul would harvest the peaches by themselves, cart them back to the barn where his mother had hanged herself, and then box them up into white cardboard boxes for shipping to the produce terminal in South San Antonio. The boxes were treated with a thin, industrial grade wax that was supposed to keep the bugs out. That wax was gritty to the touch, and slick, a lot like the stuff he had on his hands now. But that sealant wax was clear; this stuff was black. He'd managed to wipe most of it off on his pant legs, but he could still feel it, and he didn't like the memories that came flooding up with it.

He tried to sort out the fractured images in his head. He remembered the kid running from the Cadillac, weaving through the rusted boxcars. He remembered the dead goat. And he remembered seeing his father inside that boxcar, the dead kid at his feet. After that, cover officers arrived to help him. They were led to the scene by Hawkeye's spotlight shining down from above, and Paul remembered seeing them appear in the flickering bluish-white light, guns drawn, shoulders bladed off in combat stances, then lowering their weapons in confusion and disgust, looking first at the dead goat on the ground, and then at Paul, and then at the puddle of blood spreading out from underneath the dead kid.

Collins had been the first to speak. He said, "Oh shit," then got on the radio and started telling the dispatcher what they needed.

Paul climbed down from the boxcar after that and stood, trembling, while the others looked in at the mess. Seles looked at Paul, then at the dead body, and then back at Paul, and said, "He's ripped wide open. What in the hell happened in there?"

Collins spun around and snapped at Paul. "Don't you say a fucking word, Paul. Don't you dare answer him." Then Collins stuck his finger in Seles' face. "What in the hell's wrong with you? You don't ask him a damn thing. You know better than that."

"Get your finger out of my face," Seles said.

Collins dismissed him with an angry wave of his hand, a gesture that was clearly meant to be insulting. "Man," he said to Seles, "you really fucking piss me off, you know that?" He turned to Paul. "Henninger, you keep your mouth shut."

Seles got into Collins' face. Collins' eyes narrowed.

"What are you gonna do?" Collins said, clearly taunting him. "You want something?"

Paul just stood there and watched them squaring off, posturing each other. Collins' nostrils flared. His eyes were slitted, unblinking. His mouth was curled into a smile. Both men had their guns in their hand, though they were making an exaggerated gesture of keeping them tucked down, against their thighs. Paul could tell from just one look that this wasn't about him. Not directly, anyway. These two had it in for each other, and Paul was just the excuse.

"Come on and do it if you're gonna do it," Collins said.

Mike showed up then.

"Knock it off," he ordered, and his voice cut through the air like a blast of arctic air. They were all the same rank, all of them patrolmen, but Mike entered their little circle with all the clout of deputy chief, and not one of them dared to question his right to give orders.

Mike forced his way into the crowd.

"Collins," he said, "you cool it. Now! I said now! Holster your gun." He turned to Seles. "You and Barris go secure the perimeter. We're gonna have the press all over this place in a few minutes and we need to have our crime scene under control before then. Don't let anybody in here until we can get EMS to pronounce him. And nobody talks to Paul about this until he's had a chance to talk to an attorney."

"Attorney?" Paul said. "Why do I...?"

Mike grabbed his shoulder and half led, half pushed him towards the boxcar.

"Don't worry about this," Mike said. "Just go have a seat over there. Garwin will be here in a few minutes. He'll tell you what's gonna happen."

"But why do I need an attorney? I don't understand. I didn't…I didn't do that."

"Nobody said you did. Just try to relax, okay? And remember, don't say a word until you've talked to your attorney. You'll have to tell Garwin what happened, but beyond that, you keep your mouth shut, understand?"

Paul hesitated, but eventually said, "Okay."

Mike gave him a friendly smile.

"Trust me, you'll be fine."

Fine, Paul thought. *Yeah, right. Didn't you hear? I got a charge to keep?*

***

He'd been sitting in this boxcar now for a long time, and he still hadn't been able to sort it out in his head. Earlier in the evening, when he'd sensed his mother's presence staring back at him from that dead girl in the Escalade, he'd thought he was losing his mind. But what he'd just seen didn't allow him the luxury of that kind of doubt. There was no way to explain away what he had seen in that boxcar. That *was* his father. No amount of self-doubt was going to change that. And, as if he really needed anything else in the way of proof, there was that dead body over there, underneath that yellow tarp. And the dead goat. And the stick lattice sculpture they'd discovered afterward tucked back in the dark of the boxcar. Those things were as real as the coin in his hand. They couldn't be pushed aside.

The more he thought about it, the faster he moved the Barber fifty cent piece back and forth between his hands. All he wanted to do was turn his mind off, let the hands work themselves. It was easier not to think.

He forced himself to slow down and worked on a few simple vanishings.

You've got a charge to keep, boy.

"Hey."

Paul flinched.

He looked to his right and saw Wes standing there, leaning against the boxcar.

"You okay?" Wes asked.

"Yeah," Paul admitted. "Sorry, you startled me."

"Yeah, well, that's understandable. You've been through a lot."

Paul nodded.

"Garwin sent me over here," Wes said. "I'm supposed to stay with you in case the news tries to talk to you."

"Oh. Okay. Thanks, I guess."

"I'm not doing you a favor. It's required. Read your General Manual."

"Oh." Paul waited for Wes to say something, but he just stood there. "So, is Garwin gonna be coming around any time soon?"

"Eventually," Wes said.

Wes dug his phone out of his pocket and went back to his Facebook page. Paul watched him, then looked across the train yard, where CSI technicians were retracing the path of his foot pursuit with cameras and other equipment he didn't recognize.

He turned back to Wes. "So, what happens next?"

Wes looked up from his phone. He seemed annoyed. "Huh?"

"I'm sorry. You're busy."

Wes nodded, then went back to his phone.

Paul let his legs swing free, like a little kid in a big chair. He hated this, the feeling that he'd been put on the back burner and left to simmer.

He said, "Hey, Wes?"

Wes put the phone down. "Yeah?"

"I'm sorry, I just feel a little, you know...what am I waiting here for?"

"For Garwin."

"Yeah, I know that. But, why?"

"Because that's how these things are handled. You talk to Garwin, then Homicide, then the DA. I'd make sure you have your attorney with you when you talk to Homicide and the DA, though."

Paul was confused again.

"Wait. What do you mean, how these things are handled."

"These things," Wes said. "An in-custody death. You know?"

No, he didn't know. Paul felt dizzy. There was too much coming at him at one time. He wanted to scream out loud that he needed a time out, that he needed everyone to just go away and let him think. But of course, he had just spent the last twenty minutes doing nothing but sitting and thinking, and it hadn't gotten him anywhere.

He closed his eyes and took a deep breath, then made his best effort to sound focused. "So, this is an in-custody death?"

"Yeah."

"But I didn't do anything to that kid. I didn't have him under arrest. I was just chasing him. How can this be an in-custody death?"

Wes shrugged. "I'm not really supposed to talk to you about this."

Paul waited, but Wes didn't offer anything more. Just went back to his phone.

For a moment Paul managed to pull his mind away from his parents and turned to this new problem, the in-custody death. He'd heard plenty about in-custody death investigations while he was a cadet, but in almost every one of those cases, the suspects had died after a physical arrest had been made. In other words, after the guy was handcuffed. It usually happened in drug cases, where the suspect swallows a large amount of dope and the baggie ruptures inside his stomach and he overdoses in the backseat of the patrol car. But that didn't fit his situation at all. He hadn't come anywhere near putting his hands on the kid. And, worse, his suspect hadn't overdosed. He'd been murdered.

Still, despite the fact that nothing fit, knowing that the others were thinking this was an in-custody death made part of the picture a little clearer. He'd been wondering why one of the evidence technicians had come by and photographed his hands and scratched the dirt from under his fingernails into an evidence envelope.

Paul interrupted Wes. "Someone said earlier that I might get sued. You think that's true?"

"Probably," Wes said, and shrugged again. "You know what they say. You're not a real policeman until you've been sued. Don't worry about it. If somebody sues, you'll probably beat it. As soon as they throw in the bit about the guy doing the drive-by, you'll be off the hook. Plus, you saw his chest. The kid was murdered. If you didn't do that, and I don't see any blood on you, then you don't have anything to worry about."

Yeah, right, nothing to worry about. I got a charge to keep, whatever the hell that means. Tell me how that's nothing to worry about.

Paul looked down at his hands, at the Barber fifty cent piece rolling over his knuckles, and thought again of his father and all the storm of hatred and terror and love—yes, even love—that came with that.

***

Through the crowds of officers and crime scene people and Medical Examiner Investigators and contract ambulance guys in white plastic rain suits waiting to remove the body, Paul saw Sergeant Garwin.

He didn't look happy.

The sergeant stopped a patrolman walking through the area and apparently asked where he could find Paul, because the patrolman turned and pointed right at him.

"Well, there he is," Wes said.

Paul followed Garwin with his eyes as he made his way over to them.

"Yep."

"Good luck."

"Thanks," Paul said.

Wes patted him on the shoulder again and walked off, leaving Paul with Garwin.

Garwin stopped in front of him and shook his hand. "You doing okay there, bud?"

"Yes, sir," Paul lied.

"This is hard stuff to deal with. You don't ever get over it, believe me."

"Yes, sir. Thank you, sir."

Garwin crossed his arms over his chest and nudged a pebble around on the ground with the toe of his boot. He seemed to be planning his questions out in his head.

"Listen," he said, "this is complicated. A lot of stuff is gonna be happening because of what went on here tonight. A lot of people are gonna be asking you questions. You're probably gonna have to answer the same questions over and over again. You understand that, right?"

"Yes, sir."

"Good. Did anyone tell you to make sure you talk to your attorney before you give your statement?"

"Yes, sir. Mike did, sir."

"That's good. He's looking out for you." Garwin said, "Look, bud, what I'm about to ask you is different than your statement. You have the right to an attorney, just like anybody else, but because you're a policeman, you also have a responsibility to tell me exactly what happened so that we can get this investigation going. You understand that that's a condition of your employment, separate from your civil rights under Miranda, right?"

Not really, Paul thought. But he nodded anyway.

Garwin said, "Now tell me what happened."

Paul babbled something about seeing the Cadillac at the drive-by back at the Witherby Courts.

"I know about that," Garwin said. "Tell me what happened *here*."

Paul sighed. "I saw the kid in that boxcar jump out of the Cadillac and run this way. I followed him. When I got to that line of cars over there, he turned and pointed his gun at me. I ducked down behind another boxcar and waited. When I turned around, he was dead."

Garwin waited.

Paul could feel him dragging the moment out, hoping on the silence to coax more details out of him, but Paul held his silence.

"That's it?" Garwin said at last.

"Yes, sir."

"What about the goat?"

"I saw that when I started to advance on the boxcar, sir."

"And the kid, what about him?"

"Sir?"

"Did you see him at all?"

"Not until I got to the boxcar, sir."

"Did you hear anything, any screaming?"

Paul shook his head.

"The kid is ripped open less than thirty feet from you and you didn't hear anything?"

"No, sir," Paul said. But he had. He had heard the kid scream. Why was he lying? Why was he continuing to lie?

He didn't know.

Garwin looked him square in the eyes.

Paul looked down at the Barber fifty cent piece in his hand. He didn't know why he'd lied about the screaming he'd heard. There was a voice inside his head telling him to be quiet about it. He didn't understand it, but he obeyed it.

"Do you mind telling me how that's possible, bud?"

"I don't know, sir. Maybe...I don't know. I was scared. I mean I was really scared. He just pointed a gun at me, you know? I might have heard something. It's hard to say. The helicopter was right above me. It was making a lot of noise. Maybe there was a scream and I just blocked it out. I don't know."

"Did you see anyone?"

"No, sir. No one."

Garwin went silent again.

Finally, he said, "Hey bud, I want you to look at me. Look me in the eye."

Paul did. It was hard to hold Garwin's stare, but he did.

"Listen very carefully to what I'm about to say to you, okay? What happened here tonight is more important than the death of some piece of shit gangbanger. You understand that, right? What happened to that kid in there is the exact same thing that happened last night at the Morgan Rollins Iron Works. The exact same thing. You understand the significance of that, right? Tell me you do."

Paul nodded.

"Tell me. I want to hear you say the words."

Paul swallowed the lump in his throat. The connection to the Morgan Rollins Iron Works was something he'd already thought long and hard about.

Paul said, "I understand you, sir."

"Good," Garwin said, and when he spoke again, his voice was almost a whisper. "Bobby Cantrell, one of the detectives who died last night, was a good friend of mine. One of my ex-wives founded the Police Officer's Wives Auxiliary with his wife. Bobby and I have been friends for the last twenty years. I care about him. I care about what his wife is going through right now. I need you to tell me everything you saw here tonight. If you saw anything at all, it might help us figure out who killed one of the best officers this Department has ever had. Now tell me, please, if you've left anything at all out."

Garwin stopped there, and waited.

Paul felt like he was going to throw up. All he wanted to do was run and hide his head in the sand somewhere, to get out of the spotlight.

He said, "I've told you everything, sir," and then he waited for Garwin's response.

Garwin searched his face for more. Paul faced him as best he could.

"Okay, bud," Garwin said. He put a hand on Paul's shoulder. "Okay, that's fine. Why don't you come on over here with me? The Shooting Team's over there by your car. They're gonna want to talk to you, too."

***

From the top of the Kingsbury Street Bridge, Keith Anderson could see the entire Seguin Railway Yard. There were police cars everywhere, and the scene was lit up like a neon Christmas by the cruisers' red and blue LED lights. Three helicopters circled overhead. One of them, moving very close to the ground, was almost certainly Hawkeye Bravo. The other two, higher up, were bound to be news crews. They were going to be a lot more of them, he knew, as soon as word got out that they were dealing with another situation like last night's mass murder.

Anderson had always hated the east side. There were a few pockets that were really nice—ranch lands crisscrossed by slow-moving streams and dotted with thick copses of trees—but for the most part, the east side of San Antonio was densely-packed urban decay at its worst. Everywhere you looked you saw slums. Gangs and drugs and poverty had worked together on the east side, eroding it like water through limestone, until the vast majority of what was left looked more like a war-torn third world nation than something you expected to see in the seventh largest city in the United States. And it came as no surprise to him that so many of his cases came out of these streets. Life was treated cheaply here.

He looked off to his left, beyond the Seguin Train Yard, and could see the crumbling smokestacks of the Morgan Rollins Iron Works. He was, he figured, less than half a mile from where he had spent most of the previous night. What was it about this place, he wondered. What in the hell was going on here?

***

Levy was waiting for him near where the Cadillac had high-centered on the tracks, its front and rear passenger doors still hanging wide open.

He looked worn down, haggard. He hadn't combed his hair, or what little there was of it to comb, nor had he changed his suit. As Anderson got out of the car and closed the distance between them, he couldn't help but notice the bags under Levy's eyes and the sweat stains spreading across his white shirt.

They shook hands.

"Jesus," Anderson said. "You look like hell."

Levy grunted.

"I haven't been to sleep yet. I made it home at two a.m., and then they call me back for this fucking mess before I could even take off my damn tie."

Anderson nodded. He hadn't had any sleep either. "You said this might be related to the deal last night?"

Levy pinched the bridge of his nose and closed his eyes. "Keith, I got a bad fucking headache," he said. "It's this damn heat. What is it, like ninety-five degrees out here? It's ridiculous. This is no way for a man to live."

"Yeah man," said Anderson, smiling, doing his best imitation of Bill Paxton in *Aliens*, "but it's a dry heat."

Levy gave him a dirty look.

"Cute," he said. "I'm fucking dying out here and you're making jokes."

"It's your own fault, Chuck. You're working me to the bone. How else am I supposed to deal with the stress?"

Levy smiled, but without humor. A look passed between them. They'd spent a good part of the previous night at Bobby Cantrell's house, talking with Jenny. It had been horrible.

Levy put a hand on Anderson's shoulder and guided him over towards the boxcars.

"I'm pretty sure this is related to the Morgan Rollins mess last night. We got the same two East Patrol guys from last night. They're trying to make an arrest for heroin back at the Witherby Courts. They see this Cadillac here doing a drive-by at the intersection of Wedding and Hall. They chase the Cadillac to here, where they wreck out on the tracks. After that, Mike Garcia—you know him?"

Anderson nodded. There was plenty he could say, but instead he let the nod stand.

"He and his partner chase the guys on foot. Mike catches his guy over there," and pointed off to the left of the Cadillac, "while his partner chases the backseat passenger over there, towards those boxcars."

"What's the partner's name?"

Levy took a small, sweat-sodden notebook out of his shirt pocket and flipped through the pages until he found what he was looking for.

"Paul Henninger," he said. "I don't know him."

"Me either," Anderson said. "Must be new."

"Yeah, like that matters. I've been off Patrol for so long I don't recognize half the uniforms I see anymore. They all look like kids to me."

Anderson nodded.

"Was there anybody in the front passenger seat?"

"Yeah. He took off towards the north fence line. Hawkeye Bravo got him on video scaling the fence and then going into the ditch over there.

East is doing a quadrant for him now, but they're stretched pretty thin with this shit here."

"We get a name on him?"

"The driver said he only knows him as Pops, but you know how that goes. We'll get the name later."

"And Henninger's chase? What happened there?"

"Well, that's the big question," Levy said. "Henninger chases him over that way. He says the kid pulled a gun on him then ducks behind a train. When Henninger comes out from behind cover, he sees another one of those weird looking goats from last night. Then he goes inside the boxcar and sees the kid dead, splayed open, same as Cantrell last night."

"They find the gun?"

"Yeah. It's been fired recently, too. Probably used in the drive by."

Anderson nodded to himself.

"What do you suppose is up with the goats?" he asked. He remembered how strange the one from the night before looked—the long, curly whitish-gray hair, almost like dreadlocks.

"Fucked if I know. But everything was the same as last night. Both the goat and the kid were ripped open, their hearts torn out. You know, I'm wondering if it's not some sort of cult we're dealing with here."

Anderson looked out across the scene, at the acres of rusted railway cars everywhere. He could see Hawkeye Bravo making another lap over the scene.

"You said Hawkeye was over the scene during the chase?"

"Yeah. Nelson, the pilot, tells me they got the whole thing on video. I've been trying to download it to the computer in my car, but so far I got nothing."

"Figures. The Department won't hire enough people to do the job, but they don't have a problem spending too much money on equipment that doesn't work."

"Don't even get me started," Levy said.

"So Henninger's over there now?"

"Yeah. You ready to talk to him?"

"Yeah, I think so."

"Okay," Levy said. "Talk to him in your car, though. Okay? I want to get him away from all the rest of the Patrol guys as soon as we can."

***

Alone again, Paul watched as the scene started to wind down. Most of the picture takers and evidence collectors had cleared out, and the officers on post were looking bored. Helicopters continued to circle overhead, but they were up high enough that their props were barely audible. A hot wind blew through the train yard, sending streamers of brown dust between the boxcars like snakes trying to find their way out of a maze. He was sweaty and hot and mentally exhausted, and he just wanted it all to end.

He was practicing a few variations on the standard two-handed vanishings when a man in dark gray slacks and a maroon shirt came up to him. He didn't wear a tie, but his shirt had the Homicide Unit's logo on the left breast. He had a detective's silver and black badge, but no gun or radio on his hip.

"Excuse me, son. Are you Paul Henninger?"

"Yes, sir," Paul said, and he thought, *Doesn't he recognize me? He doesn't, does he?*

"I'm Detective Keith Anderson, from Homicide. You mind if we walk and talk?"

"Um," Paul said. "Are you the one who's gonna be taking my statement?"

Anderson smiled. "I was hoping to."

Paul put the coin away and said, "I was told I needed to talk to my attorney before I said anything to you."

"You were? Who told you that?"

"My partner. And my sergeant, too."

"Hmm. I wonder why they told you that."

Paul kept quiet.

Anderson said, "You mind if I see your hands?"

"No, sir." Paul stuck them out for the detective to see.

Anderson made a show of looking at them, turning them over, looking at the palms, the knuckles, under the fingernails.

"I don't see any blood," he said. "Did you clean yourself up already?"

"No, sir. I didn't have any blood on my hands to wash off."

Anderson nodded. "Yeah, you're right about that. I mean, that's obvious just from looking at them."

Paul waited.

Anderson stepped back and motioned towards Paul's police car. "Do you mind if we walk while we talk?" he said.

"No, sir," Paul said. "I guess not."

Anderson put his hands in his pocket and they walked, side by side, towards the cars. He said, "I heard that boy in there got torn wide open. That true?"

"Yes, sir. That's what it looked like."

"And there was a goat there too, right?"

Paul hesitated before he answered. "Yes, sir."

"Was it one of those weird looking ones? The ones with all the gray curly hair all over it?"

"Yes, sir."

"That's the same kind of goat that was at the Morgan Rollins factory last night. I've never seen goats like that. Must be some kind of weird Asian goat or something, you know?"

Paul said, "Asian?"

"Yeah, you know, like in the Himalayans or someplace like that. Looked like something Richard Attenborough would do a TV show on."

"It was an Angora goat, sir."

"Angora?" Anderson stopped and looked at him. "You know about goats?"

"Sure. I grew up on a farm, sir."

"Really? Where?"

"Smithson Valley, sir."

"Ah," Anderson said. He started walking again. "You're a Hill Country boy."

"Yes, sir. We raised the same kind of goats. That hair you saw, it's called mohair. Lots of folks 'round here raise Angora. You can shear it four, maybe five times a year. They're good eating goats, too."

"You eat those things? Really?"

"Yes, sir. The meat's supposed to taste like veal. I don't know about that. I've never tasted veal."

Anderson glanced at him, his smile easy, friendly. "But they taste good, that's what you're saying?"

"Yes, sir."

"Hmm."

The cars were less than a hundred feet ahead of them now. Paul could see a crowd of sergeants and lieutenants and even a captain hanging around, talking about the scene. Seeing them, realizing they were there because of him—and, though they didn't know it, because of his father as well—was almost crippling. He felt like a bug under their microscope.

"This is me over here," Anderson said, and pointed to a blue Ford Taurus, covered in dust. "You wanna have a seat?"

"Sir?"

"What?"

"What about my attorney, sir? Don't I get to...talk to him or something?"

"Yeah, you said that before. Why do you need an attorney?"

"They told me..."

Anderson waved his hand in the air like he was dismissing the whole thing.

"Look," he said, "you didn't kill that kid, right?"

"No sir."

"I didn't think so. Nobody here does. You don't have any blood on your hands. You don't have any under your fingernails. Hell, even if you had time to go and put on a pair of those big yellow dishwashing gloves before you killed him, you'd at least have gotten some blood on your uniform. Am I right?"

"Uh, yes sir," Paul said slowly. "I guess."

"So it's obvious to everyone here you didn't kill anybody. Am I right?"

"Yes, sir."

"All you did was chase some kid who ran from you, right?"

"Yes, sir."

"And you were chasing him because he broke the law, right?"

"Yes, sir."

"So you were doing your job, right?"

"Yes, sir."

"Well then, see? That's what I'm saying. You're not a suspect in anything." Anderson opened his door and motioned for Paul to open the passenger door. "So what's the problem? All I want to do is get your statement so I can find out who *did* kill that little piece of shit. You see, I'm thinking whoever killed this kid also killed those people at the Morgan Rollins Iron Works. You follow me on that?"

Paul nodded.

"Good."

He got into his car.

Paul stood by the open passenger door, looking down at him. Anderson motioned to him to sit down, and he did.

Anderson took out what looked like a digital video recorder, about the size of Bic lighter, and hit the record button.

He said, "So, Officer Paul Henninger, you've been made aware of your right to an attorney?"

"Yes, sir," Paul said.

"How do you feel about giving me a short statement about what happened?"

Paul felt his mouth go dry. He could sense what was happening, and he didn't want to be here, but it was like he couldn't stop it. He said he didn't mind making a statement.

And besides, if you do say you don't want to give a statement, you sound guilty. You can't afford that. You got a charge to keep, remember?

Anderson put the recorder down on the dashboard between them. "Good," he said. "So just take it from the top. Pretend I don't know anything about what happened. Tell me what it looked like for you."

***

Paul did just that. He started from the alley, where he and Mike had watched as the three heroin dealers made a sale, and progressed all the way through the story, telling it all in a tired, almost bored tone, as one reciting lines of memorized poetry that no longer have any meaning. It wasn't until he described rounding the corner and seeing the goat that his tone and pace changed. After that, he spoke slowly, choosing his words like they were steps through a mine field. He started to feel light-headed.

When he was done, he put his hands in his lap and sat there, staring at the digital recorder on the dashboard, waiting.

"And that's it?" Anderson said.

"Yes, sir. That's it."

"You didn't hear anything?"

"No, sir."

"No screaming?"

"I didn't hear anything, sir."

"Hmm. That's odd."

Paul waited in silence.

Anderson said, "I think it's odd because you were just a few feet away from where a kid was being ripped open. A goat, too, for that matter. Don't you think that's odd?"

"I didn't hear anything, sir."

Anderson nodded.

He stroked his chin and seemed to stare at his dashboard. Paul followed his gaze and saw an old, yellowed photograph covering the speedometer. It showed a boy with long, wavy dark hair and clothes that looked to be from the mid-nineties, sort of grungy.

They waited each other out in silence.

Finally, Anderson said, "You don't talk much, do you?"

"No, sir," Paul said. "I guess not."

"Well, that's okay. You don't have to, really. You see, whether you know it or not, you're actually telling me an awful lot."

Paul cocked his head to one side. "How's that, sir?"

"Earlier, when I asked you if you heard any screaming, you crossed your arms across your chest. Up to this point, you've been looking at your hands in your lap. You know what that little motion tells me, crossing your hands like that?"

"No, sir."

"It tells me you're getting defensive. It tells me you're hiding something. Maybe you did hear something. Who knows? Maybe you heard the kid cry out, but you didn't go to him because you were scared. Is that it? Were you scared, Paul? It makes sense you know. Being in a gunfight situation isn't like a walk in the park. It's terrifying as hell. I know. I've been there."

Anderson looked at Paul and waited for him to say something, anything.

The silence went on and on.

Anderson said, "Paul, you mind if I tell you a story?"

Paul looked up at him and shook his head.

"This was in August, 1991. I was working the warehouses around Pop Gunn Drive. You know that area?"

"No, sir."

"Run down, nasty place. Nothing but warehouses. The south side at its worst. Well, anyway, they'd been having a string of burglaries in the area, and my sergeant ordered me to drive the area all night, you know, seeing what I could see. Well, I hear this disturbance come out on the radio, shots fired in a house about two miles or so from where I am. I figure, I'll stay in the area, listen for what happens. Well, the officers get there, and the next thing you know, the emergency tone's going off. The officers are calling in shots fired, two people hit. Turns out, a husband lost his mind and took it out on his wife and youngest son."

Anderson glanced at the picture covering his speedometer, and Paul thought he saw a dark cloud pass over the detective's face.

"So of course the guy manages to get into his truck and flees the scene," Anderson said. "The officers put out his description and I start looking for the truck. You can guess what happened next, right? There I am, driving around with my thumb up my butt, and sure as hell, guess who comes tearing around the corner right in front of me?"

"The guy from the shooting?"

"Right. So I go after him. We have this little car chase around the warehouses, and the next thing you know, the guy crashes. He jumps out of the truck, and I follow him in my car. Well he stops and turns and points a gun at me, and I lock up the brakes. He runs off around a corner of a building, and I go after him on foot. I go around the corner, and I hear this loud boom, right? It's the guy's gun. I think, Oh shit, he's shooting at me. So I jump back behind the corner and I stand there, breathing so hard I can barely talk on the radio. I stand there for a real long time, you know? Just me, listening to the wind blowing through the eaves of this building above me. When my cover got there, they asked me what was going on. I couldn't tell them, I was so scared. Finally, they moved in, and you know what they found?"

"What?" Paul asked.

"They found the guy behind a pile of lumber, dead. The shot I'd heard, that was him, popping himself off."

Anderson stopped there and looked at Paul.

"Tell me, Paul, is that what happened to you? Did you hear that kid screaming out? Did you get scared and freeze? There's no shame if that's what happened. The public may think we're nothing but a bunch of baton happy racists, just living for the chance to beat the shit out of some hapless minority, but you and I know the truth. It isn't that way. Believe me, I know."

Paul didn't say anything. His mind was playing the same loop over and over again. Slowing to a stunned walk as he saw the slaughtered goat.

Turning and looking at the figure of his father crouched over the dead kid. His father talking to him.

You've got a charge to keep, boy.

"Is that what happened, Paul?"

Nothing.

"Paul?"

"I didn't see nothing, sir. I didn't hear nothing, either. I looked into the boxcar, and the kid was dead."

"Just like that?"

"Yes, sir. Just like that."

Anderson nodded to himself again. He smacked his lips and said, "Okay."

"Okay?" Paul said. "You mean...I'm okay to just go?"

"Yep."

Paul waited, but when it was obvious that Anderson wasn't going to say anything else, he opened his car door and made a move to step out.

"Hey, Paul?"

Paul stopped, half in, half out of the car. "Yeah? I mean, yes sir?"

"We're not going to be charging you with anything. Just so you know."

"Okay, sir. Thanks for saying so."

"No problem." He paused. "Oh. There is one other thing."

"Yes sir?"

"How long have you been on, son?"

"I graduated in March, sir. This is my second night off my FTO rides."

"Your second night? You're kidding?"

"No, sir."

Anderson laughed. "Lord, son. Hold on to your hat, because you're gonna have a wild ride of a career."

Paul regarded him for a moment, then walked away without saying another word.

***

Paul and Mike were in the car now, headed downtown to the Homicide Office, where the two of them would be spending the next four or five hours, at least, writing their reports. Mike was driving—calmly, for once—strumming the top of the steering wheel like it was a guitar to the song on the radio. Paul wouldn't have known it was Alice Cooper they were listening to if Mike hadn't told him. To Paul, it just sounded like noise, and if there were chords in there somewhere, he couldn't hear them.

"But this is a guy singing?" Paul said.

"Yeah."

"So...his name is Alice?"

Mike stopped strumming the steering wheel and looked at Paul in disbelief. "Are you kidding me? Alice Cooper? Paul, you remember when you gawked at me when I told you I didn't like Willie Nelson? Well, I'm having one of those moments right now. You've never heard of Alice Cooper? Really?"

"Sorry."

"You know what your problem is, Paul?"

I got a lot of problems, Paul thought. But all he said was, "What?"

"Your taste in music sucks ass. I'm serious, Paul. All that country music is gonna rot your brain. They've done studies on that, I think. Next thing you know you'll be marrying your cousin."

Paul didn't even bother to smile. He sank down into the passenger seat and tried to think. Outside the car, the sky was turning the dark purple of bruised fruit, a glow of crimson spreading across the horizon. They drove by dark, weather-beaten houses that were crammed together so densely they reminded him of a hive. Paul watched it all go by without really seeing it. His thoughts kept coming back to the image of his father's back curled over his bloody work, his hands submerged into the kid's chest.

You have a charge to keep, boy.

"Can you unlock my window?" Paul said to Mike. "I gotta get some air."

"Sure thing," Mike said. "You feel sick? I can stop if you want."

"I'll be all right. Just open the window."

Mike nodded, then went back to driving. He slowed to a stop at a red light and, to Paul's surprise, actually waited it out, rather than merely checking if the coast was clear and going on through the intersection.

After a while, Mike said, "That better?"

"A little," Paul said.

"Good."

The light turned green and Mike slowly pulled away from the stop line. "You're gonna get through this," Mike said. "It looks weird right now, I know. Believe me, I know. But you're gonna come through this smelling like a rose. Trust me."

"Sure," Paul said, though he was still looking out the window at the darkened houses slipping by, thinking that he wanted to be any place else in the world but in his own shoes right now.

***

Anderson found Levy at the boxcar, kneeling over the dead goat, its chest ripped open, same as the boy inside the car, same as Ram and Herrera at the Morgan Rollins Iron Works.

"I just don't get it," Levy said. "What's with the goats?"

"It's an Angora," said Anderson. "Apparently, you can shear these things three, even four times a year. And, according to Officer Henninger at least, they're good eatin' goats, too."

"They're what?"

Levy looked up at him then, and under different circumstances, Anderson might have laughed at the confounded look on his face.

"I talked to Henninger, got his statement. He tells me he grew up on a farm out near Smithson Valley High School. He said they used to raise these same kinds of goats out there."

"Really?"

"That's exactly what I said."

"That's a mighty handy coincidence, don't you think?"

"Maybe not," Anderson said. "According to Henninger, these things are raised all over the country."

Levy looked down at the carcass.

"Doesn't look like any kind of goat I've ever seen."

"Me either," Anderson admitted. "Of course, neither one of us are goat farmers."

"Are you gonna check that out?"

"Sure, Chuck. I'm gonna drop everything else I got going on and run out and interview every damn goat herder in the Hill Country."

Levy scowled at him. "Don't be a jerk, Keith."

They both stood over the dead goat, looking down at it for a long, quiet moment.

"It is a lead worth checking on," Anderson said. "Somebody had to bring these goats into the scene. It's not like they run wild around here."

Levy nodded. "If you don't have time for it, I'll have Massey and Vogler check it out."

"Thanks."

Levy walked back to the cars and motioned for Anderson to follow. The two men crossed under the crime scene tape and left the bluish glow of the helicopter's spotlights behind.

"Deputy Chief Allen is waiting for us back in the office."

"Okay."

"Did you learn anything else from Henninger besides a natural history of goats?"

"Not really," Anderson said. "He told me about the same thing he told Garwin."

"But? That sounds like you think there's something more."

"I do. He saw something in that boxcar. I don't know what he saw, but he did see something. I think he got scared. Maybe he froze, maybe there's something else going on. I don't know yet."

Anderson had just scaled a small embankment that led up to the tracks. He got to the top and stopped, waiting on Levy to catch up. The poor guy was dying out here in this heat. He was wheezing and his suit was soaked through with sweat.

He held out a hand and Levy took it. Once Levy made it to the top, Anderson said, "There's one other thing."

"What's that?"

"Can you get me access to Henninger's personnel records? I don't think he's directly involved with what we've seen out here, but I know he saw something he's not telling us about."

"And why do you think his personnel records will help you with that?"

"Maybe they won't, but I need to start someplace."

"I'll have to clear that with Deputy Chief Allen. He'll want to know why."

"Tell him I don't know why," Anderson said. "It's just a feeling."

Chapter 8

Rachel sat at the little card table in their kitchen where she and Paul ate most of their meals. She was angry. She was angry at Paul because he was late and hadn't had the decency to call and tell her why. It wasn't like him to make her worry like this.

But her anger wasn't directed solely at Paul. He was probably fine. Maybe he stopped off for drinks with his new buddies or something. But his little bit of choir practice meant that she was left here in their apartment to deal with a busted air conditioner. It was the second time since they'd moved in that the thing had gone out, and now their place was so hot she felt she was about to scream. The hottest month of the year and she had to sit here, roasting, the landlord nowhere to be found.

She sipped a glass of milk and stared out the open window at the backyard of the house next door. There was a sorry-looking white and black dog tied to a corner of a crumbling shed out there, its tongue hanging out the side of its mouth and a rheumy, beat-down look in its eyes. Rachel wiped the sweat from her neck and thought that poor dog looked about as miserable as she felt.

And then Paul's truck finally pulled into the drive. He pulled into the slot under the carport and shut off the truck. Rachel sighed in frustration, waiting for him to get out, already thinking of what she was going to say to him.

She watched his truck for a long time, but he never got out.

Most of the back glass was a bright, reflected splash of sunlight, but from where she was she could see through the lower edge of the back windshield to his hands in his lap, the Barber fifty cent piece moving back and forth, catching and flashing in the sunlight.

She thought back to the little house on Huisache where she'd lived for a time back in college, to a day in late September of her junior year. She'd been hired by the English Department the semester before to be Paul's tutor in Intro to American Lit, and she was all prepared to hate the stupid jock they were sending her, imagining what it would be like to sit there while some steroidal, lumbering dolt muddled his way through Emily Dickinson and Henry James and then tell her that "this stuff is stupid" and that he "just didn't get it."

And then she'd met him, and surprised herself because she found him cute and sweet and kind. They started dating midway through the fall semester of their sophomore year. And then, near the beginning of their junior year, she gave him that Barber fifty cent piece for his birthday.

She remembered handing it to him, explaining what it was and the history behind it, and then telling him how her literary hero Neil Gaiman had just written a great book called *American Gods* that she loved because the main character, an ex-convict named Shadow, reminded her so much of him. She also told him how Shadow stumbled through the book doing coin tricks, and maybe, she suggested, with what she hoped was a mischievous little spark in her eyes, he could learn a few of his own.

Well, he had learned a few coin tricks—had become damn good at quite a few of them as a matter of fact. But more than that he had gone out and read the damn book, too, which was something she hadn't even hoped he would do because she knew that reading a book for him was about as much fun as passing a kidney stone was for other folks. That impressed her more than the coin tricks ever could because he had done it for her, because he did something just because it interested her.

But now, as she stood at the open kitchen window, watching her husband work that coin back and forth, she realized that her life had grown far more complicated since those easy days in the little house on Huisache.

She looked down at her husband, oblivious to the heat and the dust in the air, wondering what he was thinking. He wasn't dumb, even though he did his best to seem that way. He just thought differently than she did. His mind was like a giant set of clock gears that you had to nearly break your back to get turning. But once those gears did begin to turn, they did so with a force that was like a rockslide coming inevitably down towards a decision.

She had come to an understanding about him, and seeing him down there, the gears starting to turn, made her feel a little afraid—not *of* him, but of something that she knew, or sensed, or felt, was coming *for* them.

***

From the front, their house looked like a quaint, Craftsman-style two story bungalow slowly being swallowed alive by ivy and chinaberry bushes. When they first found it, Rachel went crazy with excitement. She studied the architectural theory behind it. Paul remembered her trying to explain it to him, why it was such a cool place.

But Paul knew almost nothing of architecture, and cared even less, and to him the place just seemed old and overgrown. It might have been classy once, he supposed, but it wasn't much to look at now, especially from the back, which was made of sagging wood paneling, the white paint coming off in dry, feathery flakes. It was just a straight up and down wall with a few windows, the kind of feature that made you think that maybe the architect had gotten bored, or simply ran out of money and had to finish the thing on the cheap.

The only break in the monotony was a plain, unpainted wooden staircase that started at the corner of the house next to the driveway and went up to a door in the middle of the house on the second story. It was clearly an afterthought, added on at the same time the owners figured they could make more money carving the house up into separate apartments.

Paul trudged up the stairs one at a time, head bent down, each footstep bursting into a cloud of yellow dust that followed him up the stairs.

He slid his key into the lock, and stepped inside.

He headed for the kitchen, got a glass from the pantry, filled it from the tap in the sink, and then drank it down in one gulp. He filled it again, this time only downing half of it before he stopped and wiped his lips with the back of his left hand.

"Hi," Rachel said, though her tone said, "What the hell, you can't even acknowledge me?"

His eyes rolled towards her with a motion that was like an old door swinging on rusty hinges.

"Well?" she said.

"Hi," he said.

She waited for more, but when it didn't come, she crossed the kitchen floor to the phone that was mounted there on a pillar, removed it from the cradle, and showed it to him.

"You know what this is?" she said.

Again that slow roll of his eyes that was like an old door on rusty hinges, this time from her face to the phone in her hand.

The dial tone echoed from the phone.

"It's a phone, Paul. Some men use it to call their wives to let them know they're gonna be five hours late from work. Five hours, Paul. Two days in a row. What the hell?"

He drank the rest of his water. He wiped his lips again with his wrist, and this time a smear of dust appeared across his face, dark against his skin. His tongue tested the grit on his lips and he could feel the greasiness of it. For a moment, he thought he might get sick.

"What time is it?" he said.

"Time? What time...Paul, it's past noon."

He nodded to himself.

"You didn't call, Paul. What's wrong with you, you can't check your messages? I've been worried sick about you."

"I'm sorry," he said.

He put the glass down in the sink, then undid the top button on his uniform jersey and pulled the top edge of his body armor away from his chest. He could feel the heat rising off his soaked t-shirt.

"It's hot in here," he said.

That made her laugh, but it was the kind of a laugh that you hate to hear from a woman, because you know that what follows will be angry and indignant.

"You know why it's hot, Paul? You wanna know why? I'll tell you why. It's so damn hot in here because the air conditioning went out in the middle of the night. I woke up at four a.m., Paul. I wake up, and I'm covered in sweat. The sheets are soaked. I can barely breathe. It's like I'm trying to breathe the air coming out of an oven. And of course the fans don't do a damned thing."

"Did you call the landlord?"

"What do you think? Of course I called him. I've been calling him all morning. He's nowhere to be found. But then, if you had bothered to check your messages, you would have known that."

He looked past her, at the apartment. She'd been busy changing things around again. She was always in the process of changing things around, trying to match them up to the ideal that was in her mind.

"Did you hear me? Paul?" He looked at her again. "Jesus," she said. "You weren't even listening to me, were you?"

He let out a deep breath. His chin fell to his chest.

"Well?"

"I'm being investigated for the death of sixteen year old kid," he said.

That stopped her.

"What?"

"A boy died last night. Mike and I were chasing him. The car he was in crashed and the kid took off running through a train yard. He was murdered right before I caught up with him."

"Murdered? What do you mean he was murdered?" Her tone had changed. She was no longer angry. She sounded confused and frightened. "Why are they investigating...Paul, tell me what happened."

She crossed to the kitchen table and pushed a chair out for him. She patted the floral-patterned cushion on the chair and said, "Sit down, Paul."

He nodded, then sat, then went through the whole story all over again. He told her about Garwin's orders to interview heroin junkies in their district and about watching the three junkies from the alleyway and about the shooting and the car chase and the kid running and the kid turning and pointing the gun at him and him coming out and seeing the dead goat and...

***

...she could tell he was leaving something out. It was obvious. He normally used his hands when he told her stories. Sometimes he even added sound effects. He was like a kid that way, animated.

But something was different this time. Something had come inside, clung to him like the dust on his boots and taken a piggyback ride inside their marriage. She could see whatever it was moving around inside of him, swimming in the depths of his eyes.

"But what does it mean that you're being investigated?" she asked. "Are they accusing you of something?"

He shook his head.

"Paul? Do they think you have something to do with this?"

"No."

"Then...I don't understand. Why are you being investigated?"

"It's standard procedure."

Now it was her turn to shake her head.

"You say that like I'm supposed to understand what that means. Standard procedure means what?"

He closed his eyes and she could see the air bleeding out of his chest.

"Paul?"

"It means there will be an investigation," he said. "Detectives are going to look into the incident. It's a murder. They're going to take it apart piece by piece and they're going to try to figure out who killed that kid. Until they do, I'm part of the investigation. I haven't been charged with anything, but there's going to be an Internal Affairs investigation at the same time, so..."

"An Internal Affairs investigation? Why is Internal Affairs looking at you, Paul? If you didn't do anything wrong, why would they be looking at you?"

"It's standard procedure in an In-Custody Death."

"Standard procedure," she said, and huffed. "There's that phrase again. Paul, would you please stop talking to me like a cop and tell me what the hell is going on. I'm your wife, for Christ's sake, and I don't understand what you're telling me." She stopped and waited, then said, "You tell me Homicide is investigating you. Now you tell me Internal Affairs is investigating you. I ask you why and all you can tell me is that it's standard procedure."

She looked at him, really looked at him.

"What does that mean, Paul? Tell me, please. You're scaring me."

"I'm sorry," he said.

She waited.

The two of them sat there at the table, her looking at him, Paul looking off into space at something only he could see. She looked into his eyes, eyes that normally looked hazel, but seemed gray now in the late morning sunshine, and she wondered if she was merely looking at the shine off a shallow pool, like the sun reflecting off a grease puddle in the asphalt, or if the gray she saw there was some great and previously unknown and unfathomed depth.

"Paul?"

"It'll be okay," he said. "They'll do what they do. It'll all work out in the end. I want to go to bed. I'm tired."

"Okay," she said. She was too stunned to say anything else.

"Are you gonna read?"

"No."

She wanted to reach out and shake him, make him talk to her.

"I told Mary I'd meet her and her daughter for lunch. I figured it'd give you a chance to sleep."

He nodded.

"Is that okay?"

"Yeah, sure," he said. "Of course."

"I can cancel, Paul. I want to be here with you if you'll let me. I want to be here with you. You know that, right?"

He nodded.

"I just want to get some sleep, Rachel. You go out with Mary. I'll be fine. Really. Go on."

***

She showered, dressed, and did her hair and makeup. He listened from his chair in the kitchen as the hair dryer whined over the sound of Bob Dylan's *Tangled Up in Blue*, and he knew that Rachel was feeling down. She always played that album when she got this way. The last time he heard it was when they were getting ready for the move from their apartment on Chase Hill to this place, Rachel wondering if they could afford it while she searched for a new job. She'd been frustrated and irritable all the time during that move; and now, with her listening to Dylan once again, he felt guilty. He wanted to reach out and touch her, tell her everything, ask her guidance in what to do, but he knew he couldn't. Some things, they were just too much to talk about.

When she was all put together, she came into the kitchen, paused when she realized that he hadn't moved, and said, "If you want the shower now..."

"Thanks."

"I'll be back around five. Is that okay? Do you want to sleep longer?"

"Sure," he said. "Five's fine."

"I love you," she said.

"Love you, too."

She paused, waiting.

He stayed quiet, looking off again into nothingness.

"Okay, I'm gonna go."

"Okay."

She waited again, then finally turned and walked out the door.

From his seat, Paul could hear her opening the screen door, could hear its springs groaning, then the sound of her gently closing it again as it settled in the jamb. It occurred to him then that he had never lied to her before. He was breaking new ground.

***

Paul dropped his things on the side table next to his bed, his patrol car keys and his notebooks and nameplate and badge and Barber fifty cent piece. Next he stripped and threw his uniform in the laundry. And it was while he was doing that that he noticed yet another change Rachel had made to the apartment.

The whole back wall of the apartment was lined by mismatched bookshelves. On the take home pay the two of them made, they couldn't afford anything fancy, so they'd scavenged garage sales and Goodwill stores until they found enough shelving to create what Paul called their Frankenstein furniture. The shelves were different styles, different textures, different colors, and most of the time they were crammed with Rachel's beloved paperbacks. But it looked as though she'd taken a small section of books down and stacked them up on the floor next to an old recliner near the foot of the bed. A few of Paul's boxes were there, like maybe she had been planning to put up some of his stuff on the shelves.

He went to one of the boxes with the word "House" scribbled on it in black Magic Marker and opened one of the flaps. "House" meant the house he'd grown up in, the old family goat ranch out in the Hill Country, and the items inside were mainly documents related to the sale of the house and the acreage that surrounded it.

He had packed this box during the summer prior to the start of his freshman year at The University of Texas at San Antonio, gone through it again during tax time, and then packed it away, not ever planning on coming back to it. But here he was, looking into the box again. And this time, he saw something he hadn't anticipated, for there was a blue pocket folder perched right on top. It wasn't labeled, but it didn't have to be. He could see the corner of an aging photograph sticking out of the top of the folder, and he knew what was inside.

He took the folder out, crossed to the bed, and sat down on it, the folder in his lap. Without opening it he knew he was about to see ghosts from his past, those of his mother and his father, yes, of course those, but also of the land they lived on, the land that had been so much a part of who he was—the land that continued to live inside him, no matter the distance that he put between himself and that place and those people.

His mind was a mess. He felt detached, like he was groping blindly at the tattered fragments of the past while his fingers bent the exposed corner of the photograph back and forth, toying with it, teasing it until the paper slid free from the folder.

He tasted his dry, cracked lips with the tip of his tongue and could still feel the grit there. When he looked down, the photograph was on his right thigh, the folder and its contents spilled on the hardwood floor near his feet. He studied the photograph. What he saw was a family, and at first glance it could have been anybody's family, a husband, young, strong, serious, his pretty wife at his side with a baby boy on her hip.

That was his mother holding him. He looked to be around two, maybe a little younger, which would have put his mother at about twenty. She was skinny, but not to the point of emaciation, as he remembered her. Her dark, deeply tanned skin was stretched tight over a pronounced facial bone structure, and yet she didn't look fragile. His memories of her were of a woman very different from the one in this picture. In his memory, she was a wraith who haunted the front room of their house. He remembered standing by the bed she kept there, staring at the black eyed woman under the yellowed sheets who almost always responded to anything he said with a drugged-sounding, "Let me rest, baby. Momma's not feeling up to doin' much right now."

And yet, when he looked into the photo on his thigh, what he saw was a very different woman. She was pretty—pretty because all the mental hardships she was destined to endure were still in her future. This was his mother before she lost her mind, before the depression made her a mental crank case. The woman pictured here was eight years away from the woman who would run screaming into his room with a knife in her hands and murder in her eyes.

Paul didn't want to think about that. He let his gaze drift from his mother to his father. He put his finger on the photograph and touched the face of the man who had loomed over his life like the shadow of a mountain. The man was young here, maybe thirty years old, with a small waist and strong arms and an unsmiling mouth that was thin as a razor cut. His head seemed to Paul to be shaped almost exactly like a shoebox. As always, he wore his black slacks, his black Red Wing boots, his white shirt buttoned at the neck and the sleeves, starched to the point it could probably stand up on its own. And of course there was his black Stetson hat crowning that shoebox-shaped head.

There wasn't an ounce of mirth in the man's soul, a fact that was obvious from even the small glimpse of him stored here in this photograph. And yet, as Paul ran his finger over the image of the man, he could sense a window into the past opening up around him. It was a feeling like standing in a peach orchard in the middle of the summer, with the South Texas sun beating down on your arms and scorching the back of your neck and from out of nowhere you feel a breeze, a hot, sluggish breeze that plucks at the cream-colored dirt on the ground and lifts little clouds of dust a few feet into the air so that it falls onto the toes of your boots like gossamer curtains falling from a window and you realize that you are a part of this land and it is a part of you and though you make your living from it, the land is at the same time taking your living from you, drawing it out of you one drop of sweat at a time. Looking at his father's picture was like that, the feeling of having something pulled out of him that he was powerless to hold on to.

He could sense something stirring around him. The air felt gritty and waxy against his skin, and gradually he became aware that the world around him was changing. He could see the apartment, but superimposed over top of that he could also see a ghostly world that was both strangely new and at the same time vaguely familiar.

Paul sensed he could step into this new world if he wanted to. All he had to do was let it come.

***

Confused, but not frightened, not really, Paul stood and turned to take a long, slow look at this new world. It was a small, cheap motel room. There was a metal frame bed against the far wall, a yellowed mattress on top of that with the bed sheet pushed down to the foot rails. The mattress was puckered in the middle, burned here and there by the cherries that had fallen off long ago cigarettes. A small, two-drawer dresser rested against the wall at the head of the bed. The only light in the room came from the guttering candle atop that dresser and it cast an orange glow on the yellowed, floral print wallpaper behind it, giving the stains on the wall an ochre cast that might have been rust bleeding through the paper from the nails in the wall, but might also have been blood or possibly spilled rye. Any and all was possible. The room smelled of old sweat and stale smoke and over it all, pushing everything down, was a heat so oppressive that it settled in your nostrils and made each breath a matter of forced will.

Paul crossed to an open window and looked through the curtains. Below him was an empty town with narrow, crumbling streets bathed in moonlight. The architecture was old Mexico, but even if he hadn't known that by the shape of the slovenly cinderblock buildings with the red tile roofs and the glass shards embedded in the concrete on the tops of the walls he would have known it by the sounds of a dance coming from somewhere off to his left.

This was his father's room. He was certain of that. He glanced down at the dresser and saw whiskey and a pack of crumpled Mexican cigarettes and was surprised because his father had never smoked around him. And then, next to the cigarettes, he saw a small mound of fibrous, bone-white mushrooms streaked through with thick blue veins and he recognized the product from his training at the Academy as hallucinogens. Suddenly he thought back to the night six years ago, the night he killed his father, and how, at dinner, his father said he once went to Mexico looking for something, what he didn't know, but something that wasn't his father, Paul's grandfather, and Paul thought: *Huh, imagine that. My dad used to get freaked out on 'shrooms.*

A man whined in pain behind him.

He turned and, for the first time, saw his father through the open door to the bathroom. His father was naked, save for his socks, his back to Paul. He was standing over the commode, his body drenched in sweat, bruises all over his back, but darkest over his kidneys. He had one hand on the corner of the sink to support his weight. He held his cock with the other. He was trying to pee and couldn't. He stamped one foot, threw his head back and howled in pain. Then he hung his head forward and sobbed, his whole body trembling in pain.

Paul studied the man. He looked emaciated. The powerful shoulders that Paul remembered were stooped and his spine seemed to be made of rubber. The pride that had made his backbone straight as a cane pole for all the time Paul had known him was missing. This was the man who would someday work in the peach orchards from before sun up to after sun down without ceasing, the man who could lift a two hundred pound goat carcass into the air with one hand, the man whose grip was hard enough to make other men frown when they shook his hand. This was the man who would come back from the dead and tell Paul he had a charge to keep; and yet here he was, a shell, a spiritual pauper, a man with all the self-respect of one who has just been prison raped.

Embarrassed, Paul turned away. He had never known, never even suspected, that this side of the man existed. Looking back over the span of the few years of his life, he saw absolutely no indication that the man had ever been anything but cold and hard and insane. But this, this squalor, this ugliness, it humanized the man, made him seem whole somehow, or at least filled him out in some way that made the man he was to become make more sense to the boy, the son, who was to inherit the legacy of that coldness and hardness and insanity.

Paul walked to the window and stared out at the little Mexican village and listened to a dog bark and then the sound of a truck changing gears and accelerating out on a roadway far away.

There was a knock at the door, three quick, soft raps.

Martin Henninger stepped out of the bathroom, walked right by Paul, and fell face down on the bed.

The knock again.

"Go away," Martin Henninger said.

A pause. Another knock.

"I said, fuck off!"

Another pause.

The doorknob turned slowly, but when the door opened, it was with authority.

A young Indio girl stood there. She looked like she could pass for seventeen, as long as you didn't look at her too closely. She wore a simple cotton dress of faded red that stopped an inch or two above her knees. Her breasts were small and her shoulders were broad. Her black hair was long and curly, damp against her round, dark face. Her feet were small and almost round. She wasn't wearing shoes.

"You can stand?" she said.

Martin Henninger groaned. "Go away," he said.

"You must stand up, señor. The men who beat you, there is talk in the village that they are not done with you."

"Ha!" Martin said, and to Paul it sounded like the sound of a man who would welcome being put out of his misery.

"Señor, please. Stand up."

Martin rolled over in bed then and looked at her. His face was sallow in the glow of the candlelight, his expression ironic as his eyes walked over her body.

"How old are you?" he said.

"I am eighteen."

"Bullshit," he said. "Fifteen I'd believe."

"Señor, please. Do as I ask you. Stand up."

He rolled his eyes. "What the fuck," he said, and laughed. "Not like it matters, right? I mean, what the hell, far as the law down here cares, you could be thirteen and it wouldn't make a cold witch's titty of a difference, would it?"

She frowned and he smiled. Then he stood up. It was a slow, painful motion, and it reminded Paul of the morning after the day they'd played Rice in Houston back when he was in college. He'd gotten hit in the lower back, right above the butt pad, and for a blinding moment he'd seen nothing but purple and felt a screaming pain down both his legs and wondered, as he struggled to his hands and knees, if his football career was over. His father moved like that, like the morning after that hit when Paul had tried to climb out of bed and thought for a second that he wasn't going to be able to do it.

And then Martin was standing, naked as naked gets, before the girl, and his dick looked red and ulcerous, like he'd tried to pass broken glass through his urethra.

He waved his hand at the obscenity of his disease and said, "Is it worth twenty pesos to put this in your mouth, little one?" He shifted his weight to the other leg. "You see this, right? One of the other fucking hookers around here got to me first."

"You talk too fast," she said. "I don't understand all you say. But I can see what you have wrong with your pendajo. I know who can help you with that. But you must come with me, señor. It is very bad for you here."

Martin waved her off.

"Go home, girl. Let me die here."

She cocked her head at him.

"You wish to die?" she said.

He laughed, a self-deprecating laugh that was as new to Paul as the idea of a father who had lived life at the bottom, where life was cheap and short and weighted down by disease.

"There is talk in the village that you came here looking for something that will make you happy. Is that not so?"

Scratching his diseased groin, he said, "Happy. Yeah, sure," and shook his head. "I didn't come here to live it up with whores and drugs, if that's what you mean. I came here to learn how to feed my soul." He stopped there and looked at her. "What's your name, sweetheart?"

"Magdalena Chavarria," the girl said.

"Magdalena, eh? You mind if I call you Maggie?"

"My name is Magdalena," the girl said.

"Magdalena. All right."

Martin staggered slightly, then sat down on the side of the bed. He looked right past Paul, not seeing him at all, to Magdalena, who was still standing just inside the door.

He said, "You know what it means to feed the soul?"

She started to speak but he cut her off.

"No, of course you don't. Let me tell you. It's like trying to drink from a mirage. It's like that song, you know the one, how do you hold a moonbeam in your hand, how do you keep a wave upon the sand? It's like that. It's a vain hope. It's a joke the mystics played on us. It can't be done. The human soul can't be fed. And you know what? I'm beginning to think it doesn't even exist. I think it's all just darkness and trouble." He said, "What do you think of that, Magdalena? Do you think the soul exists?"

She stared at him for a long time, seeming to consider what to make of him. Was he merely a bug under glass, something to be gawked at, or was he a broken, diseased man, one of the untouchable Americans who come down here south of the border to become human shipwrecks on a sea of whiskey? Or was he none of those things? Her dark eyes were bottomless, and what she thought she thought alone.

"I can help you find the answers you seek, señor. But it is not easy. It is not something I can tell you. Or show you. It is only something you can come to know after a long time of not knowing. It is like watching a season change. The knowledge can only come on you like that."

Martin ran trembling hands through his hair, then mopped the sweat from the back of his neck with his palm.

"How do I know you're not taking me somewhere to roll me?"

"To roll you? I do not know those words. But I think I understand. You ask me if I'm taking you to those men who did this to you, no?"

"Yes."

"I am not," she said. "But if you stay here, you will die, and you will not know what you came here to find. If you come with me, you may die, but you may also learn to live again."

He gave her a waxy, unenthusiastic grin. "You mind if I get dressed first?"

She sailed right on through, or was oblivious to, the sarcasm. "Yes, put on your pants. But leave your other belongings and come and follow me."

***

Martin Henninger left his room, dressed now in jeans and a dirty blue t-shirt and old sneakers and followed the young Indio girl in the faded red cotton dress down to the street. She walked ahead of him, her bare feet slapping quietly on the pavement. Paul's father stumbled along behind, his body stiff, his gait like that of a wounded soldier marching to the rear, and as they moved through the streets Paul had the strangest feeling. He knew already that he was not a part of the events playing out here, that he was, perhaps, experiencing a memory. As the thought took form in his head he felt his physical form fading to the consistency of a shadow and merging with the diseased American man trailing behind the solid, but still pretty, Indio girl in the faded red cotton dress—if indeed merging was what he could call this feeling of losing himself within his father, of being pulled down and made to be still, for he felt very much like he had as a young boy, when his father had clamped a hard hand down on the back of his neck and squeezed to keep him from running off.

They walked until they left the town behind. Here the road was blond dirt bordered by shallow ditches where weeds grew, and out beyond the ditches was emptiness that disappeared into the night. Ahead of them, far into the distance, Paul could see a jagged row of black mountains against the faintly luminescent blue glow of the sky.

They came to a shack of crumbling white adobe with rattlesnake hides nailed to the front door and Angora goats in the yard and chickens pecking at the dirt.

A woman was inside.

She was tall and lithesome and beautifully shaped, her figure more classically feminine than the young girl who had brought him here and now stood next to him. And though this older woman lacked the heavy features of the Indio girl, there was an obvious familial similarity to their faces.

Paul guessed she was the Indio girl's mother.

"You rest now," the woman said to Martin in Spanish, gesturing towards a dirty mattress on the bare dirt floor.

"But..." Martin said, and turned toward the younger girl in appeal.

"There's plenty of time," the girl said. "Do as she asks. Rest now."

And then Martin, and Paul too, for he was inside Martin, looking out as from inside a glass jar, sat on the mattress and let the women strip him of his shoes and his shirt and finally of his pants, until he was naked on his back.

"You are in pain now," the dark-haired woman said, "but it will pass soon. We will help you."

"Your daughter told me you could teach me," he said.

"In time," she answered. "But not now. First you heal, then you learn."

And with that she took a small, white piece of waxed paper from the younger girl and used her fingernail to scrape up a reddish-brown paste that was the consistency of peanut butter from the paper.

She put her finger on Martin's tongue and his lips closed around her finger and there was something sensual about the act that even his battered body could respond to. Her eyes smiled back at his, sensing his arousal.

"Put your head back," she said. "You will feel very dizzy shortly."

He did as she instructed and closed his eyes.

Paul felt suddenly warm inside as the paste dissolved on his father's tongue—which, for the moment at least, was also his tongue.

He felt the woman's hand on his cock and his eyes sprang open. He looked down his body and saw the woman spreading dollops of black, tar-like goo onto his groin. It didn't burn like tar, though. It was actually cool feeling, like damp morning grass against the skin.

"What are you doing?" he said, and just then the dizziness hit him. His head rolled on his neck, his muscles seemingly unable to support the weight.

"Put your head down and sleep," she said, not looking at him, her hands working with the clinical disinterest of a nurse dressing a wound.

But Paul's vision had clouded over. The woman's face twisted and melted, and her voice became garbled. The corners of his vision pulled apart like taffy into streamers of light.

"You need to sleep to heal," she said.

Every syllable she spoke brought an explosion of color in his eyes.

He didn't so much put his head down as let it fall. "What are you...?"

"Sleep," she said. "For now."

***

He was awakened by the need to piss. He dreaded the prospect, remembering the pain it had been causing him over the past week, but the need was greater than the fear and he rolled over onto his hands and knees. He was still dizzy, still weak as a kitten. The young Indio girl was on her back, naked, her dark, heavy body patterned by silvery coins of moonlight that filtered into the shack through holes in the roof.

He groaned, and the girl shot bolt upright.

"You startled me," she said.

"Sorry," he answered.

He tried to lick his lips to moisten them, but his tongue was dry as a desert rock.

"Do you need to make pee pee?"

That made him laugh, and laughing made him cough. "Yeah, I need to make pee pee."

She helped him to his feet and then scratched at the corners of the black tar paste on his groin until it started to give. Then she peeled it away.

"I take you," she said, and slid her strong body under his arm.

She held him up that way as he did his business into the dirt behind their shack, and then led him back inside. She laid him down on the sheet again, her hand behind his head to guide it down onto the floor, and then, as he struggled to remain conscious, she reapplied the black, tar-like goo to his groin.

He passed out again before she was finished.

***

When he awoke there was a shaft of early morning sunlight lancing through an open window. Dust moved sluggishly in the air. He sat up in bed and looked around and was confused to find himself alone. It was his father who was confused, and Paul realized he knew that, understood it perfectly, because he was also confused, and he was, at least for the moment, one and the same as his father, a perfect echo, feeling what he felt, seeing what he saw, knowing what he knew. That was how complete the union of the two had become.

It was also how he knew that the feeling of broken glass being pushed through his father's urethra was gone, and how the shortness of breath was gone, and the ringing in his head from too much alcohol and hallucinogenic mushrooms was gone. The machine that was his father's human body was, for the first time in what Paul knew to be a very long time, free and clear of pain and fog.

A rooster crowed somewhere close by. He moved his chin to the left and then to the right, really pushing it out, stretching the muscles in the neck that had grown tight from sleeping on them wrong.

He stood and worked the kinks out of his shoulders. Then he looked down at his groin and peeled away the dried black paste. Not knowing what to do with the thing once it was off, he looked around the room and finally decided to toss it into a corner where a couple of dirty Styrofoam cups and some other trash lay.

He intended to go outside and piss, for he felt now that he could do that without fear, and in one of those funny little tangents the mind sometimes makes when it should be thinking more immediate thoughts, he told himself that it was going to be a mighty big team of wild horses that dragged him into the next dirty cantina whore's bed. That thought was all it took to get him dressed.

He walked outside, into the bright, hot sunshine, and called out Magdalena's name. He could see now that the shack was in the midst of an enormous plain of bone white dust, the monotony of it broken only by an occasional acacia tree and a patch of hearty weeds in the sparse shade. But it was mostly bone white dust and hot wind as the plains stretched off toward the black rock mountains in the distance. The girl was nowhere to be found, and neither was her mother—that lithesome, black haired beauty who had so ably cured his burning crotch. He wanted to meet her, finally talk to her, now that his eyes could actually focus. And he wanted to know if she really knew what she had said she knew when she promised him special knowledge of the ways of the world.

But first things first, he told himself. He was of the body, and as such, subject to the needs of the body. He walked around the back of the shack where he vaguely remembered pissing the night before, or maybe the night before the night before, and unzipped his fly.

He stood there, head thrown back, eyes closed, shoulders slumped, waiting for the flow, when he heard a noise, the slowly uncoiling rattle of an aroused rattlesnake.

Cock still in hand, he looked down and saw nothing but dirt. He turned around in a clumsy circle, and saw movement in the shadow of an old metal bucket up against the back wall of the shack.

He was too late to move away, for even as he back-peddled, the snake struck, punching into the calf muscle of his left leg, its fangs cutting through the denim like it wasn't even there and plunging into the meat beneath.

Martin screamed. Paul screamed, too.

The snake disengaged, fell away, and recoiled, its rattle going very fast. Martin fell backwards. He was clumsy because he was stiff and he was scared and now he could feel the burn of the venom coursing through his body, like somebody was trying to push a lit cigarette through his arteries.

Paul felt like he'd just run his head into a wall. His vision was all heat shimmers, the ground tilting up at wrong angles, like he was walking across the deck of a boat on rough seas.

He collapsed to his knees and there were more rattlesnakes, all around him now. They were big ones, with bodies as big around as his legs and diamond-shaped patterns on their creamy brown hides and heads the size of a slice of pie. He felt another punch into his legs and he went down on his side, screaming. Another bite caught him in the back of the thigh, still another on the shoulder, and one more in the belly. The pain was so immediate, so intense, he no longer felt fear. There was only the burning inside him.

Face down in the dust now, he turned his head toward the black hills in the distance and saw a form walking towards him. It was the woman, he knew that, though her form had changed, so that she no longer seemed the beautiful, lithesome black haired young mother with the supple midriff and the long, slender fingers. Now she was a wire-haired Indio grandmother, short, squat, heavyset, and as she stood next to his head and looked down at him, he could see the coarse black hairs on her legs.

She held a rattlesnake by the middle and knelt down next to him and said, "You are not going to die."

"I'm bit," he said, and groaned. He was crying. "Please help me..."

"You are not going to die," she repeated. "Be patient."

***

Time rolled by. It could have been a long time, or it could have been no time at all. He wouldn't have known the difference even if there'd been a clock staring him in the face. What he did was lay there in the dust, expecting to die. He lay there until Magdalena came along and lifted him to his feet. He moved like an arthritic old man. But she took his weight on her shoulders just as she had done that first night that she took him out to urinate into the dust, and she led him on.

The old woman was sitting on the ground nearby, rocking back and forth, while her hands worked at a furious pace, twisting baling wire around sticks and twigs, assembling them into odd, lattice-like structures. She was chanting something, the words hardly distinguishable in the flood of slurred syllables.

The air smelled of burning wood, and he noticed a small brass bowl on the ground behind her, a piece of charcoal and some grass smoking there.

Martin said, "What are—" and stopped there, for at the same time he felt Magdalena squeezing his arm in warning and saw the old woman turn her face up at him. Her eyes had rolled up into her head and showed nothing but yellow streaked through with red, threadlike veins. But her chants never stopped and her hands never stopped flying over the sticks, building them into the shapes he saw all around him.

The lattices formed a semicircle. In his haze, he turned his eyes from one to the other and counted five in all. The old woman was working on the last station of this semicircle, but in the middle, not far from where he hung on Magdalena's arm, was an Angora goat thick with gray mohair tied to a post in the ground. Its black eyes were wide, perfectly round, and though they showed no real sense of understanding, and though the animal hardly moved, he could tell it was terrified by the short, tentative bleating it made.

The whites of the old woman's eyes stayed on Martin as her hands finished their task. And then, without so much as a pause after the last stick was secured in place, she rose to her feet and approached him, pulling a long carving knife from her apron as she came.

"Is it true you have come here to learn the ways of the world?" the old woman said.

"Yes," Paul heard himself say.

"You have lain with many women, no?"

"Yes," the voice that spoke for both Martin and Paul said, though it sounded ashamed.

The old woman cleaned the blade on her apron.

"You have taken the mushrooms that grow in the shadow of the acacia trees. I could smell them in your sweat when you first came here."

"Yes."

"These are traps set along the way for the foolish. There is no wisdom in a woman's crotch, no more than in the crotch of a tree. And the mushrooms are more foolish even than the woman's crotch, for at least with a woman you have a little fun, no?" She laughed. "But the mushrooms...ah, the mushrooms. Many Americans come here to buy them." She shook her head. Her face was the color of old leather and deeply creased, her forehead smeared with ash. Her lips were white and crusty with chapped skin. A strand of wiry gray hair fell down across the symbols on her forehead and she let it stay. "The mushrooms are a fool's paradise. They make you sick and they make your body smell of damp wood and the doors that they open do not lead anywhere but to twisted versions of the things you already know. There is no wisdom there. Only the illusion of wisdom."

"Where is wisdom?" Paul heard himself say.

The woman touched the tip of the knife to his chest. "If I were to cut out your heart and hold it in one hand and wisdom in the other, and told you I could only put one of the things back in, which would you have me do?"

"Wisdom," Paul said. "I want to know everything."

"As you wish," the woman said.

And with that the woman turned and picked up the smoking bowl from the ground. She stuck the first two fingers of her right hand into the bowl and got them black with charcoal soot. Then she came back to him and touched his forehead with her sooty fingers and painted her symbols there.

"This marks you, Martin Henninger. *emet. emet. emet.* It is a symbol that will allow you entry into the mysteries you about to witness. Those who lack this mark can go no further."

She turned away again and picked up the goat by the throat and raised it to its hind legs with one hand. The fearful grunting it made was silenced like it had been chopped off with an axe. Then, with a fast, precise overhand motion, she jammed the point of the knife into the goat's throat and cut downwards, flaying the animal open. With two fast cuts she removed the animal's still beating heart and held it in her hands.

She held it up before him and said, "We are merely conduits for an ancient, primitive power that is more fundamental even than our most basic notions of good and evil. In exchange for our service as conduits we are allowed to glimpse the forces that control existence. It is a hard service you now undertake. It is a terrible charge you have sworn to keep. But the reward is vast knowledge."

She worked toward him, the still-beating heart dripping slick blood between her fingers, streaking her knuckles.

"Open for me now, and accept the symbol of your charge, for the end of man is knowledge, and part of you ends today so that another part may begin."

And with that she stepped forward again and held the beating goat's heart towards him. He felt something moving in his chest, and when he looked down, saw a vaginal gash opening there, its labial lips shining with his blood, quivering for the seed about to be planted there.

He watched her hand and the heart she held in her hand slip into his chest. And then the hand came out empty. The gash sealed again, leaving no trace of its presence, though he could feel the new beat echoing through his body. He tried to breathe and succeeded only in making a stuttering, coughing sound. But then the breaths did come, and when they did, he felt strong, stronger than he had ever felt before.

Half-smiling, he looked down at the old woman.

She did not return the smile.

"You have been marked," she said.

He nodded slowly.

"Come," she said, "we will eat, for there is so much still to learn."

***

Paul blinked several times and then gasped. He was in his own apartment, the air hot and stale smelling. Rachel's mountains of paperbacks were on the floor before him, and he was still sitting in the recliner.

He glanced over at the digital alarm clock on the bedside table and groaned. It was 3:18 in the afternoon, and he was exhausted.

He forced himself to stand up.

The memory, or the vision, or whatever it was still echoed in his head, but he didn't try to interpret it. Not just yet. It was all too fresh, too violently raw, for his thoughts to make sense.

He unsnapped the keepers that held his gun belt to his pants belt, then removed the gun belt and stuffed it under his side of the bed. After that he unlaced his boots and stowed them in the corner of the room. They were filthy with dust and would have to be cleaned and polished before his next shift on Tuesday night. Then he unzipped his jersey and let it fall on the floor.

Next came his body armor, with its multitude of Velcro straps. His sweat had formed a sort of vacuum seal between the panels of his vest and his white t-shirt underneath, and when he peeled the panels away he saw black all over his shirt.

He swiped at it with his fingers, noticing only then that what he was touching was the same greasy dust he had seen pouring from under his father's shirt in the boxcar.

"Oh shit," he said, and started beating at his chest and stomach with both hands.

The dust fell away in clumps, and only when he got most of it off his shirt, and it lay in peppery piles on the floor next to his socks, did he realize that it had coated nearly every inch of his skin with a fine layer of grit.

Chapter 9

It was Sunday afternoon, about one o'clock, and Anderson was in the car, headed for the Medical Examiner's Office. His cell phone rang and he fished it out of its holster on his belt and checked the caller ID. It was Margie.

"Hey," he said.

"Hi," she whispered.

He caught the tone of her voice and figured she was still at Jenny Cantrell's house. She'd been there since nine that morning.

He pulled off the road and into a KFC parking lot.

"How is she?"

"It's hard," she said. "There have been so many phone calls. I wish people wouldn't call like they do. I know they're just trying to help, but it makes it so hard. The phone just won't stop."

"Maybe you ought to take it off the hook," he said.

"Yeah, maybe," she said. "Her mother called this morning. She's coming down tonight around six. I'm gonna stay here with her until then at least."

"Okay. I'm gonna be later than that, I'm pretty sure."

"Yeah," Margie said. "Listen, that's what I was calling about."

"Oh?"

"Can you talk to Jenny for a sec? She wants to talk to you."

Before Anderson could answer, before he could prepare himself, he heard Margie say, "Here he is, dear," and then there was a pause as the phone went from one woman to the next and then, suddenly, Anderson found himself talking to Jenny Cantrell. He remembered how awkward he'd felt the first time he'd seen her after she heard the news of Ram's death, holding her while her whole body shook against his, how totally inadequate he'd felt to the task of comforting her.

"Hi," she said.

"Hey, Jenny," he said. "You want me to tell my wife to clear out of there?"

"No," she said, and he heard a laugh in her voice that was not really a laugh at all, but great sadness trying to sound brave and strong to the rest of the world. "She's been great. Can I keep her a while longer?"

"Sure," he said. "Long as you need."

There was silence between them for a moment, then she said, "You're going to his autopsy today."

It was not a question. She already knew.

"Yes," he said.

"I was wondering..." Her voice trailed off there, but he didn't speak up. He let her find her own thread to follow, let her get the words out at her own pace. She said, "I was wondering...his wedding ring. I want it."

"Okay," he said, and said it right away, without bothering to tell her that the Medical Examiner's Office had strict rules about the dispensation of property and how things like that simply weren't done. He said it right away because he didn't care about those things. They didn't seem to matter.

"Thank you," she said.

He closed his eyes and let his chin fall to his chest.

And then Margie was back on the phone.

"It's me," she said.

"I don't know how long I'll be," he said. One autopsy could take the better part of two hours. He had forty-six to attend. Even with multiple examiners working...

"I could be real late," he said.

"It's okay. I'll either be here or at home."

"I'll call you."

"Love you," she said.

"Love you too, babe."

***

The Bexar County Medical Examiner's Office was tucked far back into the northwest corner of the University of Texas Health Science Center's campus. In order to get to it, he had to pass by a guard's shack, where he was waved through with a nod and smile because they knew him there. From there he drove down a winding two-lane private road lined with neatly spaced crepe myrtles on both sides. During wet summers, the crepe myrtles were laden with pink blossoms. But it had not been a wet summer, and the trees that Anderson passed were so starved for water they almost seemed skeletal.

Anderson parked his car as close to the front doors as he could get, which was about three rows back. Sundays were usually dead around the morgue, but not so today. He figured they had brought in most of their off-duty personnel to handle the extra workload the killings at the Morgan Rollins Factory had created. He looked at the cars and the sickly looking shrubs lining the walk that led to the morgue's front doors and he told himself he was ready to do this thing.

But he didn't get out of the car right away. He sat there and watched the heat shimmers rising off the black asphalt and thought about John, his youngest son, thought about what it had been like to show up here with his arm around Margie's shoulder and wait in the waiting room until somebody recognized him for who he was and brought him back to the back where an investigator came over and told them about the results of the autopsy on his sixteen year old son.

And then at once he was back in those days, feeling the rage and frustration and helplessness as he fought with his youngest son nearly every single day, trying to get the kid back on the right path. Margie had found some pot in his room over the summer. That by itself wasn't so bad. Anderson dismissed it as a phase, something kids did and then left behind when their real life got started. After all, his grades were good, he got his stuff done.

But that next school year, things got way out of hand. It was like John boarded a rocket-sled headed downhill, and nothing they could do could stop him. He started skipping school. He started drinking—or, as was more likely, had been drinking for some time already and simply stopped trying to hide it. He snuck out all the time.

And then, one night in October, the lieutenant in charge of the Traffic Investigations Detail showed up at his house and told them about the crash—how John was ejected from the front passenger seat of a friend's car that rolled off the freeway at a high rate of speed and into a field of cedar trees.

At the Medical Examiner's Office, the investigator told them John's blood alcohol level was a .331, more than four times the legal limit.

Margie said, "What does that mean?" and looked from the investigator to her husband.

The investigator hung his head.

Anderson wrung his hands together in his lap. He hadn't heard the boy sneak out, and he was beating himself up for that now. It didn't have to happen. It shouldn't have happened. If only he'd heard the boy sneaking out.

"What does that mean?" Margie said again.

"It means he didn't suffer," Anderson said, and prayed to God that was true.

And then that moment was gone and he was looking again at the plain tan-colored brick building that housed the Bexar County Medical Examiner's Office. He swallowed the lump in his throat, then touched his fingers to his lips and pressed them against John's photograph that covered the speedometer.

"Love you," he said. "I miss you."

He grabbed his sweater, his Mr. Rogers sweater, and went inside. It was cold down there with the dead, and he was going to be spending quite a lot of time with them.

***

He met Dr. Allison Mise down in the chill chest. She was an athletically built black woman in her late forties who tied her graying black hair into a tight ponytail. Her face was thin, with high, pronounced cheek bones and a smallish mouth with pale, wrinkled lips that reminded Anderson of a country preacher. He had never seen her wearing makeup.

Today she wore a white smock, which was standard for all the doctors and technicians in the morgue, and a plain white blouse under that and tan slacks without a belt and leather Birkenstock sandals on her feet. Her assistants all wore thick black rubber wading boots that went up to their knees.

She said, "Kind of tight quarters around here, huh?" and shook his hand.

Her grip was firm, solid, almost mannish.

"Yeah," he said, trying to force himself to relax, as he did every time he came down here and found himself suddenly in the presence of the dead. "Looks like you got your hands full around here."

"Max capacity is supposed to be sixty, but we're way over that now. You should see the coolers. We've got them stacked like cord wood against the back wall."

The look he gave her must have said volumes.

"A joke," she said.

He smiled.

"But seriously," she said, "you should see it in there. We don't have a single gurney left. We've had to store them on the floor."

They were filled to capacity, no question about it. He had never seen the place like this. Several years before, the Mexican Mafia and the Aryan Brotherhood had been involved in an all-out war, and hardly a day had gone by when a body didn't turn up in some farmer's cow pasture down in the southern part of the county. But even back in the wildest of those days the morgue had never looked this crowded.

Anderson buttoned his sweater. It was cold down here, but that wasn't the first thing you noticed. It wasn't even the smell, which was bad, but not *that* bad. What you noticed when you rode the elevator down from the main floor, where you wouldn't have been able to tell the place apart from any one of a thousand doctor's waiting rooms or law offices, to the basement, where the bodies were kept, was the grunginess of the place. All the lighting down here was done with fluorescents, and that gave everything a bluish tint. The accumulated grime that blackened the caulk between the tiles and balled in the corners seemed to almost shine under it. This was a filth that had moved in to stay, like in a prison, where the janitor's mop does little more than push it from one side of the hallway to the other.

And it was small. Or maybe, he thought, that was just because there were so many dead bodies crammed into it. He was less than five feet away from a little wrinkled old man whose jaw had set into a teeth-baring grimace that made it look like he was trying to push out a bowel movement. The man was nude, and his sunken chest and frail-looking arms and jutting collar bones and waxy yellow skin reminded Anderson, with all the force of a cement block thrown at his head, that the dead are denied their pride.

Fortunately, he thought, they feel no shame.

Six more gurneys, really nothing more than white-colored plastic tables that could tilt down at the feet to allow the blood to run into the sinks along the back wall, were on the other side of the old man.

All of them had bodies on them.

Some of the bodies were rolled up in bloody white sheets, others were uncovered, staring with dead, glassy eyes up at the ceiling.

Off in the far corner, two of Dr. Mise's assistants were putting the finishing touches on a body. One held a garbage bag open while the other poured organs into the bag from what looked like a plastic iced tea pitcher. When the last of the slop was in, the assistant holding the bag, a tall, lanky kid with sunken, sleep-deprived eyes, tied it off and crammed it into the open chest cavity of the body on the table. He went to work suturing up the chest while the other, a short, muscular Hispanic guy in his early thirties, went over to the sink and washed off his gloves.

Billy Joel's "She's Always a Woman to Me" played on a radio along the back wall. Anderson probably wouldn't have even noticed it had the short, Hispanic guy not suddenly said, "Jesus, I hate this fucking song," and went over and fiddled with the dial until he came up with the opening drums of Led Zeppelin's "When the Levee Breaks."

"There you go," he said, and smiled at Anderson as he bopped his head to the beat. He turned it up a notch.

Allison Mise said, "You ready to get started, Keith?"

"Yeah," he said.

"Xavier," she said to the shorter guy. "Let's set up the table."

"Sure thing, Doc."

Xavier hustled over to the empty table next to Anderson and spread a white sheet over it. Then he took a blank evidence card from the desk and put it in one corner of the table. Mise put a hand on Keith's shoulder, something he hated her to do while she was down here, and guided him to one side so Xavier could do his thing. It wasn't until she moved that Anderson realized the body on the table behind her was Bobby Cantrell.

Anderson sucked in a breath, and when he looked away, Xavier was writing Robert Bradley Cantrell on the evidence card in the corner of the table.

**

Ram was wearing a blue t-shirt that had curled up on his right side to show a wide swath of his hairy belly. His empty holster had shifted so that it was partially curled over the belt and the top of his jeans and was digging into his flesh. He had pale, cream-colored dirt on his pants and his right shoulder and in his black hair. There were paper sacks over his hands, secured at the wrists with string. The sacks had been put there by the evidence technicians at the Morgan Rollins Iron Works Factory in order to preserve any evidence that might show up in a Gun Shot Residue test. Anderson's eyes drifted from his best friend's bagged hands and over the jagged, ugly hole in his chest to the blood that had splattered up into the nape of his neck and dusted his goatee. The blood made him look like he was wearing a bib.

Xavier walked around the body, taking pictures of the injuries as he made little screeching noises that, Anderson guessed, were supposed to mirror what Jimmy Page was doing with his guitar.

"Got what you need, man?" he said to Anderson.

Anderson said, "Huh?" and looked at him, and it was only then that he remembered he was supposed to be writing his observations down in his steno book.

Anderson shook himself and said, "Yeah, I got it. Go ahead."

"You sure?"

"Sure," Anderson said.

"Cool."

While the bags were being removed from Cantrell's hands, Led Zeppelin faded out and Three Dog Night's "Jeremiah Was a Bullfrog" started up.

Xavier said, "Ah man, change that shit," to the tall, sunken-eyed kid across the room.

From behind Anderson, Mise said, "Billy, don't you dare. It's about time we had some decent music in here."

Anderson looked back at her.

She was whistling to herself as she wrote out her notes on a clipboard, her pale, wrinkled mouth not quite warped into a smile. Anderson liked Mise, respected her, but it didn't change his opinion that you had to be a weird duck to work in this place.

A loud thud from the autopsy table made him turn around.

"Fuck," Xavier said, panting, "he's a heavy bastard. Hey, Billy, come here and give me a hand."

Xavier pushed Ram over on his side so that his face was smashed up against the lip of the table. Billy came over, and the two of them rolled him over far enough that they could get a wooden block under the body's shoulder blades.

"Yeah, that'll do it," Xavier said. Then he started taking off Ram's jewelry and bringing it over to the table, where he laid it out and photographed it.

Anderson turned to Mise and said, "Allison, his wedding ring, I need it."

She looked up at him, still humming to the music, and said, "Huh?"

"His wedding ring. His wife and my wife are over at his house right now. She called me this morning and wanted me to get the ring."

He could tell she was right about to quote chapter and verse of the Bexar County policy that said he couldn't take personal property out of the morgue, but she stopped herself.

Then she nodded.

"Thank you," he said.

There was another loud thud from the table as Xavier dropped one of Ram's arms onto the plastic bin.

"Jesus," he said. "This guy's huge, man. Must weigh a fucking ton."

Anderson winced.

"Xavier!" Mise said sharply, and shook her head at him meaningfully when he gave her a *what did I do?* look. To Anderson she said, "I'm sorry. I didn't know he was a friend of yours. This must be terrible for you."

"Thanks," he said.

She nodded.

She walked over to the body and looked at Bobby's right arm. Anderson watched her lift it, turn it over, and feel down the length of the ulna and radius. It looked like she was trying to squeeze the last bit of toothpaste from the tube.

"He saw it coming," she said. "That's for sure."

"What do you mean?"

"Look at his arm," she said. She held it up, and he could tell that the bone was busted up inside. "That is a Grade Four comminuted fracture," she said ominously. Then, by way of further explanation, "A spiral break."

He had a blank expression on his face that said she had left him at the starting line.

"We usually see fractures like this in skiing accidents," she said. "The foot gets planted and rooted in one direction by the blade of the ski, but when a sudden force twists the rest of the body you apply torsion, like this." She made a motion with her hands like she was twisting a towel into a snake. "You end up corkscrewing the bone. You see?"

Sort of, Anderson thought. "It looks like it hurt."

"I'll say," Mise answered. "Now look at this." She held up Bobby's arm to his face, so that it looked like he was shielding his eyes from the sun or trying to block a blow. "He had his arm up like this. You see?"

"I think so. What? He got grabbed, where, by the wrist?"

"Looks like it from the bruising. And the arm was twisted to cause this break."

"Okay," he said, and felt like he was supposed to be understanding something that he wasn't even aware of yet.

"You don't get it, do you?"

"I guess not," he said.

"Do you have any idea how much torsion it takes to break a bone?"

"A lot?" he said.

"Yeah," she said, and snorted. "A whole freakin' lot. It's not something you just do—" she snapped her fingers "—like that." She said, "A skiing accident I can understand. A full grown man breaking a baby's arm...yeah, I've seen that, too. But look at your friend here. He's a huge guy. You have any idea how strong you'd have to be to do this to a man his size?"

"Hmm," he said. "Good point."

***

Anderson's feet started to hurt midway through the autopsy. He watched with mounting irritation and restlessness as Ram was stripped and poked and prodded and photographed and washed off and cut open and washed off again.

Jimmy Buffet was on the radio now singing "Son of a Son of a Sailor," one of Anderson's favorites, and one he never heard on the radio. But not even the wistful contentment that Buffet's music usually brought him could penetrate the malaise that had formed in his mind.

It all seemed so disgusting, so cheap. He watched as they flipped Ram's nude corpse over and stuck a thing that looked like a T-square over him, one end over the head, the long end wedged into the crack of his butt. Then they flipped him over again and worked at the rib cage to open it further than whoever had killed him already had.

Xavier hummed to himself as he reached into the chest with a ladle and started scooping out organs into a plastic iced tea pitcher, stopping every so often to ask permission from Dr. Mise to continue.

Anderson closed his eyes and waited for it to be over.

"Hey, Doc," Xavier said.

Anderson opened his eyes.

Mise crossed the tiled floor and stood next to Xavier, the two of them looking into the open flesh canoe that was Bobby Cantrell like two boys who have just found a coral snake in the bottom of a hollowed out tree stump.

"What is that?" Xavier said. "It feels gritty."

"It's the same stuff he had on the outside of him, too."

"What is it?" Anderson said, coming closer, standing just behind them.

"It looks like transfer, don't you think?" Xavier said.

"Has to be," Mise said.

"What is it?" Anderson said again.

Mise moved to one side. "Here look," she said, and grabbed the flap of Cantrell's chest wall and pulled it down so Anderson could have a look. "See here, around the heart? All that black stuff. It's the same stuff he had on the outside."

Anderson thought of the junkie in the interview room, the black, waxy stuff he had spent a long time washing off into the sink.

"What is it?" he asked again.

"I don't know," Mise answered. "Carbon soot maybe, mixed with some kind of wax."

"How did it get there?"

"I don't know," she said, and then stopped. She leaned forward and said, "Oh my God." She ran her finger around the bulge of the heart. "Oh my God."

"What?" Anderson said.

Mise looked at Xavier. "You didn't notice this?" The heat in her tone was unmistakable.

"What?" Xavier said. And then he looked, and for a moment he didn't see what she was talking about. And then he did and his eyes bulged.

"What is it?" Anderson said.

Mise reached in and wrapped her hand around the heart and scooped it out. She held it up and said, "I can't believe this."

"What?" Anderson said. "Tell me."

"This is not a human heart."

That stopped him. He looked at the heart in her hands and then at her. She looked back at him.

"How can you tell it's not human?"

"Here," she said, and put the heart down on a cutting board that rested across the sink at Bobby Cantrell's feet. She led him to one of the other tables, where the tall, sunken-eyed kid named Billy was cutting into a fat white woman with tattoos all over her arms and neck. Billy stepped aside and Allison Mise reached into the chest cavity and pulled out the heart. "See this beard of fat that's hanging on here?"

He did. It looked like yellow candle wax.

"You only see that on human hearts. Other mammal species, no fat. But on every human heart, you see this little beard of fat."

He turned away from the human heart and looked at the heart on the cutting board at Bobby's feet.

After a long silence he said, "What is it?"

"You mean, what kind of animal did it come from?"

He nodded.

"Can't be sure just looking at it. Only that it came from a mammal, one about the size of a man."

"A goat?" he said.

"Could be," she said. "That'd be about the right size. Could also be a big dog or a—"

"It's a goat," he said.

***

Out came the white, knotted, sausage skin-looking snake that was the colon. The smell of shit was overpowering, and Anderson had to shake his head to void the smell from his nostrils as the ball of guts was dropped into the sink.

The hits just keep coming, he thought.

Xavier had a white, circular saw in his hands, similar in size and shape to what Anderson, who sometimes watched cooking shows on the Food Network with Margie, had heard celebrity chefs refer to as a stick blender. He turned it on and began to cut into the scalp over the top of the head, working from ear to ear across the ash symbols on the forehead. AC/DC was doing "Back in Black" on the radio, and Xavier seemed to be happy again, shuffling his feet and moving his shoulders to the beat while he worked.

Then he put the saw down and started working the skin back from the skull, over the face, helping it along by slicing it from the bone with a scalpel.

He turned to Mise as the song faded out and said, "Permission to cut?"

"Go ahead," she said.

Xavier picked up the circular saw again and it started to whine and scream as metal dug into bone. White powdery bits of dust flew from the saw, and Anderson couldn't believe that the man didn't use a face shield. Somehow, it seemed even less sanitary than Mise walking around in her Birkenstocks.

Xavier turned to Anderson while he was sawing away and, smiling, said, "Fuck, this guy's sure got a hard head."

His smile was meant to be breezy but looked obscene to Anderson.

And then, thankfully, the whine of the saw stopped. Anderson looked away. Mise was at the sink, using a huge knife to slice the liver into thick steaks.

"He's got rocks," she said.

"Excuse me?" Anderson said.

"Rocks," she said again. "Gall stones."

Anderson nodded. Ram had never been one to turn down a beer.

A few minutes later, they bagged all the organs into a black trash bag and stuffed them back down into the body cavity. Xavier wheeled him over to the walk-in coolers on the side wall nearest the door.

"Well, that's that," Mise said. "Just forty-five more to go."

Anderson groaned inwardly.

"Relax," she said. "I got six more doctors coming in at four. Things'll speed up pretty fast from here."

He nodded, but he was thinking, *Goddamn it, I hate my job. I really, really do.*

***

It was past midnight when Anderson finally walked back to his car. The night air was hot and close and dry, but at least it didn't smell like the air inside the morgue. He reached in and turned the ignition over without getting in. Waves of heat were pouring out of the car, and he wanted to give the AC time to do its thing.

While he waited, he took out his cell phone and dialed Deputy Chief Allen's home number.

Allen picked up on the second ring.

"I didn't wake you up, did I, sir?"

"Hell no," Allen said, and Anderson believed him. The man sounded sharp as ever. "What did you find out?"

Anderson told him about the autopsy. He told him about the spiral fracture to Bobby Aaronson's right arm, and about the strange, carbon-like soot that was all over the inside of his chest cavity, and lastly, he told him about the goat's heart. Then he waited to hear what Allen had to say.

"I can't fucking believe that. A fucking goat's heart. What is that, some kind of devil worshipping stuff?"

"I don't know, sir. Maybe."

"It's fucking obscene is what it is."

Anderson climbed into his car, held his hand up in front of the AC vents to make sure it was blowing cold air, and closed the door.

Allen said, "And what about this black shit you told me about? You said the kid from the train yard had it all over him, too?"

"Yes, sir."

"But we don't think he was ever at the Iron Works?"

"No, sir. But the freight yard where he was killed is right next door to the Iron Works. You can see the smokestacks from the tracks."

"So what does that prove?"

"I don't know, sir." And he really didn't. Beyond the obvious, that whoever did the murders at the Iron Works also did the kid in the freight yard, he didn't have a clue. He felt helpless.

Anderson waited in silence, and after a moment, Allen said, "I approved your request this afternoon to get a hold of Officer Henninger's personnel file. I also authorized you to see his psychological file as well."

"You did?"

"Yeah," Allen said. There was another long silence, and Anderson could feel Allen building up to something. He said, "Keith."

"Yes, sir?"

"Keith, listen, before I put these files in your hands, I need you tell me something."

"Okay," Anderson said, but slowly, like he was mentally gripping the arms of his chair and bracing for bad news.

"I need you to tell me what...what specifically set you off on this kid? What was it he said that made you link him in here?"

Anderson had expected that question.

"It wasn't anything he said. Not really. I can't explain it, sir. All I can tell you is what I already told you. When I looked into his eyes that night at the freight yard, I could just tell that he saw more than he was saying. That's it, really." Then he said, "Why? Did you already go through his files?"

But Anderson already knew the answer. Allen, Anderson knew, had been a homicide detective back in the day. He wouldn't have been able to resist.

"Yeah, I did," said Allen. "And the only thing I can tell you, Keith, is that you got good instincts."

Anderson shifted the phone to his other ear. "Tell me what you found, sir."

"You remember when we went through the application process? Remember how, during the background check, if they found out you'd smoked even so much as a joint you were out?"

"Sure," Anderson said. It was a sore subject these days with the old timers, the ones who felt the Department's scramble to hire new officers was driving the standards way down. The way Anderson understood it, these days, a recruit could admit to doing cocaine and still had a chance to get in—just so long as it wasn't in the past seven years.

"Well, you're not gonna believe what this kid's got in his file."

"What?"

"He's a mess. Get this. He killed his dad during his senior year in high school."

"What? No. You're kidding me."

"It's the truth. The Comal County Sheriff's Office did a full investigation and the thing was written up as a justifiable homicide, self-defense. He was cleared because apparently the dad was a real piece of work, but it's right there in his folder. You'll see it before you take off tomorrow."

Anderson was still thinking about Paul Henninger killing his dad, wondering how someone manages to become a policeman after doing something like that, even if it was in self-defense—

I mean, Christ, don't they at least still have to take a complete psychological exam?

—and it took him a moment to catch up to what Allen had just told him.

"Where are you sending me?" he said.

"Comal County," Allen said. "Short trip—but I need you to visit with their investigators to follow up on the deal with Henninger's dad. Even if it turns out to have nothing to do with this case, if the press hears about this and we can't tell them we've followed up on it—shit, we'll look like fools."

"I agree," Anderson said. He could see that, but then, he would have done that anyway. There was no need for Allen to give him a direct order to do it.

Allen spoke before he had a chance to say anything, and it was like he had been following Anderson's interior monologue word for word.

"I got another reason I want you to go up there," Allen said.

"Yes sir?"

"You know those weird stick things we found all over that inner chamber at the Iron Works?"

"Yeah?" he said.

"I looked over some of the crime scene photos from where Henninger killed his dad. Those same stick things, they're everywhere. They're all over the barn and in the inside of the house and out in the yard. They're everywhere."

"No," Anderson said. "Are you sure they're the same?"

"Of course I'm sure," Allen said. "Exactly the same."

My God, Anderson thought. *Oh my God.*

Chapter 10

Paul was on Rachel's mind all that morning. All afternoon, too. A day of shopping with a friend hadn't shaken the image of him coming home and trudging up their back stairs, every inch of him covered in dust and sweat and smelling like he'd been touched by something corrupt. It scared her a little, seeing him like that. He was her man, her rock. He wasn't supposed to fall apart. But he had. And what was worse, he had lied to her. Hadn't he?

She believed him when he said he hadn't hurt that boy. So no, maybe he hadn't technically lied to her. Maybe she shouldn't call it that. But what then? Maybe he hadn't told her a lie outright, but he certainly hadn't told her the whole story. That was what upset her, the evasion. She had seen the doubt in his face, the trepidation, and she wondered what would make him hold back like that. Was it fear? Shame? Or something else that was just too big to put a label on?

Rachel pulled into the carport next to Paul's truck at a quarter of five that afternoon and went upstairs. She heard the shower running. She put her things down on the couch and walked over to their bed. Paul's uniform was crumpled up in a black dusty ball in the corner. His boots looked tired, the tongues yawning down across the instep, a ring of cream-colored dirt around them.

She knocked on the bathroom door and called his name through the crack.

No answer.

"Paul?"

She pushed the door open. A steam mist hung in the air. He was leaning over the sink, completely nude, his hands on either side of the bowl. His skin was wet. His hair was wet, uncombed. He was looking into the mirror. She tried to meet his gaze there, and that was when she realized that he wasn't looking at himself in the mirror. He was looking *beyond* the mirror. Into nothing.

"Paul?"

His eyes focused and met hers in the mirror. "Hey," he said. "How was the day?"

"Good." And then, almost as an afterthought, "I bought a blouse."

He nodded.

Rachel studied his face. He looked exhausted, even more so now than he had when he first came home.

"How about you?" she asked. "Did you sleep?"

"A little," he said. "Not much, actually. I've been thinking."

"Thinking? Paul, you didn't sleep at all while I was gone?"

"Not really, no."

"Oh, Paul."

"Rachel, I have something kind of big I need to tell you."

She swallowed. "Okay Paul," she said. "What is it? Is it about last night?"

"In a way, yeah. But it's more than that. More than just what happened to that kid." His breath hitched in his chest. He said, "I'm sorry, Rachel. This is in so many pieces. It's hard to tell it."

"Just start at the beginning, Paul. I'll listen."

"Rachel, I've been thinking a lot about my father."

"Your dad?"

Rachel went inside the bathroom then and took him by the arm and led him out into the bedroom. She handed him a pair of his boxer shorts and said, "Here, put this on."

He looked down and seemed surprised at his own nakedness. He took the boxers from her, stared down at himself, and laughed at some private joke. Only then did he slide on his shorts.

"What is it?" she said.

"I was thinking about Mexico," he said.

"What?"

He guided her to the bed. "Here, sit down, would you. This is gonna be hard for me. It may take me a while to get out."

"Paul, you're scaring me. If you're in trouble..."

"I'm not in trouble. Not like you mean it anyway. But some things have been happening to me lately. Some things that involve my father. My mom, too. There's so much I need to tell you about, but I don't even..." He threw up his hands as if to say, *It's all too much.*

During their four years together he had said very little about his dad. Even less about his mom. Looking at him now, Rachel was struck by how serious he looked, how genuinely confused he was by the enormity of what was going on in his head. It made him look more vulnerable than she had ever seen him look before. She almost reached out then and touched his face, but a part of her held back. He wouldn't want that. He wouldn't take her hand away, but it might amount to putting a stopper on whatever he was about to say. Instead, she said, "What do you mean, some things have been happening? Paul, are you okay?"

He looked at her. She met his eyes and hardly recognized the man she saw there. Her Paul was quiet, calm. She had seen him confused before. She thought back to him as a cadet at the police academy, leaning over a book at their apartment's kitchen table, trying to pull the sense out of a sticky passage or memorize a statute, and realized that wasn't the same thing as whatever this was at all. He was adrift now in a way she had never seen before. He was shaken.

"What is it, Paul?"

"Rachel, I saw my father last night. In that boxcar."

He blurted the words out, and for a moment she didn't know how to respond.

"Paul, your father's dead."

"I can't tell it to you all at once. There's too much."

"Paul, I don't know what to say to that."

She said the words and just as quickly wished that she could take them back. But as it turned out it didn't matter. He had gone this far. He intended to tell it, and once he went that far, his words took on a momentum that wasn't going to stop.

***

Paul sat there with Rachel on the side of their bed, wondering how he was going to say everything that needed to be said. And then he saw the box that he had gone through earlier that day, the photograph that had opened up so much to him still leaning against one flap of the box lid, and all at once it was clear to him. He knew he had to begin with that Sunday morning back in early September so many years ago.

He had seen his mother curled up on the sofa in the darkened corner of their living room. He saw the shabby kitchen piled high with dishes, the carcass of last night's chicken still on the table. He saw his father sitting on a chair in the lawn outside the screen door. He had a cylinder head from their tractor in his hands and he was turning it over and over, studying what was wrong with it.

Paul was standing next to the screen door, listening to the shrill drone of the cicadas in the tall grass, waiting for the sound of Steve's dad's pickup to come up the road and take him away.

Paul was dressed in his football gear, white pants with red and black striping, a red jersey paid for by Bob White's Marina. He held his helmet by the face mask in one hand, his shoulder pads on the floor at his feet. He was impatient, full of a twelve-year-old boy's urge to just *go*, get gone from this place and get onto the football field.

The phone rang.

It caught him by surprise, because the phone almost never rang. A flutter of panic went through him. *It's Steve*, he thought, his good mood crashing. *They're not coming.*

He heard his mom say, "Baby, if it's for me, tell 'em I ain't feelin' up to talkin' on the phone."

The phone rang a third time.

It wasn't for her, Paul knew that. No one ever called for her, not anymore. Not in a very long time.

Another ring.

From outside, his father shouted, "Answer the goddamn phone," and Paul did.

"Hello?" he said.

There was a click and a static-filled silence. And then, a woman's voice, speaking in rapid Spanish. Paul said, "Ma'am, I didn't catch a word of that. You're gonna have to talk to me in English." More Spanish, but this time he caught his father's name somewhere in the jumble. He said, "You wanna speak to my dad?"

"*Si. Tu Padre*. Martin Henninger."

Paul so rarely heard his father addressed by his first name that at first he could only stand there and look dumb. The woman sounded young, but he wasn't a very good judge of those kinds of things. Not yet anyway. He only knew that he had heard a note of sadness in her voice.

"Who is it?" his father said from the doorway.

"I don't know," Paul said. "She's talking Mexican. I can't understand a word she says. She asked for you though."

"Me?" his dad said. He looked at the phone in Paul's hand. "Here, give me that," he said.

"Hello?" he said, and then stood there listening. Paul watched his father's face. He saw the look of annoyance dissolve and reform itself into first recognition, then shock, then something that must have been sorrow, for his father hung his head and listened silently for nearly a minute, barely breathing at all.

When he spoke again, it was in Spanish. The words poured out of him, and Paul stood there, gawking at his father. He had no idea. The man had never even hinted that he could speak Spanish.

He heard his father say, "*Que dijo ella?*" Then he fell back against the wall and leaned his head all the way back and let out a long sigh. "*Si, te oi,*" he said. "*Yo tengo que guardar un cargo.*"

None of it had made any sense to Paul at the time. It had just been a confused jumble of foreign words, the sense of them overwhelmed by the realization that his father could speak them. But he had some Spanish in college. He had some survival Spanish in the police academy. And he had picked some up while he was working the largely Hispanic neighborhoods west of downtown that the officers on Central Patrol not so lovingly referred to as Little Mexico. That last phrase, *Yo tengo que guardar un cargo*, he knew what that meant.

I have a charge to keep.

He thought about that now, about the memory suddenly laid bare like that, how a key piece of a sprawling puzzle seemed to have fallen into place, and he thought, *Yes, that phone call, and what happened afterwards, makes a whole hell of a lot more sense now.*

***

"Now you make sure it's all right with your folks, you hear?"

"Yes sir, Mr. Sullivan," Paul said. He turned and beamed a smile at Steve. They were twelve, sitting side by side in Steve's dad's truck. It was the same truck—minus the oversized off-road tires and the aftermarket sound system that Steve would get for his own six years later—Steve would use to cart them back and forth to school. But for now it was your standard issue farm truck, plain as the day is long, idling quietly on the side of the road in front of Paul's house.

The two boys jumped down from the truck, reached into the bed to grab Paul's shoulder pads and helmet, and ran for the screen door on the side of the house. Paul's mother was there in the kitchen, washing dishes in the sink.

Paul stopped when he saw her, surprised to see her on her feet.

He said, "Hi, Mom."

"Hey, baby," she said. Her voice sounded weak, but not like it usually did. Normally, she sounded like she was speaking from inside a fog bank. She looked from Paul to Steve, the two boys covered head to foot in dust and grass stains and sweat. "Hello, Steve," she said.

"Hi, Mrs. Henninger."

The two boys looked at each other, Steve nudging Paul with one elbow.

"Go on, ask her," he said.

"Okay, okay," Paul said. He turned to Carol Henninger. "Hey, Momma, Steve's dad's outside. He said if I wanted to I could eat at their place tonight. Can I, Momma? Please?"

Carol Henninger picked up a dishtowel and dried her hands. She took a quick look over her shoulder, back towards the darkened living room, then looked back at Paul.

"I don't see why not," she said. "That might actually be a real good idea, Paul. Go on now. Get yourself upstairs and get changed. Be quiet, though."

Even at twelve, Paul wasn't deaf to the caution in her voice. He looked past her, into the living room, and saw his father's lattice-like stick sculptures all over the floor. His heart sank. As many of them as there were in there, his father had to have been at them all day. Even after making one or two, his father's moods were unpredictable, though they usually veered towards violence. After making the number Paul could see from the kitchen (he counted four, five), there was no telling what was in store for the rest of the night.

A silent understanding passed between mother and son. "Hurry it up," she said.

He turned without another word, ready to sprint quietly up the stairs, when his father appeared in the doorway. Martin Henninger was dressed in his usual, starched-white shirt buttoned at the neck, black slacks, worn black Stetson hat, though he didn't seem to be put together as well as usual. A quick glance told Paul that. His underarms were soaked with sweat. His fingers were shaking.

Paul met his father's eyes and had to look away again almost immediately. They were nested in a web of wrinkles, and he saw a crazy intensity there that was like that of a man who has just won a fist fight, but expects to get jumped from both sides at any moment.

"Where you going, boy?"

"Daddy, I..."

Martin Henninger looked down at his son. Then he looked past Paul to Steve, said nothing, didn't even show signs of recognizing the boy.

He turned back to Paul.

"I asked you a question."

"Daddy, I—Steve asked if it was all right for me to eat at their place tonight. His dad's outside."

"What's wrong with eating here?"

"Nothing, Daddy. I just thought it'd be fun is all."

Martin Henninger pushed the bill of the Stetson up his forehead and scratched his hairline.

"No," he said. "I want you here tonight."

"But, Daddy—"

Martin Henninger gave Paul a look that stopped him cold, mid-sentence.

He said, "I want you here with your family tonight. Now go on upstairs and get that shit off and get changed. You need to go feed the goats."

Paul looked away.

"Yes sir," he said. He turned to Steve and said, "I gotta go, Steve."

Steve looked like he wanted nothing more than to get gone himself. "Sure," he said. He turned to Carol Henninger and offered a little wave. "Bye, Mrs. Henninger. Bye, Mr. Henninger."

"Bye, Steve," Paul's mom said.

Paul watched Steve slip out the screen door and kept watching him until he turned the corner at the front of the house and was gone from sight.

Then he turned back to his parents, head down.

"Go on," his father said again. "Get out of that shit and get changed. There's something I want to show you."

"Yes sir," Paul said, and sprinted up the stairs.

***

He was back downstairs in less than two minutes. His mother was standing off in one corner of the kitchen, her arms crossed over her chest, eyes down on the floor. Paul looked at her and realized how small she had become, how frail. Her face, though she rarely went out into the sun anymore, was dark, and there were wrinkles at the corners of her mouth. *She isn't* that *old*, he thought. *But she looks ancient, like this house and the land and that man out there in the yard have sapped her of everything she needs to feel alive.*

"Hurry up, Paul."

Paul glanced through the screen door and saw his father out in the yard, standing with his face to the sun, a corona of light dancing around his silhouette.

"I'm coming, sir," he said, and sprinted through the door and out into the yard.

He trotted up next to his father and waited. Paul knew that when it came to this man, it was best to just stand there and wait to be told what to do. Guessing, if you were wrong and ended up doing the opposite of what he wanted, only made him angry, and the man had a very short temper when it came to that sort of thing.

"Come with me," his father said, and walked off towards the barn.

Paul followed him.

The big sliding door was open, and enough light filtered through the gaps between the boards that Paul could see one of his father's stick lattices in the middle of the floor. A rush of anxiety made his face feel hot. He had seen his father make the lattices many times since that night when he was five and came down the stairs to spy on the man and saw him so horribly changed, and he had learned to keep his distance.

"Daddy, what...?"

His father stared at the lattice. He had his hands in his pockets, a bit of hay in his teeth. He said, "You know what that thing is?"

Paul answered quickly. He said, "Momma told me to leave your stuff alone, Daddy. I ain't done nothing to it, I swear."

"Hush," his father said. "I know you ain't done nothing to it. I'm asking if you know what it is."

"No sir."

"I don't think they have a name. At least they ain't got none I ever heard. This woman I used to know taught me how to make 'em years ago. Don't really know how it happens either. I just start to feel this sort of red haze in my mind and I know it's time to go gathering wood. Lot of times that's the last thing I remember about making them. I'll snap out of it a few hours later, hungry with this feeling like every part of me is starving. Not just my belly, but every part of me. And then I'll look at what I've done and I'll see one of these things."

Martin Henninger trailed off into his own thoughts, and Paul waited. The waiting grew uncomfortable, and Paul said, "But what are they for? What do you do with them?"

"Sometimes I don't do nothing with them. Just throw them away. Those I think must be duds. You know what a dud is, Paul?"

Paul thought of the Wiley E. Coyote cartoons, the coyote staggering around punch drunk from having a giant rock dropped on his head, a hammer in his hand, some sort of artillery shell next to him. The coyote starts banging on the shell, once, twice, and then *boooom!* the thing explodes in his face.

He said, "A dud's like sometimes when one of them Black Cat fireworks won't explode when all the others around it do."

Martin Henninger looked at his son and almost smiled. "Yeah, that's right."

Paul looked at the stick lattice in the barn. "Is that one a dud?"

"No," his father said. "Not that one."

"So what's it supposed to do?"

"Well, that's the thing, Paul. It ain't so much what *it's* supposed to do, as what *I'm* supposed to do. You see, that thing over there, what it does is act like a magnifying glass. You ever held a magnifying glass up to the sun and burned up ants with it?"

Paul said he hadn't, but he had seen kids at school do it.

"Well it's the same thing," Martin Henninger said. "Same idea anyway. The only difference is the kind of power that's being channeled." He paused there and smiled to himself. "It's funny though. Now that I think about it, the results can be the same. If that power gets channeled into the wrong man, it'll burn him up sure as the sun burns up an ant." He turned to Paul and tapped the side of the boy's head. "But if it goes to the right man, that man can use that power to do great things."

Paul didn't understand. He looked from his father to the stick lattice in the center of the barn and just didn't get it. His father had said he could use the power that thing gave off to do great things, but when he looked at the lattice, he just saw a pile of sticks cobbled together at random. He couldn't feel any great power emanating from it. And as for great things, well, they didn't exactly have it easy around this place. They scraped an existence out of a mangy herd of Angora goats and picked peaches in the summer and repaired tractors in the winter and, for all the work, could barely afford to eat fried chicken but once a week. Where was the great power in that?

Paul's father smiled then, and it caught Paul by surprise. He smiled back, and only then did he realize that his father wasn't smiling at *him*, but because he knew exactly what Paul was thinking.

His father said, "It ain't that kind of power I'm talking about. What I'm talking about is spiritual power, and spiritual power *will* feed a man's body and soul. It won't pay the rent, but—well, that's a hard lesson to learn. Took me a long time to figure out that power and wealth ain't the same thing. Not true power, anyway."

Paul nodded, though he had no idea why.

"Come here," his father said. "I want to show you something."

He walked out of the barn and over by where the goats were feeding in the grass.

"Grab that big old son of a bitch right there. The one with the black on his ears."

The goat he pointed out was Oscar's great great grandfather. Paul stepped into the yard and grabbed the animal by the scruff of his neck and pulled him over to his father. He was dusty, head to foot, a rheumy glaze in his eyes.

His father said, "What did I tell you about fleas?"

Paul thought for a minute, not wanting to say the wrong thing and spoil his father's relatively good mood. But the only thing he could think of was an old quip his father tossed out every once in a while as they were shearing the goats.

Cautiously, he said, "You said where there's one there's gonna be a thousand."

"That's right. Here, watch this."

Martin Henninger put his palm on the animal's head and ran his hand down the length of its back. As he did so, one black speck after another leapt onto his hand. By the time he had reached the tail, his hand was covered with a swirling black mass of fleas.

Paul had been kneeling next to his father, but he was on his feet now, scrambling backwards.

"It's all right," Martin said. "Come here."

Paul hesitated.

"I said get over here. *Now.*"

Paul came forward, Adam's apple pumping up and down in his throat like a piston.

"Put your hand right here next to mine."

"Sir?"

"Do it." He hadn't raised his voice yet, but he wasn't far from doing so, Paul knew. "Put it here next to mine. Hurry it up."

With his skin crawling, Paul did as he was told. Instantly the fleas jumped from his father's hand to Paul's, swarming it, enveloping it.

But he wasn't getting bit.

Paul turned his hand over, looking at the insects so thick there that he could only see his skin in a few places.

"How come they're not—"

"I want you to remember something, Paul."

Paul looked at him.

"I want you to remember that it took me a long time to learn what I know about the world. It took me a lot of heartache, too. One day you'll understand that. And one day I'm gonna come to you and I'm gonna teach you these things that I've learned. You are gonna be called upon to take certain responsibilities upon yourself. Do not fail me when I call upon you."

Paul sensed right away the ominous tones in his father's voice, though little of what he said made sense. He started to ask his dad why he thought he might fail him, when suddenly his hand began to burn.

He let out a whine.

Looking down at his hand, he saw the swarm attacking him. He felt them biting him, felt the searing pain, like his hand had been pressed into a hot cast iron skillet and held there. He screamed and swatted at the swarm on his hand, batting the insects away with his left hand even as he beat the right one against the thigh of his jeans.

By the time he had them all off, his hand was covered with red whelps and the fingers had already started to swell slightly.

Holding his wrist, he looked at his father, his expression asking why, why did every lesson have to hurt so badly.

"Go wash that off," his father said. "Then feed the goats. And I want the barn cleaned up before you go to bed tonight, you hear?"

"Yes sir," Paul managed to say.

He turned and headed for the water trough on the side of the barn, still holding his wrist. The pain was getting worse, and tears were coming freely down his face. He dunked his hand into the water that filled the trough and the coolness of it felt good. His breathing began to slow back down to normal, but the fingers were so stiff and swollen that he could barely flex them. He tried, and nearly screamed from the pain.

Then, glancing up towards the house, he saw his mother watching him from the shadows of the kitchen doorway. Her face was stern, almost like she was accusing Paul of doing something nasty. She looked away and retreated back into the darkness.

***

Paul went into the barn and took down the feed buckets from the wall, where they hung from a pair of old railroad spikes that his grandfather had driven into one of the wall studs. The swelling in his right hand had gone from bad to worse. It was an unnatural, angry shade of red now, and the pain was intense. He couldn't even close his fingers over the feed bucket's handle. When he tried, a pain shot through the injured hand and up the length of his arm. He let out a gasp and dropped the empty bucket onto the dirt floor.

"How's your hand?" his mother said from the doorway.

"It hurts," he said. He didn't want her to see him crying, but there was no helping that. His eyes were welling up, and he could feel a few runners going down his cheeks.

"Here, let me see it."

She came closer, and he held out his hand for her to look at. She grabbed it and turned it over, looking at it front and back.

He let out another gasp at the rough handling. "Momma, that hurts."

If she heard him, she made no sign of it.

"Momma, stop."

He tried to pull his hand back.

She tightened her grip and pulled his hand back to where she could look at it. Her strength was surprising for such a small, frail woman.

"Stop, Momma. Please."

"Hurts, don't it?"

"Yes, ma'am."

"Well, it serves you right for being so stupid."

"But, Momma, I didn't do it on purpose. I was just doing what—"

"Stop whining," she snapped.

She let his hand drop, then looked out into the yard. It was getting late, and sunlight was settling down through the oak trees. The goats were moving around restlessly on the dirt road that led down to the horse pasture, bleating for their dinner.

"Go into the kitchen," she said. "I'm gonna put some meat tenderizer on that. Works on scorpion and wasp stings, should work fine on whatever you got yourself into."

"It was fleas, Momma."

She stared at him, and for just a moment, there was a change. The hard shell seemed to fall away from her, and Paul saw the woman he had always known. *But that's not right,* he thought, because the woman he saw just then wasn't the same woman he had always known. Not quite. This woman was alert, her eyes clear and focused, yet kind.

"Go on," she said. "Get inside. I'll be there directly."

He ran for the house.

***

Paul waited for her inside the screen door of the kitchen. Her thin, crudely cut brown hair was down, and a sluggish breeze caught it and lifted it off her shoulders. Her body was thin, ill-looking, though she was moving with a purpose now. Her head was down, watching the ground in front of her, her shoulders set forward like a person walking into a strong wind. He glanced at her hands. The fingers curled into fists. Opened again. Curled again.

Paul's smile fell away. The bright glowing segment of kindness he had seen in her was gone, a cold blue-steel hardness in its place. When she entered the kitchen she walked right past him to the pantry. She pulled down a glass bottle of meat tenderizer and poured it into a small bowl. She added some water and made a muddy red paste of the spices.

"Come here," she said, and nodded at the counter. "Put your hand there."

Paul came forward. He put his injured hand on the counter where she told him to and watched her.

"Momma?"

She ignored him. She scooped out a small handful of the paste with her fingers and spread it over his swollen hand.

It hurt, but Paul bit his lip and didn't cry out. He watched her working.

"Momma?"

She kept working on his hand, working the meat tenderizer into the folds between his fingers and over the humps of his knuckles. She was using the ball of her thumb to really press the paste into him, digging into the skin. Paul's tears came again, though he refused to make a sound.

"My God," she said under her breath, almost hissing it as she dug still deeper into the back of his hand, "what is wrong with you, you stupid boy?"

"Momma?"

"Don't you know that man is a mean, evil bastard?"

She was talking about his father, of course. Paul grew very scared, both for her and because of her. If the old man heard her talking like that, he'd like as not beat the crap out of her. He had seen him do it once, a few years earlier when she refused to do something he asked. He didn't know now what it was they had fought over. He only remembered his father knocking her down with a backhanded slap to the face, kicking her in the hips and thighs as she tried, at first, to claw at him, and then merely tried to bat away the boot that kept coming at her.

But he was also scared of her now. She was looking at him with wide-eyed fury, white spittle on her lips. This was a creature that wasn't supposed to be capable of this kind of rage. Where was it coming from? Was she testing him?

That must be it, he thought. Hadn't his father said he would be called upon to take on certain responsibilities, that he best not fail when the time came? He said, "Daddy told me he's gonna teach me what he knows about the world. He said I got a lot to learn. Momma, I want to learn it." Paul said this earnestly, both because he believed it was what she wanted to here, and, on some level at least, because it was true. But what happened afterwards caught him by complete surprise, for he knew as soon as the words left his mouth that he had badly misjudged his mother's fury.

Her mouth fell open.

Then she closed it and clapped a hand over her mouth to stifle the gasp forming there. Her eyes shone with an emotion that even Paul at twelve recognized as betrayal. He started to speak, but never got a chance to get it all out. Her hand went to the counter, to the rolling pin there. "You little bastard," she said. "You want to be like him? Do you?" She scooped up the rolling pin and brought it back. Paul somehow managed to duck out of the way before she brought it down on the spot where he had just been. The rolling pin hit the counter and sent up a cloud of flour dust. Plates clanked in the cabinets. A Mason jar turned on its side and rolled off the counter and onto the floor, where it shattered at Paul's feet. His mother swung the rolling pin again. She was screaming now. "You little bastard! You fucking little bastard! Burn in hell, you stupid, you stupid, you stupid little bastard!" She swung again. Paul managed to spin past her, reached the screen door, and tumbled outside. He fell on the cement steps and landed face first into the grass. Carol Henninger emerged from the doorway behind him. She still had a death grip on the rolling pin and there was a crazed look on her face that chilled Paul more than anything else he'd ever seen. "You little..." she said, trailing off in her rage, her lips trembling.

Paul got to his feet and ran. He ran as hard as he had ever run in his life, going full tilt for the oak covered hills out beyond the barn. He ran until he could no longer breathe, and there he stopped. Looking behind him, towards the house, he waited and listened. Nothing. He was alone.

He rolled over onto his back and closed his eyes and cried.

***

It was dark when Paul awoke, and there was a slow, even pounding in his head. The pounding reminded him of the steady rhythm of a hammer, or the sound a metal door makes as it's blown open and closed by the wind. And then he remembered where he was and what he was doing here and he jumped to his feet and spun around in terror.

He was alone.

Moonlight filled the trees.

He heard an owl hooting off in the distance. A crumbling limestone outcropping a hundred-fifty feet high rose above him, and he knew exactly where he was. He hadn't come as far as he thought he had, for there was a road a few hundred yards to the west of him, and he knew it was only a short distance to his house on that road.

What are you gonna do? he asked himself. *Ain't got nowhere to go. Ain't got nobody to take you in.*

And that's when he realized that there was really only one place he could go. Never one to lose himself in a book, he had never bothered to read stories of kids running away from home on big adventures, but he nonetheless understood the concept. He got it. He saw the attraction in it, and if there was ever a time in his young life when that attraction seemed at all tempting, it was right now. But he was too practical even at that early age to believe he could survive on his own. There was, really, only one choice he could make.

He walked to the road, pointed himself towards his house, sighed, and started the walk back home.

***

His parents were yelling at each other in the living room. Actually, his father was doing most of the yelling. He listened at the screen door, standing there with his hand on the rusted handle, trying to work up the nerve to walk inside.

"It ain't your choice to make," his father yelled.

"It is, too," his mother yelled back. "He's my boy."

There, in the shadows of the living room, Paul could see his father standing with his back to him, his mother on the couch before him. Paul saw the man's head tilt forward, and he had to strain to hear what his father said to that.

"He's mine, Carol. And don't you ever forget that."

"I will stop this," she said, and stood up. "I'm stopping it now. I will not let him turn into something I detest."

"Sit down, Carol."

"Go to hell."

"Sit down, woman, before you piss me off."

She tried to push her way past him, but he threw her back. She slapped him. Paul heard the echo of it ring through the house. He saw her standing there, hand still raised in a posture that suggested she was finishing a salute, her eyes narrowed on her husband's.

Martin Henninger punched her then. His fist cracked into her jawbone with a boxer's speed and power. It sent her sprawling backwards onto the couch. She was very still after that, like a pile of clothes somebody had thrown there and forgotten about.

Martin Henninger turned and looked right at Paul. Paul looked back at him and at that moment there was no doubt whatsoever in his mind that his father knew exactly what he was thinking.

His father came to the door and pushed it open. He stepped to one side and let Paul come in.

"Go on upstairs," he said.

"Why is she acting this way, Daddy?"

"Don't you worry about it," Martin Henninger said. "Just go to sleep. You got school in the morning."

***

His mother's screams filled the house. Paul lay awake in bed, listening to her rant, listening as she tore around downstairs like she'd gone rabid. What she said didn't make any sense to him. She was confused, screaming about Mexico and sticks and iron and Paul all in one breath. There were too many threads for Paul to follow, too many thoughts breaking down mid-sentence, changing into something else before the meaning could be made clear.

The fight spilled over into the kitchen. Paul could hear his parents down at the foot of the stairs. He heard his mother scream, "You stay away from me! I swear to God I'll cut your fucking balls off!"

And then there were footsteps on the stairs, coming up fast.

Paul rolled out of bed, got down on his back, and scooted underneath the bed. He lay there, listening, his fingers clutching the metal webbing that held up the mattress. He looked out on his room. He could see the black metal ghost of an old trash heater that had been in this room since before he was born. He could see the legs of his writing desk and his chair, still and serene. His eyes followed the uneven wave in the floorboards. For a moment, everything was quiet.

And then his door burst open and his parents were inside his room. He watched their feet as they moved across the floor. They might have been dancing they were so close. His father was probably holding his mother in a bear hug. His mother was grunting as she struggled to break free. He saw her kick his father's shins. He heard the sound of something swishing through the air as his father jumped backwards.

His mother screamed, and one of her knees buckled. Paul heard the sound of a fist or maybe the blade of a hand striking her body. Once, twice, two more times after that. Paul saw a flash of white, and only realized what it was a moment later. His father's hunting knife, a big five and a half inch long blade with a hooked tip, landed point-down into the floorboard beside his face. His eyes widened on it, absorbing the sight of it. He saw it vibrating.

He tried to cram himself into the far corner of the bed, but his fear had cut off his brain's communication with the rest of his body as surely as that knife would have sliced his life away. As it was, all he could do was stare at it.

His mother sagged to the floor. She landed with her own face near the knife. Her mouth was bleeding, and one side of her face was puffy and red, the beginnings of a bruise forming along her jawline. Her eyes were closed, and for that Paul was thankful.

His father's hands scooped up the body and hoisted her into the air. Paul watched his father's feet as the man turned towards the door and then disappeared down the stairs. He told himself to move, but he might as well have been asking stones to speak.

***

Sunlight was coming in through his window before he finally found the courage to move—though he couldn't bring himself to go anywhere near the knife. He slid out from under the bed and looked around. Two of his trophies had been knocked down during his parents' fight and he righted them. He looked around the room then and ran a hand through his hair. So much had happened. He didn't understand any of it.

He walked down the stairs as quietly as he could. He stopped at the bottom of the stairs and listened. Nothing. He went into the kitchen and that's when he saw the destruction. The house was a wreck, so many things broken, so many things not where they were supposed to be.

Have they gone? he wondered.

He looked around and figured they probably had. The house seemed to be deserted.

Paul made an effort to clean up here and there, mostly by throwing the broken stuff in the trash. There was a broom in the pantry and he used it to sweep up the broken glass from the Mason jar.

When he was done he still had ten minutes to go up to the road and catch his bus for school. He went back upstairs and changed his clothes, then went downstairs and ran some water through his hair at the sink. He stood at the screen door and looked in on his house. It felt like there was something he needed to do, but he was only twelve, and for the life of him he didn't know what, so he turned and ran up to the road to catch his bus. He would only find out later that his mother was already hanging by a rope from the rafters out in the barn, and that within hours of his leaving for school, the wild hogs would find their way to the body.

***

After telling Rachel all of that, Paul told her about the crash between the Escalade and the fire truck, about seeing his mother in that dead seventeen-year-old kid's eyes. Then he told her about the boxcar, about the dead goat and the dead kid and his father leaning over the body, elbow-deep in gore. He told her what his father said, that he had a charge to keep, and he told her about the mark on his forehead and where he thought that really came from.

Rachel listened to all of it without speaking. He couldn't see anything in her reaction. Outside it was getting dark, and she turned towards the windows along the south wall of their apartment and muttered something about closing the drapes.

"Rachel?"

Paul had been working himself up to telling her this, and he was uncertain how she would take it. He figured she would say something about how crazy it all sounded. Maybe she would try to rationalize what he said, make the square pegs go into the round holes. He thought maybe she would try to convince him he was wrong, tell him he was under stress, but she would help.

But Rachel didn't say anything to him at all. Instead, she crossed the room and closed the ugly avocado-colored drapes and then went to the kitchen to make their dinner. He sat on the bed and watched her. He watched her go through the motions, like a robot.

When she put the dinner on the table he took his place next to her and they ate in silence. Paul hardly touched his, hardly tasted what he did eat. He spent most of the meal looking at the tablecloth between them, figuring she would say something, eventually.

But dinner came and went, the plates went into the sink, got cleaned, and got put away, and still she said nothing to him.

He was unable to wait any longer. He said, "Rachel, will you talk to me, please?"

"I want to read for a while," she said. "I'll probably go to bed after that."

"Okay," he said, scared to go further with what had happened between them, and put his hand over hers.

She pulled her hand away.

"I want to go read for a while," she said, and got up and got a book and went outside on the patio.

***

Rachel woke up soaking wet. Her skin felt hot. Her clothes were drenched in sweat. The air in the apartment felt hot and close and smelled stale. She threw back the covers and tried to catch her breath.

She was dressed in white pajama shorts and a pink tank top that read, "Tinkerbelle" across her breasts. Paul, in his boxers next to her, was sleeping on his side, facing away from her.

Just as well, she thought, and right away hated herself for thinking it. She hated Paul at that moment, too, because he had made her think it, but that was something else.

She got out of bed and went to the thermostat on the wall. It was almost ninety degrees in the apartment. The air conditioner had stopped working again at some point after they went to bed.

She hit it with the flat of her palm, and when that didn't do anything, she said, "Come on, dammit," and hit it again.

Still nothing.

She stood there listening to the apartment around her. She could hear the wind blowing up against the corners of the house. It made the walls creak with a plaintiff moan. She could hear the floorboards beneath her as she walked. Outside, she could hear traffic going by, tires slapping the pavement, an occasional loud exhaust or the high revving drone of a motorcycle accelerating away into the night.

There was a shabbiness about this place that bothered her in a way the little house on Huisache never had. In that house, she had felt a sense of belonging, a sense that she was exactly where she needed to be for that point in her life. But now, in this place, she didn't feel that way. There were waves of anger and regret and confusion and love all going through her in a rush that was too tangled to pull apart. She couldn't pick one thing to isolate and think about. Her mind felt scattered.

Paul rolled over onto his back and groaned in his sleep. She watched him sleeping, then moved to her boxes of paperbacks and picked one out at random, a collection of Terry Bison's short stories entitled *Bears Discover Fire*. But as she stood there, peering into the box, a thought went through her head like the single crack of a gun across a quiet field.

This is what heartache feels like.

It was Paul, of course. His story had done this to her. He had knocked her off balance, and she hated him for it.

And she loved him in spite of it.

This is what heartache feels like.

"Damn it," she said, and got up and went out on the patio to read.

Though it was the same temperature outside as inside, it felt better to be outside, because of the breeze. She dropped into a chair and pushed her sweat-soaked bangs out of her eyes. She sighed and opened her book and began to read.

But she found her mind wandering off the page. It wasn't an unpleasant feeling though. She was thinking about the trip to Corpus Christi she and Paul had taken right before the end of their junior year to visit her parents. She remembered the look on her dad's face when he saw how big Paul was. Her dad was a comfortable looking man with a slight paunch and incipient jowls and a gray donut of hair around the back of his balding head. He was a kind man, a gentle man. And now he was meeting a giant who appeared to have been carved from solid rock.

Her mother's reaction had been even more telling. She had peeked around Paul's back and mouthed the word *wow* to Rachel, then laughed at the shocked look on her daughter's face.

The whole family, cousins and all, had joined them later that day, and the boys went out on the lawn for a pickup football game. Rachel and the girls watched from the sideline, drinking iced tea and talking about the boys. Her younger brother flubbed a pass to Paul, throwing it a few feet behind him. But then Paul did something amazing. Without breaking stride he reached behind him with one hand, spun, caught the football with his fingertips, and came down in the end zone. He moved like a tiger playing with house cats, so effortlessly graceful, and yet so powerful.

The men on the field just gawked. Rachel and her mother stood and cheered.

That had been a great weekend for them. She remembered the two of them floating on rafts in her parents' pool, Paul in his Hawaiian print shorts and Rachel in a yellow bikini that she hoped her dad wouldn't freak out over. Rachel had turned to him and said, "Paul, what do you want to do?"

Paul, not understanding, had turned his head towards her, lifted his sunglasses, and said, "Do when, tonight?"

"No. I mean, what do you want to do, you know, after school? What are your plans?"

"You mean like a job?"

"Well, yeah. I guess."

He squinted at her, and not because of the bright sunshine. He seemed to give a lot of thought before he said, "I'd love to play pro ball. But I know that ain't gonna happen. What I always figured I'd do is be a cop. I've got in pretty good with this internship to S.A.P.D. The pay's good. Benefits are good, too."

"Oh," she said. "Yeah, I remember you saying that."

"But I don't think that's what you mean, is it? What you mean is: who am I looking to spend my future with. Rachel, there is no doubt at all in my mind who I want to spend my future with."

She tilted down her sunglasses and looked at him.

"Rachel, you're my center. I have never met anyone who can focus me the way you do. It's like, the way you know something is so completely right that all the rest of the world can fall away, but what stays here between you and me will always be whole. That part's indestructible. That's how certain I am that I love you."

Rachel smiled inwardly at the memory and longed for a little of that security now. The rest of the world had certainly fallen away, but she was far from convinced that the two of them were whole. The indestructible felt like it was starting to crumble.

This is what heartache feels like.

Something caught her eye down on the lawn. She put her finger in the book to save her place, stood up and walked to the railing. She had seen a man there, she was almost sure of it. A man in a white shirt and dark slacks, an old cowboy hat in his hand. But there was no one there now. Just the junipers dancing in the breeze.

Damn it, Paul, she thought. Paul and his stories about the homicidal maniacs who were his parents. *Now you've even got me rattled.*

Chapter 11

At first, Magdalena Chavarria didn't recognize her own living room. Her head was ringing and it was hard to concentrate. There was a film over her eyes that she couldn't wipe away. She'd been sitting in the same position for a long time and her back and hips ached. There was blood in her mouth. She touched her fingers to her lips and winced.

In front of her was a stick lattice, only the third one she'd ever been called upon to make. The first was twelve years ago, in Mexico, right after the death of her Abuela. After that lattice, she'd buried the woman in the rocky white soil near their home and gone into town to call Martin Henninger, the young man from Texas who had stayed with them for so long while he learned the secrets of the way, and told him that it was her Abuela's instructions that the power now pass to him.

After that she made the trek northwards, first crossing the border into Texas with six other illegals. From there she'd made it to this little house on the east side of San Antonio, where she hung the sign of the curandera above her door.

Her first year had been a lean one, but certainly no harder than her life in Mexico had been. She told fortunes for the old women in the neighborhood. Sometimes she offered herbal remedies and prayers for aching joints or helped the younger women with the cramps that came with their monthly visits. Business was never enough to make her rich, but it was steady enough to live on—and it seemed like a fortune after Mexico.

And then, on a cold, rainy morning in early September, an old woman from down the street came to her house, pounding on the door, begging for help. Magdalena went with the frantic woman to her house and was ushered into her living room, where the woman's fourteen year old granddaughter was on the couch, naked from the waist down, screaming in agony from the depths of her labor pains. A group of woman knelt around the young girl's head, mopping the sweat from her face with towels and trying to reassure her, though from their faces they all knew that death was coming.

"Please help her," the old woman begged in Spanish. "She's bleeding so much. I don't know how to stop it."

Magdalena looked from the old woman to the girl on the couch. She was writhing in agony, and there was blood all over her legs and running down the skirts of the couch. Magdalena felt ice forming in her belly. She felt angry, too. These women wanted too much from her. She couldn't do this. She couldn't wield the power. Not really. She looked at the dying girl on the couch, the poisonous beads of sweat popping up all over her face, and she knew the girl was going to die. Death was already crouching on her chest, licking at her lips.

The other women stared at Magdalena. She could hear them muttering to each other. Magdalena wanted to turn around and run out the back door, anything to get away from here. She came close to losing herself to anger. She hadn't asked for this. These women, they'd brought her here to do the impossible. If the girl died, it wouldn't be because of some complication resulting from a child having a child, but because Magdalena had failed her. That wasn't fair. She hadn't asked for this.

"Please do something," the old woman said.

She grabbed Magdalena's hands in hers and went down on her knees. "Please."

Magdalena touched the wrinkles in the old woman's skin and felt the fragile bones in her hands, and all at once her Abuela's words came back to her. *Life and death are reflections of each other. If you trust in this power that I'm teaching you, it won't matter what side of the mirror you're standing on.*

"On the way in, I saw some chickens in your backyard," Magdalena said. "Are any of them sitting on eggs that are about to hatch?"

"Yes. Several."

"Go and get me one of those eggs, please."

"Of course," the woman said.

The woman left and Magdalena went to the girl's side. The other women parted for her.

Magdalena touched the girl's forehead and felt how hot she was. The girl's breathing was ragged and her pulse was out of control. A big blue vein throbbed in her forehead.

"Can you hear me?" Magdalena said.

The girl opened her eyes. There was madness there for a moment, bloodshot crazed madness, but it faded.

The girl nodded.

"Good. I want you to breathe with me."

Magdalena was aware of the power flowing between them, and in that moment she knew that she could help this little girl. She could feel the little one taking strength from her, the energy flowing down her arm and out her fingertips like a living thing.

"Breathe with me," Magdalena urged.

The girl's ragged breathing began to slow. Magdalena breathed in, breathed out. Breathed in, breathed out. Her hand was steady on the girl's cheek. The girl's convulsions were easing, her fear ebbing away from her like she was shucking off a heavy wet coat. The big blue vein stopped throbbing.

"Good," Magdalena said. "Breathe with me."

And then they were breathing together, the two of them in perfect time.

The old woman came back in with the egg and handed it to Magdalena.

"Thank you," Magdalena said.

To the girl, she said, "I'm going to lift your shirt now. Keep breathing with me."

The girl nodded.

Magdalena lifted the girl's shirt and revealed the swollen belly beneath. She could see what she thought was the baby moving, low in the birth canal, fighting for daylight.

"Good," she said, "you're good, child. Keep breathing. In and out, in and out."

She placed the egg on the girl's stomach and rolled it across the downward swell of her belly with the flat of her palm. There was no more doubt in her mind now. She could feel the circuit forming between the fetus in the egg and the fetus in the girl's belly, one life taking shape, one life going away.

Magdalena said, "Do you feel it? Do you feel it?"

The girl nodded eagerly. Her breathing broke with the sound of snot bubbling in her nose and Magdalena said, "Easy girl. Breathe deep. Breathe with me."

Magdalena took the egg away. She was suddenly dizzy and had to steady herself on the side of the couch. She turned and looked for the old woman who had brought her here.

"Bring me a bowl," she said.

Someone handed her a bowl, and Magdalena put the egg inside it and stood up.

She turned to the old woman and said, "She's ready for the baby. Help her."

Magdalena stood on unsteady legs and stumbled away from the couch. She stood in the middle of the room, watching the egg, glancing at the girl who was now pushing her baby out of the birth canal. She saw the bloody baby emerge. She watched as the old woman cradled the still, purple-skinned child in her arms.

The old woman looked from the still baby to Magdalena, her face a ruin of grief.

Magdalena turned to the egg in the bowl. She muttered, "One life goes in, the other out. All things in balance."

And almost as though on cue the egg burst with a sound like that of a gunshot. The old women who had gathered around the young girl's head spread like startled birds, all of them looking at the bowl.

Inside it, a fetal chick lay dead in a flower of blackish red blood.

Magdalena was also looking at the bowl. She was aware of the sounds of the girl crying, though these were not tears of pain, but of a relief so complete it seemed almost spiritual.

And then there was the sound of a baby crying.

Magdalena let out a long sigh. The women turned from the bowl to the baby in a flood of ecstatic voices, and Magdalena stumbled out the door.

From that day forward, Magdalena's reputation as a curandera was secure.

***

That first lattice she made all those years ago in Mexico was like a slowly burning pile of coals. She had felt its power for years, burning within her with a slow, steady heat that was as reassuring as her Abuela's touch had been when she was just a child.

The second lattice, though, had felt very different. That one, made only four days ago, was like a bonfire in her chest. The need to make it had come upon her with all the unexpected force of a car crash, and when she was done with it, she had staggered out the back door and into the yard where she kept a small herd of goats and vomited all over the grass.

She came to with the goats pressing their noses against her mouth. Slowly, like an old woman, she rose and staggered back inside. It was then that she saw the lines of Hebrew scrawled across her walls.

There was a black magic marker on the floor in the kitchen, the cap off and probably lost during her fugue state. She picked it up and went to a bare spot on the wall and tried to copy some of the script. She couldn't. For some reason her hand wouldn't work, wouldn't make the necessary movements. It felt like so much work just to keep her chin up, and soon she gave up on the pen and dropped it to the floor.

After that she stumbled into the living room and stared at the lattice in the middle of the floor. It was not very large, certainly no bigger than the one she had made in Mexico all those years ago, but this one resonated with a power that terrified her. She could feel a heat coming off it. Magdalena put out a hand to it and just as quickly pulled it away. Apparently, now that it was made, she was not to touch it.

But she did know what she was supposed to do. She went out back again and led two of her goats to her truck and tied them up in the bed. Then she drove them to the old Morgan Rollins Iron Works, said the prayers her abuela had taught her, killed one of the goats, and set the other free inside the complex.

"Come back with the priest," she said to the goat in Spanish.

When she was done, she drove home and poured herself a glass of water. She was so thirsty. She downed her first glass in a gulp and poured another. That one went down in another gulp. As did the third and the fourth. After that she felt a little better, though she did pour yet another glass and took a few swallows from it before setting it down on the counter.

She fell asleep on the couch, still wearing all her clothes, and dreamed of the man who had come to live with them all those years ago. She hadn't thought of him in a very long while, but she could see him clearly enough in her dreams.

Magdalena also dreamed of the dead goat, the one she'd gutted on the dirt floor of the circular chamber inside the old factory. In her dream, it began to convulse. A man's hands emerged from inside its ribcage. She knew who the man was, even before she saw his face, and when Martin Henninger pulled himself out of the animal like a man pulling himself up through a hole in the floor, she wasn't surprised. Terrified, but not surprised.

But then he went about ridding the old factory of the men who did their drugs there, and that was terrible to watch.

So many men died, and in her dreams, she saw every one of them.

***

Magdalena went to the sink and washed the blood off her fingers. Her muscles still ached and her head was ringing, but she knew what she had to do. It was like a line drawn on a map in her head. She dried her hands on a paper towel and took her keys from the basket near the back door and got in her truck and drove to the Mulberry Green Mental Health Rehabilitation Center.

The building was on the fringes of the Vista Verde District just north of downtown, and didn't look like much of anything from the curb, just a crumbling white brick structure with windows of smoked glass. There was a small brick wall near the front walk that had the name of the clinic printed on it, but the floodlights at its base weren't working and it was impossible to see what the sign said from the street. Some kids had scrawled graffiti on the left side of the building. On the opposite side, a large copse of walnut trees separated the clinic from a three story Victorian style wood-framed house. The house was painted a light egg-shell blue and had evidently been converted into a law office.

That meant it'd be deserted.

"Good," she said. She didn't want to see anybody else hurt. Ever since her dream of the old factory, the dead had haunted her. This was an abomination that she was doing. The power her Abuela had taught her, it was not for this. It was meant to heal. Her Abuela would not approve, though of course her Abuela was no longer here. Martin Henninger was the conduit for the power now. Magdalena had no choice but to serve.

On the other side of the big blue Victorian was a washateria and a convenience store, both evidently open all night but deserted at the moment. Two gay men were walking across the parking toward the club down the street. Magdalena waited for them to walk out of sight, then got out of her truck and walked to the vacant lot across the street from the clinic.

Once she was in position, she began to mutter the commands Martin Henninger put in her head. The swarm started as a hum in the distance, but the sound grew steadily louder, until it was like the roll of a bass drum. From within the din, Magdalena could hear the steady clicking of millions of insect wings. There was a surge of wind at her back and then the sky above her darkened, filling up with wave upon wave of cicadas, their shrill drone elevated now to a deafening roar.

They swarmed past her and descended on the clinic, pounding against the building's backup generators. It only took a few seconds for the smell of smoke to drift across the street to her. She watched as the first tentative puffs of smoke darkened into columns and began to swirl into the night's sky, and when the front doors to the clinic burst open and a pair of nurses emerged, coughing and spluttering, waving away the still swarming cicadas, Magdalena got ready to move.

***

David Everett's body was in full revolt. It wanted heroin and it wanted it right now. He was shaking. He ached everywhere. His skin was wet with sweat and his teeth rattled from the waves of chills that swept through him.

They had him on suicide watch. Though his mind had been chewed to honeycomb by the drugs, he could still tell what these people thought of him. They weren't cops, but from where he was sitting there was little difference. He was still a prisoner.

The room—not a cell, but a room—had been stripped of anything that might conceivably be used as a weapon. There was no furniture besides a bare mattress. They took the sheets so he wouldn't hang himself with them. His clothes, too. Now he was wearing a green paper hospital johnny. It was soaked through and torn. He would have ripped it off if he'd had the energy. As it was, he could barely lift his eyes from the mattress to the door. The effort was too great.

Something was going on outside. Had been for a few minutes now. He'd heard voices and the sound of people moving fast in the hallway outside. The lights flickered but held. There was a faint smell of electrical smoke coming from the vent in the wall above him, but he wasn't thinking fire. He wasn't thinking about anything except heroin.

The lights flickered again—and then went out. He held his breath for a moment, listening to the dark outside his room. There was someone standing there.

He waited.

The door opened, and the figure of a woman appeared in the chalky gray outline of the open door.

David Everett managed to push himself up into a sitting position.

"Who are you?" he asked.

"A friend," said the woman's voice. Her Mexican accent was strong.

She came forward and knelt beside him.

"These are your clothes," she said. "Put them on."

"Where are you taking me?"

"Away from here."

"Where?"

"Don't ask questions," she said. "There isn't time."

The woman helped him to his feet, then kept a hand near as she let go, as if uncertain whether or not he would remain upright.

Everett wasn't so sure about that himself.

He steadied himself and waited to see if it would last. It didn't. A wave of nausea tore through his gut like a punch and sent him pitching forward. The girl grabbed him and held him, but wisely held off trying to make him stand up again.

"I'm sick," he said, wheezing.

"Heroin," she said, and even through his convulsions he could hear the contempt in her voice. She reached into her pocket and took out a wad of wax paper that held a black, sticky goo not unlike uncooked Mexican black tar heroin. She took it out and forced it into his mouth.

He sputtered at the bitterness of it, and tried to spit it out, but she wouldn't let him.

"Chew it," she said.

"What is it?"

"Not heroin. But it will help you. Chew it."

He did chew it, and almost immediately felt a flood of warmth in his throat and belly. It felt good. Not like heroin, but good. He could feel the crazy urgent need for the drug growing quiet, like it was being forced down into a box somewhere deep inside him.

"What is that?" he said.

"Just put your clothes on. We have to go right now."

"Okay." He let go of her arm and stood on his own, both surprised and sobered to find the convulsions and the pain were gone. And his vision was clearer, too. He took a deep breath, expecting a fit of coughing, and found only air.

"Hurry," she said. "Get dressed."

***

Now they were standing in the shadows outside the Bexar County Medical Examiner's Office, watching the darkened building.

"What are we doing here?" Everett asked.

Magdalena didn't answer him. She was swaying, her eyes half-closed, the eyelids fluttering as she muttered what sounded like nonsense to Everett.

"Who are you? What's your name?"

Again, nothing from Magdalena.

He gave up on her and went back to looking at the quiet building. It looked closed to him.

"They're not closed," Magdalena said.

Her voice startled him. Everett looked at her, wondering if he had asked the question aloud or not. He didn't think he had.

"Tell me who you are," he said.

"They're not closed," she said again. Her eyes were open now. She was staring directly at the building without blinking. "Inside, you'll find three people—two women and a man. The man has a gun."

"A gun? What are you talking about, lady? I'm not going in there."

"Look at me," she said.

A police car rolled by at a crawl on the road on the far side of the building, and Everett ducked down deeper into the shadows.

"Look at me," she said. Her voice was flat but stern.

"There are cops all over the place," he said.

"The police won't bother us. Look at me."

He glanced at her and started to say, "Fuck this, let's get out of here," but the look on her face stopped the words in his throat. Her face had changed. It was still her, but there was something else there with her, inside her. He stared into her eyes and felt himself slipping away.

"Look at me," she said.

"Okay," he said. But he may not have said the word out loud. He couldn't tell, and his mind wasn't paying attention to that now anyway.

"Use a large rock to break into the front door. The people inside will try to stop you. Don't let them. There will be towels inside. Use the towels to hold open the doors leading down to the basement. Do you understand?"

He nodded, his mouth hanging open.

"Go," she said.

***

Everett walked up to the front door and looked at it. The whole thing was made of glass. When he put his face against the glass he could see into the waiting room beyond. There was a table, a couple of small couches, a plant in the corner. On the far side of the waiting room was another door. It looked solid.

The door in front of him had no handle. Confused, he blinked at it until he realized it was one of those automatic doors meant to slide open when someone was standing in front of it. He looked to his right and saw a buzzer on the wall, a rock garden beyond that. He went to the rock garden, picked up a stone the size of a cantaloupe, and tested its heft. Good and heavy.

He went back to the door, lifted the rock, and broke out the glass.

***

They hadn't had a call all night, and for that Melinda Sanchez was grateful. It gave her a chance to catch up on her reports, and after the mess at the Morgan Rollins Iron Works, there was still a stack of them standing about a foot high in the In Box on her desk.

The only trouble was she couldn't make herself do it.

"Thinking about Wayne?" Julia asked.

Julia was Julia Culpepper, who had the desk across the aisle from her. They were both twenty-five, pretty, well-built. Julia was dating Dylan Hodges over at Bexar County Homicide, and the two of them introduced her to Dylan's partner Wayne Taliaferro at a triple shooting the week before. She and Wayne had hit it off. There'd been a date, a couple of phone calls since, another date next weekend. Things were going well.

"You were, weren't you?"

Melinda just smiled.

"You're going out with him again, right?"

"Maybe."

"Maybe. Jesus, Mel, spill the beans, would you? Did you guys…?" She looked around to make sure their other partner, Randy Sprouse, wasn't listening. "You know?"

Melinda tried to sound sufficiently shocked when she said, "Julia! No, of course not. I just went out with him once."

"Oh, lighten up, Mel. There's nothing wrong with fucking a guy on the first date. If it feels right, you gotta do it."

"Julia!"

But despite her best efforts, Melinda couldn't keep the snicker out of her voice. It *had* felt pretty darn right, and it had almost come to that.

Randy muted the commercial that had just come on the TV and got up and stretched. He was older by far than the two of them—had actually been a cop longer than the two of them had been alive—and regarded just about everything and everybody with a weary, if not a little sour, indifference. He was nice, though.

He saw the conspiratorial looks on their faces and said, "What?"

"Nothing," Julia said.

Melinda shrugged, and they both giggled.

"You girls are talking about dating cops again, aren't you?"

"Why, Randy?" Julia asked, hitting him with her fluttering eyelashes. "You jealous?"

Randy laughed. "Yeah, right. Girls, Randy is too old to be feeling randy these days. I get all the sex I can handle just watching my wife do housework. Who's the guy this week?"

"Same guy," Julia said. "Smartass. It's been the same guy for the last two months."

"Oh, well, who can tell around here? You girls make me feel like I work in Peyton Place sometimes."

Melinda arched a questioning eyebrow at Julia.

Julia said, "That's like *The O.C.* for old people."

"Cute," Randy said. But before he could say anything else they heard the sound of glass breaking.

"What was that?" Julia said.

"It sounded like it came from up front," Melinda said.

They were all standing now. Randy moved to the video monitors near the opposite end of the room, and Melinda and Julia followed him. The three of them looked at the monitor that showed the front door. The camera there was mounted on the outside and pointed down across the plane of the doors so that it would give a profile view of anybody standing there. Melinda studied the screen, but all she saw was a pile of glass shards on the ground.

"Call Campus Police," Randy said to her. "Julia, come with me."

"Okay," Melinda said.

Randy and Melinda went out into the hallway while Julia went back to her desk and picked up her phone, but couldn't get a dial tone. She punched another line, but that was dead, too.

"What the...?" she said, and picked up the phone on Julia's desk. That one was dead. So was Randy's.

"Oh shit."

She grabbed her purse and took out her service weapon, a short-barreled Glock 27. Then she made her way towards the front.

On the nightshift, they left most of the lights off, and the hallways leading from the Investigations Office to the front lobby were dark. Melinda moved through them, wincing every time her heels clacked on the floor, trying to hear what was going on up front.

All she heard though was thudding of her heart against her chest.

"Randy? Julia?"

No answer.

"Randy?"

She was almost at the lobby now. It was around the next corner. She went to the wall and inched her way closer to the corner. Straining to hear any kind of sound at all, she took a deep breath and waited in silence.

A long moment passed.

Finally, unable to take it anymore, she called out, "Randy, answer me. Julia?"

Nothing.

Come on, girl. Get it together. You can do this. You can do this.

She took a deep breath, then slipped around the corner, gun up and ready for whatever was there.

Or so she thought.

Julia's leg was sticking into the hallway, holding the door open. Beyond her leg she could see Randy slumped onto the floor. Neither of them was moving. Melinda's breathing was coming fast and ragged now, her fear overriding her training. In her mind she kept telling herself to run. She had been to the schools, sure. She had a peace officer's license, yeah, but she wasn't a real cop. The closest she had ever come to a tactical building sweep was watching a video on it back in school. She wasn't made for this.

Stop that. You can do this. You can do this.

She peered into the shadows of the lobby. From here, it looked empty, but her eyes kept turning back to the unmoving bodies on the floor. Then she caught a glint of light on the floor and saw a puddle of blood spreading away from Julia's head.

"No," she said, and lowered her weapon. "No, Julia."

She knelt down next to her friend and searched her neck for a pulse. There was none.

"Julia, no! Wake up, baby! Please."

Crying, she rocked back on her heels and covered her mouth. Her gun felt like it weighed a million pounds in her hands. She could barely lift it.

Glass crunched behind her.

She gasped as she spun around. There, in the shadows, standing perfectly still and watching her with the cold, dead eyes of a psychopath, was a bone-skinny man whose long, greasy hair hung over his face like a curtain. In his hands, he held a big rock, and even in the darkness, Melinda could see the blood dripping from it.

"What did you do?" she said.

He was on her then, and he moved fast. She put up her hands to block her face, but she never had a chance.

***

Everett dropped the rock and it hit the carpet with a dull thud. He looked at the three bodies on the floor without any real sense of what had just happened. It was almost like there were two David Everetts. One was in a red haze, full of strength and purpose. The other was a balloon floating in the air above the red one. Balloon Everett was barely conscious, and when the red Everett moved, balloon Everett was pulled along behind him, almost like there was a string tied to his belly. He felt the tug and he went. There was no fighting it.

The red Everett went down a hallway, opening doors and throwing rolled-up towels down as door stoppers to hold them open, until he reached a stairwell. Balloon Everett could feel cold air coming up from the stairwell, and maybe a smell as well, though it was faint.

Red Everett used a chair to wedge open the stairwell doors, then went down another hallway and into the morgue. Balloon Everett watched sleepily as Red Everett opened the freezer doors, and he continued to watch as naked corpses rose from the racks of tables, sloughing off their sheets and staggering out through the open doors.

When the last of them was gone, Red Everett turned and headed back upstairs. He stayed well behind the long line of dead men, and Balloon Everett bobbed contentedly in the air, watching the parade as it made its slow way towards the waiting night.

At last Red Everett reached the front room, and there he stopped amid the broken glass. He reached down and picked up one of the guns from the investigators on the floor. Almost like he was studying it, Red Everett turned it this way and that before jamming the muzzle under his chin and pulling the trigger.

As the sound echoed away, Balloon Everett felt the cord that held him to Red Everett let go, and he went floating, bobbing away into nothingness.

***

Magdalena watched the dead melt into the darkness. One by one they left the building and then dissolved, like soap bubbles riding the wind. They were headed for the Iron Works again.

"Travel fast," she said. "There is much to do."

Chapter 12

Anderson and Levy were in the car, headed for the Bexar County Medical Examiner's Office. Anderson was driving. Levy was on his cell phone, talking with a detective named Carl Vince from the Night Utility Unit who was over at the Mulberry Green Mental Health Facility looking into David Everett's escape. Whatever Vince was telling Levy wasn't making Levy very happy.

Anderson said, "What's going on?" Levy just held up a finger for him to wait.

Off to the east, the sky was beginning to lighten. A copper pool was spreading across the horizon, dappling the rooftops of the shallow east side. It was going to be another hot and cloudless day, one of those relentlessly hot summer days that smothered the city and made you feel like you were being cooked inside your clothes. The dawn wasn't even here yet, and already the temperature gauge on the dash was reading in the low nineties. Anderson searched his memory, thinking back to the last time San Antonio had gone through a draught this bad. What had it been, five or maybe six years ago?

Beside him, Levy hung up his phone and tucked it back into his belt. He had to lean over almost into Anderson's seat to do it, and even then he had to pull his stomach up and out of the way as he searched for the clip.

Anderson said, "Well?"

"Just a second," Levy grumbled as he fought with his phone clip. "God, I'm getting so fucking fat."

Anderson waited.

"There," Levy said. He settled back into his seat, trying to get comfortable, then said, "They don't know shit down there. Vince said from what they could see Everett just walked right out the front door."

"How is that possible?"

"I don't know," Levy said.

"Well, what did he say?"

Levy shook his head. "Apparently they had some kind of bug problem. A whole bunch of them got into the generator and it started a fire. The building filled up with smoke and the staff went around opening up doors. You know, standard fire drill. There were only two nurses working, I guess. They escorted their patients into a secure area behind the building and waited on the Fire Department. By the time Fire had the place secure, Everett was gone."

"Just like that? Gone."

"Apparently. Looks like he just walked off."

"Jesus H. Christ," Anderson said. "A bug problem?"

"That's what Vince said. Crickets or cicadas, some kind of bug. They're all over the place down there."

"That's just great," Anderson said.

He drummed his fingers on the steering wheel and thought about the timeline for this fiasco. Anytime a Patrol officer was dispatched to an incident involving a dead body, he was required to contact the Medical Examiner's Office so that one of their investigators could make the scene and decide whether or not the body would need to be taken to the County Morgue for an autopsy. The Communications Unit supervisor told them he had first tried to contact the Medical Examiner's Office at three a.m. Patrol had been trying to raise the ME's Office for two hours before that. When the Communications Unit supervisor was unable to raise any of the ME investigators, he dispatched an officer to their location to find out why they weren't answering their phone. That officer had arrived at the morgue at thirteen minutes after three and found the murder scene Anderson and Levy were on the way to now.

"What time did Vince say this invasion of the crickets happened?" Anderson asked.

"Around eleven thirty. The Fire Department got there at eleven thirty-seven. Why? What are you thinking?"

"Just doing the timeline. Everett slips away sometime between eleven thirty and eleven forty. We know Patrol tried to raise the Medical Examiner's Office at around one o'clock. That means Everett had less than an hour and a half to get all the way across town, kill three armed people, and steal forty-three bodies."

"And kill himself."

"Yeah, and kill himself."

Levy made a deep sigh. "You're saying somebody had to have picked him up from Mulberry Green and taken him to the morgue."

"They would have to, don't you think? The morgue's what, about thirty miles away from Mulberry Green? Somebody picked him up and drove him to the morgue."

"Yeah," Levy said. "That makes sense."

"But who? If it was the same people who stole the bodies from the morgue that raises kind of an interesting question."

"What's that?"

"How'd they know Mulberry Green was gonna get swamped by bugs? That's not the kind of thing you plan for, you know? And it's not the kind of thing you do yourself."

Levy thought about that. "Yeah, I see what you mean," he said.

"So, for some reason, the people who did this got Everett out of Mulberry Green, brought him up here, stole a whole bunch of dead bodies, and then left Everett to kill himself."

"But why would Everett kill himself? If he did kill himself. I mean, we don't know that, do we?"

"No, I guess we don't. Not conclusively, anyway."

"We could get that off the morgue's cameras, though."

"Yeah," Anderson said, but he was lost in thought.

They exited the freeway and headed up Wurzbach to the main entrance of the University of Texas Health Science Center campus. The campus police department had three cruisers blocking the roadway, and when Anderson turned into the driveway, two officers stepped forward to flag him down.

"Too bad they didn't have this kind of security before this happened," Anderson said.

"Yeah. Well, at least the press won't be getting in. God, can you imagine this footage playing out on the six o'clock news?"

Actually, yeah, Anderson thought. He'd been thinking about exactly that, as a matter of fact. He'd been thinking about Jenny Cantrell sitting on her couch, trying her best to hold it together after learning of Ram's death, then having the news come on with this mess. Jesus, what was he going to tell her about this?

He rolled down his window, and the campus police officer leaned in.

"You guys from SAPD?"

Both Anderson and Levy held out their IDs. "Homicide," Anderson said.

"Okay, sir," the officer said, and stepped back. He waved them through, and Anderson drove on.

"Chuck," Anderson said, "what in the hell are we gonna tell Jenny? Have you thought about that yet?"

"I thought about it," Levy said. "I thought about it, and I have absolutely no fucking clue."

They drove in silence down the winding tree-lined road that Anderson had driven just a day before. Ahead of them they could see a circus of red and blue lights. There were police cars and evidence technician vehicles parked all over the place. Uniforms were setting up barricades and marking off safe lanes for entering and exiting the scene. Anderson parked out of the way and watched the show.

"There's Allen," Levy said.

Anderson spotted the deputy chief easily enough. He was the only suit in a sea of uniforms, and he looked agitated. *Poor guy's probably had even less sleep than me last couple of days,* Anderson thought. *And that ain't much.*

"You ready for this?" Levy asked.

"I guess. Ready as I'll ever be." He shook his head. "Jesus, this is something else."

***

As Anderson stepped through the barricades and onto the lawn in front of the morgue, he saw Allen talking with a group of people in plain clothes. He recognized several of them as investigators with the Bexar County Sheriff's Office Homicide Unit. A few he knew by name; others, he just recognized their faces.

Levy joined him on the front steps and together they walked inside the lobby. Anderson stopped just inside the doorway and waited for a pretty young evidence technician to get the picture she was trying to take. He stood there and took in the scene.

There were four bodies in all, and he knew all of them. The two young women both had their eyes open. One of them, Julia Culpepper, was on her stomach in the middle of the doorway that led back into the rest of the building, one leg holding the door open. The other young woman was slumped against the wall to his left. Her head was turned towards them, her eyes and mouth open in a gesture of surprise that Anderson found both disturbing and pitiful. He could only imagine what she must have been thinking at the last moment, how scared she must have been. There was a nasty gash on the side of her head that Anderson guessed was caused by the melon-sized rock in the middle of the floor. They'd have to confirm that during her autopsy, of course, but it looked pretty obvious to him. A few feet in front of her, one hand close enough he might have been able to touch the heel of Melinda's right shoe, was the body of Randy Sprouse. He'd known Sprouse for twenty years, and as he stared down at the body he thought, *I was at your retirement party. Jesus H. Christ.*

Off in the far corner, sagged down between two heavy couches, was the body of David Everett. He was dressed in a filthy white t-shirt and blue jeans and sneakers with no socks. The t-shirt had a bib of blood and brain matter down the front. There was a hole under his chin and one arm was slung limply over the arm of a couch.

Melinda Sanchez' gun was on the floor in front of him.

"Whose footprints are these?" Anderson asked, pointing at the tread print on a piece of broken glass in the middle of the room.

Levy looked at the glass. "Looks like a Hi Tech boot print. Probably from one of the Patrol officers who made initial entry. I talked to him out front. He said he came here, saw the scene, then called for backup. Once they got back up, they did a protective sweep of the rest of the building."

Anderson nodded. "I'd like to confirm his print just the same."

"Okay."

"I saw you talking with Bexar County Homicide. What are they doing here?"

Levy walked on his tiptoes through the crime scene. He made it to the door held open by Julia Culpepper's left leg and turned back to Anderson.

"You know Dylan Hodges and Wayne Taliaferro?"

"I know Dylan."

"Apparently, Dylan Hodges was dating this girl here." He pointed at Julia with his toe.

"Oh man, that sucks."

"Yeah."

Anderson knelt down in front of David Everett and looked into the man's eyes. He was staring off into the nothingness beyond Anderson's right shoulder.

"What are you thinking?" Levy asked him.

"I'm thinking how badly we misjudged this one. Looking at him in the witness room, I never would have thought he could do this."

"None of us did, Keith."

"Yeah, but it still doesn't make it any easier, you know?"

Levy said, "Yeah, I know."

Anderson rubbed his chin, deep in thought.

After a long silence, he said, "You played us, didn't you? That whole time you were sitting in the interview room, pretending to be all spaced out, you were playing us. You were a part of this the whole time."

***

Down in the autopsy room, there were three bodies on the waiting tables. The doors to the coolers were standing open. They were propped open with towels, just like every other door between here and the front lobby. Anderson stood in the middle of the autopsy room and looked around. From where he stood, he could see into the coolers. There were a few bodies in there as well.

"My guess is these bodies that are still here didn't come from the Morgan Rollins crime scene," he said to Levy.

"Do you recognize any of these guys from there?"

"No," Anderson said. "We'll have to check it for sure, but I'm willing to bet that whoever took the bodies from here knew who they were looking for. I don't think we'll find any of our Morgan Rollins victims here."

"Why would they take the bodies?" Levy said, and shuddered. "That doesn't make any sense."

"Maybe not to us."

"But you think it makes sense to somebody?"

"It must. Why else would they do it?"

Anderson walked over to the coolers. The fluorescents in this place were cheap, or maybe just old, and they cast a sickly bluish light on the tiled floor. But even in the bad light, Anderson could see there was something there.

He knelt down next to the cooler door and stared at the floor.

"What is it?" Levy asked.

"Can you get one of the evidence technicians down here?" he said. "It's more of that black soot we found on Everett's hands."

***

Anderson watched an evidence technician dab the tiled floor with a cotton swab. He held the swab up so that Anderson could see and said, "You think that's enough?"

"Yeah, I think so," Anderson said.

"Okay."

The technician, a young man with GUERRA written in bold white letters above the pocket of his utility uniform, dropped the swab into a clear plastic envelope, peeled off the self-adhesive strip, folded the flap over to seal it, then wrote his initials across the seal with a magic marker.

"Is there any more of it?" Guerra asked.

"No, I don't think so."

Guerra walked towards the door that led to the upstairs, and Anderson watched him go, his mind starting to drift. He was thinking about his oldest son, Keith Jr., and the weekend he'd spent a few years ago helping the boy move into his first college dorm room. Keith Jr.'s room had been on the third floor of a shabby 1950s era building, and the weekend he'd moved in, the elevators had been out. They'd moved a pickup truck full of stuff up three flights of steps, back and forth, all day long, and by the time they were done, they'd worn a black trail into the carpet with all the dirt they'd dragged in.

"Stop!" he yelled. "Hey, hold it a second."

Levy gave him a look. "What is it, Keith?"

"Hold on a second, Chuck." Anderson went to the doorway. To Guerra, he said, "Come back here a second, will you?"

"Sure," Guerra answered. "What is it?"

"Let me see one of your swabs, will you?"

He handed Anderson an extra swab from his kit and Anderson knelt down and rubbed it on the floor. It came away with the same black soot as the first swab.

"Damn it," he said. "Let me see your flashlight."

Guerra took a Mini Stinger from his belt and handed it to Anderson.

Anderson knelt down again and shined the light at an oblique angle to the floor. In the beam, he could see more of the soot. He moved to the doorway and did the same thing down the hallway.

"What is it?" Levy asked.

"Damn it," Anderson said. He hung his head and muttered, "Damn it." Then he stood up and handed the flashlight back to the evidence technician. "Any idea how many people have been through here since this incident started?" he asked.

Guerra said, "I don't know. Probably about fifteen."

"Damn it," he muttered.

"You mind telling me what the problem is?" Levy asked.

"That soot is everywhere down here. There's a trail of it that leads from here all the way down the hallway. Probably goes up the stairs and out the front door, too. But we've walked all over it now." He laughed at himself. "Damn it," he said. "Sometimes I feel like such a fucking amateur."

***

Anderson and Levy walked back up to the lobby. The bodies had been moved, all but Everett's, and now there was nothing in the lobby but broken glass and a spent shell casing and a bunch of numbered metal tents to mark the various locations of pieces of evidence.

Levy said, "Well, what do you think? Allen's gonna want your first impressions."

"First impressions, huh?" Anderson thought, *My first impression is that I don't have the slightest fucking clue what's going on.* But what he said was, "I think it's pretty obvious we're dealing with a group of people here. How many I don't know, but those bodies had to go someplace, and that means somebody had to load them into some kind of vehicle. My guess is they had some kind of van parked out here in the parking lot. They used those towels we saw to hold open the doors, and they came and went through here like you would if you were moving furniture. That's why that black soot was spread out like it was. They must have traipsed it in with them as they were moving the bodies out of here."

"Okay," Levy said, "I can see that. But what about Everett there? How does he play into this?"

"Beats me," Anderson said. "It looks like he shot himself, but why he did it, and when he did it, is anybody's guess at this point."

Anderson scanned the crowd in the parking lot and his gaze found Allen. He was with two other members of the SAPD Command Staff and they were talking to a fourth man Anderson didn't recognize. Actually, they weren't really talking. Allen was doing the talking, nearly yelling, in fact, and the fourth man was standing there with his head hung low like

186 | Joe McKinney

he was a kid about to be sent to his room.

"What do you mean, *when* he did it? We have it on the video monitor. Well the sound of it anyway."

Everett had been standing in a spot the video cameras didn't cover, though they had picked up the gun's report.

Anderson turned back to Levy. "I was just wondering if he helped the others move the bodies. I don't see any of that black soot on his hands."

"You think it's possible he didn't shoot himself?"

"At this point I just don't know, Chuck. Hey, who's that with Allen over there?"

"No clue. He doesn't look happy, though."

"No, he doesn't."

Anderson took a deep breath. He was thinking about Jenny Cantrell again and what this was going to be like for her. Poor woman; it just kept piling up.

"Hey Keith?" Levy was at Anderson's side now, talking low, almost in a whisper. "Tell me something. We got goats with their hearts cut out. We got a detective with a goat's heart stuck in his chest cavity and his own heart God knows where. Now we've got missing bodies. Tell me, do you think we're dealing with some kind of cult?"

Anderson thought about that. It did make more sense than any other idea they had come up with so far. A lot of the sickness of all this was easier to digest when you started talking about cults. Cults were strange. They got people to do things they would never do on their own. Look at the Heaven's Gate people killing themselves so they could join up with the UFO mother ship. Look at Charles Manson talking his "family" into committing mass-murder. Look at Jim Jones talking nine hundred and something people into committing mass-suicide. You saw that kind of craziness, and the things they were dealing with suddenly seemed a little less crazy.

"Certainly seems like a cult thing, doesn't it?" Anderson said. "We ought to get somebody from the office to contact the FBI and see if they can crosscheck their files for similar crimes. If it's a cult, there's bound to be some kind of precedent."

Allen joined them then. He was wearing a crisp gray suit, white shirt, and blue and gold tie. His expression was smooth and reserved, but there was anger in his eyes.

"You guys find anything," he said.

"More of that black soot," Anderson said. "Whoever took the bodies must have had it on them."

Allen looked at the body of David Everett in the corner and shook his head. "This is unbelievable," he said. "Un-fucking-believable."

"Yes, sir," Anderson said.

"Do you know who that guy is over there? The one in the blue suit?"

He was pointing at the man Anderson had seen him talking to. Anderson told him that he didn't recognize him.

"That's Edgar Gantz. He's the Chief of the campus police. You know what he just told me?"

"What?"

"You're gonna love this. I figured whoever took those bodies had to have brought a van or something in here to do it. Am I right? You don't move forty-something bodies in a fucking Hyundai, right? So I ask him if he can have somebody go through the records. You know, try to get a list of all the vans that came and went through here tonight."

"And?" Anderson asked. He was almost afraid to hear the answer.

"He tells me they were short-handed last night. They only had three guards working, and he was at the main gate. You know how many other gates there are to this place?"

Anderson shook his head.

"Eight. They had one patrol car working last night. You know what that means?"

Levy said, "Sounds like nobody saw a damn thing."

"Bingo," Allen said.

Anderson said, "I'm almost afraid to ask about the video cameras."

Allen pointed at the three buildings behind him. From where they stood they could see the backs of each. There were generators and Dumpsters and loading docks and a paved runway leading straight on through between them.

"There are no cameras back here," Allen said. "Can you believe that? This is supposed to be a secure facility. God, we're gonna look like fools when this gets out."

Allen scanned the scene again, then turned back to Anderson. "You said you found some more of that black soot. What's that all about?"

Anderson glanced at Levy, and he would have laughed if it hadn't been happening to him.

***

As they were heading back to the car, Anderson's cell phone rang.

"Hold on a sec," he said to Levy. "This is Margie."

He answered. "Hey babe, what's up?"

"What's up? Jesus. How about you fucking tell me, Keith. Jesus Christ, why in the hell didn't you say anything to me about this when you left this morning? You knew, didn't you? Didn't you?"

"Margie, wait. Hold on, would you? What are you talking about?"

"You know damn well what I'm talking about. Jesus, Keith. I get over here to Jenny's house this morning and I find her crying her eyes out. She tells me Ram's body's missing from the morgue. Is that true, Keith? Tell me that's not true. Somebody's playing a really shitty joke on her. Tell me that."

Anderson stopped. He didn't answer for a long time. Levy was already at the car, but when he saw Anderson wasn't with him, he stopped and looked back.

"What is it?" he asked.

Anderson held up a finger for him to wait.

"Keith?" Margie said.

Anderson took a deep breath and said, "Yeah, Margie, it's true. Somebody, a group of people, we think, killed three Medical Examiner's Office investigators last night and took all the bodies from the Morgan Rollins crime scene."

"Including Ram?"

"Yes, including Ram. Raul Herrera, too. The other detective who was with Ram."

"Oh my God," Margie said. "Why? Why would anybody do that?"

"We don't know."

Levy was standing next to him now. He said, "What happened? Does she know?"

Anderson nodded.

"Fuck! How? Who told her?"

"Margie," Anderson said. "How did Jenny find out?"

"What difference does that make? You should have told me, Keith. She deserves more than that, Keith?"

"Margie, please. I know. Just tell me. How did she find out?"

"Steve Garwin called her an hour ago. Keith, you knew about this before that. Why didn't you tell me?"

Anderson could feel another migraine coming on, and the morning sun wasn't helping any. It already felt like it was ninety-five degrees out here. He was sticky with sweat and upset and now he had to deal with this.

He closed his eyes and pinched the bridge of his nose and tried to will away the looming headache.

"Well?" Levy said.

Anderson opened his eyes. He put a hand over the phone and said, "Garwin called her about an hour ago."

"Garwin? Jesus, why? Why would he do that?"

He shrugged angrily. "Why the fuck you asking me? I don't know."

"Keith?" Margie now. Some of the volume had gone out of her voice, but none of the heat.

"I'm here," he said.

"I can't believe you'd do this."

"Margie, please. I'm sorry, all right? I had to get out here, and I didn't want to say anything until I had the facts."

"Well, what are the facts?"

"I don't know, Margie. I really don't."

"That's great, Keith. Are you coming over here? She wants to talk to you."

"I will, Margie. Later. Chuck and I have a nine o'clock appointment up at the Comal County Sheriff's Office. I'll come by after that. I promise."

"After your appointment? Jesus, Keith. Jenny is our friend. She needs us here."

"Margie, come on."

"Okay, fine," she said. "All right, fine. I'll see you later."

She hung up without another word. Keith stood there, looking at the phone.

To Levy, he said, "Fucking wonderful. I can't catch a fucking break."

***

They were in the car again, this time heading out to the Hill Country north of San Antonio. The suburban sprawl of San Antonio's north side fell away and became wide tracts of cedar and oak forests that went off as far as the eye could see in every direction. From the highway, Anderson saw vast clouds of dust and cedar pollen hanging in the valleys between the countless hills, and he was struck by the quiet of it, the peaceful ease that seemed to settle over him as he took in the view.

"It's beautiful, isn't it?" Levy said.

"Yeah. It takes your breath away."

"Yeah, it does at that. You ought to think about moving out to Pipe Creek. It's even prettier than this. Land is cheaper, too."

"We've thought about it," Anderson said. "But I've got three years left on my mortgage. I don't want to have to go through all that crap again. You know? Another loan, more bills. When I retire I just want to take it easy, read some books."

Levy nodded. "It'd be nice to put all this behind me. No more calls in the middle of the night. No more stress. No more getting hammered in the press. You know what I can't wait to do when I retire?"

"What?"

"I am gonna buy some cows."

"You're kidding?"

"No, I'm serious. I've been thinking. I got all that land out there. If I start raising some cattle on it, I could get an agricultural exemption on my taxes. I could save four or five thousand a year."

"Yeah, but cows? That's a lot of work, isn't it? If you're gonna do that agricultural exemption, don't you have to butcher them?"

Levy shrugged. "What else am I gonna do with my time?"

Anderson thought about that. He couldn't see himself butchering cattle, no way. But at the same time, he had no idea what he was going to do with his own time after his career was over. But the more he thought about it, the more he came to realize that, for the first time since it began, he was actually looking forward to the end of his career. The thought of retirement, of putting all this behind him, of shuffling off all this mind-numbing responsibility and letting somebody else worry about it for a change, suddenly seemed like the most welcome thing in the world.

"Is this us up here?" Levy asked.

"Yeah, looks like it."

Anderson slowed the car and turned into the main gate for Smithson Valley High School. From the main road, they could see the entire campus, and it was enormous. The school itself was made up of seven large yellow brick buildings with metal roofs. The baseball fields and what looked like horse stables were off to the right. The football stadium, where they were going, was off to the left. Though school was out, there were trucks and cars parked in the grass near the field house. Levy pointed that way and said, "Walsh said he'd meet us down there."

"Right," Anderson said. "Let's hope this guy can tell us something good. After that disaster this morning, it'd be nice to come back with some good news."

And that's exactly what they found.

***

The stretch of lawn between the field house and the northern entrance to the Smithson Valley High School stadium was packed with people, parents mostly, but quite a few teenagers as well. Somebody had backed a flatbed trailer up to one edge of the parking lot and men were busy off-loading hay bales. Beyond the rows of hay were food booths and smoking barbeque pits. A cloud of smoke drifted over Anderson and Levy carrying the heavenly scent of slow-roasting meat.

"Looks like a festival," Anderson said.

"That's what Walsh told me," Levy answered. "He said they were doing some kind of fundraiser to pay for their new scoreboard."

"Did he say how we're supposed to find him?"

"He said he'd be the only black guy out here. Shouldn't be that hard."

They found Detective-Sergeant Julian Walsh at one of the barbeque booths. He was shorter than Anderson, about Levy's height, but built like the front of a truck, with broad shoulders and a chest and arms that were obviously the product of several hours a week in the gym. His face was flat and almost completely round, and when he smiled, Anderson got a mental picture of a body-building cherub. He wore jeans and a green t-shirt with the Comal County Sheriff's Office logo above the left breast pocket, and over that a white apron with the words "Chef of Police" printed on it.

"Sorry I couldn't meet you fellas at Headquarters," he said. "But I'd already committed to doing this for our Association."

"It's no problem," Levy said. "I'm just glad you could meet us on such short notice."

"Always happy to help a brother out."

"So this is your Association's booth?" Anderson asked. "What are you guys cooking?"

"Pork butt, my man," Walsh said proudly. "Sixteen hours in the smoke and it'll dissolve on your tongue. Hey, you guys ought to come by later. I make about the best pulled pork sandwich you are ever gonna have. My grandma's recipe."

"Sounds great," Anderson said. "But we're kind of swamped." Then Anderson nodded toward Levy. "And besides, he's Jewish."

"Oh, man," said Walsh. "Hey, I'm sorry."

Levy waved it away.

Recovering, Walsh said, "I heard about the Morgan Rollins thing on the news. Sounds like you guys got your hands full." Walsh slipped off his apron and said, "Well, come on over to my truck. I got the info you guys wanted."

"I appreciate that," Anderson said.

"No sweat. So, Paul Henninger is a San Antonio Police Officer now, huh? How's he doin'?"

"He's having a busy career so far," Anderson said.

"Yeah, I bet. Say, he's not in trouble, is he? I know you said you were looking into his father, but he's a good kid."

"I don't think he's got any problems," Anderson said. "We're just interested in the stick lattices you guys found at his father's death. They may not be related to what we're doing, but we need to check it out. Did you know Paul pretty well?"

"Well, just in passing. My little brother played football with him in high school. Of course, everybody 'round here knows who Paul is. When you're in Smithson Valley, Detective, you're in football country. And Paul was about the best ballplayer Smithson Valley ever turned out. Some folks 'round here thought he might even go pro one day."

"Really?" Anderson said. "He was that good? He's definitely big enough."

"Oh yeah. My kid brother said there wasn't nobody could hit harder than Paul Henninger. Lot of people were rooting for him, too. You know, on account of his parents."

"I don't really know anything about his parents," Anderson said. "I was kind of hoping you could tell us about them."

Walsh took his keys out of his pocket and said, "This is me over here." He stopped at a yellow Chevy pickup and opened up the driver's side door. He took out two bankers boxes from his backseat and took them around back.

"Open that tailgate, would you?" he said to Anderson.

Anderson folded down the tailgate, and Walsh put the boxes down on top of it.

"That's everything," he said. "Go ahead and take a look."

Anderson and Levy opened up the boxes and started flipping through them, looking for the crime scene photos.

Walsh said, "About the nicest thing I could say about Paul's parents is that they were just plain weird. The mother hanged herself when he was twelve. Did you know that?"

"No, I didn't," Anderson said.

"Yeah, I was there that day. It was one of the first calls I ever made as a policeman, if you can believe that." He shuddered. "Still gets to me, too. She'd been hanging in their barn most of the day. By the time Paul's daddy found her that afternoon, a bunch of wild hogs had got after her. God that was a nasty sight. She was nearly picked clean from the hips down."

"Were you the detective on his father's death?"

"No, I was still a patrolman when that happened. The lead detective on that one was a guy named Wayne Cotton."

"Is he still around?" Anderson asked.

"No, he died two years ago."

"Oh, I'm sorry."

"Don't be," Walsh said. "The guy was headed for an early grave anyway. You know those people who are so fat they have to be buried in piano cases? That was Cotton. Guy never ate a vegetable in his life." Walsh paused, and Anderson got the feeling he had only just noticed how truly fat Levy was. He looked like a man who has just figured out his foot in his mouth. Twice in a row. He added, "He smoked, too. I don't think he was planning on a long retirement, you know? Those are his reports in there. I think he took most of those photos himself."

Anderson kept looking through the stack of crime scene photos until he found a series that showed the stick lattices. His eyes widened as he flipped through them, one by one. He nudged Levy in the shoulder and said, "Hey, look at this."

Levy looked at the photos and shook his head. "I'll be damned. Exactly the same as Morgan Rollins and the train yard."

"Yeah," Anderson said. He turned to Walsh and said, "What can you tell me about these?"

Walsh looked at the photos and shrugged. "Nothing much. I remember seeing those things in the barn, but I didn't really pay 'em too much attention. I just thought it was one of the crazy things Paul's daddy did. The man kind of had a reputation, if you know what I mean."

"You said that," Anderson said. "I'm afraid I don't know what you mean? What was so weird about him?"

"Well, I guess it was mainly because he and his wife kept to themselves so much. Folks around here are pretty friendly. We're getting big population-wise, but we still got that small town kind of personality, you know?"

"Like this fundraiser," Levy said.

"Exactly. Just about everybody knows everybody around here. Paul's parents, though, they didn't ever do anything like this fundraiser. Here they had this star athlete of a kid, this kid that was on the front page of the newspaper almost every day during football season, and they never showed up to his games, never took part in the booster club. They just stayed on that farm of theirs and kept to themselves. His momma was supposed to be a manic-depressive or schizophrenic or something like that. I remember, the night before she killed herself, one of their neighbors nearly ran her over on the road in front of their house. Apparently she was running in the middle of the road screaming nonsense about her husband being the devil. A couple of our guys took her home, but Paul's daddy wouldn't have anything to do with her. Just told the deputies to drop her in the back room and close the door."

"Nice guy," Anderson said.

"Yeah, he was a piece of work. Of course, I don't really know too much about him. Just that his daddy was a preacher over the Baptist church on Farm Road Three-sixteen. I know they used to fight a lot. Then Paul's daddy went off to the Army, and when he came back here he stayed around for a few months before heading down to Mexico and lived there for a while. When he came back here he worked at the Morgan Rollins factory until it closed down, and after that he took over the family farm and hardly ever left it."

Anderson looked at Levy and shook his head. He said, "Paul's daddy worked at Morgan Rollins?"

"That's right. Worked there for three or four years, if I remember right. You guys didn't know that? I thought I mentioned that to you on the phone."

"No," Anderson said. "No, we didn't know that. Seems like we're learning all kinds of new things."

***

"So do you think Paul Henninger is part of some kind of cult?" Levy asked.

They were in the car again. It was almost noon, and the highway into town was filling up with lunch hour traffic.

"I suppose it's possible," Anderson said. "You saw those pictures. There's an obvious link between whatever Henninger's father was doing with those stick lattices and what happened at Morgan Rollins."

"Plus he used to work there."

"Yeah, there's that, too."

Levy said, "Of course, Martin Henninger is dead."

"Yep."

"So where does that leave us? The son picks up where the father left off. He's part of some sort of cult that's killing heroin junkies and stealing their bodies from the morgue."

"Yeah, maybe. I suppose. Of course, Paul Henninger has a pretty good alibi for the night of the Morgan Rollins killings. He was on duty, after all, with a partner."

Levy turned his wedding ring around his finger. It was a nervous gesture with him, one Anderson had seen him do a lot during long investigations.

He said, "So, where does that leave us? Do you think Henninger is involved with this or not?"

Anderson said, "Chuck, you should have seen him that night at the rail yard. He was really shaken up. Like he'd just had the scare of his life. You don't fake that kind of look."

"Okay, so he was shaken up. How does that fit in with all the other stuff we know about his family's link to this? I mean, he'd just had a gun pointed at him. He'd just been in his first car chase. Maybe he was just rattled from that."

Before Anderson could answer, his phone rang. He scooped it off his belt and checked the caller ID.

"It's Margie," he said, "let me take this." He flipped the phone open and said, "Hey, babe."

"Hi."

She sounded calmer. At least he couldn't hear any anger in her voice. Now she just sounded tired.

"What's going on?" he asked.

"I'm still here at Jenny's," she said. "She's been getting visitors all day from the Association and the funeral home. God, Keith, there's so much to handle."

"Did Deputy Chief Allen come by?"

"Yeah, he was here."

"How did that go?"

"Well, not so good. He apologized for what happened, but what can you really say in a situation like that, you know? She's devastated, Keith."

"Yeah, I can imagine."

"She's come to a decision, though."

"Oh? About what?"

"She wants to go ahead with the funeral. She talked with Raul Herrera's wife earlier today. They both want to go ahead with it."

Anderson was stunned. Margie was silent, waiting for him to say something, but he didn't have any words for it.

"Keith?"

"Yeah, I'm here," he said.

"What do you think?"

"I don't know," he said. "I don't even know if you can do that. Can you bury an empty coffin?"

"Allen was here when she made up her mind. So was the guy from the funeral home. Allen said he would make it happen."

"He did. Huh. Well, I guess he will then."

Margie was quiet after that, and Anderson got the feeling that the call was over. He said, "Hey Margie."

"What is it, Keith?"

"Are we okay?"

"I don't know, Keith. I just don't know. I'll talk to you later."

"Okay," he said. "I love you."

"Love you, too," she said. "See you tonight."

"Okay," he said. But she had already hung up.

Chapter 13

San Antonio's endless summer rolled on. The sun grew hotter each day, hanging in the sky like a swollen white eye, scorching all but the thinnest clouds from the upper atmosphere. The earth turned brittle from the heat, going from green to yellow to brown. Dust was everywhere, thick and depthless where the air was too dead to allow a breeze.

And the nights weren't much better. As Paul and Mike roved the streets, baking inside their body armor, soaking their uniforms with sweat before they even completed their first call, they watched the world around them wilting beneath the heat. The homeless and the junkies lounged on discarded couches in the ubiquitous vacant lots and watched them cruise by with rheumy, empty expressions, not even bothering with their usual routine of pretending to move along. Diseased dogs roamed the streets and alleyways of their district, rooting out their dinners from garbage that accumulated behind buildings and in the gutters. But even the scavengers were sluggish and lazy and disinterested to the point that they couldn't be bothered to get out of the way of passing patrol cars. The heat that gripped San Antonio during the July days and nights of that summer was slow and constant and unrelenting, a prolonged smothering that sapped the will and dulled the mind.

In the passenger seat of the patrol car, the window open and the dry and dusty and sour garbage smell of San Antonio's east side drifting into his nose, Paul watched the landscape slip by and was surprised to realize that he had a pretty good idea of where they were.

It was nearly two in the morning now, and they had spent much of that night drifting through the southern part of their district—an area Mike lovingly referred to as Heroin Town—looking for junkies to shake down for information about the Morgan Rollins killings. But now they were headed north along Lee Hall Boulevard, leaving their district. A few minutes earlier they had received a message from Wes and Collins on their MDT that read simply: *Ready*. And Mike had turned the car north and sped away.

Paul didn't ask questions. He read the message, looked at Mike, who had a wicked smile on his face, and waited to be told what was up.

He was still waiting when they entered the warehouse-lined streets in the middle of Barris and Seles' district. Paul watched the buildings slip by.

198 | Joe McKinney

Their corrugated metal roofs and tubular construction reminded him of airplane hangers. The street was quiet and dark. Large oak trees filled up the spaces between the warehouses. A black dog trotted into the street and watched them as they drove around it.

"What are we doing here?" Paul finally said.

Mike's smile got bigger, but he didn't speak. He slowed the car to a crawl, blacked out the lights, and turned into a driveway that led up a steep incline and then curved around the back of one of the warehouses.

Wes and Collins were already there. Their car was blacked out and idling smoothly beneath the eaves of a large Spanish oak.

Mike parked the car a short distance from Wes and Collins and opened his door. But before he could get out, Paul stopped him. They usually parked driver's side window to driver's side window, 69ing, as it was commonly called.

"What are we doing here?" Paul asked.

"Just get out. There's some things you need to know in order to become a well-rounded policeman."

"A well-rounded policeman?"

"Just get out," Mike said.

***

Mike popped the trunk, reached inside, and came up with a handful of rubber surgical tubing. He handed it to Paul and said, "Hold this."

Paul looked at it. "What's this for?"

Mike kept digging through the trunk. Without looking up he said, "Show him, Collins."

Collins laughed. He gave Paul a good-natured slap on the shoulder and said, "Come on."

They crossed the parking lot to the back edge. Wes was already standing there, waiting for them.

From where they stood, they could see over a sea of oak trees. The metal roofs of the surrounding warehouses looked like rafts floating in the midst of a gently undulating green sea.

"What am I looking at?" Paul asked.

Collins pointed at a parking lot some two hundred feet away. "There they are—right there," he said. "See 'em?"

It was dark, and the cars were blacked out, but once Paul knew what he was looking at, he could see plainly enough two SAPD patrol cars parked next to a three story building made entirely of corrugated tin.

"I see 'em," Paul said. "Who is that?"

Collins laughed. But it sounded like a mean laugh. "Barris and Seles. The other car is their daddy, Garwin."

Oh no, Paul thought.

"You almost ready, Mike?" Wes said.

"Got it," Mike said.

Paul turned back to him and saw Mike holding a blue plastic cup with a handle on each side and a faded picture of SpongeBob Squarepants on the front. In his other hand, he had a small Igloo cooler.

"Is that a baby cup?" Paul asked.

"That depends on how it's used," Mike answered.

He took the surgical tubing from Paul and cut it into two equal pieces with his pocket knife. As Paul watched, recognition gradually sinking in, Mike tied off one piece of tubing to each handle. Then he opened the cooler, revealing a dozen or so baseball-sized water balloons, and Paul's suspicions were confirmed.

As a freshman member of the UTSA football squad, and before he had met Rachel, he went to Corpus Christi with a busload of guys from the team for spring break. They stayed in a weathered little three bedroom house about a block from the beach. The house was surrounded on three sides by high rise hotels, and the balconies were crammed with college students all shouting out at each other, everybody ready to party. Some of the guys took a homemade water balloon launcher a lot like the one Mike had just made and shot balloons at the people on the hotel balconies.

At the time, Paul had had no idea that water balloon slingshots were so popular. But within moments, the people on the balconies began to shoot back with their own water balloon slingshots, and because the house was in such a poor tactical position, it only took a few minutes for nearly every window in the house to get broken out by flying balloons. It was Paul's first practical lesson on the tactical virtues of the high ground.

Paul said, "That's a slingshot."

"Well what do you know?" Mike said. "It can learn."

"Nice to know he's got more than muscles," Wes said.

Collins gave his partner a dirty look. "Dude, shut up. You really gross me out with that gay shit, you know that?"

Wes rolled his eyes.

But then Paul's smile wavered as a stray thought crossed his mind. "But Garwin's down there," he said.

"Your daddy will be just fine," Collins said.

Mike led the others to the edge of the lot. Paul looked across the tops of the trees and had a perfect view of their targets. The planning that went into this was impressive, he realized. A lot of pieces had to fall into place to make it work.

He stood off to one side as Wes and Collins each grabbed an end of one of the tubes. Mike stood between them, the cup in his hands. He pulled it back so that the ropes were taut and the slingshot ready to fire.

"Hand me a balloon," he said to Paul.

"We're not gonna get in trouble for this, are we?" Paul asked.

"Just hand me a balloon, Paul."

Paul handed him a yellow one.

"Now stand over there," Mike said, pointing to the left of Wes with his chin. "You're gonna be the spotter. Tell me where it lands."

Mike let the slingshot go, and the balloon went into a high arc over the trees. It landed somewhere off in the trees to the right of the target.

"Too far right and short," Paul said.

Mike loaded the slingshot again and let his second shot fly. It went straight, but too long. It hit the side of the building behind the police cars and made a loud cracking sound that ripped through the quiet night air like a shotgun blast.

Collins snickered and said, "Oh shit. That was loud."

"Do it again," Wes said. The small gap between his round eyes was creased with laugh lines. "One more time."

But they didn't get the chance. Before any of them could get back into position, they were interrupted by Barris' panicked voice on the radio.

"44-50," he said, and didn't wait for the dispatcher to respond. "I got shots fired. Shots fired! Eighteen hundred block of Court Street. Unknown direction."

Collins and Mike looked at each other, then back at Mike. Mike just stood there, his mouth hanging open.

"Oh that fucking idiot," Mike said. "I can't believe he did—"

The dispatcher set off a city-wide emergency tone that drowned out the rest of Mike's sentence. Then her calm, businesslike voice came over the radio. "I have 44-50 out with shots fired in the eighteen hundred block of Court. Cover is Code Three. 44-60, 44-70, 44-40, start that way."

Before any of them could answer, Garwin got on the radio. He sounded strangely calm. "44-100, I'm ten-six with 44-50."

They all looked at Mike, who was staring at the two police cars below them and shaking his head.

"Mike?" Wes said.

Mike said, "One of you get on the radio and tell them that—"

But he was cut off by a second emergency tone. Their dispatcher came on the radio again and said, "9217 Lincoln for a robbery of an individual. 9217 Lincoln in 44-70's district, clearing all but East." There was a pause as the dispatcher switched from the all-route citywide channel to the dedicated East Patrol channel. When she spoke again, her voice was as calm as ever, almost bored. "44-80, I know you're on break but you're all I've got. Start that way, Code Three. I'll get you some cover as soon as I can."

"10-4," said a rather irritated-sounding officer. "Coming from a long ways off."

Paul looked at Mike for guidance. Lincoln ran right through their little heroin town off of F.M. 78. Lots of dope, lots of guns, lots of messy calls.

"Mike?" he said.

Mike turned away from Seles, Barris, and Garwin's cars. To Wes, he said, "Tell them a bunch of kids did it. The robbery's in our square. Paul and I will take that."

Wes looked doubtful, but he cleared his throat and keyed up his radio anyway.

"44-60," he said.

Looking at Mike with an *okay, here it goes* expression, he said, "44-60, tell 44-50 and 44-100 no shots fired. Repeat, no shots fired. It's just some kids with a water balloon shooter. I saw them running east of Court towards Mittman."

The pause that followed seemed to go on forever. Finally, the dispatcher spoke. "44-100, do you copy that, sir?"

"10-4," Garwin answered.

Another long uncomfortable silence followed.

"44-70," Mike said.

"Go ahead, 44-70," the dispatcher said.

"44-70, if that's gonna be a bogus call, we'll be on the way to 9217 Lincoln for that robbery of an individual."

"10-4," the dispatcher said. "44-100, do you copy?"

"I copy, 44-100," said Garwin. "Have 44-70 divert. And ask 44-60 if they've still got those kids in sight."

Wes looked at Mike. Mike shook his head.

"Uh, negative, 44-60," Wes said. "We lost them."

"Okay," Mike said. "We're outta here. Paul, get in the car. I'm driving."

Paul didn't argue. He got in the passenger seat and a moment later he was holding onto the dashboard for dear life as Mike gunned the Crown Victoria down the steep slope of the drive and out onto the street.

Over the howling of the Ford's engine, Paul heard Garwin's voice on the radio.

"44-100, have 44-60 make my location."

"Shit," Mike said.

"10-4," the dispatcher said. "44-60?"

There was a long pause before Wes answered. "44-60, 10-4. Can you ask 44-100 for his twenty, ma'am?"

"44-100?"

Garwin said, "44-100, tell him to get down here *now!* He doesn't need my twenty because he knows exactly where I'm at."

"Oh shit," Mike said.

"44-60, you copy?" the dispatcher asked.

"10-4," Wes answered, and when he spoke again he sounded like a condemned man being led to the gallows. "We're on the way."

***

Two hours later, the four of them were together again, sitting at an open-air picnic table behind an all-night grease pit called The Cave. It served burgers, fries, and fried chicken, and, according to Mike at least, was just about the only place in the whole 44 section where they could go to eat and be reasonably sure the cooks weren't doing something obscene to their food before they served it.

But, like everything else on the east side, the Cave was an eyesore. Grass grew up through cracks in the concrete. Graffiti was scrawled all over the fence that circled the lot. Burglar bars sealed every window and door in sight. And he was pretty sure he'd seen rats or mice running around behind the Dumpster not twenty feet from them.

Paul looked around the table. Wes was smiling that creepy smile of his at him. Collins was pissed off, as usual, and pushing his French fries around in a puddle of ketchup. Mike was eating a hamburger that oozed mustard and wilted lettuce and seemed as happy doing it as a goat munching clover.

Paul watched them, listened to them, and he thought about Collins. Mike he was beginning to understand. Wes, too, in a way. But not Collins. He was a contradiction in so many ways. He loved being a policeman, but he obviously felt like he deserved something better. He thought policemen were the only members of the human species worth bearing the name *human*, and yet he hated most of the cops he worked with—like Barris and Seles and Garwin. He was constantly complaining about how bad the Department sucked, and yet his bitching and moaning provided an outlet for the others and in the process, and ironically, Paul realized, raised everybody's morale.

"44-70," said the dispatcher.

Mike was holding some fries in one hand, his radio on the table in front of him. "Go ahead, 44-70," he said.

"44-70, make 1212 Formund Street for a sexual assault report." There was a slight pause, and Paul could have sworn he heard laughter behind the dispatcher's ordinarily glassy voice. "Your complainant states his girlfriend has done something to his penis. Unknown what."

Mike put down his fries when he heard the part about the guy's penis. "Why do they do this to me," he said, sounding thoroughly harassed. "10-4," he said into his radio. "We're on the way, ma'am."

***

The house they responded to was about the size and shape of a school bus. It had once been white, and there were still traces of a canary yellow trim around the roofline and around the front door, but years of neglect had turned large patches of the outside to gray, and the front porch had a rotted sag to one side that reminded Paul of the brim of an old hat. The lawn was a weed patch. There was what looked like a broken down and thoroughly rusted Trans Am up on blocks in the front lawn. In the driveway was an old Chevy pickup with metal racks in the bed that held paint-splattered buckets and a few ladders.

They parked in the street, but almost as soon as they got out, a tall, gaunt-looking white guy in loose fitting blue jeans and nothing else came running out of the house. His chest was covered with tattoos. He had long, stringy blond hair that hadn't seen shampoo since the first Bush was in office. Paul guessed he was six-two or six-three, but he was so skinny he couldn't have weighed more than a hundred-thirty pounds. Ropey veins showed through the skin up and down his arms.

As he stumbled into the street, waving his arms in the air above his head and screaming nonsense, Paul realized the man had the wild, bloodshot eyes of a meth head.

"Jesus," Paul said. "I've seen goats cough up stuff that looks better than that guy."

Mike chuckled.

"That fucking bitch!" the man screamed at them. "She done tore my pecker to pieces!"

Paul glanced at Mike, hoping to clue off his reaction, but didn't see what he expected. Mike was strolling casually toward the man with an almost bored expression on his face.

"She's inside," the man said, pointing to the house. Tears were welling up in his eyes. "That fucking whore. She done tore me up."

"And how did she do that?" Mike asked.

"Fuck if I know. I think she put sand in her pussy," the man said. "When I was fucking her, I got all tore up. It was like she was rubbing me with sandpaper down there."

The man was squeezing his cock through his jeans, and now he was crying.

Without even the barest trace of a smile, Mike said, "So if it was hurting so bad, how come you didn't stop fucking her?"

The man looked at Mike like he was speaking another language.

Mike said, "That never occurred to you?"

The man was confused now. "Look at what she done to me," he said. He unzipped his pants and let them fall to his feet, his junk hanging out for the whole street to see.

Paul groaned and turned away, but Mike never even blinked. "Pull your pants up," Mike said.

"Look at this," the man said. "Look at it. It's all tore up. I'm bleeding."

"You got more problems than sand," Mike said. "There's a free clinic over on Carlton. Tell your girl to go to it. The doctor can give her a shot and then put her on some pills that'll clear that up."

The man stood there, staring dumbly at the two of them, his pants around his feet.

"You ain't gonna arrest her?" he asked incredulously.

"For what?" Mike asked. "It ain't a crime to get an STD."

"What about my pecker?" The man grabbed it with one hand and pointed at it with the other. "What am I supposed to do with this?"

"Give it a rest for a few days," Mike said. "Maybe both of you need to get that shot. Just between us guys, you might be having some real problems later...I mean, you know, with the whole fidelity thing."

"Huh?" the man said.

Mike turned to Paul and motioned for him to get back in the car. As they drove away, steering around the almost completely naked man in the middle of the street, Paul felt so thoroughly confused that he couldn't even laugh.

***

They were headed down Hickman Street now, the hot night air blowing in through the open windows, carrying the scent of magnolia and dust. Outside, the slum houses of Heroin Town rolled by. They were quiet now, and dark. Even the hardest of the hardcore junkies had fled indoors or crawled back under their rocks and there seemed very little to do but wait for the coming daylight to spread across the horizon and mark the end of their tour of duty.

Paul was feeling good. It had been a fairly busy night, and a fun one, and as the events of the evening played out again in his head, he had the feeling that he was becoming a part of something really good with Mike and Wes and Collins. He almost forgot the mess that was his real family and his life outside of the Department. Paul still had the image of his dead father elbow-deep in that kid's guts, but it seemed like a bad dream now. Something that was too distant and too horrible to be real.

Certainly Rachel had thought so. She had dismissed it outright, not in so many words, or in any words at all in fact, but through her silence. For her, it was a non-occurrence, a hole that could be smoothed over by ignoring it. He told her everything, and she rejected it. Her silence was painful and confusing, but it was muted now by this new thing, this camaraderie, this feeling of belonging to something good. Football had never made him feel this way. His home life with his father was certainly never this good. The only thing that had ever made him feel better was loving Rachel, and the fact that he could equate the two in his heart both scared and thrilled him.

But it wasn't to last. Something big was waiting for him, and like so many big things in life, it started as something small.

***

"44-70."

Paul answered the radio this time. "Go ahead, 44-70."

"44-70, make 642 Utley Street, 642 Utley for a disturbance. Complainant states her neighbor is fighting with her."

Utley, Paul thought. *On the fringes of heroin town, closer to the eastern edge of their district, over by the Morgan Rollins Iron Works.*

"44-70, 10-4. We're on the way."

Mike turned left on Crowder, one of the four major surface streets that ran north to south through their district, and headed south. They turned left again onto Banks and headed east to Utley.

Paul had figured the location almost exactly, he realized. They were close to the Morgan Rollins Iron Works. He could see the tops of its smokestacks peeking out above the trees behind Utley.

As they drove, Mike told him about houses in the area to watch out for. The family at 756 Utley sold heroin. The shemale prostitute at 714 was HIV positive. The kid at 651 was a car burglar and known to deal in stolen guns. There were a handful of vacant houses scattered up and down the street, all of them known shooting galleries.

Mike was in the middle of telling him a story about the schizophrenic woman that lived at 634 when he suddenly broke off mid-sentence. His eyes grew wide and he said, "Oh shit!"

Paul followed Mike's gaze to the houses on the driver's side of the car. A dark-haired Hispanic woman in her late forties was running right for them. She was waving her arms and screaming and she was covered from head to foot in what looked like blood.

Paul and Mike jumped from the car at the same time, both of them with their guns drawn.

Mike was faster. He got to the front of the car and yelled at the woman to stop. Paul took a few steps that way, following Mike's lead. He had no idea if the blood-covered woman was running to them for help, or running at them because she had just done something horrible and was still in a frenzy. From the way her eyes were rolling wildly from the houses behind her to the cops in front of her, Paul thought it was equal odds either way.

"Stop!" Mike yelled. His voice split the night with absolute authority. He had his pistol in the low ready stance, not pointed at the woman, but only a flick of the wrist away from being in position to put her down if he needed to. "Stop right there," he said.

206 | Joe McKinney

The woman skidded on her heels in the street. As she did, the wild look in her eyes cleared a little, and anger took its place.

"She did this to me," the woman said. Her voice was a mix of rage and self-pity and contempt. Blood dripped from her matted hair. "Look at me," she said. "Look at what she did to me."

"Are you hurt?" Mike asked, lowering his weapon.

"She did this to me." The woman started to bounce up and down on her toes, and from her face Paul could tell the thought of being covered in blood was making the woman's skin crawl. "She did this to me."

"Are you bleeding?" Mike asked.

Paul glanced at Mike. What a weird question to ask somebody covered in blood.

"She threw this on me," the woman said. "It's all over me."

"Why did she throw blood on you?" Paul asked.

The woman wheeled around on him, like she had only just realized he was standing there.

"Because she's a fucking witch," the woman screamed. "She cursed me. Oh Jesus, what am I gonna do?"

"She's a what?" Paul asked.

But the woman didn't answer. She stood in the street and shivered, her arms around her chest and her eyes on the pavement. The temperature was in the high nineties, and she was shivering.

"Paul," Mike said.

Paul glanced at Mike, who pointed back at the house where the woman had come from with his chin. Paul looked at the house. It was a lot like every other house on the block: small, falling into the dust, paint peeling like dead skin. A waist-high hurricane fence ran around the perimeter of the yard, and the section of fence that separated the woman's yard from the house to the left of hers was lined with brightly guttering votive candles and draped with what appeared to be dried chicken bones. There was trash all over the woman's yard, and her front door and most of her porch were covered with blood.

"Where's this other woman at?" Mike asked the still shivering, blood-stained woman.

But she didn't answer. She didn't get the chance. Before she could say anything, the screen door of the house to the left of hers flew open and another woman came running out.

All at once the vision Paul had experienced of his father in Mexico came crashing back in on his mind. The crazed Mexican woman running at them from the next house over was older and heavier and grayer than the young girl who had led his father out of his hotel room and carried him out behind her grandmother's shack to piss among the goats, but she was unmistakably the same woman. She was Paul's past and his visions and his present all crashed together.

"That's her," the blood-stained woman said. She ran behind Paul for cover. "She did this to me."

"You're damn right I did," the second woman said.

Paul found himself in the middle of the two women, and the distance was closing fast. They were screaming at each other in Spanish now, and Paul couldn't understand a word of what was said. He only knew that things were about to get violent.

Paul pushed away from the blood-covered woman and said, "You stay there! Don't you move." Then he turned to the woman from his father's past and said, "Stay where you're at! I'll come talk to you in a second."

But the woman didn't stop. She kept on coming, her hands raised, fingers spread out like they were claws and she meant to dig the other woman's eyes out of her skull.

"Stop!" Paul ordered her, trying to copy Mike's tone of absolute authority.

It didn't work. The woman ran right over him, slicing at his face with her fingernails, clawing her way over top of him to get to the blood-covered woman. Paul grabbed her by the arm and slung her back into her yard. Then he grabbed her again and pulled her hands behind her back.

The woman kicked and spit and screamed that she was being raped. Paul couldn't understand much of her rapid-fire Spanish, but he definitely heard the word rape.

He was so shocked he let her go.

She faced him long enough to spit on him and then ran for the blood-covered woman again.

But before he could chase after her, Mike stepped in front of her and punched her in the solar plexus, the bundle of nerves at the base of the sternum, with the heel of his palm. She flew backwards, landing on her knees, and leaned forward and nearly vomited. Mike didn't give her a chance to get back on her feet. He grabbed her by one arm and threw her face down into the dirt. Then he put one knee into the small of her back and handcuffed her hands behind her back with all the ease of a rodeo calf roper. She had been screaming at Paul, and she was still screaming, but now those screams were coming through mouthfuls of dirt.

He had her on her feet again by the time Paul got to him. With an expression that was more annoyed than angry he handed her to Paul and said, "What the fuck's wrong with you? You put your hands on somebody you better make damn sure you don't let go until the job's finished. I don't care if it's a woman, a kid, whoever. You put your hands on them, you make damn sure they're secure."

Paul nodded.

Mike pushed her towards the car. "Here, take her. Put her in the car and get her information. We're booking her for assault."

Humbled, Paul did what he was told. He led the woman to their patrol car and stuffed her into the backseat despite her screaming. Then he got into the front passenger seat, took his metal clipboard down from the dashboard, and took out the yellow page, the arrested person supplement to the offense report they were going to be writing.

He checked off the blanks for Hispanic, female, black hair, and heavy built. Then he took a deep, nervous breath, and looked at the woman in the sun-visor's vanity mirror. She wasn't screaming now that the door was closed and they were alone. She was looking right at him, her eyes unblinking as she pushed dirt and grass out of her mouth with her tongue.

"I know who you are," she said.

Paul felt the blood run out of his face. He swallowed the walnut-sized lump that had suddenly formed in his throat and tried to sound like he hadn't heard her.

"What's your name?" he said.

"Magdalena Chavarria. But you already know that, don't you?"

"How tall are you, Ms. Chavarria?"

"I was with your father when he got a mark like the one you bear on your forehead. I was there when my Abuela put a goat's heart into your father's chest."

Paul put the clipboard down on the dash and slowly turned around. He was looking at her over his shoulder now, through the plexiglass prisoner cage, but he had the feeling that it was she who was looking at him, that he was the bug under the glass. He felt small and scared and confused.

"Your father made me help him," she said. "I needed to see you. I needed to tell you what kind of danger you're in. Do you understand what your father has done?"

Paul shook his head.

"Your father is very powerful, Paul. Stronger even than my Abuela. She could not have returned from the dead the way your father has. And she would not have wanted to."

"I don't understand," Paul said.

"Your father is evil," Magdalena said. "What he is doing, it is not what my Abuela taught him. It is an abomination. It is a sin. He has made me raise the dead, and he means to do it again. Have you seen those visions? Do you know what he has planned for you?"

"No," Paul said, full of disbelief, and yet also of a sense that what this woman was saying was true.

"Paul, it is very bad. You must fight against him. I believe that you are stronger even than your father. If he is able to corrupt you it will be very bad."

It was too much for Paul. He wanted to throw up, and he scrambled from the car. When the hot night air hit him he gasped. Then he stood there trying to catch his breath. Inside the car, Magdalena Chavarria slowly turned her gaze toward him and stared without expression.

"What the fuck's wrong with you?" Mike said.

"What?" Paul said.

Mike squinted at him. "You all right?"

Paul nodded. "Yeah. Fine."

"You don't look fine." Mike crossed into the street and opened the driver's side door. He seemed to regard Paul for a second before deciding it wasn't important enough to worry about. "Get in," he said. "Let's get the fuck out of here. We can do her paperwork downtown."

Paul glanced at the backseat again. Magdalena nodded to him, and Paul was sure he was going to throw up. He felt it rising in his throat.

"Hey," Mike said. "You coming?"

Paul closed his eyes and forced it down. *Master it. Master it*, he ordered himself. Then he opened his eyes and climbed into the car.

He caught her gaze in the vanity mirror as he slammed it back into its upright position, and in that fraction of a second, he almost came undone.

Chapter 14

Keith Anderson stood under the colonnade of the Oak Meadows Church of God, cursing the heat and the harsh blue glare of the South Texas sky. Anderson had never been one for wearing sunglasses, but he would have killed for them now.

He stared up at the ceiling, where a row of thirty immense columns rose into the shadows sixty feet above him. It was an absurdly huge church, four stories of red brick and polished white concrete treated to look like fine European marble. Maybe it was meant to be imposing, even awe-inspiring, the way medieval cathedrals were to the peasants, but to Anderson it just looked gaudy. It seemed to put into architectural reality all that was distasteful and pompous and hypocritically commercial about fundamentalist Christianity in America.

Marked patrol cars from all over Texas filled the parking lot in front of him. On his way in, he'd even seen a few honor guard detachments from places outside the state, like Oklahoma and Tennessee and Alabama. He'd heard one of the Traffic sergeants say there were a thousand patrol cars out there, and more were showing up every minute.

At the near edge of the parking lot was a circular drive that curled around an island of grass, and in the middle of that island was a pair of flagpoles, the US and Texas flags both flying at half-mast. Closer in still was an emerald-green lawn big enough to host a baseball game.

Everywhere he looked, Anderson saw officers in their dress blues walking in small, sober groups with their wives and girlfriends. His own uniform felt tight and uncomfortable, the gun belt digging into the small of his back and reminding him why he had been so thankful to leave Patrol all those years ago. The long-sleeved black cotton blouse was hot, and even though he didn't wear body armor like most of the younger officers and detectives did, he still felt a strong impulse to tug at the neckline and let out some of the trapped heat that massed next to his chest.

A police whistle split the somber tone of the morning and Anderson looked down at the circular drive to see Traffic officers in their white hats and black gloves clearing the way for a line of shiny black Crown Victorias. The Fords pulled up to the walkway that split the lawn and led directly to the imposing flight of white concrete steps at Anderson's feet.

Okay, he thought, *here comes Allen.*

He scanned the command staff as they exited their vehicles until he found Deputy Chief Allen. Allen cut an imposing figure in his dark blue, thigh-length great coat. His shoulders and chest gleamed in the sun with reflected brass, and around his neck was the San Antonio Police Department's Medal of Valor, which he had won as a lieutenant fifteen years earlier for pulling a family of four out of a burning restaurant. His hair was a perfect gray helmet, every strand in place. He was smiling, but the smile was solemn and sincere, like a politician at a wreath-laying ceremony.

Anderson watched him walk forward to the lead car, put a hand on the chief's shoulder and say something that brought a nod from the chief. Then Allen was walking across the lawn and towards the steps. Coming up them now, almost trotting, not even noticing the climb that had left Anderson winded when he made it.

Allen nodded at the officers he passed on his way up, calling most by their first names. And then he was standing in front of Anderson, extending his hand.

"How are you, Keith?"

"I'm good, sir. You?"

"Okay."

Anderson nodded, though he secretly wished he had some of Allen's reserves. The man had to be working on absolutely no sleep, and yet he still managed to look fresh and rested.

"I've only got a minute or two, Keith," Allen said. "Tell me what you found out from Comal County."

Anderson told him. He laid it all out in order, right down to Paul's father working for a time at the Morgan Rollins Iron Works.

"And so you still hold with the idea that we're dealing with some kind of cult?"

"I do, yes sir."

"Why?"

"Well, it's the logistics of the thing, really. One man couldn't have killed all those people at Morgan Rollins, not even if they were all browned out at the time. And someone had to get Everett out of his holding cell at the clinic and drive him all the way across town. And then there are the bodies. One man, hell, even two or three men wouldn't be able to move forty plus bodies up two flights of stairs and onto a truck in less than an hour. Well, maybe they could do *that,* but when you put the bodies together with everything else we've seen, a cult is about all that makes sense."

"Hmmm," Allen said. "Okay, I can buy that. The thing is though; all you really got is a guess. I mean, are we talking some kind of religious cult, or something like the Manson Family?"

"I don't know, sir."

"Have you checked any federal resources yet? I know the Bureau of Justice has got the National Criminal Intelligence Resource Center. Maybe they've got something on similar crimes."

"Yes sir, I checked them. I also checked Law Enforcement Online and the National Center for the Analysis of Violent Crime and VICAP and the FBI's Behavioral Analysis Unit. Nobody's seen anything like this."

Allen stared down the steps towards the line of black Crown Victorias waiting in queue. A pair of lieutenants walked by with their wives and Allen nodded to them.

When they were gone he said, "So basically you've got nothing?"

"That's about the size of it," Anderson said.

"What about Paul Henninger? Give me your honest opinion. Is he involved? I don't want this guy in uniform for one second more if you think he is. I mean it. I'll have his ass on administrative leave if you've got any reservations at all."

"You want my *opinion*?"

"Well, you don't have any facts, so that's about all I can hope for at the moment, isn't it?"

Anderson flinched. "Yes sir. I guess so." He watched the flags resting against the flag poles. They looked limp, like dead bats hanging from a pole. "Well, if you want my opinion," he said, "then no, I don't think he's involved. I mean it sure is tempting to connect him, and maybe he is connected somehow, but I don't think he *knows* what's going on. When I talked to him that night at the train yard, I could tell he saw something that shook him real bad. Whatever it was he saw, it made an impression. But I could tell that whatever it was, he hadn't expected to see it."

"You think he'll talk to you about it?"

"I don't know, sir. Maybe. All I can do is try."

"Yeah, well, do us all a favor and hurry up with that, would you?"

Anderson frowned. "He was my friend, sir. I'm working as fast as I can."

Allen started to speak, but stopped himself. He nodded instead, then glanced back at the rest of the Command staff. They were waiting for him.

"So where do you go from here?" Allen asked. "What's your plan?"

Anderson thought about that. He said, "I guess the best thing to do is to follow the bodies. I find it hard to believe that anybody, cult or not, could commit a triple murder and steal that many bodies without leaving some kind of physical evidence behind."

"I agree with that," Allen said. He shrugged his shoulders inside his great coat, then grabbed the hem of the white long-sleeved shirt underneath and tugged at it so that it showed the regulation one-quarter of an inch from the hem of the coat. Then he stared down the steps at the throng of officers moving across the lawn and, in a voice so low he might have been talking to himself, said, "You know, I'm glad we could do this for Jenny. I think going forward with this gave her some power over the situation. I think she needed that."

Anderson was shocked.

Allen saw it and raised an eyebrow at the expression on Anderson's face.

"What?"

"Sir, you've got to be kidding me. You don't honestly believe this is a good idea, do you?"

"Yes," Allen said, a little defensively, "I do."

"I just..." Anderson trailed off, shaking his head.

"You just what?"

Anderson sighed.

"I just look at all of us out here, and I can't help but think we're fooling ourselves. Like this is some kind of sick joke."

Allen turned and faced him. Anderson could almost feel himself shrinking under the weight of the man's hard stare.

"Excuse me?" Allen said. "What did you say?"

"Look, sir, I just—"

"I helped set this up, Keith. And you know why I did it?"

Anderson didn't say anything.

"I did it because it's going to help Jenny. And you know who else it's gonna help?" He pointed at the crowd marching towards the church. "You see them, Keith? That's who it's gonna help. Those men and women out there. They need to see the Department honoring its own. They need to see that we give a shit. We won't leave an open wound, which is exactly what postponing this funeral would have done. We need to heal."

"I know that, sir. That's not what I mean. What I'm trying—"

Another Traffic officer's whistle cut him off. Both men turned towards the circular drive and watched as a marked police car pulled into the drive, its overhead red and blue strobes blinking slowly.

"Damn it," Allen said, looking at his watch. "She's early." He turned to Anderson. "That's Jenny. I know she'd like to see you before she has to go in. And I know she'd appreciate you not calling her husband's funeral a sick joke."

Anderson didn't blink. He had no idea how to express himself, how to say why he felt this was so wrong. He only knew that he hated it.

"He was my friend, Robert."

"Yeah," Allen said harshly. And then, more gently, "Yeah, I know, Keith."

Allen left him then and walked down the long flight of white concrete steps and across the wide sea of emerald grass to the circular drive, where a patrolman in an honor guard uniform was getting out of the driver's side of the patrol car and walking around to the passenger side to let Jenny Cantrell out. Anderson watched the deputy chief's back as he walked away, and he couldn't help but feel the sting of someone whose good intentions have been misunderstood. Yes, he did think this funeral was a sick joke. They were burying empty coffins for Christ's sake. How useless was that, how fake? And no, it didn't feel like healing. Hell, it didn't even feel like a step in that direction. It just felt like a lie, both to the living and the dead.

And then Allen was standing there at the patrol car, taking Jenny Cantrell's hand as she stepped from the passenger seat in a black dress. Officers and wives turned that way and a hush fell over the lawn.

Anderson watched Allen guide Jenny toward the walkway, and he thought, not about Jenny, but about Allen. There was a man who had done just about every high-profile job the Department offered. He was a founding member of the SAPD SWAT team. He had been the leader of a twenty-six county narcotics task force. He had won just about every medal and commendation the Department gave, some of them twice. He was a graduate of the FBI's National Academy. And yet he had paid a heavy price for all those honors. For everything he'd put into the Department, he'd lost more than that from his personal life. It had cost him a marriage. He had two children he hadn't seen in ten years. When he left the office at the end of the day he stepped into a void that only going back to work could fill. Anderson looked at the man, the legendary Deputy Chief Robert Allen, and he wondered what he thought about as he led a sobbing widow to the church.

***

Anderson turned away and saw Margie staring at him from the shadows. She was leaning against one of the columns that made up the colonnade, and the look on her face suggested that somebody had just pulled the mask off her husband's face, revealing a man she never knew existed, and a man she didn't like.

He said, "Margie, I...Do you want to go down with me?"

He held out his hand for her to take.

She didn't even look at it. She walked right by him.

He said, "Margie, wait."

She turned around and stared at him. Waiting for him to speak.

He didn't know what to say.

She said it for both of them. "A sick joke?" She shook her head in disgust. "You bastard."

And with that she walked down the steps to be with Jenny Cantrell.

***

When Paul was a cadet at the Academy, he had a Patrol Tactics instructor named Ernie Lambert who used to take a sick glee in telling the cadets what a stupid choice they had made in joining the Department.

"Three things are gonna happen to you your first year on the job," he said. Paul and the rest of his cadet class were in the courtyard while this was going on, the rain coming down in buckets on their back while they were knocking out pushups, Lambert walking between them under his umbrella. "Number one: you will buy a new truck. Number two: you will buy a new house. And number three: you will get a divorce. And trust me folks, Sweet Susie Rottencrotch will take everything you worked so hard for. This job is a bitch, gentlemen, and she does not allow you a mistress. Some of you will try to chase tail. Some of you ugly mutts might even catch some. But mind my words, you will find you have become a rocket with the jets burning at both ends. And the part in the middle? Well, that part's you, and that part just gets crushed. Why did you idiots take this job? Go on—leave! Get out while you can. Pack your shit and leave, you worthless piss ants!"

At the time Paul had thought the man was an asshole, nothing more. He did his pushups and yelled out his "Yes Sirs!" and "No Sirs!" at all the right times and just let what was said roll off his back like the rain.

He hadn't thought of Ernie Lambert since graduation, but this morning Ernie's three warnings were on his mind. They hummed around in his head like bees trapped in the wall. He had bought Rachel a new truck. They had moved into the new apartment on the second floor of that Craftsmen-style bungalow. That left what, a divorce? A week earlier, the thought never would have entered his mind. But today, walking across the parking lot toward the Oak Meadows Church of God, it suddenly seemed like a very real and very terrifying possibility.

He looked back over the events of the past few days and he felt like kicking himself for telling Rachel what he had seen. It would have been so much easier to lie. But he had been too naive in his belief that his absolute love for her would equal absolute trust in him on her part.

And that wasn't fair. He pictured the situation turned around the other way, him standing in Rachel's shoes, and he realized that it wasn't merely a case of him being too simple, or too naive. He had been a first rate asshole. All things considered, the silent treatment she gave him after he spilled his family baggage in her lap was pretty gracious. Probably better treatment than he would have given her.

He tried to take her hand in his, but she pulled away.

She wouldn't look at him, and Paul, not knowing what else to do with his hands, reached into his pocket and rubbed the Barber fifty cent piece, feeling the chips and cracks along its edges that had been worn smooth through years of contact with his fingers.

"Paul," Rachel said, "how come everybody else is wearing their long sleeves?"

He had already noticed that. He had noticed it as soon as he got out of the car. Every policeman he could see, and there had to be thousands of them, was wearing the long-sleeved Class A uniform. Most had the optional clip-on tie attached. Everybody wore their hats. But Paul was in his short-sleeves, the routine patrol utility uniform. It was clean and pressed, the creases in the sleeves sharp enough to cut paper, but it was still the wrong uniform, and Paul suddenly felt sick, like he had been exposed as an outsider, as somebody who didn't belong in *this* family, who didn't share their right to grieve the honored dead.

"Why didn't you wear your long sleeves?" Rachel whispered to him.

Some of the other officers were staring at him. Paul nodded back and tried to look natural.

"I didn't know," he said weakly.

Paul touched his fingers to the soot-colored mark on his forehead and he groaned. *This marks you. You don't choose this. It chooses you. And you have a charge to keep.*

For a moment, he thought he was going to be sick.

***

They saw Wes and Collins on their way to the church. Collins had a girl with him, a slim, pretty, dark-eyed blonde. Wes was by himself, hands in his pockets, hat cocked to one side. He looked bored.

Collins gestured at Paul's uniform. "What the fuck's that?"

"Yeah, yeah, I know."

"No, seriously, dude. What the fuck's that? Where's your Class A?"

"I didn't know we were supposed to wear it," Paul said. "Nobody told me."

Collins looked disgusted.

"Leave him be," Wes said.

"No way, fuck that," Collins said. "You always wear your Class A to funerals. Always." He turned to Paul and said, "They should have told you that at the Academy."

"Nobody told me. I'm sorry."

"Uh huh."

Paul reached for his Barber fifty cent piece. Wes patted him on the shoulder. "Don't worry about him. He's just pissed about Barris and Seles."

"What do you mean?" Paul said.

"You didn't hear?"

Paul shook his head.

"They're getting medals for meritorious conduct."

"Really? For what?"

Collins snorted.

Wes said, "A couple of weeks back they pulled up on this guy stopped in the middle of an intersection. He's had some kind of stroke. They pull him out and take turns doing CPR on him until they get a pulse back."

"Wow. They saved his life."

"Yeah, right," Collins said. "Dude died ten minutes later in the ambulance. They ought to call it the Nice Fucking Try Award."

Paul smiled. He looked at Rachel and saw she wasn't smiling. She looked uncomfortable, like it was causing her some effort to keep a friendly expression on her face.

"Rachel," Paul said, "this is George Collins and Wes Stokes. They work the district next to me and Mike."

Rachel smiled. "Hi," she said.

Wes and Collins nodded. Collins didn't bother to introduce his date.

"Say, you guys seen Mike out here anywhere?"

"Yeah," said Collins, "he's over there."

"Cool. I'm gonna introduce Rachel to Mike. I'll talk to you guys later, okay?"

Paul put his hand on the small of Rachel's back and they walked off to where Mike was standing, talking with Garwin and two other sergeants that Paul didn't recognize.

Rachel said, "Well, they were, uh, nice."

Paul laughed. "Yeah, well, Collins can be a little rough around the edges."

"Yeah," Rachel said.

They walked through the crowd, and Paul felt some of the hurt and anxiety leaving him. Her little show of affection towards him, letting him leave his hand there on her back, her warm smile as they walked together, had made him think that maybe they weren't as far apart as he'd feared. He smiled at her and then let his gaze wander over the crowd. There were a few faces he recognized, but not many. He nodded to the people he knew and to a few of the ones he didn't who made eye contact with him, and he started to relax.

And that's when he saw her, his mother.

She was standing still in a crowd of moving people. Officers and wives walked right by her, nobody noticing the rail skinny woman in the potato sack of a yellow dress with the haze of dust obscuring her face.

She was looking right at him, and that was what made Paul stop in his tracks. He could see her through the constantly shifting gaps in the crowd, and though he couldn't see her face, he knew who it was.

"Momma?"

She was trying to speak. Through the cloud of dust he could see her mouth moving, her body shaking with the effort to reach out to him. A group of sergeants stepped in front of him, blocking his view, and he half-stepped, half-pushed his way around them.

"Excuse me," the sergeant said, and gave Paul an irritated look, but Paul ignored him.

He walked towards his mother.

"Paul?"

Rachel had stopped. She was looking back at him now, and she looked confused. "Paul, where are you going?"

Paul's gaze was locked on his mother, trying to see her face behind that veil of dust. She looked so small, so cold, standing there with her pipe-cleaner arms hugging her chest. A strand of her long brown hair fell across her face and was lost in the swirling dust of her face.

Paul walked forward, and he might have been sleepwalking, or drugged, for all the attention he paid the crowd moving past him. She was speaking to him, her voice like a hiss of static, the words lost behind the blur, and at the sound of that familiar voice he felt some vital part of him going numb.

Whatever it was she was trying to say, she wasn't coming through. Paul could sense the effort, the desperate effort to push through the dust haze over her face. And then her head tilted forward and her whole body went into a stoop, like the effort was just too much and now she had nothing left.

"Momma," he said, and didn't bother to notice the officers around him cock their heads back in surprise. "Momma, no." But even as he closed in on her the crowds continued to cross in front of him, and when at last another gap opened, his mother was gone. Paul stood there, looking at the spot where she had been, and swallowed the lump in his throat.

What in the hell is going on?

"Paul?"

He turned away, feeling out of synch, like the world was moving too fast.

Rachel put a hand on his bicep. "Paul? You okay, baby?"

He blinked at her. She was looking into his eyes now, clearly worried.

"Why did you go off like that? Are you okay?"

He nodded. "Yeah," he said, and did the best smile he could muster. "Yeah, I'm fine now."

***

Later, after the service, Paul and Rachel were walking across the lawn towards the patrol car they'd been assigned for motorcade to the cemetery. Paul had taken his Barber from his pocket and was rolling it over the back of his knuckles. He was still thinking about his mother, how small and sad she looked, how she could even be there at all, and that numb feeling that had first started to spread inside him when he saw her in the crowd was still there. Was there something wrong with him? He wondered about it, and the Barber flashed back and forth across his knuckles.

They ran into Mike in the parking lot. He was talking and laughing with a few other guys. The bill of his peaked Patrol cap was pushed high up on his forehead, and he was wearing sunglasses. The glasses made his face look thinner, not as boyish-looking as Paul was used to seeing him, but the Class A uniform and black tie he wore couldn't obscure the width of his shoulders or the muscles in his arms. He still looked like a brown-haired tank.

Paul introduced him to Rachel and they shook hands all around.

Mike said, "Paul's told me a lot about you, Rachel. He said there's one and a half brains in your marriage, and he's got the half."

Rachel smiled and glanced at Paul, who was making an effort to look like everything was fine. He'd put up the Barber, at least.

"Paul's told me a lot about you, too," she said. "He says you're some kind of master practical joker."

"I disavow all knowledge of any practical jokes," he said. "Here at the San Antonio Police Department, we take this shit seriously."

"Spoken like a real public service announcement."

Mike slapped Paul on the shoulder and said, "Hey, she's good."

Paul nodded. He glanced at Rachel and saw her smile, and it was almost enough to put him at ease. She was truly beautiful. There were moments when he looked at her and was shocked at how beautiful she was. Her smiles were like finding money on the ground.

Mike said, "Hey, did you hear about Barris and Seles?"

"I heard they were getting a medal for meritorious conduct for doing CPR on somebody. Collins called it the Nice Try Award."

"Yeah, that about sums it up. Hey, listen, you mind if I ride with you guys to the cemetery."

Mike was glancing over Paul's shoulder, like he was expecting to hear a commotion at any minute.

"Why?" Paul said. "What did you do?"

"Well," Mike said, "you know those stink bombs? The ones in the foil packets with the vial inside, you bust it open—"

"I think I get it, yeah."

"Well, we probably ought to get going. Somebody might have, you know, set one off in Barris and Seles' car. Sitting out here in this heat I imagine it's probably gonna be pretty nasty-smelling in there."

"Nice," Paul said.

***

It took them twenty minutes to get out of the church parking lot, and there was still more than half the parking lot left to empty out behind them by the time they got on the road. Paul looked out the windshield and saw a long line of bumper-to-bumper police cars proceeding at a snail's pace down the road, all of them with their emergency lights flashing. In the rearview mirror, the line was even longer. Traffic officers were stationed at the intersections along the route to the cemetery, and at one point Paul saw them bring traffic to a stop, spin on their heels, snap to attention, and cut crisp salutes as the widows' cars drove by. He was baking in this heat, even though he was wearing short sleeves and had the air conditioner blowing full blast. He could only imagine what those guys were going through, directing traffic in their Class As and black gloves.

Rachel watched one of the Traffic guys as they rolled through the intersection, and she said, "*Put crepe bows round the white necks of the public doves. Let the traffic policemen wear black cotton gloves.*"

"Huh?" Paul said.

"It's a line from a poem by W.H. Auden," she said. "I always thought the white and the black in that line was just a symbol of his grief. I didn't know they really wore black gloves."

"They don't, usually," said Mike from the backseat. He had given up the front seat to Rachel so she could sit next to Paul while he drove. He said, "Most of the time they wear orange or green glow-in-the-dark gloves. Or none at all. Today is special."

"Oh," said Rachel.

There was a long moment of quiet, the only sound that of the straining air conditioner and the faint whir of the lightbar on top of the car.

But then Rachel turned to Mike in the backseat and said, "You're gonna take care of my husband, aren't you Mike?"

"Rachel," Paul said.

Rachel ignored him. Still looking at Mike she said, "You will, won't you?"

"Sure," Mike said. "But you know, Paul doesn't have as much to worry about as you think. He's got good instincts. He knows when to keep his mouth shut. A lot of officers, they get in trouble because they let their pride get in the way of their common sense. It's easy to do. Hell, I've done it before. But not Paul. He knows when it's best to just shut up and let it roll off his back."

"Like how? Give me an example."

"Rachel, come on," Paul said.

She turned almost all the way around to face Mike. "Let him talk, Paul. I want to hear what my husband is like on patrol."

Mike said, "Oh crap. Sorry, buddy."

"Yeah right," Paul said.

"Tell me," Rachel said. "Paul says you've got a story about just about everybody on the Department. I bet you've got one on Paul."

Mike laughed. "Yeah, all right. The other night. We arrested this crazy lady for throwing goat's blood all over this other lady. He tell you about that?"

Rachel shook her head. "Goat's blood?"

"It was pretty gross. Anyway, Paul gets her in the car, and the whole time this woman is telling him all sorts of stuff about how he's been marked and how he has a charge to keep and all this other witch crap. I swear I was ready to brake check her, you know? Slam on the brakes and let her take a face-first dive into the prisoner cage. But not Paul. He just reaches up and closes the vent window, lets it all roll off his back." He leaned forward and gave Paul a slap on the shoulder. "You're doin' good, buddy."

He smiled at Rachel and went back to looking out the window.

Rachel slid back down into her seat and spent a few moments looking at her hands folded in her lap. Then she turned to Paul. Paul stared back at her, and he could almost read her thoughts in her eyes. *That's what you said to me the other night. What your father told you, that you have a charge to keep. It can't be true, can it?*

***

They arrived at the San Antonio Municipal Cemetery some twenty minutes later and shuffled to the graveside. A tent had been placed over a row of chairs so that the widows and their families could sit in the shade and listen to the service and be close by to receive the neatly folded flag handed to them by the chief.

Paul stood between Rachel and Mike, shuffling uncomfortably beneath the relentlessly bright sun that burned the back of his neck. He could smell Rachel's perfume, and that was nice. But he could also smell all the other bodies crammed in around them, and that wasn't so nice. He touched Rachel's hand and she closed her fingers around his. He looked down at her, and she smiled back at him and gave his hand a little squeeze.

There was a breeze moving through the trees, but it was barely strong enough to jostle the leaves. Paul looked out over the endless stretch of white marble grave markers, and he remembered the funerals he had attended for both his parents. Both were miserable, quiet affairs, with only a priest and one or two local folks there to show their support for Paul, nothing at all like the very public show that this double funeral was designed to be. The little country graveyard where his parents were buried could probably fit in one small corner of this place. And yet, for all the added show, for all the pomp and circumstance and size of the spectacle, it was just as quiet here as it had been at both of his parents' funerals. There was an occasional cough. Sometimes a baby would cry. But for the most part, it was silent. Everywhere he looked Paul saw people with their heads turned down to their feet. A few had their eyes closed. Others were murmuring prayers.

And then one of the chaplains was speaking again.

"From the Gospel of Matthew," he said, his voice carrying easily in the still air. "And if I have prophetic powers, and understand all mysteries and all knowledge, and if I have all faith, so as to remove mountains, but have not love, I am nothing."

Paul found himself drifting, partly out of tiredness, partly out of distraction. The image of his father in that Mexican motel room flared up in his mind. He saw the man leaning over a muddy toilet and screaming in pain as he tried to pee because he had thought the combination of hallucinogenic wild mushrooms and peyote and a whore's crotch would force open the doors to perception. Paul wondered what would make a man crave knowledge like that, like he wanted it more than he wanted his own life. It was a dangerous question, he knew; for once he understood that impulse, once he knew what had driven his father to be the kind of man he was, to make the kind of choices that he had made, he would understand the man. And Paul had enough sense to know that understanding is the same thing as becoming. Understand the man, become the man.

You have a charge to keep.

The chaplain went on. "Love is patient and kind. Love is not jealous or boastful. Love does not insist on its own way. It does not rejoice at wrong, but rejoices in the right. Love bears all things, believes all things, hopes all things, endures all things."

Out of the corner of his eye, Paul saw the color guard readying their rifles for the salute. He saw the line of chiefs standing by patiently, ready to offer their sympathy and support to the sobbing widows.

Paul squeezed Rachel's hand. She had seen them, too, for Paul heard her gasp, and when he looked at her, he saw a woman whose sensibilities had just been fiercely shaken.

"Oh my God," she whispered under her breath. She was looking at Herrera's two year old son, standing next to his mother. Somebody had dressed him in a miniature version of his daddy's uniform, and he stood stiffly, picking at the seat of his pants, uncomfortable in the heat and mystified by the spectacle going on around him.

He turned slightly and tugged at the hem of his mom's dress, and Rachel clapped her hand over her mouth.

"Love never ends," said the chaplain. "When I was a child, I spoke like a child, I thought like a child, I reasoned like a child. But when I became a man, I gave up childish ways. For now we see through a glass, darkly, but then face to face. Now I know in part, but then I shall know even as I am known. And now abideth faith, hope, and charity, these three, but the greatest of these is charity."

There was a stir as the color guard called out their commands. At the first volley, Rachel jumped.

Paul looked at her and saw she was crying.

The color guard fired twice more, and both times Rachel jumped.

***

When the service ended, the assembled crowd moved as a slow, somber wave across the lawn of the cemetery towards their cars. Rachel had stopped crying. She had retreated inward again, though this time Paul knew it wasn't because of him, and he felt a little ashamed at himself for feeling glad about that.

Paul remembered a time when he and Rachel were in bed one night in the little house on Huisache, watching a documentary on JFK. The show replayed the famous scene of John F. Kennedy Jr., a toddler of maybe two or three at the time, coming to attention and saluting his father's casket as it passed by. The scene had made Rachel groan in her pity for the boy, and she had said something under her breath about the sadness the boy had just inherited. Paul thought back on that moment now, and he thought of Herrera's little boy, and he thought he understood exactly what she had meant that night.

And then somebody bumped his shoulder, hard. He turned, an annoyed expression on his face, and was shocked to see Magdalena Chavarria standing there in a simple black dress, a black shawl draped over her shoulders. She didn't speak, but she did stuff a note into his hand. Paul looked down at it, a simple piece of folded-over white paper no bigger than a bookmark, and back to Magdalena. But she was gone that fast. She just melted into the crowd.

"Paul?" Rachel said.

The crowd was trying to move around him, but they were packed in shoulder to shoulder, and he got bumped more than a few times.

"Paul?"

He looked down at the paper and opened it. Eight words were printed there. Just eight words, but they took his breath away.

Come see me. I can answer your questions.

"Paul?"

He looked at the paper, then folded it over and stuffed it into his pocket.

"Coming," he said.

Chapter 15

Paul and Rachel sat at the little folding card table in their kitchen. Rachel was drinking a cup of coffee, Paul a glass of milk. The morning sun was coming in through the windows, and as Paul looked across the room towards their bed the stillness of the place irritated him. He was covered in sweat and dust from his shift the night before, and he was exhausted. Between the funeral the day before and working all night he had slept little. And yet, for as tired as he felt, he was still restless. He felt like there was something calling to him, waiting for him, only it was too faint, too distant to get his mind around.

"That thing on your forehead still worries me," Rachel said.

"Hmmm?"

"That bruise. Shouldn't it have started to get a little better by now? It's been a week."

"I don't know," he said. "It doesn't hurt."

"Yeah I know, but...Paul?"

"Hmmm?"

"Are you listening to me?"

"Yeah," he said, though in his head he was miles away, thinking about the past. "It doesn't hurt, Rachel. I promise it doesn't."

"Okay." She sipped her coffee and watched him. "Paul?" she said.

"Yeah?"

"I was thinking about what Mike told us in the car. That woman you arrested?"

He looked at her.

"Magdalena Chavarria."

"Is that her name?"

"Yes."

Rachel looked down at her coffee. "That woman said you have a charge to keep. Was that what she said? Those were her exact words?"

Paul didn't say anything.

"What does that mean, Paul?"

"It doesn't mean anything," he said. "Like Mike said, she's just a crazy old lady."

"But you said...Isn't that what you told me your dad said when you...when you saw him in that...?"

He just stared at her. He wasn't trying to make this difficult for her, but he couldn't do anything about the way it was unfolding either. There was so much she didn't know, even after all he had said to her. And he wasn't even sure it made sense to him. As soupy as his head was, he could probably babble on for a million years and not get any closer to explaining it for her.

"Paul, I want to talk to you about this. I think it's fair for you to know that I just can't make myself believe it. I want to believe what you've told me, but it's just so...so strange." She waited a beat, then said, "I have to go to work now, but I want to talk to you, Paul. Can we talk tonight, before you go to work?"

"Sure," he said. He traced the curve of her face, the delicate point of her chin. "Sure," he said. "Tonight. We'll talk then."

***

Paul watched her go through the kitchen window. He had the Barber in his hand and he was practicing a few simple vanishings. Down below Rachel paused and looked up towards the window. She raised one hand in a wave that seemed hesitant, almost cautious, then turned and got into her pickup and backed out. He listened to the sound of her pickup accelerating into traffic, and when that sound was gone, he got up, crossed the apartment to the bed, and began to peel off his sweat-soaked uniform.

He took a shower, and though it felt good to clean off the grime of the east side, it didn't do anything to settle the restlessness that filled him. He thought about eating something. Some fried chicken maybe. But he knew it wasn't food he wanted. What he really wanted was to feel the way he'd felt during his vision of his father in Mexico. He wanted to experience more of that bond with the man that he realized he was only now starting to get to know. And wasn't that funny? Paul had to kill the man to understand him.

No, he thought, correcting himself, *No, that really isn't all that funny. None of it is. Not all the death. Not the confusion. Not the fear. Not the unknowing. None of it is all that funny.*

He put on a pair of boxer shorts and a t-shirt, then went around the apartment turning on the box fans that he and Rachel had started using because the air conditioner just couldn't be counted on anymore. Rachel said she woke up four or five times a night because of how hot she got. During the day he sometimes had to go to the kitchen and put a wet rag in the freezer box so he could put it on his forehead while he slept. The landlord had promised to get the unit fixed, but so far they were still baking.

Once he had a good cross breeze working through the apartment he went back to the recliner next to the bed and put the box of stuff from his father's house on the floor in front of him. He went through the contents one by one, taking each picture out and holding it in his hands, waiting for that certain image to rent the veil between this world and the other, the one where his father waited. He paused for a long time over the picture that had set his last vision in motion, the one of his father and mother and him on his mother's hip in front of the house in Smithson Valley, and when nothing happened he grew irritated with himself, angry that he wasn't doing something he was supposed to know how to do.

"What is it?" he asked. "What's wrong?"

Finally, frustrated, he tossed the pictures back in the box and kicked it away from him. The box slid across the hardwood floor and struck the wall, where it made a small, dark hole.

"No," he said, thinking about the three hundred and fifty dollar security deposit they wouldn't be getting back now. "No."

He crossed the floor to the box and pushed it aside. Then he probed the hole in the wall with his fingers and was surprised at how mushy the drywall felt. Almost like it was rain-sodden.

"Fuck," he said. Then, almost shouting it, "Fuck! Stupid, stupid, stupid."

Wait. Maybe I can fix it.

He threw on a pair of jeans and went down to his truck to get his toolbox. When he came back up he sat Indian style on the floor in front of the hole and opened the toolbox. He pushed a hammer and some screwdrivers aside, looking for a retractable blade. But when he picked up a battered old Craftsman socket wrench, he went numb.

He raised it to eye level and saw "M.H." scratched into the handle. His father's wrench. He swallowed the lump that had formed in his throat, and when the world around him started to turn hazy and dark and a different world began to take its place, Paul Henninger smiled and let it come.

***

It took him a moment to realize where he was. The floor beneath him was a metal mesh catwalk. The walls were not walls, but metal railings. Metal pipes crisscrossed above him, throwing striped shadows across the catwalk. Ahead of him the catwalk joined with the floor of a large, circular chamber. Paul heard the sounds of men working, voices yelling on the catwalks around him, heavy trucks straining in low gear down below him. The smokestacks gave it away. He could see them peeking out over the rim of the chamber ahead of him and to the left, and he realized this was the Morgan Rollins Iron Works—not as he knew it, but as it had once been.

228 | Joe McKinney

A transistor radio was playing one of his favorite songs, The Steve Miller Band's "The Joker," and it brought a smile to his face. He followed the music into the chamber and saw a big diesel generator hunkered down in the middle of the room like a sleeping dinosaur. Machine parts were scattered everywhere. The place smelled like dust and oil, but it wasn't an unpleasant smell. Sunlight filled every corner of the room, but it wasn't hot. It felt like springtime.

He caught a flash of movement and saw a man's legs sticking out from under the generator, black slacks and black Red Wing boots. A black Stetson leaned against the man's narrow hips.

"Daddy," Paul said.

There was no fear. Not this time. He knew the man couldn't see him, couldn't hear him. Whatever was about to happen was for his benefit, but he was not an active player in the show. He was a ghost in a theater.

Martin Henninger worked on the generator with calm, steady determination. Paul knelt by his father's hat and watched him work the wrench onto a bolt and dog it down, and he could almost hear the man's mantra of *You do one thing at a time and you do it until it's done; you try to do more than one thing at a time, nothing gets done* in every swing of his elbow. Growing up, his father had worked that philosophy into him with the same relentless single-mindedness with which he did everything in his life. It didn't matter if he was eating fried chicken or reseating a cylinder. It was always the same. *How do you eat an elephant? You take it one bite at a time.*

Now Paul sat watching him, remembering the things he told him, and he wondered why it had taken him so long to appreciate the man's ability to focus, his gift of being able to immerse himself in a problem for as long as it took to reason it out. He was a man to whom distraction was a cardinal sin, willpower a religion.

But then Martin Henninger's concentration broke. Paul saw it happen, and for a moment he was terrified. His father's gaze left the tool in his hand and seemed to lock with his own. His expression turned hard, almost violent. He grabbed a bar above his head and pulled himself out from under the generator, still looking right at Paul.

No, not right at me. Through me.

Paul rocked back on his heels and then rose to his feet. He backed away hurriedly as his father got to his feet. Martin Henninger stepped into the space where Paul had just been standing and stopped. He looked one way and then the other. The Steve Miller Band faded out and Janice Joplin's "Me and Bobby McGee" started up. Martin Henninger reached over to the radio and turned it down.

"What is that?" he said, and turned to face the ground behind Paul.

Paul spun around. Skeins of dust were moving over the chamber floor, curling around one another like fine silk scarves caught in the wind. Paul watched the dust take shape, saw it settle onto the floor and form an unmistakable image. It was his own face he saw, but his face as he had been twenty years earlier, a boy of four.

His father stepped past him, eyes fixed on the image.

"Paul," he said.

Paul looked at his father, and he saw the man's eyes had rolled up into his head. His hands fell to his side and the wrench he held slipped from his fingertips and clattered to the metal floor.

"What does this mean?" Paul asked.

At first there was no sound but the breeze through the superstructure, the distant, muted voices of men working. But then Martin Henninger began to mutter, and Paul turned to face him.

He was rocking on the balls of his feet, his upper body moving in a circular sway. His lips moved, but the sounds weren't in English. They weren't Spanish either. He continued to sway, and soon he was moving in such large circles that Paul couldn't stop himself. He reached for his father and grabbed his shoulder.

The feeling was like putting his finger into a light socket—so much power, so much energy concentrated in one blast. He felt his body go numb and his bowels nearly let go, but somehow he kept his feet.

He staggered backwards. His eyelids fluttered. He looked at his father. And then his father turned and looked at him.

"Paul?" his father said.

"Daddy? You can see me?"

His father nodded.

"It's me," Paul said. "I saw it, there in the sand. It's not you...it's me. I'm the one that's supposed to..."

"Yes," Martin Henninger said. "You see it."

"Yes."

"I didn't understand when she first told me, all those years ago in Mexico. I was vain. I thought I was the one. But it was always you. I was meant to keep the power burning. But you are the one who is meant to wield it. Do you know what that means, Paul?"

Paul shook his head. He was too stunned to speak.

"You'll be able to see into men's souls. You will know their fears and desires like they were written on their face. No one will ever be able to hide the truth from you. Men will be drawn to you like a lodestar. I spent my life trying to see what lies beyond the doors to perception. But I was never meant to see that country. It was meant for you."

"My inheritance," Paul said, his voice barely a whisper.

"And your charge. You'll make a kingdom of this world."

Paul looked at him intently, and it was like he was seeing the man for the first time. "You knew, Daddy. You knew about this the night that I...that I..." He swallowed. "Daddy, why? Why did it have to be this way?"

Martin Henninger touched his chest where the aerator's spikes had pierced him and black soot poured from his fingertips.

"Do you see this soot, Paul? Every time I appear to you, a little more of me burns away. I can't hold the gates open for long."

"Just tell me why, Daddy. Why did you have to die?"

"I can't tell you everything, Paul. I had to learn it on my own. You do, too."

"I don't understand, Daddy. I want you back."

"I could tell you what I know, but you wouldn't understand it. That's the whole point, Paul. Knowledge without experience is impossible. Do you understand that? Paul, you're meant to do some great things, but you won't be able to get any of it done if you don't learn how the power works. There's only one way to do that, and that's the hard way. The way I learned it."

"Daddy..."

But there was nothing else. The world melted away in a flash of daylight...

***

...and became the living room of the family ranch house in Smithson Valley. His parents were standing just inside the doorway that led to the kitchen, and Paul could tell by their faces that they had been arguing.

"And what are we supposed to do for money while you're hanging around the house all day?" his mother said. She was staring at his father with wide, unblinking eyes. Her mouth was set in a stern thin line, and there was a forcefulness to her that shocked Paul. He had never seen her like this, so solid, so totally unafraid, not a trace of fragility. "Huh? Did you think about that?"

"Money ain't gonna be a problem," his father said. "The land's all paid for. We ain't got nothing but the county taxes, and that ain't nothing with our agricultural exemption. We can make it work on what we get from the peach crop during the summer."

"And food? Electricity? We got bills to pay, Martin. You didn't think about that when you quit your job, did you? How are we gonna put food on the table?"

"We ain't gonna starve, Carol."

His mother waited, her hands balled into fists and resting on her hips.

"That's it?" she said. "We ain't gonna starve. That's the best you got? Martin, you aren't a bachelor any more. You got me. You got that boy out there."

"It's for him that I'm doing it, Carol."

"For him? What the hell does that mean? This home and this land, they're his birthright. You're gonna risk losing his birthright for him? You tell me if that makes sense to you. Huh, does it?"

"I made my decision, Carol. This is the way it's gonna be."

"Oh, okay. That's great, Martin. Fuckin' fantastic."

She reached behind her back and untied the apron she wore. She pulled it off and folded it and put it in a cupboard next to the stove. Then she fell back against the wall and ran her hands over her face.

Martin Henninger walked through the kitchen and leaned against the doorway that led outside. Paul walked up beside him and looked out the doorway. What he saw there took his breath away. It was him. It was Paul at four, playing in the cheatgrass that came up to the middle of his thighs. He had a stick in one hand and he was using it to slash at the tops of the grass like it was a pirate's cutlass.

"So much depends on that boy," he said to himself.

Carol Henninger looked at her husband, made a disgusted noise, and turned away.

Paul watched her, still shocked at the obvious strength in the woman. He reached back into his memories but couldn't think of a time she had looked so well put together. In his mind, she was always the frail little stick of a woman who lived in the shadows of their home, too fragile to step into the light. What happened to her? he wondered. Why did she change?

His father stiffened beside him. Paul turned around and looked at him, then turned to where he was looking, at his younger self playing in the grass.

"Paul, get over here! Now!"

Martin Henninger jumped down the concrete steps onto the grass and ran for his son, yelling his name the whole way.

Paul followed him, though he couldn't see what had excited the man so much. His father was sprinting at full speed now. Behind him, Paul saw his mother coming down the steps. Her expression was stricken with panic.

He heard his younger self let out a high-pitched yelp, and then he was tripping over his feet and screaming as he tried to dodge something on the ground at his feet. Watching the scene, Paul felt his gut tighten. He knew what this was. He remembered now. He remembered the snake, the way it kept coming after him, the dusky gray of its body in a constant state of unfolding. He remembered the milky pink of its open mouth.

And with the memory he felt himself back there in that time, moving like a dancer to get his feet away from the charging snake. He felt his father's iron grip on his shoulder. He felt—not remembered, but felt—his father lift him off the ground and move him out of the way. Paul watched the man from the boy's eyes, watched his father put himself between the child and the snake. He looked into his father's eyes and saw fear and anger and love all in one hard glare.

"Goddamn it, boy!" Martin Henninger shouted. "Damn it. Get your ass inside. Move!"

Paul staggered backwards, and as he did, he watched his father reach down into the grass and come up with the snake. He held the limp animal by its middle, doubled over like it was a rope. The thing had to be six feet in length and as thick around as Paul's thigh, but in his father's fist it was docile.

His father turned to him, the snake hanging from his fist. "I told you to get inside, boy. Move your ass."

"But Daddy..."

"Move!"

The boy turned and ran to his mother. He ran into the house at full speed and threw his hands around her. She put an arm down across his back and stroked his shoulder while she watched her husband walking down the white dirt road that led out to the horse pasture.

"Come on inside," his mother said. "I'll make you some dinner."

She led him inside and he followed her without another word. Paul stood near the back door, watching them, watching his mother as she moved through the kitchen, gathering up flour and salt and an egg and a big, ancient-looking chef's knife. They had had chicken fried steak that night. He remembered that clear as a bell. He didn't know how he knew that, but he did.

His father was coming back up the road now, and he was carrying sticks. Lots of them. Paul watched him come on to the house, watched him carry the sticks inside. There was a skein of baling wire wrapped around his fist.

"What are you making for dinner?" he asked.

"Chicken fried steak and mashed potatoes."

"How long's that gonna take."

"I don't know. Forty-five minutes maybe."

Martin Henninger grunted, then walked into the living room, where he dropped the sticks and the baling on the floor. He came back to the kitchen then and said, "Paul, you hurry up with your dinner. I want you in bed early tonight. You hear me?"

"Yes, Daddy."

He grunted again, then went back outside for more sticks.

Paul watched the man walk away, the bill of his Stetson like a black halo in the fading evening sunlight, and he realized that he remembered what came next. This was the night his mother had told him it was best to steer clear of Daddy when he got this way. That it was best for everybody if he didn't bother his Daddy while he assembled his stick lattices. This was the night Paul stayed awake in anticipation, the night he came down in the middle of the night to see what the fuss was all about and saw the man with his eyes rolled back up into his head, an unknown language on his murmuring lips.

***

Darkness fell around him. He was standing on the bottom stair of the house in Smithson Valley. The kitchen was dark. So too was the flight of stairs leading up to his room. From around the corner, in the living room, he heard the sound of his father mumbling, the faint clatter of oak sticks fitted together and tied with baling wire.

He heard the stairs creaking above him. He turned and saw himself at four, a bright, mischievous glint in his eyes as he quietly walked down the stairs. The adult Paul stepped into the kitchen. Off to his left he could see his father working on the lattice, rocking back and forth in the dark, mumbling to himself. Even in the dark he could see the man's eyes were turned up into his skull, his hands working independently, as though they were on remote control. The murmuring stopped. His mouth stayed open in an O.

Four-year-old Paul stepped into the kitchen. He was barefoot, wearing a t-shirt and his underwear. He stepped into the kitchen and stopped.

"Daddy?" he said, and Paul thought, *Freaked out, definitely freaked out.*

Martin Henninger turned to face the boy, and the boy started to scream loud enough to fill the whole house with his fear. Paul watched the boy scramble up the stairs to his room, ass over elbows, just like he remembered. He would be up there for the rest of the night, hugging his knees and shaking.

But it was the adult Paul that got the real shock. His father was standing inches from his shoulder, eyes still turned up into his skull, and there was a humming noise coming from somewhere deep down in his throat. Paul gasped and fell back, and for a second he was unable to catch his breath.

He said, "Daddy, holy—"

But the shock faded fast. What took its place was a vaguely familiar giddiness, like the thrill he used to feel just before he took the field back when he was playing football. He was nervous, but not scared.

He recognized the word struggling to take shape in his father's humming. The word was *build.*

Build it, Paul. You know how.

And he did know how. He knew exactly what to do.

***

Paul went down to his truck and got some baling wire from the cab. He wrapped the baling wire around his fist and went into the yard and gathered together a bundle of sticks.

Upstairs, he put the sticks in a pile on the floor between the bed and

Rachel's boxes of paperbacks and sat down Indian-style in front of them. For a moment he was confused, unfocused, but then he realized that he was trying too hard to make something happen. He stopped, took a deep breath, and let that part of his mind go. He put his hands down into his lap and thought about breathing.

In and out, in and out. Just let it come.

And it did come. His head rolled back on his shoulders and his mouth fell open and his hands started to move on their own.

A hot breeze touched his face and he opened his eyes. He tasted dust. He was standing on a limestone outcropping, looking down over a vast desert plain of caramel-colored sand and scraggly vegetation. The ground shook beneath him. In the distance, a wall of static energy rushed towards him, eating up the desert and the sky at a speed almost too fast for his mind to absorb. Miles of desert disappeared in seconds. The entire summit of the sky melted into a roaring, frenetic static. The wall stopped just beyond his reach, and he stood like a primitive man at the foot of an advancing glacier, looking up at the ice walls of its world-destroying face.

He stepped forward and put a hand into the wall. Light and energy slipped through his fingers like sand. He turned his hand over and stared at the grains of light pooling in his palm and all at once he saw the pieces of the puzzle coming together, the big picture forming into a coherent whole. He saw his father unable to cross over, unable to hold the door open between his world and Paul's. He saw Magdalena Chavarria in her home, small and alone before a force she had never truly understood. She was scared, confused, terrified by the things Paul's father had made her do. She was working against him, doing everything she could to keep the doors between the worlds closed.

And Paul could also see into the years ahead. He could see himself as his father had described him, a lodestar to men, a light to shine into the corners of even the darkest minds. He saw himself as a latter day Jeremiah, a prophet turning a hard eye on the destruction of one world and the birth of a new one.

He was aroused by the destruction. But he was not without love for what was lost.

All things in balance.

***

When Rachel walked in the door to the apartment she was aware of three things more or less at the same time. The first was the unbearable heat of the place. It was like stepping into an oven. As soon as she opened the door she got a blast of it in her face and she thought, *The air conditioner's out again. Goddamn this place.*

The second thing she noticed was the curious stick lattice next to her bed. It was a beach ball-sized collection of oak twigs lashed together into a shape that seemed to defy any readily discernible purpose. They jutted away from each other in odd directions, like an erector set put together by a brilliant, but insane, child. Had she encountered it in a museum, she might have thought it a weak example of modern art, some vaguely humorous attempt to merge the abstract sculptures of Charles O. Perry and Bathsheba Grossman. But here, in her apartment, it seemed grotesque. And a little frightening.

But the third thing she noticed was really the thing that tilted her over the edge. It was Paul, in his jeans and a loose t-shirt, his hair all over the place as though air dried after a shower. He was shining. There was no other word for it than that. Looking at him, she could see a glow coming off his skin. She thought of Claire Danes in the movie version of Neil Gaiman's *Stardust*, light emanating from her skin. Though unlike Danes, it was not beauty that caused him to shine. He was shining from love and joy and pride, but it from violence, and the end of things. The apocalypse shining forth from the face of a man.

"Paul?"

He blinked, then looked at her. "Hey, you're home."

"Yeah," she said. "Are you...okay?"

"I'm fine."

"What are you doing on the floor?"

He nodded to himself. He said, "I made this today."

"Yeah, I noticed. Um, what did you do today?"

"Just this."

"Oh. Did you sleep?"

He didn't answer.

She said, "It's hot in here. Did the landlord call today?"

"No."

"Oh. You didn't happen to call him, did you?"

"No."

She waited for more. She hoped for more, something to break the weirdness of the moment.

Nothing came.

"Paul?"

He almost snapped his answer at her. "What?"

The suddenness of it surprised her. She stepped inside and put her purse on the bookshelf near the door. The shine in his face was going away, but she could still see it, and he was still sitting on the floor. He wasn't looking at her.

"Did you think about what you want for dinner?"

"No."

"Oh, okay. Do you want to go someplace? We haven't been to dinner in a while."

"I don't care," he said. "I'm not hungry."

"Oh."

He rose from the floor and dropped into his favorite recliner. She crossed the living room and sat on the edge of the bed. She hadn't planned on discussing this so bluntly. Her idea of how it would go was more subtle. She would come in to the apartment and get dressed into something more comfortable, jeans and a light blouse maybe. They would sit next to one another on the couch. She would hold his hands in hers. She would say something like, "Paul, I've been thinking about this all day, and I have to tell you, I just don't believe in ghosts. I don't know if you do or not, but I know that you've told me you've seen your father. You've told me he's killed somebody. That black boy in the train car. I'll be as honest as I can be and say I don't believe that. I'm not calling you a liar, but I just don't believe the dead walk beside us. I don't believe they hurt people. But that doesn't mean there isn't some other explanation. Tell me everything. Maybe together we can figure it out."

Her days were spent filing billing statements at the dentist's office where she worked. It was mindless work. She could turn off all but one percent of her brain and still look like the best bill-filer in the business. Normally she thought of anything else but work. She and her friends laughed about their stupid husbands or their thoughtless boyfriends or books they were reading or patients who deserved the toothaches they got because they were such assholes, but all day long she had been thinking about that speech. She had worked it out, more or less word for word, hoping it would be enough to get Paul talking. Sometimes he was so hard to get talking.

But now, in the face of his complete disinterest in her, all that came out was, "Paul, can we talk about what you told me? You know, about your father?"

He said, "You know what, I am kind of hungry. Make me some fried chicken."

That caught her off guard. She said, "What?"

"Fried chicken. You know, a little egg, a little flour. You fry it up in some oil."

"Um, yeah," she said. "I know."

"Good. Make me some chicken."

"O-okay," she said. "Sure, Paul. Anything you want."

He turned away from her.

She said, "Paul, I'm sorry. I didn't mean to—"

"Just make me the fucking chicken," he roared. He stood up and glared at her. When she didn't move, he waved her off with a disgusted flick of his hand. "Goddamn it, Rachel. It ain't that fucking hard. You complain about the goddamn air conditioner. You complain that I never take you out to eat. For fuck's sake. Do me a favor, would you? You wanna fucking complain? Go outside and tell it to the wall so I don't have to fucking listen to you."

Rachel was so stunned she couldn't answer him.

He gave her another disgusted glare, then crossed to the little closet next to the bathroom door and took down a fresh uniform.

"Where are you going?" she asked.

"I'm goin' to work."

"Paul, it's not even six thirty. You don't have to be at work until—"

"I'm going to work," he said.

And then he shouldered his uniform, took up his gun belt and boots, and walked right out the door.

Rachel watched him go, speechless.

Chapter 16

Paul stood beside a junked Buick in the vacant lot next to Magdalena's house. From where he was he could see her moving around inside through one of her kitchen windows. She was pacing her floor, grinding her hands together, looking like someone who has realized too late that they are in far over their heads.

Off to the west the sky was the color of rust and copper. Dust tails curled over the cracked and wrinkled street. Paul had the sensation of standing outside himself, almost as though he was floating above his body, watching what happened with a drugged disinterest. He wanted to pull himself loose from what was happening, but it was so hard. He felt so sleepy, and it was so easy to just float and watch and not fight.

Inside the house, Magdalena was moving from the living room, towards the front door, and out of sight. When she reappeared, she went to the window in the kitchen and looked outside. She was definitely expecting something.

"Time to go," a voice inside his head said.

***

Paul slipped over the hurricane fence that surrounded Magdalena's backyard and walked through her herd of goats on his way to the backdoor. Male goats piss on each other's heads as a show of dominance, and the urine smell was strong here. These were Angora goats exactly like the kind his family had raised, though the pen these goats were kept in was much smaller than the one his family had used on their farm. The goats had eaten all the grass from the ground and there was a muddy pit in the middle of their pen. They had been rolling in the pit, and the goats that watched him cross the yard to the house were crusty with dried mud. He cooed at them to keep them quiet, looked around to make sure no one was watching, then knocked gently on the door.

He had heard Magdalena moving around inside, pacing the hardwood floors of her living room, but when he knocked that noise stopped. He reached out with his mind and was surprised by what he could see. She was in there, her fingers touching her lips, her eyes darting this way and that like a mouse in a room full of sleeping cats, and he could see it all as clearly as if she had been standing right in front of him, no door in between.

He knocked again.

When she didn't answer, he jumped the fence and crossed to the kitchen window that had given him such a good view of her before. She was standing there, watching the backdoor in exactly the same pose as he'd seen her in his mind. He knocked on the glass with the backs of his knuckles and watched her jump. She stared at him through the glass, and though there was recognition on her face, it was like her feet were nailed to the floor.

Paul glanced towards the street. Earlier, there had been a two- or three-year-old little boy out there, playing with an empty beer bottle in a weedpatch yard. Now, there was an ancient looking heroin junkie staggering down the sidewalk. He couldn't see the kid.

He turned back to Magdalena and said, "Open the door."

She nodded and made for the front of the house.

He tapped the glass again with his knuckles and said, "The backdoor."

"Oh," she said, and turned around and went to the back of the house.

A moment later, Paul was standing in her living room.

***

She was a nervous wreck. She paced and muttered and squeezed her hands together like she was trying to scrub them clean. Paul sat on her couch, leaning back casually, one leg crossed over the knee of the other, watching her. With every step she took he felt his feelings hardening towards her. More and more of his father was seeping into him, taking control of the situation, and as that happened, Paul began to lose interest in what was about to happen to her.

"You said you could answer my questions," he said. "You mind sitting down to do that? You're making me dizzy."

"Oh. Yes. Yes, of course."

She pulled up a chair and sat down in front of him. She wore a purple blouse and brown pants with a frayed and muddied hem, like they were too long for her. Her face was round and splotchy with pencil eraser-sized blemishes. Deep crease lines were etched into the corners of her eyes. Her lips looked gray. Paul supposed he could still see traces of the girl in the red dress that had come to the Mexican motel room all those years ago, but only with effort.

"The last few days have been hard on you," he said. Not a question.

She nodded. "Yes, very hard."

"It shows in your face. When I saw you at the funeral you didn't look this way."

"Much has happened," she said.

Paul picked at a loose piece of skin at the corner of his thumbnail. He said, "You told me you had answers. What kind of questions am I supposed to ask you?"

"You have had the visions, yes?"

"A few, yes. I know how you know my father, if that's what you mean."

"You know that I was raised by my Abuela, my grandmother."

"The woman with the rattlesnake. Yes, I know."

Magdalena sounded alarmed at that. "You have seen her with the snake?"

"In a dream, yes. I saw her. She was trying to hand me a live snake. She was speaking a language I didn't recognize."

"Oh. I didn't know."

He shrugged.

"It is true then." There was awe and terror in her eyes. "You are meant to inherit this power."

"That's what I'm told."

"Paul, I am very scared. Your father possesses great power. Power far beyond my own. Even from the grave he is powerful. But your father is a dark man, Paul. A bad man. I think he has corrupted the power that he inherited from my Abuela, the power he intends to pass on to you. He is using what he knows to do horrible things."

Paul sighed. "What are you saying, Magdalena? My dad is Darth Vader?"

"I...I do not understand."

"You know, big dude, black helmet, sounds like James Earl Jones? Is that what you're trying to say, that my dad is strong in the dark ways of the force? I guess that makes me Luke. Who does that make you? Are you supposed to be my Obi-wan Kenobi or my Yoda?"

She looked thoroughly confused.

"I do not know what you mean. I do not know these people."

"Are you kidding me? You've never seen *Star Wars*? Who in the hell hasn't seen *Star Wars*?"

"Paul, I am being very serious with you. You have seen the visions. You have seen your father. You know the power is real."

"Yes, I know it is."

"Paul, I am very scared. My Abuela taught me how to use this power when I was little girl. She told me it was meant to heal. It is used to strengthen the soul. So long as all things are in balance, it can accomplish anything."

"Yes, that's part of it."

"Part of it, yes. But your father, Paul. He has done many horrible things. He has murdered many men. He has taken that which is good and strong and balanced and made it a force for wickedness." She hung her head, like a spy who's just been made to talk, a heretic admitting her crime. "He made me raise the dead, Paul. Do you have any idea what a great transgression that is?"

She looked down at her hands and he could tell she was willing them to stop shaking.

She looked back over her shoulder, then down at her hands again. "Paul," she said. "You are not alone in this. Others are trying to help you. But they cannot do it alone. Your father is too powerful for that. In the end, fighting him will be up to you. To do that, you have to find something to help you stay in this world. He will try to lead you into his world; you must fight that. You need to center yourself in this world. Find something worth holding on to, because the dead will take you over when you quit being a part of this world."

"Well, that certainly sounds serious," he said.

She looked shocked by his flippancy. She stared at him for a long time, and as he stared back at her, he could see the knowledge of what was going to happen dawning within her.

She swallowed hard.

From somewhere behind her came the sound of windows breaking. She jumped to her feet and spun around to face the noise. Paul kept his seat. He looked at his fingernails and waited.

"Oh my God," Magdalena said.

"Something like that," Paul answered.

The backdoor blew open. Paul heard the sounds of bare feet walking over broken glass on the hardwood floor. He heard the moans of the dead coming closer. They were stepping out of the shadows, taking shape as they stumbled from the kitchen to the living room.

Magdalena saw them and gasped. There were four of them. Each man was completely nude, their chests bearing the Y-shaped stitching of an autopsy. Their bodies had the faintly yellow tint of dead flesh. Their eyes were completely vacant. Paul had attended an autopsy as a cadet and he knew the doctors bagged all the organs that had been slopped out of the torso into plastic trash bags and then stuffed the bag back inside the body before stitching it up. The memory came back to him now because the dead man who was first through the door had a scrap of trash bag sticking out from one corner of the Y-shaped seam in his chest.

Magdalena turned on Paul and her eyes were pleading for help. She said, "But he hasn't turned you yet. You can't do this. You have to protect me."

Paul stared back at her with cold indifference. A small part of him did feel uneasy, but that part was buried deep down, and it couldn't compete with the thundering echo of his father's voice coming out of that wall of static.

"Please," she said.

Paul's expression didn't change.

Magdalena shook her head no, like it wasn't fair, then ran for the front door.

She never made it.

The dead moved fast. They swarmed over her like piranha on a sinking carcass. From his place on the couch, Paul listened to her screams. He could hear the dead men tearing her apart, ripping into her with their hands and their teeth, and then, with awful suddenness, all was quiet—save for the sound of wet body parts being tossed onto the hardwood floor.

It didn't last long, hardly five minutes. When the dead passed through the living room, bound for the backdoor, one of them was dragging Magdalena's left leg. There was a long, ropy piece of tissue hanging off the severed end, painting a thick blackish-red smear across the floor.

The dead man dropped the leg in the middle of the floor and walked out the backdoor with the others. They faded into nothingness as they stepped outside.

Paul watched them go and that static voice inside his head told him it was time for him to vanish as well.

Chapter 17

Paul drove to the Eastside Substation, showered, and changed into his uniform. He barely remembered the drive. The entire evening was a dim blur, vague images moving behind a red veil. He knew he had built a stick lattice. He remembered the feeling that had come over him as he touched the wall of static that appeared in his vision, but that was the last clear thing he could remember. Everything after that, from leaving Magdalena's house to the start of his shift and the six calls they'd made so far, was a blur.

Mike said, "You want some?"

He was holding up something that looked like a giant pork rind. They were at The Cave again. Paul had barely touched his burger.

"What is that?" Paul asked.

"Chicken fried bacon," Mike said. "You want some? It's a heart attack waiting to happen, but this shit is good."

Paul shook his head. "You really eat that?"

"Hell yeah. Don't worry about the heart attack part, Paul. They put EMS on stand-by every time somebody orders this. Try it."

"No thanks."

Mike shrugged and took a bite. "Suit yourself."

"44-70," the dispatcher said.

"Damn it," Mike said. He keyed up his radio. "Go ahead, 44-70."

"44-70, make the south entrance of the Morgan Rollins Iron Works and contact 85-07. He's standing by."

"85-07?" Paul said. "Who's that?"

"Homicide," Mike said. "Remember, Homicide is the 85 series?"

"Yeah, I guess." He rubbed his eyes, trying to force himself to think. "Sorry. Just tired."

Mike gave him a worried look.

"44-70."

"Yeah, yeah," Mike said. He keyed up his radio. "44-70, I copy, ma'am. Who is that by name, please?"

"Homicide is all he said, 44-70. He requested you and your partner by name though, sir."

"Great. Well, pull yourself together there, sleepyhead. Let's go see what Homicide wants."

246 | Joe McKinney

***

For the past week, Keith Anderson had been working his way through mountains of paperwork. He and his team had gone through every document of government record that mentioned the original forty-five murder victims and every report mentioning David Everett. They'd gone back through every report Bobby Cantrell ever wrote. They poured over autopsy reports and crime scene photos and anonymous CrimeStoppers tips and patrol-initiated field contacts, and so far, they had a big handful of nothing.

None of their leads amounted to anything useful. None of the strange, ritualistic behavior they had seen matched anything in any of the law enforcement information clearinghouses—federal, state or otherwise. The only thing he did have was a mounting pile of handwritten to-do lists and a page of stick figure diagrams with Paul Henninger in the center. It made him feel like a blind man trying to grope his way out of a maze.

But in all the rush to gather information, in all the long, endless hours spent thinking about unspeakable crimes, the one thing he hadn't done was revisit the initial crime scene. He had been over the photographs and blueprints of it countless times, but he hadn't actually seen it since that first night. And that gave him an idea. He still needed to talk to Paul Henninger alone, and Paul was working the area around the Morgan Rollins factory. He was going to need a patrol escort while he explored the scene, so why not call Henninger and kill two birds with one stone? Talking to Paul in that environment might put him in the right frame of mind, certainly more than another trip downtown to Homicide would. So he made a call to the East dispatcher and had Paul and his partner meet him at the south entrance to the factory. By the time they arrived, he was waiting by the trunk of his car, flashlight in hand.

Anderson shook hands with Mike Garcia first. "How you been, Mike?"

"Good, sir. You?"

Anderson shrugged. "Fair, I guess. Busy."

"I bet. You mind telling us what we're doin' out here?"

"Just wanted to go over the scene again." He extended his hand to Paul and said, "How are you, Officer Henninger?"

"I'm okay," Paul said.

Anderson studied the younger officer, and couldn't help but feel a little intimidated by his size. He was a wall of almost pure muscle, and his hand completely swallowed Anderson's. It wasn't much of a stretch to see this kid playing college ball. Maybe even in the pros. But he looked tired. Anderson could see black shadows under his eyes, and that bruise on his forehead was still there. He must have taken a hell of a hit to get a mark like that.

Anderson said, "You know, I've been doing some research on those goats you told me about. The Angoras."

"Oh yeah?"

"Yeah. Turns out you were right about it being a common livestock animal around these parts. Apparently, Texas leads the nation in mohair production. I was kind of surprised about that. You know, it being so hot down here. Don't the animals ever just keel over and die from the heat."

Paul shrugged. "I suppose it happens."

"Of course, it may be they're just used to this kind of climate. The information I found said they're one of the oldest known breeds in existence. Started all the way back in the Middle East, and it is hot as hell there, too. Did you know there's mention of them as early as the time of Moses?"

Paul didn't answer. Anderson watched him, and he could sense the younger officer bringing up a defensive wall. He backed off a little. He smiled and tried to look disarmingly dumb.

He said, "So, I bet you guys were probably trying to get something to eat, weren't you?"

Mike laughed.

Anderson said, "Yeah, I thought so." He took out a small digital camera and said, "Come on, we'll make this quick. You ready to go exploring?"

***

They were inside the superstructure now, walking the catwalks. Anderson stopped at the foot of a ladder that Paul and Mike had scaled without difficulty and groaned at the prospect of going up it. They hadn't made it very far, and already he was breathing hard and sweating.

He wondered how anybody, especially a bunch of browned out heroin junkies, could have possibly moved through the rusted tangle of bent steel and collapsed walkways that he was looking at now without killing themselves. Pipes and wires and hulking pieces of busted machinery seemed to poke out in every direction, and the place was a maze of dark, blind alleys. Some of them were part of the original superstructure, but others had been made by the hundreds of junkies who had called this place home. When he got near the top of the ladder Mike offered him a hand up and he took it. They were perched on a two foot wide metal ledge. Behind him was the ladder. In front of him was a twenty foot drop off. At the bottom of the drop off was a dangerous looking pile of metal rods and rusted scrap that reminded Anderson of some kind of metal insect monster trying to crawl its way up from an abyss.

"Thanks," he said.

He dusted the rust off his pants and tried to look like this was the kind of thing he did every day.

"You guys make many calls in here?"

"Sometimes," Mike said. "Suspicious person calls, mostly."

"Who calls them in? There're no houses around here."

"Different people," Mike said, and shrugged. He found a clear path into the superstructure on a walkway a few feet above them. He jumped up first, then gave Paul and Anderson a hand up. "Probably just people passing by on Morgan Rollins Road. If you keep going south past the factory the road comes out onto Walters Avenue. It's a straight shot to the freeway from there."

"Yeah, but how do you see them from all the way down there? I barely saw a thing when I was down there waiting for you guys."

"You'd be surprised," Mike said. "In the moonlight, you can see people up on these catwalks without too much trouble."

"I'll take your word for it, I guess."

They moved on in silence after that, climbing through and over the debris until they reached the inner network of corridors that led to the circular chamber where Herrera had died. Provided he had his bearings right, they were also pretty close to the spot where Bobby Cantrell died. Some of what he was seeing looked familiar from the crime scene photos. Ahead of him were four corridors. The one to his far left went nowhere. He could see that from where he stood. The one to the right of that led to a catwalk that skirted around the circular inner chamber. It was on that catwalk that they'd found David Everett. The two on the far right both led to the circular chamber, but he was more interested in the one to the extreme right because that was the one Cantrell and Herrera had taken the night they died.

He pointed it out to Mike and Paul. "That one leads to where we want to go."

"Okay," Mike said. "If you say so."

Anderson looked at Mike. "You've been here before, haven't you?"

"I don't come in here unless I have to. Usually we just drive by and hit the place with our spotlights. That's about all it takes to get the junkies off the catwalks."

Anderson raised an eyebrow at him. "Good to know things haven't changed since I was on patrol."

"What are you looking for anyway?" Mike said.

"That's a good question," Anderson said. He turned his light down one of the corridors and took a couple of steps into it. "I don't really know what I'm looking for. I hardly ever do. If something grabs me, I pay attention. You know?"

Silence.

Anderson turned around, pointing his flashlight back the way he'd come.

"Mike?" he said.

He peered into the darkness, trying to make out the shapes that were just beyond his flashlight beam.

"Officer Henninger?"

No answer.

"Hey guys?"

He trotted a few steps in the direction he had come and emerged into the open area where he had last seen the two patrolmen.

"Hey! Where are you guys?"

Nothing.

He turned his flashlight in every direction, but saw absolutely nothing—only metal and dirt and trash.

"Mike?" He was yelling now. "Officer Henninger?"

Still nothing.

He felt the heat of panic rising in his cheeks. A darkness had settled over the corridor. It was a darkness so heavy the flashlight beam could barely reach into it.

"Hey guys?"

His voice sounded small and weak in the darkness. He felt the sudden urge to run, but fought it down. That wouldn't do here, not as dark as it was. He'd pitch over the edge of a catwalk and drop God knows how far down to his death. Probably find out what happened to all the junkies who didn't make it out of here alive.

Out of the corner of his eye, something moved.

He spun on his heel and turned his flashlight beam down one of the corridors.

"Mike? Officer Henninger?"

He took a few steps into the darkness, walking slowly, his right hand resting on his gun. Except for some trash and old rotten blankets and a few makeshift lean-tos, the corridor was empty. At least the little of it he could see was empty. He followed the path to another corner, rounded it, and stopped. His mouth fell open in shock. There, standing not fifteen feet from him, was Bobby Cantrell. He was nude, his chest stitched in black from his autopsy, but it was Bobby Cantrell. He stared Anderson square in the eye, his face an absolute blank, no emotion whatsoever.

"Bobby?" Anderson said.

He was surprised he wasn't scared. Confused, a little dizzy, and he was even a little giddy at seeing his friend again. But he wasn't scared.

Cantrell said nothing. His eyes gave away nothing. They stared into Anderson's, but there was no recognition there, no mirror of the emotion Anderson was feeling. It was like looking into a bottomless hole.

"Bobby?"

Cantrell turned and walked off into the darkness. Anderson trotted after him, his flashlight bouncing around the man's bare shoulders and back and he called out his name, begged him to stop.

"Jesus Christ, Bobby. Stop, would you?"

He never even stopped to think that this couldn't be happening. That part of him that knew this man was dead, that had seen the body carved up on the autopsy table, was silent. Instead there was simply a need. He needed to talk to the man. He needed to hear his friend's voice, and that need was too powerful to shake off.

"Wait a minute, Bobby. Stop, please."

But the dead man kept on walking. He stepped over debris and stepped through holes in the walls and even climbed a ladder onto a catwalk like it was perfectly natural. He didn't need a light to show him the way. He moved like a man at perfect ease with his surroundings. They emerged onto a catwalk, away from the rest of the superstructure. They were walking towards the dark gray smokestacks that loomed over the rest of the factory. The catwalk was rickety and whole sections were missing, eaten through by the rust. It leaned precariously to the right, and there was no handrail.

Had Anderson been looking anywhere but at Cantrell's back, he would have seen the ground was at least sixty feet below them. Had he not been so lost in the haze of confused feelings that had overtaken him, he would have felt a rough, hot wind whipping dust all around him, rippling his white golf shirt and khaki slacks like a flag in a storm. But he didn't see any of that. All he saw was what had been ripped from his heart, and he walked where his dead friend walked, followed where he led, calling his name the whole way.

Years of decay and neglect had collapsed an entire section of the catwalk immediately ahead of him, just beyond a metal stairwell. The collapsed section was a massive tangle of rods and wires and metal lattice works far below him, and had he looked down he would have seen it there, yawning up at him. Cantrell paid no attention to the missing section. He walked across the air to the middle of the gap between the sections and turned around. He beckoned to Anderson.

He followed eagerly. He didn't see anything but the dead man, and he was oblivious to the shouting beneath him.

***

Paul was the first one up the stairwell. The detective was already dangerously close to the edge. Another few steps and he'd go tumbling to his death. Paul watched him getting closer and knew this was what was supposed to happen, that his father intended for this man to die in this way. He knew it in the same way he had known Magdalena was meant to die.

Though now he was not so sure. He hadn't felt the need to stop Magdalena's death from happening. She had known what she was doing when she defied his father. This man, he didn't know the truth.

He and Mike had been searching for him for the last ten minutes. Or rather, Mike had been searching for him. Paul knew exactly where he was. He had climbed the stairs to this point knowing that the detective would be here. Now he was only a few feet away from him, fighting with himself about what to do. Mike was still below, yelling up at Anderson to stop. Paul glanced down at Mike, then back to the detective. He watched the man staggering forward in a trance, his flashlight swinging uselessly by his side, and he said, "Stop, Anderson. Come on, hear me. Stop."

But the detective kept walking.

"Stop him, Paul!" Mike shouted. "Stop him!"

Mike's voice was like a siren in his mind. It shook him loose from his own trance, and he ran forward just as Anderson stepped over the edge of the catwalk.

Paul dove for him and caught him by the foot. Most of Paul's upper body was hanging over the edge. He held Anderson's ankle in his right hand, the metal lattice of the catwalk with his left. A furious voice in his head was ordering him to let the man fall, to just let go. Drop him, damn it!

Paul felt the man's foot sliding through his fingers. He could feel his body armor sliding over the jagged edge of the catwalk, the buttons popping off his shirt one by one. Anderson was dead weight. His body spun like the corpse of a hanged man, rotating slowly one way then the other, a plaything in the breeze. Paul was breathing hard now. His eyes were rolling from Anderson to the twisted metal on the ground below them. He heard Mike yelling.

"Help me," he yelled, and as he did he felt his voice growing stronger. "Mike, I'm slipping."

"I've got you," Mike said. And the next moment Paul felt Mike's powerful grip on the back of his gun belt. "Just hold him tight," he said, his voice strangely quiet and calm. "Don't let go. I've got you."

Paul groaned from the pain in his arm. He could feel his muscles screaming at him, almost like a force was trying to pry his fingers loose.

"I can't hold him!" Paul screamed.

"Don't let go, Paul," Mike said.

Mike ran his hand down Paul's arm and grabbed hold of his wrist. He pulled up, then grabbed hold of Anderson's leg with both hands.

"Stay still," he said to Paul, and a moment later was hoisting Anderson's inert body over Paul's back.

Mike pulled Paul up onto the catwalk next, and afterwards, they sat there, inches from the edge, looking at each other. Paul was breathing hard, his eyes half-closed. He was exhausted. Mike had Anderson's unconscious body across his legs. He was breathing hard, too.

Mike said, "Holy shit, dude. That sucked."

And they both laughed.

Chapter 18

Thirty minutes later, Anderson was standing next to his car, trying to reassure the two young patrolmen that he was feeling fine.

Mike looked at him doubtfully.

"Really," Anderson said, "I'm okay."

Mike had practically carried him down from the superstructure, and even now, as they stood at the remnant of the gate that marked the south entrance, the night winds blowing dust clouds down the road below them, he was still trying to hold his elbow. It made Anderson feel like an old man whose grandkids are afraid he might fall down the stairs.

He gently, but firmly, pulled his elbow away from Mike and straightened himself up.

"Really," he said. "It's okay."

"You sure?" Mike asked.

"I'm sure. I should have known better than to go crawling around up there as tired as I am. I haven't gotten much sleep since all this started."

It sounded lame and Anderson knew it, but luckily Mike didn't try to take it any further.

"I owe you guys," he said. "I really do."

He looked at Paul. Henninger looked unfocused, like he was thinking about something else and wasn't quite able to get his mind around it.

"Especially you, Officer Henninger. Thanks."

Paul merely nodded.

The three of them stood looking at each other in an uncomfortable silence, then Anderson said, "All right, well, I'm gonna take off. Thanks again, guys."

"Not a problem," Mike said.

Anderson nodded, got into his car, and got out of there as fast as he could.

***

But he didn't go home. Instead he headed to a little Dunkin Donuts stand at the corner of Rigsby and Houston and ordered a large cup of coffee and sat in a booth and drank it black and thought about what had just happened.

He *tried* to think anyway. But what came to mind was all the senseless, ignoble death he had seen in his long police career. All the hacked up, burned, raped, strangled, mutilated, and decomposing bodies strolled through his mind like the cast of a Romero movie on parade.

For a long time he sat there thinking about murdered hookers and gang members shot full of holes and wives strangled by their husbands and babies beat to death by their parents and he felt some essential, deep down part of himself going numb. He had seen so much, so much misery and grief, and for the longest time he had managed to keep it separate from his own soul. But he wasn't so sure he was succeeding anymore.

And then he thought of Bobby Cantrell on the autopsy table, his chest opened up so that he looked like a canoe, and it occurred to him that the essential thing that death denied to the dead was their dignity. You could live with dignity, and many people did, but you could never die with it. Even the best of us get treated like meaningless meat on the autopsy table.

He looked up at the counter, and Bobby Cantrell was standing there in a white apron, wiping down the counter with a dishrag.

"You need something, buddy?" Bobby Cantrell said.

Anderson just stared at him. He stared into Cantrell's eyes and a long moment passed. The light around Cantrell's face turned from a soft blue to an aqua green, like the ocean with sunlight passing through it. Bobby Cantrell's mouth was moving, but there were no words coming out. Anderson didn't try to answer back. He couldn't anyway. There wasn't enough air in his chest for that.

"Hey look, man, if you're drunk you're gonna have to leave."

The sound startled him.

"What?" Anderson said. The man behind the counter wasn't Bobby Cantrell anymore. He was just some guy, the guy who had sold him the nearly untouched cup of coffee on the table in front of him.

"If you're looking to sleep it off, you're gonna have to do it someplace else."

"I'm not drunk," Anderson said. He shook himself mentally. "I'm sorry. I...just had kind of a hard day. I'm okay now."

The man behind the counter seemed to consider him, then shrugged. "Whatever," he said, and went back to wiping the counter.

***

He was sitting in his car in the Dunkin Donuts parking lot when his cell phone went off. It was Levy, and for a moment he thought about not answering, but that didn't last long.

"Keith, you there?"

"Yeah, I'm here," Anderson said into the phone. "What's going on, Chuck?"

"Where are you?"

"The corner of Rigsby and Houston, the Dunkin Donuts."

"What are you doing out? It's three in the morning."

"I know what time it is, Chuck."

A pause.

"Well, seeing as you're already over here, I need you to come by 642 Utley Street."

Anderson closed his eyes and sighed. He slid down into the seat and thought of Bobby Cantrell.

"You there, Keith?"

"Yeah, I'm here. Where in the hell is Utley Street?"

"Well, from where I'm standing in the front yard I can see the smokestacks of the Morgan Rollins Iron Works."

Anderson sat up straight.

"What have you got, Chuck?"

"I thought that'd get your attention. Just come down here. I think we may have gotten a break in this thing."

***

When Anderson arrived at the scene, he was surprised by how low key the police presence was. There were police cars at either end of the block, turning away the occasional car that tried to turn down the street. Closer in, somebody had run a cordon of yellow crime scene tape around the house and across the street. There were a few patrol cars parked along the curb and an evidence truck just inside the crime scene line and two unmarked Ford fleet cars, one of which belonged to Chuck Levy, but that was it. Usually, a murder scene got a much bigger response than this.

Even the neighbors had, for the most part, stayed indoors, and that really surprised him. It was nearly four in the morning, but that hardly made a difference when it came to crowds gathering to watch a lurid scene. You could usually count on the streets to flood with people during an incident like this, even in the wee hours of the morning.

From the car, he scanned the small crowd of about twenty people standing around outside the crime scene tape in their t-shirts and blue jeans and nightgowns and every man he saw was Bobby Cantrell, staring right back at him. "Oh Jesus," he said, and closed his eyes. *Go away. Go away, please.* When he opened them again, the crowd was just a crowd again, the occasional woman holding a sleepy-eyed baby wearing nothing but a diaper, the men talking to each other about how the cops were doing it all wrong.

Anderson turned off the car, got out, and looked around. Mike Garcia was leaning up against the front of his patrol car, his thick arms crossed over his chest, chatting up a pretty young evidence technician.

The girl looked to be about twenty-two or twenty-three, right out of college, with shiny black hair, and a figure that looked absolutely amazing, even in the black, BDU-style uniforms of the Evidence Unit. She had the biggest, roundest pair of doe eyes Anderson had ever seen, and the glory of their radiant innocence was pointed straight up at Mike. Her lips were open just a bit, just enough for the tip of her tongue to touch the bottom of her upper lip. She giggled at something Mike said, and Anderson forced himself to turn away, out of decency. The poor thing had the hook in her mouth and didn't even know it.

He looked toward the house and saw a simple, humble eyesore huddled in the dark behind a weed patch yard. It was surrounded by a sagging hurricane fence, and the bottom of the fence was lined with unlit votive candles. Stuff that looked like dried dog turds on a string were tied to the tops of the fence, and he thought, *Dried herbs and chicken bones. Oh great, a fortune teller.*

Paul Henninger was standing in the shadows of the porch. Even from the street, Anderson could tell how pale he looked. There was something flashing in his hands.

Anderson walked up to him and said, "Officer Henninger, how are you?"

Paul looked at him but didn't respond. He simply stared at Anderson, though Anderson felt more like he was being looked through than at.

"You want to tell me what you got here?"

Paul said nothing. He just put the coin—that's what it was, Anderson realized, a coin—back in his pocket and walked off. Anderson watched him go and didn't try to stop him. He could have ordered him to stop, of course, but he didn't. There was something deep inside that man that wanted to get out, that wanted to tell a story, but Anderson knew that this was not the time for it. It would come out, but not just yet.

He turned back to the street and caught Mike's eye. He waved, and Mike nodded back. Mike said something that made the pretty young evidence technician giggle, and then he came over to meet Anderson halfway across the yard.

They shook hands. "I didn't see you pull up," Mike said.

"Yeah, well, you were busy."

Mike smiled.

"Any chance with that one?"

Mike shrugged. "Maybe."

"Poor girl has no idea what's in store for her, does she?"

"Oh, I don't know about that. They all pretend to be innocent, but she knows."

Anderson tried to smile. He thought of something he'd once heard a police cadet ask a K9 officer. The cadet clearly loved dogs, the way he was looking at the German shepherd that had just pulled a murder suspect out from under a house. The cadet stroked the dog's neck behind the ears, then turned to the K9 officer and said, "So how disciplined are these dogs? I mean, I know they're not neutered. What happens if a female dog in heat comes by?"

The K9 officer had tugged on the dog's leash and said, "He's a policeman, ain't he? He sees a bitch in heat he's gonna go fuck it."

But not even that memory could call up a full smile. He looked back at the house and said, "Did you at least give her a chance to process the scene before you charmed her out of her panties?"

"Hey, come on now," Mike said. "Here on East Dogwatch we like to screw around same as anybody, but we always get the job done first."

"Fair enough. You wanna tell me what you got?"

"Sure," Mike said.

He told Anderson they got a call for a found 10-60, a dead body. The neighbor called it in. She said she'd heard something earlier in the evening, just after sunset, like somebody screaming. She'd been trying to look in through the windows ever since, trying to see what was going on inside, but couldn't. Then, at about two o'clock, she'd gone around back and found the backdoor blasted apart.

"You got the neighbor somewhere secure?"

"Yeah, she's with Sergeant Garwin. He's consoling her."

"Great," Anderson said.

"You know Garwin, when the complainant cries, he cries."

That did bring a smile to Anderson's face, in spite of all the crap he had going on in his head. He had never heard Garwin described better. And he still hadn't forgiven the man for running to Jenny Cantrell with the news that her husband's body was missing from the morgue.

"Something you should know about your witness, though."

"What's that?"

Mike told him about the call he and Paul made a few days before. He told him about the woman running into the street covered in goat's blood. He told him about the screaming the two women had done back and forth.

Anderson listened to it all. "It was goat's blood, you said?"

"Yep. The lady's some kind of witch doctor or something."

"A curandera?"

"Could be, I don't know what the hell that is."

"Mexican folk healer. Okay, thanks."

Anderson started to walk towards the house, but stopped, looked over his shoulder, and said, "Where'd she get the goat's blood from, any idea?"

"Yeah, as a matter of fact I do know. She's got a whole bunch of them out back. We've already called Animal Control. They're supposed to be sending somebody as soon as they come on at seven."

Anderson nodded.

"You might want to put on some rubber boots before you go in there," Mike said. "It's a bad one. Whoever did her really fucked her up. We found a foot near the front door, part of her leg in the living room, part of her hand next to the couch. You get the idea. There's blood everywhere. Human blood, this time."

"Great," said Anderson. "Can't wait."

"Oh, and your sergeant's waiting for you inside. He told me to tell you to contact him as soon as you get here."

Anderson nodded. "Okay. Thanks, Mike."

"My pleasure."

***

Chuck Levy was waiting for him just inside the front door. They shook hands, and Levy started to tell him something, but Anderson wasn't listening. He was too busy looking at the scene.

It was every bit as gory as Mike described. There were body parts and blood everywhere. Anderson saw three fingers and part of a palm on the floor at his feet. Part of an arm was festooned from an umbrella stand in the entryway. A lower jaw and a long tattered flap of bloody skin that Anderson figured was probably from the front of the victim's throat was resting under a sideboard table. There was a vast puddle of coagulated blood on the floor, and four sets of twin bare spots around the perimeter. He looked at them, at the way the blood was textured inside the bare spots, like you would see after a paint brush is pressed against a wall and lifted straight away.

"What are those?" he said, interrupting whatever Levy had been saying. "They look like knee prints."

"Probably so," Levy agreed. "That would fit, right? Four suspects. They've got her on the floor right here. They're on their knees around her, tearing her to pieces, tossing the body parts away like peanut shells."

"Like peanut shells?"

"You know what I mean."

Anderson sighed. "Yeah, I guess so."

He turned away and looked in at the rest of the house. It was steeped in shadows, even though most of the lights were on. He was about to ask if somebody had turned on the lights, or if they'd had the good sense to leave the crime scene intact when Levy brushed past his shoulder and said, "Come with me, Keith. There's something you need to see in here."

Anderson put his questions on hold and followed Levy into the living room. What he saw there staggered him, and it took him a good long minute just to catch his breath. It took him another long minute to absorb it all.

There was a long smear of blackish red blood on the floor from the entryway to a leg left in the middle of the floor. But that wasn't what caught his eye. What made him gasp for breath was the collection of stick lattices along the back wall. They were the same as the ones he had found at the train yard and in the circular chamber at the Morgan Rollins Iron Works. And they were the same ones he'd seen in the Comal County crime scene photos of Martin Henninger's death.

"My God," he said.

"You ain't seen nothing yet," Levy said. "Go into the kitchen and look at the walls."

Anderson drifted toward the grungy kitchen in a haze. What he saw there was writing all over the walls, though he couldn't read any of it.

"What language is this supposed to be?" he asked.

Levy said, "That, my friend, is Hebrew. Or, rather, it looks like Hebrew. A lot of it is kind of archaic looking."

"You're an expert on ancient Hebrew now?" Anderson asked.

"Hey, I told you, I may not be a practicing Jew, but I had to learn Hebrew same as every other kid who ever had a bar mitzvah."

"Yeah, but how can you tell this is ancient Hebrew?"

"Remember when they tried to teach us to read Chaucer back in high school?"

"Yeah, my teacher made us memorize the opening lines of the Prologue of the Canterbury Tales."

"Exactly. You look at that stuff, and you can tell it's in English, but it's obviously old, you know? The words are spelled funny. The syntax is all wrong. It's the same thing here with this writing."

"The syntax?"

"The way the sentences are put together."

Anderson shook his head. "Chuck, you never cease to amaze me, you know that?"

"Yeah, well, that's why I make the big bucks."

"You have any idea what it says?"

"Some of it." He walked over to the stove and pointed at the backsplash behind the burners. "This part here sounds like it's from the Day of Atonement ritual in Leviticus."

"Leviticus? Like in the Old Testament?"

"You mean the Torah, Keith. We Jews don't call it the Old Testament."

"Whatever you call it it's over my head. I haven't been in a church since my wedding day. What's the Day of Atonement ritual, anyway?"

"The Day of Atonement is Yom Kippur."

Anderson just looked at him, waiting.

"Keith, are you shitting me? One of your oldest friends is Jewish and you don't know what our major holidays are?"

"I'm an insensitive bastard. Does that make you feel any better?"

"Loads."

"Good. So what's the Day of Atonement and why is it on this woman's wall?"

"Well that's the thing. This isn't the Day of Atonement passage from Leviticus. Not exactly, anyway. It's close, but...Look, you've heard the word scapegoat, right?"

"Of course. Hell, Chuck, of course I've heard it. I've been a policeman for twenty-five years. I'm used to being blamed for other people's problems."

"Yeah, that's true. Well, the word scapegoat comes from the Day of Atonement ritual in Leviticus. Moses called Aaron and the others together while they were living in tents out in the desert and ordered them to bring him two goats. He put a hand on each goat's head and prayed. One goat was sacrificed to Yahweh. The other got all of the sins of Israel placed on its head and was led out into the desert and given to Azazel. It's the goat that escaped, or the 'scapegoat.' Get it?"

"Yeah, I got that. Who in the hell is Azazel?"

"I don't know. Nobody does, really. It's a name, that's what my rabbi told me. It means something like 'angry god,' but nobody really knows for sure."

Anderson looked at the writing again. He couldn't make heads or tails of it.

"You said all of this is similar to Leviticus?" he asked.

"Similar, yes. But not exact. You had to memorize Chaucer. In synagogue I had to memorize parts of the Day of Atonement passage. This stuff here changes it around, though. There's no mention of Moses in here. And it reads Azazel everywhere that the scriptures say Yahweh. And the goat that's supposed to be sent out into the desert for Azazel is here being told to bring back the souls of the dead."

"The souls of the dead?"

"Yeah, you know, like ghosts. That's what this looks like it's saying. I got the evidence technician to do detailed photographs of all this. I figure we could let a rabbi or somebody look at it and hopefully translate it for us. What do you think? Keith?"

***

Anderson was looking out the backdoor. Or where the backdoor had been. Now there were just shattered pieces of wood hanging from the hinges. Paul Henninger was standing out there, looking off toward the Morgan Rollins Iron Works. He had that coin in his hands again, and the goats were clustered around him, looking up at him expectantly.

"Excuse me for a second," Anderson said to Levy. "I want to go talk to..."

He trailed off there and walked outside without giving Levy any further explanation. He came up behind Paul and the goats bleated at him irritably before walking off.

"What do you see when you look up there?" he said to Paul.

Paul didn't answer, didn't even look at him.

"I've seen you work that coin. That's pretty impressive the way you do those tricks. How'd you learn to do that?"

The coin vanished, but Paul still didn't speak.

"Paul, what does the name Azazel mean to you?"

At that, Paul turned his head towards Anderson and gave him a hard look, a glare that made Anderson fight the instinctive impulse to take a step back.

He said, "I guess it means something to you, doesn't it? You know a whole lot more than you've been telling me so far, don't you?"

"I don't want to talk to you," Paul said.

"Hmmm, maybe not. Not now, anyway. Pretty soon though, you're gonna have to talk to me."

"Oh yeah? How do you figure that?"

"Because pretty soon there isn't going to be anybody else."

"Am I supposed to know what that means?"

"I think you know."

Paul went back to watching the night sky slide by the smokestacks over at Morgan Rollins.

"You mind if I tell you something, Paul?"

"This another one of your war stories?"

"No," said Anderson, "not quite."

Paul was quiet. Anderson drew in as deep a breath as he could and said, "I had a son named John who died very young."

"I'm sorry," Paul said.

"He was fifteen. He was sneaking out a lot, doing drugs, drinking. We yelled at each other constantly. One night he's out with another kid and they fly off the freeway and into some trees doing over a hundred miles an hour. The Traffic lieutenant who told me about the crash said that he didn't suffer, that death was instantaneous, but I can't help but think that he had been suffering for a long time before that."

Anderson glanced at Paul, then followed his gaze out to the Morgan Rollins smokestacks. They were beautiful in their own way, the way cities turned to rubble can be beautiful.

He went on. "After John died, my wife and I had a pretty hard time. I thought our marriage was gonna crash land. It didn't, but it sure felt that way. One night, I'm sitting on the couch watching TV. My wife is in the bedroom crying her eyes out. Well, I'm sitting there, and this commercial comes on. I don't even remember what it was for. I just remember it had all these kids in it, all of 'em about John's age. I looked at the screen, and I swear to God, every kid in that crowd had John's face. I felt like I was gonna die that night."

"I don't see your point," Paul said.

"My point is this. I knew—well, I figured it out later, actually—that I was so emotionally invested that my mind was playing tricks on me. Lately it's been happening to me again, only this time it's Detective Bobby Cantrell that I'm seeing. He was my best friend, Paul. Aside from my wife."

"I remember you telling me that."

"Yeah, well, the reason I'm telling it to you again is because of what happened to me up there at Morgan Rollins." He waited to see if Paul would say something to that. When he didn't, he said, "But you know what happened to me up there, don't you?"

"I don't have a clue," Paul said.

"No, I think you do. As a matter of fact, I know you know what happened up there. That wasn't a figment of my imagination I saw, was it? That wasn't stress. That was real."

Paul inspected his shoes.

"Nobody's gonna believe you if you say a dead man tried to kill you, Detective."

"No, they won't, will they?"

"Nope."

"But you would believe it, wouldn't you, Paul?"

Paul looked at him then. His eyes had a glassy shine to them. He said, "Detective, I just don't know what I believe anymore."

Chapter 19

Rachel awoke around three a.m. to a miserable, suffocating heat. She had been sleeping with her knees tucked up against her chest, but now she threw off the scrap of covers still clinging to her feet, rolled over onto her back, and groaned. Her face was wet with sweat. Her entire body was wet with it. She was exhausted but wide awake, and she knew she'd never be able to get back to sleep now. She turned on a few lights and went into the kitchen wearing only a t-shirt and a pair of blue panties and fanned herself with a paper plate, trying to cool down. When that didn't work she traded the paper plate for a glass of ice water and went over to her boxes of books. She'd finished Bruce Boston's *The Guardener's Tale* before she went to bed and it left her hungry for more science fiction, something dystopic and angry, like maybe Philip K. Dick's *A Scanner Darkly* or George Orwell's *1984*, maybe even Paolo Bacigalupi *Shipbreaker*. She'd been meaning to read that for months now.

But what she found instead was an open cardboard box, pictures and papers inside. Curious, she took out a stack of the pictures and looked through them. Not a one of them was familiar, though she figured the little white house with the rusted metal roof and rangy yard was where Paul had grown up. The man and woman in the pictures had to be his father and mother.

One by one she flipped through the pictures. Paul had told her painfully little of his past, and what he had told her was primarily about his father. The only time he ever mentioned his mother, beyond what he told her the other night, was to say that he remembered her as one step above a vegetable. Someone who lived in the shadows, spiritually mired in depression. Looking at the pictures, though, she found that description hard to believe. The woman she saw was no vegetable. She looked strong, sturdy, and she reminded Rachel of the women from Louis L'Amour's westerns. Here was a pioneer woman raising kids in Apache country, her face burnt by the sun, her hair tied back into a simple ponytail with a scrap of fabric.

It was impossible to tell what year the photos were taken, though she guessed Paul couldn't have been more than one or two in most of them. One in particular made her smile. It showed Paul—and God, he was a huge baby—sitting in the grass, wearing only a diaper, his mother touching the tip of his nose with her finger. Neither one was smiling, but there was still a warmth to the photo, a sense of love that was almost spiritual in its intensity. And then she caught a glimpse of something written on the back, and her smile dimmed.

She read—

They fuck you up, your mum and dad.
They may not mean to, but they do.
They fill you with the faults they had
And add some extra, just for you.

But they were fucked up in their turn
By fools in old-style hats and coats,
Who half the time were soppy-stern
And half at one another's throats.

Man hands on misery to man.
It deepens like a coastal shelf.
Get out as early as you can.
And don't have kids yourself.

—and recognized it by its first line as one of Philip Larkin's poems. That sense of a life filled with missed opportunities and the harsh reality that existence is mean and shabby and rarely lives up to its promises always left her feeling unsettled and a little queasy, and she had, as a result, steered clear of most of Larkin's work. But she knew this poem, and finding it here, *this* poem especially, on the back of *this* photograph, made the goose flesh prickle across her skin.

It was creepy, and wrong. What was it supposed to be? She could tell that the clean, gracefully looped letters in which the poem was written were those of a woman, and she could only imagine that Paul's mother had copied it out here. But why? Was it supposed to be her apology to Paul? Or was it an expression of her own guilt and self-hatred in the face of a rising tide of depression that she knew would one day overwhelm her completely? Maybe none of that was right. Maybe it was a warning she left for herself, a message in a bottle sent out to her future self who perhaps might forget the elegant simplicity of this moment she shared with her child. Rachel felt her mouth turn dry. There were too many possibilities, and not enough clues.

And then the picture moved.

At first the movement was so subtle she couldn't tell for sure whether she had really seen it or not. But the figures in the picture were moving. The woman touched the boy's face and pressed the ball of her finger against his lips. Then she turned and looked straight at Rachel.

Rachel wasn't scared, though. If anything she felt dizzy, like she might fall over. She put out a hand to steady herself and blinked, and that was all it took.

She was drifting...

***

...into the darkened living room of a house she didn't recognize. There was a kitchen behind her, small, dingy, the floor in front of the screen door discolored by years of brought-in dirt and mud. To her left was a narrow, almost tunnel-like stairway that led up to a closed door. In front of her was the main room of a country home. Disassembled machine parts were scattered around on the floor and on a few of the chairs here and there. She saw an ancient couch, the arms worn to a smooth shine. There was a box fan clicking noisily in the corner. A battered, man-of-the-house style recliner in plain brown fabric lurked next to the couch. The walls were bare. There wasn't a book in sight, but there wasn't a TV either.

A sudden panic swelled within her. This was somebody's house. Somebody lived here. She was in somebody's house in the middle of the night.

You get shot for that in Texas.

She turned to run out the screen door, but it was too late. A man in a white, long-sleeved shirt, black pants, black boots, and a worn Stetson cowboy hat was coming in the screen door, carrying an armload of sticks.

She screamed. Then she put up her hands, palms towards the man, and started babbling. "Please," she said. "Mister, I don't know where I'm at. I know I don't belong here. I'm leaving, okay? I didn't take anything. I swear. I'm leaving."

But the man gave no sign of hearing a word she said. He didn't even look at her as he strode through the kitchen, passed within a foot of her shoulder, and went straight into the living room.

Rachel trailed off and turned to watch the man, for now that her initial terror had subsided, she realized she knew the man—and she couldn't believe it. He was Paul's father, Martin Henninger.

But that's impossible, isn't it? Martin Henninger is dead. Has been dead for at least six years.

"Mister, I'm just gonna—"

He dropped the sticks and they clattered against the wooden floor. She half-expected him to turn around on her then and start yelling.

But he didn't.

Instead, he dropped to his knees and picked up the sticks and put two of them together like a cross and began to twist some kind of wire around the intersection of the two pieces.

It would have been the perfect time to leave. Every instinct in her body told her it was. *Get out and go! Run as far and as fast as you can.* But something held her there. It was the hypnotic speed of the man's hands as they worked on the sticks, grabbing them seemingly at random, assembling something, something familiar—

A lattice of sticks. Oh my God. Just like Paul made in our apartment.

It seemed like the world had suddenly dropped away beneath her and she was caught in that terrifying moment just before freefall.

Oh my God.

A woman's screams snapped her back to the moment. They were coming from her left, from the room towards the front of the house that she hadn't seen until just then. And it was a horrible sound, a banshee wail of a woman angry and in pain and full of lunatic fury.

Rachel turned in time to see a woman waving a huge knife in the air as she sprinted towards her. The woman's thin, wiry hair was streaming out behind her. Her face was gray and emaciated, like a corpse's face. Her eyes were rimmed with red and so full of craziness they were enough to freeze the blood next to Rachel's heart. She was too stunned to move, too stunned to do anything but throw her hands over her face and scream.

The woman darted past her and entered the living room, still screaming, still swinging that knife like the very air around her was full of devils and she meant to hack them all to pieces.

The man in the black cowboy hat rose and turned on the screaming woman. His eyes had rolled back into his head. His mouth was open in a wide O, and for a single, incongruously funny moment, he reminded Rachel of Donald Sutherland in the final scene of *Invasion of the Body Snatchers*, pointing an accusing finger at Veronica Cartwright and raising the terrible, high-pitched howl of the alien hue and cry that announced an intruder among the faithful.

But the man made no sound. There was no scream coming from him, not even a glimmer of surprise in his features. He extended one hand and then drew it back again as the woman—Paul's mother, Rachel realized—slashed at it with her knife.

She slashed again, this time at the man's face. The knife whistled harmlessly past him, not even jostling his hat.

He stepped forward and punched the woman square in the mouth.

She crumpled to the floor and stayed there.

"Don't move," the man said. His voice was cold, implacably calm. And it sounded so exactly like Paul's that Rachel, for a moment, saw her husband standing there.

"I won't let you have him!" the woman said, though it was hard to understand her. Her mouth was full of blood and she was hysterical, practically spitting the words at the man. "You can't have him!"

"It ain't your choice to make," the man answered, still calm, unmoved.

She slashed at his knees with the knife. He took a step back, and when he did, she jumped to her feet and slashed at him again and again and again, screaming as she did, "I won't let him become like you. I won't, you bastard!"

Then she took off running for the kitchen. Paul's father chased after her. He caught her just as she entered the kitchen and knocked her to the ground with a punch to the back of her head. The woman hit the ground, bounced up, and staggered backwards onto the stairs. The man reached for her, then dodged back to avoid another knife slash.

"Don't you do it," the man said. "Don't you go up there."

He stepped onto the bottom stair.

"Don't you do it."

Rachel heard the woman scream, "You stay away from me! I swear to God I'll cut your fucking balls off!"

And then he ran up the stairs, chasing after the screaming woman. Rachel walked towards the stairs, aware, on some level at least, that she wasn't part of this, that the man and the woman couldn't see her, didn't know she was there. She stopped at the bottom of the stairs and looked up. The door at the top of the flight was open now, and she could hear the woman screaming from somewhere beyond it. She could hear the beating that ensued.

Feeling queasy with fear she climbed the stairs and stopped in the doorway of a young boy's bedroom—Paul's bedroom. The man stood with an iron hand clamped down on the back of the motionless woman's neck. She was doubled over at the waist, arms hanging limp, a puppet in his hand. The beating had stopped. The knife was sticking into the floor next to the woman's feet.

There was an empty bed in front of the woman, the covers tossed back hastily, as though Paul had scrambled away from it at the last moment. Off in the opposite far corner was an old pioneer trash stove, probably eighty years old. Next to that was a wooden desk and chair, a small window above that, the blue moonlight pouring into the room. There was a child's set of football shoulder pads at the foot of the bed and a poster of a mean-looking black pro football player on the wall and another poster of a blonde in a pink bikini standing in a hot tub, her hips cocked to one side, a thumb tucked under the waistband of her bikini bottom. The room was almost quaint in its juvenile simplicity, its perfect statement of what was important in the world from the eyes of a teenage boy, and the horrible domestic violence superimposed upon it was all the more terrifying in contrast.

"You're done, woman," the man said, and dragged her past where Rachel stood and down the stairs, leaving the knife where it was.

Rachel was near tears, watching the knife and listening to the sounds

268 | Joe McKinney

of the man moving through the house below her. She had never seen a man beat a woman so viciously before. She had read about it plenty of times, but never seen it, and she never wanted to see it again. So much cruelty.

And then she became aware of a small, sad sound coming from under the bed. She took a few steps forward and knelt down and looked under the bed. Paul was there. A twelve-year-old Paul, curled into a fetal ball, his whole body shaking.

"Oh my God," she said, and reached out for him.

***

But he was gone. The vision was gone. She was sitting on the floor, back in the apartment she shared with the Paul she'd married. She felt the heat trying to smother her. She could smell the dust in the air. She was back again, and the cloud was lifting from her mind. But the picture of Paul and his mother was still in her hand. She let it fall from her fingertips and it tumbled back into the box. She couldn't bear to look at it now.

"Maybe you're going nuts," she told herself.

She shuddered. She couldn't accept that. It had felt too real, the images too vivid and detailed to be anything but a vision of events that had actually happened.

So then why those events? Why was I shown that nasty little scene?

She walked over to the couch and sat down heavily. Her mind chased itself in circles. Lately the apartment had become so much of a burden. It was infinitely nicer than the little house on Huisache, and it had far more room than the Chase Hill apartment she and Paul had shared briefly after graduation, but none of that made her feel better about what she was looking at. The appliances would have been antiques in her mother's kitchen. The floors creaked and groaned with every step. The traffic on the main road outside sounded like a marching band moving through her head. And of course there was that damned air conditioner. What a joke that thing was. And, almost as if the apartment could hear her thoughts and was trying to add insult to injury, the lights flickered and then went out.

"Damn it!" she shouted at the dark. "Come on."

She forced herself to think. *The air conditioner burned out the fuses. Paul told you that might happen. Okay, so what do I do?*

Ah, the fuse box.

The fuse box was in the kitchen, inside the pantry. Her eyes had adjusted to the dark enough for her to see the outlines of the living room furniture, and she made her way there, half-seeing, half-groping her way through the obstacles. She opened the pantry door and reached inside, fumbling along the wall until she found the latch on the far edge of the metal faceplate. She opened the metal door and reached inside and her bowels almost let go as she realized the switches were covered, not with hardened plastic, but with what felt like human skin.

Not real not real not real not real, she thought, and threw the breaker switch.

The lights came on. She drew her hand away and turned back to the kitchen. And walked straight into the woman from her vision. She was small and weak and sadness poured out of her. Rachel felt it like the smell of putrescence washing over her. Her hair was gray and wiry and uncombed, her face gray, the lips cracked and peeling. She had her arms wrapped around her chest, her body covered in a loose-fitting yellow house dress that made her look like a beanpole with a sack on it.

Rachel covered her face and screamed. She fell backwards into the pantry, landing on the trash can, spilling a wall of cans onto the floor and into her lap.

***

And when she opened her eyes, there was nothing there.

***

When Paul came home he found Rachel sitting in the passenger seat of her truck. She was staring out across the backyard, looking at nothing.

He tried the door, but it was locked.

He tapped a knuckle on the window.

"Hey, Rachel?"

No response.

He used his keys to unlock her door. She turned to look at him, and the sickened expression he saw in her eyes startled him. He noticed what she was wearing, a damp sleep shirt and blue panties. Nothing else.

"Rachel, are you okay?"

She shook her head slowly back and forth.

"What's wrong?"

"I..." she began, but trailed off with the rest of it unsaid.

He touched her shoulder and she flinched away from him.

"Whoa!" he said. "Rachel, what the hell?"

She blinked rapidly, and some of the fear and confusion seemed to go out of her eyes. She touched her tongue to her lips and took a deep breath.

"Are you okay?"

She nodded.

"Need a hand?"

"Yeah. Thanks."

He stepped back from the truck and let her climb out. He offered her a hand up the stairs to their apartment, but she shook her head and climbed up without his help. She was unsteady on her feet at first, her legs wobbly beneath her, but by the time they reached the top of the wooden staircase, she appeared to be walking normally.

He did notice her pause with her hand on the doorknob, almost as if she was steeling herself to go inside, but he didn't say anything to her. He let her take her time. Once they were inside she went to the bed and sat on the end of it, her hands folded in her lap, her face ashen. Paul glanced at her over his shoulder as he emptied his pockets onto the bedside table next to his side of the bed. He unsnapped his belt keepers and removed his gun belt and dropped it onto the floor beside the bed. Then he untucked his uniform jersey and unzipped it.

Rachel still hadn't moved.

"Rachel, what happened to you?"

She didn't look up, but she said, "Paul, what the hell is going on?"

"What do you mean?" he asked. "Rachel, did something happen?"

She laughed. "Did something happen? Yeah, Paul, something happened. Things are pretty screwed up, actually. Your family is screwed up."

Paul's expression hardened. "What happened, Rachel? Tell me." But she was getting up now, not looking at him, holding up the palm of her hand towards him as she walked away.

"Rachel! Wait, damn it. Tell me. What the hell's wrong with you?"

He went after her. He grabbed her by the shoulder and turned her around to face him.

"Don't touch me!" she screamed. Her eyes were wild with fear now. She had her hands up, her fingernails poised like claws, a cornered animal. "Don't you touch me!"

"Rachel? Rachel, I'm not gonna hurt you."

But she was backing away.

He stopped where he was and let his hands fall to his side.

"Rachel, I—"

"Get out."

"What?"

"You heard me. Get out, Paul. Leave. I can't take it anymore. I can't take you with all this...this...I don't know...with all this shit you've brought into our home. I can't take your father and your mother and the whole damn thing. It's too much, Paul. It's too much."

"Rachel, what are you talking—"

"Just leave. Please. Go."

"Rachel, let's talk about this. Come on. Tell me what happened."

But she exploded on him instead. She pushed him towards the door, screaming at him to leave, just leave damn it. And he let her push him out the door. He was too stunned by her ferocity, too cowed by his confusion and her rage to do anything but step out the door and down the first few stairs.

He turned back towards her. "Rachel, I—"

"Leave!" she screamed.

She slammed the door in his face. Paul stood there for a moment, wondering what in the hell just happened, when suddenly the door flew open again.

Rachel had his gun belt in her hands. The thing weighed twenty pounds and she handled it like a heavy coil of garden hose. With a great effort she heaved it over the stair railing.

"Hey," he said, and ran down the stairs to pick it up. The screen door flew open again and he looked up at her, his gun belt hanging from his fist, in time to see her toss a huge arm load of his clothes over the side. Shirts and t-shirts and jeans and socks came raining down on top of him.

"Jesus, Rachel. Stop!"

She disappeared inside. He stood looking at the clothes all around him. The old man in the backyard next door was watching him, a dog bowl in his hands, a wide-eyed look of surprise on his face at seeing a half-dressed San Antonio Police Officer getting tossed out of his own home.

"Shit," Paul muttered.

Rachel appeared above him. He started to call out to her, but she wouldn't have it. She tossed another armful of his laundry over the railing and he had to jump out of the way to avoid being hit by one of his boots.

"Rachel!" He screamed it at the top of his lungs. "Rachel!"

"Go away!" she shouted back from behind the screen door. "Leave me alone."

"Goddamn it, Rachel. What the—"

"I'm calling the cops!" she screamed. "Leave me alone. Go away!"

Paul was stunned into silence. He heard a window slide open. Rachel was there, watching him, her face an inscrutable mask.

Then she turned and walked away.

He looked down at his clothes. He looked at the old man watching him from the next yard over. He shook his head and said, "Shit," and then bent over and started picking up his clothes.

***

Inside the apartment, Rachel was trembling. She could feel her heart beating so hard in her chest that it scared her. For a moment she'd wanted to run down there and throw her arms around Paul and tell him to make it all go away. Then the anger overtook her again and she wanted to slap his face. She didn't know what to think. She felt like something inside her had been knocked out of gear, and now she didn't know how to put herself back the way she had been.

So she turned away from the window and walked back to their bed and stared at the rumpled covers and tried to think.

She noticed Paul's Barber fifty cent piece on the bedside table. Rachel ran to it and scooped it up. She almost ran back to the screen door at that point and yelled down for him to come back up.

Almost.

Instead she sat down on the bed and looked at his empty recliner and the box of photos on the ground and the emptiness of the apartment all around her, and she began to cry.

Chapter 20

Somewhere, a horn was blaring.

Paul looked up and for a moment was blinded by the sunshine. He was in his truck, still wearing his white t-shirt and uniform pants. He was drenched in sweat. His right foot had fallen asleep but was still on the brake pedal. His mouth was dry, and he could taste metal shavings on his tongue. He wasn't quite sure where he was.

The horn sounded again.

He looked into the mirror and saw a guy in a blue Honda making an angry gesture at him. *Get your ass movin'.*

"Alright, alright," Paul said. He blinked at the green light in front of him. He was at the intersection of West Avenue and Alhambra. West Avenue was a major street. He knew that one. The other one though, the one he was on, was unfamiliar.

How in the hell did I get here?

He took his foot of the brake and carefully accelerated onto West Avenue. The guy in the Honda shot past him, honking and shouting something indistinct out the window as he flew by.

Paul let him get away.

He was tired beyond belief. He had slept maybe a total of five hours in the last four days, and it was taking its toll on him. A curious sensation, like he was floating, had settled over him, and as he drove on he couldn't make himself focus on anything in particular. Not Rachel. Not his father. Not even the charge he had to keep. The things that had happened at Magdalena's house, both before and after her death, kept getting in the way and scattering his thoughts.

He turned onto the freeway and drove for a long time. He headed away from town, barely noticing as the hive-like congestion of the city gave way to oak forests and rocky hillsides and the occasional hillside cow pasture. He turned off the highway and onto the rolling two lane country road that led to the house where he was raised. He was heading home. The impulse to head there to the old house had been vague at first, like a smell he couldn't quite place, but it got stronger the closer he got to the Hill Country. There were no businesses out here, and very few homes. Massive oaks formed a green tunnel over his head. Sunlight pierced the canopy and made checkerboards of light and shadow that blinked on the windshield and lulled him even further into a blissful sort of stupor that was like drifting. For the first time since his troubles began two weeks earlier he had a sense of being without apprehension. It wasn't that he felt at ease, or even comfortable. Far from it. There was so much hanging over his head, so very much. But for the time being, driving down this country road, with its slow, rolling hills and gentle curves and hazy morning sunlight that gave everything it touched a sodden, dreamlike quality, it was as if a weight had been pulled off him.

And then, just like that, he was slowing to a crawl in front of his old family home, turning into the driveway, hearing the familiar muffled pops of loose rock beneath his tires.

Paul Henninger was home.

***

He climbed down from his truck and closed the door. After his father's death, there had seemed nothing worth keeping about this place, and so he had sold it. At the time, Paul hadn't thought he'd ever come back. There wasn't any reason to. Everything about it was a bad memory. Plus, he needed the money to live on. The scholarship would only go so far, and he had the rest of his life ahead of him. Better, as Steve Miller so eloquently put it, to just take the money and run.

So he sold the land and the house for a pittance, maybe sixty cents on the dollar for what it was worth, and at the time it seemed like a good idea.

Now he was not so sure.

The man who bought the property had never been very specific about his plans for it. Only that he planned to divide it and sell it to the neighboring ranches to allow them access to County Road 131, which would shave a good twenty minutes or more off their route when it came time to transport their livestock to the Comal Stockyards.

At eighteen, Paul hadn't quite understood this plan, but he did know that the neighboring ranchers were living off their daily sweat and their nightly prayers, and that it would be a frosty day in hell before they scraped up enough hard cash to buy more land.

Now, looking at the land as a twenty-four year old who had felt more like a man than a son for a very long time, he was overcome by an unfocused restlessness that made him want to punch somebody in the face. The old house, which had never been much to look at anyway, was now nothing but a derelict almost completely swallowed up by the vegetation around it. The roof was rusted and coming apart. The wooden walls were weathered to a mealy gray. Quite a few boards had fallen away, so that from where he stood he could look into the darkness inside the house. Almost every single window was broken out. The front door was hanging by its bottom hinge. Machine parts and the battered remains of furniture littered the yard. Everywhere he looked the cheatgrass had grown tall. The yard swarmed with crickets and butterflies. Ball moss hung thick from every tree. At one time, there had been a path that led from the driveway to the screen door that opened onto the kitchen. That path was gone now, grown over.

Well what did you expect to happen? It's not yours anymore.

But it was his. He didn't own it, not legally anyway, but he still had more of a claim to it than anybody else. Even more of a claim than the man who'd bought it. After all, this was his past, his memory. This was the part of him that was supposed to be inviolate. And it was just sitting here, forgotten, rotting.

But he hadn't seen the worst of it.

Two enormous oaks flanked the backyard. When Paul was growing up, they had shaded the yard where the goats roamed at feeding time. He and his father had spent a great deal of time keeping those trees trimmed up so that they wouldn't damage the roof of the house or the barn. Walking the property in the morning after hard winter freezes, Paul had often heard the ice-laden oak limbs snapping and cracking beneath the weight of the ice. And once, down in the horse pasture, Paul had seen a sixty foot high oak split completely in half by the weight of the ice. He could only guess that something like that had happened to the oak nearest him, for a large limb that had grown over the eaves of the house had broken away from the tree and crashed through the roof and into the living room.

From the screen door at the edge of the kitchen he could see the dead limb on the living room floor. It had broken through the ceiling just behind the wall that separated the kitchen and the living room, and it had hit with enough force to knock all the cabinetry on that wall forward, so that the doors and the drawers yawned open.

He walked inside, glanced up the flight of stairs toward his old room, then continued on into the living room. Paul stood in the doorway, lost in a sort of nostalgia-induced sadness. The floors felt spongy beneath his boots. The hole in the ceiling was considerable. Trash was everywhere, beer bottles and soda cans and empty bags of chips and papers and even a few condom wrappers.

Kids from the high school, he thought. He couldn't blame them, not really. He probably would have done it too back in his day if he'd had a place like this to party.

He turned and went down the short hallway that led to the front of the house. There were two rooms here, one on either side of the front door. The one off to his left had been intended as a sitting room, but over the years had become a receptacle for all the machine parts his father had accumulated. The room to his right was a small bedroom, and the sight of it raised the gooseflesh on his arms. This was the room where his mother had spent most the years of Paul's youth. It was completely empty, save for a metal framed bed bolted to the floor. The mattress was still on it, though the moths and the mice and the raccoons had chewed it to pieces. He saw a pair of metal rings bolted into the wall, one on either side of the bed. The wood around the rings was gouged and scratched. He turned and saw the yellow wall. His father had painted this wall just before his mother got sick and started her rapid slide into depression, and even then Paul had hated the color. It was a sick-looking yellow, the color of bile, broken only by a strange, looping pattern of gray lines that curved around each other and chased each other into dead ends or trailed off into nothingness. There was a worn, blackened area that went the length of the wall near shoulder level, and as he stared at it, Paul remembered the long hours his mother had spent pacing back and forth in front of that wall, dragging her hand along it.

He walked toward the wall and reached out to touch one of the gray lines, wondering if he could trace its path through the yellow field and if it might somehow tell him something about the many secret and powerful things his father knew. There was still so much to learn, so many things he didn't understand. Every connection he could make with his father now was a possible bridge to the knowledge he needed if he was ever going to be able to keep his charge.

But as he grew nearer, he began to see something moving in the yellow field behind the gray lines. At first it was too vague to make out. A shadow moving across the wall? But that wasn't what it was at all. He could tell that now. It was taking shape. He barely had time to draw a breath before the shadow finished resolving itself into the form of his mother, wild-eyed and dirty, her face warped with anger. She grabbed the gray curling lines painted on the yellow field of the wall like they were prison bars and she began to shake them with a lunatic fury that left him too stunned to move.

She screamed his name, over and over and over again, only there was no sound. The house was quiet as a country field.

"Paul!" she shouted, and shook the bars so furiously the whole house should have collapsed around them. He took a step back, slowly shaking his head, denying her. "Paul!"

And then something seemed to give. She exploded outwards with a crash that was like a mountain of glass shattering. She reached for him, her hands gnarled and filthy, and grasped his shoulders. He screamed and fell over backwards to get away, hitting his back on one of the bed's foot posts. The impact knocked the wind from his lungs, and for a moment, before it all slipped into darkness, he saw the room changing.

***

He stood in a room he had never seen before. It was the same room in the same house, but it had never looked like this—at least, not in his memory. There was a small loveseat in one corner, an end table next to that. His mother, young, pretty, healthy-looking, but sad, sat reading a book by somebody named Philip Larkin, her legs tucked up under her the same way Paul had seen Rachel do a million times. The room was filled with sunlight. It felt warm and comfortable. The faintest trace of a smile creased the corner of his mouth.

He heard something topple over and crash in the living room. Paul looked from the doorway to his mother. She lowered the book and frowned. Then she closed the book and set it on the end table and walked out of the room. Paul followed her, amazed at the woman's grace, at the easy feminine way she moved. How long ago was this? Where was the frail, drugged-looking woman who seemed like she was constantly about to fall over and hurt herself?

He rounded the corner behind her and saw her rushing toward his father. Martin Henninger was crumpled on the floor in front of one of his stick lattices. Even at a distance, Paul could feel the power coming off the lattice.

"Martin?" his mother said, kneeling at his father's side. "Martin, are you okay?"

Paul could hear his father breathing. It was the sound of man pulling himself together, dragging himself up from a depth.

"I'm fine," he said. "Let me be."

He got to his feet. He straightened the black Stetson on his head. His white, long sleeve shirt was sopping wet with sweat. His face was milky pale.

"What happened?" she asked.

"Go into that room up there and clear it all out," he said. He was out of breath, but he managed to get that under control. "Everything goes. Pictures off the wall. Your books out of there. Everything."

"Clear it out? But why?"

Paul watched his father's face. He saw the man clenching his teeth. He could see the muscles twitching along the ridge of his jaw.

"Goddamn it, Carol. Go clear out that room. I want all your junk out of there. Go, now!"

Almost by instinct, Paul took a step back. He knew that look. Growing up, he had become an expert at reading his father's moods, at studying the shifting emotional weather inside the house. He knew there was a point, a sort of middle ground between his father's wide ranging plains of calm indifference and his sudden, mountainous peaks of inexplicable and uncontrollable rage. That middle ground came and went with the suddenness of a spark off a flint rock. Failure to catch that spark and back away in time meant you were gonna get hurt.

He wondered what was wrong with his mother, why she couldn't see it.

And then it was too late for her. Martin Henninger shoved her into the wall. Slapped her face hard enough to send an echo ringing through the house.

Her head hit the wall and her knees buckled. She slid down the wall.

"Do it now!"

When she still didn't move fast enough for him, he grabbed her by the armpit and dragged her into the break room. He threw her onto the floor in the middle of the room.

"All of this crap goes," he said. "Get it cleaned out."

His mother held her bruised cheek in silence, not daring to look at him. He recognized the look on her face. Paul had seen the look plenty of times while out on patrol handling domestic violence calls. It was the look of a woman who's been hit before. But it had been a long time since he'd seen it on his mother's face, and it made something unpleasant move in his gut.

"Move!" his father shouted.

Martin Henninger crossed the room to the far wall and grabbed a framed photograph off the wall and threw it at his wife.

"Get this crap out of here! All of it."

He began to dismantle the room, tearing everything off the walls, throwing books out into hall.

"Martin, stop!" his mother cried. But it did no good. The man was possessed by rage. He was like a ferocious and terribly strong two year old in the middle of a fit. He didn't hear anything. You couldn't reason with him. His world had turned red.

"Do it now!" he shouted, and took a small picture from the end table and slammed it down on the floor. The glass over the picture shattered, and Carol Henninger turned her face away from the spray of glass shards.

"Pick it up," his father said. "Get it out of this room."

Paul watched her scramble toward the busted picture frame. He saw her face as she picked up the picture and separated it from the wreckage. He saw the picture. It was him as a baby, sitting in the grass, his mother kneeling forward to touch the tip of his nose with her finger.

"I'm gonna be gone for about an hour. Make sure this room is empty by the time I get back. You hear me?"

Paul felt a mixture of love and fear and pain as he watched his mother tuck the picture up into the folds of her skirt.

"You hear me?" Martin Henninger roared.

She nodded.

"Then say the Goddamn words."

"Yes," she said. "I hear you, Martin."

"Better," he said, and stormed out of the house, the screen door slamming behind him.

***

The view shifted again, and this time Paul found himself on the opposite side of the room. Everything was bare save for the metal framed bed bolted to the floor. His father stood near the far wall, a paintbrush in his hand, a bucket of gray paint at his feet. He was working steadily, drawing the strangely curling gray lines onto the yellow field he had just finished painting.

His mother stood in the doorway, crying quietly to herself.

"Why are you doing this, Martin?"

His father didn't answer, didn't even look at her, but Paul knew the answer. At least a part of it. He had felt it when he stared at the stick lattice his father had been working on shortly before he forced his mother to empty out the room. He had seen a flash of what his father had planned.

"Martin, what's happening to you?"

Nothing.

Just then Paul heard footsteps in the hallway. His mother turned. Paul was there. Paul as he had been at three or maybe four years old.

"I taked out the feed like you said, Momma."

She made a furtive glance towards Paul's father, then back to the boy.

She said, "That's good, baby. Why don't you go outside and play for a little, okay?"

"I don't wanna."

"Please, baby. Just do as I ask."

But Paul walked past her and stared into the room. He stared at the sickly yellow and the gray lines his father was painting and he said, "That looks yucky."

"Baby, please," his mother said, and grabbed him by the shoulder and guided him back to the hallway. "There's some peach baskets out in the yard, Paul. Can you go gather them up for Momma and put them in the barn, please?"

"Ah, Momma, I don't wanna."

"Go, Paul. Do what Momma says."

The boy ran off. She watched him run, then turned back to her husband, who was still painting the gray lines onto the yellow wall.

"It's Paul, isn't it?" she said.

Martin Henninger went on painting.

"What have you got planned for him? What kind of twisted shit are you planning to drop on our son?"

Martin Henninger didn't answer. Never even looked away from the wall. But he didn't have to. Paul knew the answer to that question, too.

***

A power drill went off behind him. Paul turned and saw his father tightening down the screws on one of the metal rings on the wall next to the bed. His mother sat on the edge of the bed. She had lost weight. Her hair was unwashed and straggly, and in the dusty shaft of sunlight that came through the window Paul could see that it was starting to turn gray.

His mother was staring at the rings on the wall with a sick look on her face. "What are those for?" she said. "You don't need those."

Paul looked away. The yellow wall was already starting to show black scuff marks where his mother had rubbed it with her hands while pacing back and forth. He sensed that the wall was like a movie screen, showing his mother visions of her future. Something his father had created as a constant reminder of his power over her. Paul knew that she had spent long hours in this room, and the images she had seen in that wall had left her shaken. It was the gateway to her depression. She had seen herself sapped of vitality, of life, estranged from her child, bled dry by depression. She had seen so much that it had become her reality.

"You don't need those things," she said again to Paul's father. Paul turned back to the two of them. "I'm not going anywhere, Martin. You know that. I can't."

He finished mounting the ring and put away his drill and got up and crossed to the doorway, leaving her on the side of the bed without looking back.

"I don't understand you, Martin. Why are you doing this to me? Why are you taking our son away from me? Why don't you just kill me and be done with it? I don't fight you anymore."

And then the four-year-old version of Paul came running down the hallway and stopped in the doorway. He tried to enter the room, but his father put a hand on his chest and held him back.

The child version of Paul looked at his mother sitting on the edge of the bed and said, "Momma, I'm hungry."

But Carol Henninger didn't look up. She was staring down at her hands in her lap. She sagged into herself like she was drugged, a limp shell, empty on the inside. But the adult Paul knew better. He could feel what his father was doing to her, holding her down, forcing her to be silent with the strength of his mind. Paul winced. All this had been going on, would continue to go on, for years, and he would live in the same house with this and never suspect a thing. How could he have been so blind to it?

Martin Henninger pushed his child back into the hallway. "Go outside for a bit," he said.

"What's wrong with Momma?" the boy said.

"Momma ain't feeling good, Paul. Go on now. Get yourself outside for a while."

The boy looked from his father to his mother and then back to his father, his expression uncertain. "Yes sir," he said, and gave his mother another worried glance before walking away.

***

Paul felt dizzy. He put a hand to his head and blinked, and when the feeling left him, the phone was ringing. He was still in the old house, still in the vision, but things had changed. The house was dirty, the floors littered with machine parts. It was dark, too. Heavy drapes hung over the windows, and the air was thick and musty with the taint of a protracted sickness.

Paul walked out of the room with the yellow wall, down the hallway to the living room, and saw his mother curled up on the couch. Twelve year old Paul was standing in the kitchen next to the screen door in his football gear, waiting on Steve's father to pick him up.

His mother said if the phone was for her to tell them she wasn't feeling up to talking.

His father was outside, yelling at him to answer the Goddamn phone.

The boy answered, and Paul remembered it all again as he watched the boy try to make sense of the Spanish Magdalena Chavarria was firing at him.

And then his father was standing in the doorway, demanding to know who it was.

Paul watched his father take up the phone and fire back in Spanish, speaking it like a native. He watched his father lean back against the wall.

He heard him say, "*Si, te oi. Yo tengo que guardar un cargo,*" and the words shot a chill down his spine.

I have a charge to keep.

And then his father hung up the phone. The twelve year old Paul said, "Daddy, I didn't know you could talk Mexican."

"Go outside, Paul."

"Huh?"

Martin Henninger's eyes flashed. "I said, go outside! You're waiting on Steve. Go do it in the driveway."

Even from across the kitchen, the older Paul could hear his father's teeth grinding.

The twelve-year-old Paul just looked confused, and a little sad now that he knew they weren't going to talk about how his father knew Spanish.

He hung his head and said, "Yes sir."

When the boy was gone, Martin Henninger stepped into the living room and stared at his wife on the couch.

"Get up."

His mother stirred. Paul watched her move. She was so sluggish, like her body was stiff and achy. Every move seemed to bring her pain. He watched her, and he realized something. She had been reduced to a puppet. Her body had been broken. Her thoughts were not private. Her will was almost completely gone. His father controlled her absolutely. She was basically a faucet that he could turn on and shut down whenever he needed something from her. Clean the house. Cook for the child. Feed the child. Put the child to bed. Dress it, care for it, maintain it for the greatness it will one day inherit. She was a slave to her husband's will, and in that horrible moment Paul realized that his father had been keeping her around solely to care for him, and the knowledge made him want to vomit.

When she was on her feet, he said, "I want the kitchen cleaned. I want everything in here cleaned up. You hear me?"

"Yes, Martin. I hear you."

"You've got two steaks in the freezer."

"Yes."

"Cook them both. One for me, one for Paul. He's got a big night ahead of him."

A long pause. Too long.

"You hear me?"

"What are you gonna do, Martin?"

"That ain't your concern. Just get this place cleaned up."

"Martin, that's my son. I won't let you corrupt him. I won't let you make him into what you are. You're evil, Martin. You're a sick, evil man, and I won't have my boy being anything like you."

Paul's mother was breathing hard, her mouth twitching with barely contained rage. But his father was calm. He almost looked amused.

"I got big plans for Paul, Carol. He's gonna be powerful one day. You don't know how powerful. When he's a man he's gonna lead nations. Nations, Carol! Do you understand that? He will be a prophet, and his words will be as sweet in their ears as honey on their tongue. Can you picture that? Can you picture this world passing away, and my boy ushering in a new age?"

"I don't want him being anything like you."

Martin Henninger did something then that surprised Paul. He walked across the room to where his wife stood cowering and he put a hand on the back of her head and he stroked her oily gray hair almost like a master strokes a dog.

He said, "Carol, he ain't gonna be like me. He's gonna be bigger, stronger, more powerful. And sweetheart, it ain't your decision to make."

She pulled herself away from him.

"It is, too. I'll take him away from here. Away from you!"

"What you're gonna do is clean this kitchen. After that you're gonna—"

"You go to hell, Martin Henninger!" She was nearly spitting the words at him. "You go to hell, you bastard!"

"Carol, you're gonna clean this kitchen up. Now if you wanna get the shit kicked out of you before that happens, well, that's your decision to make. Either way it's fine by me. The job will get done regardless."

They stood there, staring at one another. Paul watched them both. He could feel his father exerting his power over her, and he could feel her fighting against it. Her whole body was quivering with the effort.

Finally, she broke.

Her shoulders sagged.

Her eyes turned down to the floor.

Martin Henninger smiled, turned, and walked out the door.

His mother left the kitchen and went to the room with the yellow wall. Paul followed her, wishing that he could say something to her. He wanted to tell her that he had misunderstood, that he had screwed up so very badly. He had no idea what she had been fighting against, and the fact that she had lasted as long as she did spoke to the depth of her feelings for him. All this time, she had been acting as a buffer between him and his father, keeping the man at bay by sacrificing herself. She had fought to save him, and all he had thought to do was hate her for taking the coward's way out.

She went to the bed and reached under it and came up with the picture Paul had seen her secret away in the folds of her skirt. She sat on the edge of the bed and held the picture in her lap and sobbed quietly. Then she sniffled and wiped her eyes with the back of her hand and flipped the picture over.

She took a pen from her blouse and started to write something on the back of the picture.

She was writing from memory, and writing quickly.

He only saw the first line before the room around him started to shift, but that first line was like a punch in the gut.

They fuck you up, your mum and dad.

***

Whatever it was she had written on the back of that picture had been some sort of victory for her. Every stroke of the pen had been another step towards standing up straight and taking back a piece of herself from the black pit that was her marriage to Martin Henninger. She was stronger now. Paul could feel her strength echoing through the house. And it wasn't just coming from her as she walked through the kitchen, cleaning, smiling, even whistling a tune that, to Paul at least, sounded like vintage

Patsy Cline. It wasn't just that. He could also feel it as a sort of positive energy, an eddy breaking the smooth flow of his father's power. Martin Henninger watched her moving through the house, and he was trying to reassert his sway over her, but somehow the connection had shorted out. His control was slipping, and he knew it. He was flustered, uncertain, even a little scared of her now. She was still a dog in his eyes, but a dog who no longer cowers just because the master raises his fist.

Martin Henninger came up behind her as she did the dishes and stroked the back of her hair. She stiffened for just a moment, an almost imperceptible moment, but never stopped scrubbing the pot in the sink.

He said, "You don't like it when I touch you like that, do you?"

"I'm working."

"That ain't what I asked," he said. And as Paul watched, his father curled his mother's hair around the back of his fist and yanked her head back until her face was pointed up at him.

In a breathless whisper, she said, "You're gonna do whatever you want to do."

He didn't let go. He said, "That's right," and grabbed one of her breasts with his other hand and squeezed. It was a violation, a prelude to a rape. Paul felt his arms tremble with rage, his fingernails digging into the palms of his hands as they curled into fists.

His mother remained perfectly still. Her arms stayed limp at her side, and white, sudsy water dripped from her fingertips and onto the floor.

Just then there was the sound of a truck slowing out on the road.

Paul looked up. *Steve Sullivan's truck. I'll be coming home soon. I'll find her in here, and she'll be smiling. She'll say, "Hey baby. Hello Steve," and I'll think something is wrong because for the first time in God knows how long, she won't be a wasted vegetable curled up in the shadows. She'll look almost healthy, and I'll think something is wrong, but I'll think what's wrong is that she looks healthy. I'll never guess the truth. My God, I never had a clue.*

Martin Henninger's lip curled into a sneer of frustration. Carol Henninger just laughed. He said, "Damn it," and threw her to the floor.

Then he stormed out the screen door and let it slam behind him.

***

It was nighttime now, and he was standing in his old bedroom. Moonlight filtered in through the window above his desk, silvering the wooden floor. The air felt cool. On the bed a younger version of himself huddled beneath the blankets, listening to his parents screaming at each other down below. Paul, the boy, whimpered. Paul the man took a deep breath and walked out of the room and down the stairs and into the kitchen, where he saw his father slapping his mother to the floor.

She looked up at her husband and sneered through her bloody lips.

"You can't stop me," she said. "You can't. He's mine, and I won't let you have him."

"You ain't got no say in it," he said.

"I won't let you have him," she said again. There was no fear in her voice. Nothing in her eyes but contempt.

He raised the back of his hand to her, but she just laughed.

"Go on," she said. "Hit me. Hit me, you dumb bastard. You think you can break me. You can't break me. You've tried. For six years you've tried, and you still haven't done it. You hear me? You haven't!"

He lowered his hand and said, "You don't understand."

"Then tell me what it is I don't understand, Martin. I see you're trying to corrupt our son with your witchcraft. I hear you claim he's going to be some kind of god among men, but I can't think you actually believe that. You'd have to be insane to believe that. Are you, Martin? Are you really that fucking crazy?"

He regarded her with a cold intensity that made Paul's bowels quiver.

"You don't understand, Carol. You won't ever understand. Not fully. But I can show you."

He bent down, grabbed her by the hair at the back of her neck, and dragged her into the living room.

Once again Paul fought back the urge to intervene. But he knew that would be pointless, maybe even impossible. Whatever was about to happen had already happened twelve years ago. He couldn't change the past. And besides, he was being shown this for a reason.

His father dropped his mother onto the floor next to one of his stick lattices.

"You can close your eyes if you want. It don't matter. You'll still see."

He grabbed Paul's mother by the arm with one hand and placed his other on the stick lattice.

"Watch," he said, and focused on opening the doorway that led into the visionary landscape Paul had seen when he made his lattice.

Paul could feel a rush of energy swirling around him, moving through him, filling him up with its power and giving him a high like endorphins coursing through his veins. His father was feeling it, too. His eyes were closed, his head thrown back, his mouth open in ecstasy.

And then the world fell away and they were standing in a rubble-strewn street in the middle of a ruined city. Whole city blocks had crumbled into heaps of concrete and dust. Those buildings that still stood had been reduced to their frames. The sky above them was a swollen, unhealthy red that was filled with windblown ash. Towering columns of oily smoke rose all around him. The columns entered the sky and trailed away into black shoestring clouds. Everywhere about them, scared, dirty people scattered like mice for shelter.

Paul didn't recognize the city, but he knew that didn't matter. What he was seeing was happening all over the world. It was the same lowering sky over every living thing.

Strange, keening moans filled the air.

Paul turned toward the approaching moans. On top of a tabled slab of concrete not far away he saw a much older version of himself, scarred and bent-backed, but still obviously him, chanting, arms raised high over his head as an army of the dead poured into the streets. They came from every direction at once, rooting through the rubble, pulling the screaming people from their hiding places, devouring everything they touched. This was the end here. This was the turning point his father had promised him, the new world devouring the old.

Screams filled his ears.

Paul wanted to vomit. Beside him, his mother was covering her eyes with her hands. But Paul knew it wasn't making any difference. Eyes shut or eyes open, she saw it all just the same.

She was sobbing helplessly, and when she spoke, her voice was so shaken Paul could barely understand her.

"Why?" she said. "Why would you want something like this?"

***

When the scene cleared Paul realized he was crying. Could he really be responsible for what he had just seen? Even if he was only some sort of conduit for the power his father worshipped, it was still unacceptable. Even now he could smell the smoke and the ash in his nostrils and he hated it. He spit on the floor, and he gagged on the oily taste of his own saliva.

He was standing in the darkened living room of his old house, his father on his knees in front of a stick lattice, rocking back and forth and muttering to himself.

Somebody was banging on the screen door in the kitchen.

Martin Henninger rose to his feet and walked to the door. A pair of Comal County Deputies were standing there at the foot of the concrete stairs, Paul's mother between them. She looked utterly defeated. She was barefoot, wearing an old yellow housedress that accentuated the thin frailty of her body. She looked as unhealthy as an old used up crack whore.

Paul's heart went out to her. The vision his father had shown them had sickened her to her soul. It had sickened Paul, too, but it had affected her even more. It had sickened her so thoroughly that she had left Paul alone with his father, despite her promise to never give him up. Looking at her, he sensed that that was why she felt defeated. She had drawn a line for herself that she said she would never cross, a low to which she would never sink, and she had promptly sunk below it.

"We found her walking along County Road 131," one of the deputies said.

"Yeah?" said Martin Henninger. "So what?"

"She looks like she's had a pretty good scare, Martin. Anything you want to tell me about that? You guys have a fight?"

"She's fucking nuts," Martin said. "She wanders off sometimes and ain't got a clue what planet she's on. What the hell you want me to do about it?"

The two deputies looked at each other. The one who had spoken first, a white-haired, big-bellied man with a walrus mustache said, "We brung her back to you, Martin. How about you take her inside and get her some water or something? You could make her comfortable. That'd be the decent thing to do?"

"Fuck that," Martin said. "Leave her dumb ass there. She'll be all right." And then he walked back inside, letting the screen door slam behind him.

An awkward moment passed. The fat deputy whistled. His partner put his hands in his pockets. Paul's mother never moved. She just stood there, sobbing quietly.

The fat deputy said, "Ma'am, you gonna be all right if we leave you here?"

She didn't answer.

"Ma'am?"

The cop in Paul knew what the deputies were thinking. He'd been there himself. It was a bad situation. She didn't have any obvious injuries, and she wasn't saying anything to help them help her. All they had was a woman who appeared to be off her rocker and a husband with a reputation for being a first rate prick. But there were no obvious signs of family violence, and it wasn't a crime to be an asshole. They had no choice but to leave her here with this guy. There was nothing else they could do.

The fat deputy muttered something about calling them if she needed anything, and then the two men walked away, leaving her there in the dark.

Paul watched them get in their car and drive away.

He said, "Momma, how come you didn't tell them? You could have taken us both away."

But she gave no indication that she knew he was there.

His father swung open the screen door then and said, "You need to get yourself inside, Carol. I'm about ready and I don't want you hanging around out here. I want you up in the front room where you can't cause any trouble."

She looked up at Martin, her eyes vacant, like the eyes of the dead.

"Go on. Get inside."

"I don't wanna," she said, and the sudden, country girl twang in her voice surprised Paul.

Martin's voice was hard, but he hadn't started to yell yet. He said, "I don't care what you want. What you're gonna do is get your ass inside."

For a moment, her eyes cleared. Paul's father must have seen it, too, because he sprang forward and grabbed her by the wrist and pulled her inside.

"You wanna give me shit?" he said. "You think you can give me shit?"

He yanked her off her feet.

One leg went sprawling and hit a chair and knocked it over.

She pulled herself up and she fought him all the way up the hallway and into the front room. She kicked and bit and screamed as he handcuffed her to the rings on the wall, but he was too strong for her, and she never had a chance.

"I'm gonna stop you, you son of a bitch!" she screamed at his back as he walked away. "I'll stop you, I swear it!"

***

And the scene shifted again.

Paul was standing at the foot of his mother's bed in the front room. She was still fighting, still struggling to pull her hands loose from the handcuffs that held her to the rings in the wall. Her face was distorted by an almost animalistic rage.

Somehow she managed to get one hand free.

She looked at it with a mixture of rage and pain and victory. Then she stood in front of the other ring and began to pull her hand through the cuff. It took her several long minutes of grunting and screaming and hard breathing to get her other hand loose, and when it did finally come, her wrists and hands looked like they'd been dipped in red paint.

She could barely move her fingers, but somehow she found the strength to reach under the sheet and pull up the corner of the mattress and come up with a knife.

Paul gasped. He recognized that knife. Even after twelve years, he still recognized that knife.

***

Paul was numb as he watched the scene that followed. His mother raised the knife over her head and went screaming down the hallway.

His father was in the living room, preparing to make a lattice.

He turned and caught her arm and they fought.

She slashed at him the knife and missed.

He knocked her to the ground with a loud, echoing slap.

She scrambled to her feet and ran for the kitchen.

He hit her in the back of the head and knocked her flat. Paul followed them, an icy ball forming in his stomach as the most terrifying moment of his youth got closer and closer. Even as the fight rolled into the kitchen, he couldn't help but think what that kid up there in that room was going through. Right about now he'd be climbing out of his bed and ducking under it. He'd be curled up into a ball, convinced that his mother's insanity had finally crested into some kind of unstoppable, homicidal rage.

His mother climbed the stairs on all fours. His father was chasing her, screaming at her, "Don't do it, Carol! Damn it, woman, don't do it!"

And then she was inside the room, lunging for the bed. From the top of the stairs, Paul watched her stop when she realized the child wasn't where he was supposed to be. He saw her hesitate for just a second, and that second was all it took. Martin Henninger was on her. He hit her in the back of the head and caught her by the back of her neck before she sagged all the way to the floor. Paul watched the knife drop from her hand and stick into the floorboards.

There was no ceremony, no drama, after that. His father hauled her back down the stairs like she was a sack of goat feed, and Paul was left standing alone at the head of the stairs. And he guessed that was the way it should be. He had traveled back into a past that he always thought he understood, and was only now realizing that the water was deeper than he ever imagined.

But of course the worst was still to come.

***

Now he was standing in the barn, the scene lit by the silvered light of the moon. The night was cool. A breeze drifted through the gaps in the wood siding and sent bits of hay into the air.

He heard his father's voice behind him.

"Go on, Carol. Get in there."

He turned and saw his father shoving his mother into the barn. She had regained a little of her sense now, but she was still wobbly on her feet.

"You can't stop me, Martin. They'll see what you did to me. Look at my hands. You caused this. The cops see this, they'll take Paul away from you sure as Sunday. What do you think of that, you bastard? You lose."

Martin Henninger walked forward and grabbed her by the wrists.

"Is this what you mean?" he said. And as he held her wrists in his hands, the wounds began to heal.

It happened fast enough to make Paul's mother gasp. She looked at her hands, healed now so thoroughly that not even a speck of blood remained. The light went out of her. She wasn't going to be able to fight him like this and win.

"Don't look like that," he said. "You wanted to stop me? Well, you stopped me tonight."

She looked up at him, a question on her face.

"That's right. I'd wanted to tell Paul about his inheritance tonight, but you've made that impossible. It's gonna be six years before I can do it again. It'll take that long for the cycle to come back to this point. Six years. That's what you bought this miserable existence we call the world. Tell me, Carol, was it worth it? Was it worth dying to give the world six more years?"

"What do you mean?" she said. "Martin? Martin, please. Stop this."

But there was no stopping, not for her, and not for Paul. For even as she pleaded with her husband, he took control of her body, bending it to his purpose. Carol Henninger's hands took a long length of hemp rope from the wall and looped it into the coiled pattern of a noose.

"Martin, please..."

The rope went over a rafter. She secured one end to the steering wheel of a dilapidated tractor and pulled the noose over her head. She climbed onto the back tire of the tractor and tried to plead one more time with him for her life. But her pleas were in vain. With his mind he nudged her, and she stepped off the tire...

***

...and Paul gasped as he came to. He was standing in the barn. The daylight was failing, though it was still hot and the air very close with the smell of rotting wood and weeds.

For just a moment he had a vision of his mother swinging by her neck from the rafters, and the vision was so startlingly vivid that he even imagined he heard the creaking of the rope and the moaning of the wood that supported her weight. She seemed to waver in front of his eyes like a distant figure walking down a road filled with heat shimmers, and then she was gone. Everything was still again, and he was alone.

He turned away from the cavernous hold of the barn and walked out into the yard where the goats had once grazed. It was full of sunflowers now, and many of them had grown as tall as Paul. The road that led down to the horse pasture was carpeted over by weeds.

He turned away from it and walked back to his truck. There was a stiffness in his lower back and a soreness in his muscles that surprised him. He felt tired and old before his time. It was the vision his father had shown his mother that had done it to him. He knew that now. A long time ago his father had told him that his inheritance was a power money could not buy, the kind of power that changes the course of history and stamps itself upon the minds of men forever. Paul realized now that he had never truly understood what that meant. He'd listened to his father's promises and he'd envisioned a quiet, peaceful revolution spreading over humanity, a sort of glimmering golden age of prosperity and justice and good sense.

He was only now realizing that the vision his father had in mind was nothing short of an apocalypse, an end to this world and the birth of a new one populated by the risen dead. Power, true power, he saw now, had to be by logical necessity absolute, or it was not power at all. It was not enough to teach a man what to believe, or tell him what he should hear and say and do. It was not enough to punish him for doing or even thinking wrongly. It was not even enough to reprogram him from the inside out when the threat or application of force failed to compel total submission. The Inquisition had tried to do just that. And they failed. The totalitarian states of the communist block had tried also, in their way, and they had failed. All across the world cult leaders were continually trying to assert their own brand of absolute power upon their little communities, but each of them were destined to failure, as well.

Every system invented by man to control other men was, by the virtue of being created by a man, inherently flawed, for men lacked the capacity for absolute control. No matter how efficient the system, that system could not obliterate the spirit of man that was synonymous with life. As long as a man lived, that spirit was with him. It drove him to create art, to speak, to love, to accept the possibility that the world was not lost, not yet, and that the future for which he fought today and may never see was still, nonetheless, worth fighting for. Only death could stop that. Only death could erase the individual and make him truly one with the whole. It could clean a man's mind of all erroneous thought and make it a blank slate upon which that new perfect whole could be created. And Paul was the means to make that happen.

He was sitting behind the wheel of his truck, crying quietly to himself. He understood now why his mother had cried when his father forced his vision into her mind. She had seen right away what it meant. She grasped intuitively that it was more than the loss of life. It was more than the suffering and the pain and the sky smeared red and black by fire. She mourned those things also, but it was for the loss of the spirit of man that she cried. And the thought that the one person she loved more than all the world, more even than her own life, her child, was to be the agent of that loss, was emotionally crippling beyond anything Paul could imagine.

"You miserable bastard," he said to the picture of his father that suddenly appeared in his mind. "My inheritance—you want me to do to the world what you did to me. It's a lie, all of it, and I won't do it. Do you hear me? I won't."

He banged his fists down on the steering wheel. "Do you hear me? I won't do it!"

Chapter 21

She'd called Paul half a dozen times at least during the day. At first she was angry. Rachel told herself that when he finally answered his damn phone she was going to lay into him and say all the things she didn't get to say when she threw him out the first time. But as the day wore on, and he still hadn't answered his cell phone, she started to fray at the edges.

The air conditioner was blowing, but not doing much of anything to cool down the apartment. She sat in a kitchen chair with a box fan blowing over her and tried calling him again.

She got his voicemail.

"Paul," she said, "I'm sorry. Please call me back. Just talk to me. I was scared earlier. God, I was so scared. So much has happened in the last few days and I don't know what to do about it. But I know I love you. Please believe me on that. I don't want you to leave. I want you to come home. Please, if you can get off work tonight, come home. I don't care if we have to stay up all night, just come home. We can talk through this." She swallowed the lump in her throat and sniffled. "That's all I wanted to say, Paul. Just know that. I want you home with me."

Then she hung up.

She thought of calling him right back, leaving another message to tell him that she believed him now. After seeing his mother—God, after touching the breaker switches covered with human skin—she believed him. But she didn't call back. Calling him too many times before he was ready to talk might only serve to drive him away, and she couldn't afford that.

When he finally decided to call her, she would tell him she believed it all now. She would talk to him, and she would keep the whiney little girl buried deep down inside her. Paul didn't need to deal with that. He needed someone who would stand by him, and that was going to be her.

Their love was worth it.

***

And she was still telling herself that at 11:45 that night, though her brave face was starting to crumble. She was in bed, reading a book upon which she couldn't concentrate. The pages just looked like a blur. She folded the book down across her stomach and looked around the apartment.

Something was wrong, and it took her a long moment of staring out across the apartment to figure it out.

It was so quiet.

She listened to the silence and thought how strange that was. No matter what time of day, there was always traffic going by on the street below. Three o'clock in the morning on a Tuesday and you could still count on a car or two every couple of minutes. And that dog next door—about the only time of day that thing was quiet was in the heat of the afternoon when it was too hot to do anything but lay in the shade and pant.

She waited and listened and the silence stretched out interminably.

Finally, she couldn't take it anymore.

She went to the patio door and opened it and walked out onto the covered patio. The night was still, but not in a peaceful way. A faint breeze brushed against the Italian junipers that flanked the yard. Her bare legs were damp with sweat but she felt no chill from the breeze. If anything it was more stifling out here than it was inside. It was almost like a giant black blanket had been draped over the world. She could feel its smothering presence.

She was about to walk back inside when a car passed on the street below. Rachel watched it glide by, but didn't notice until it was out of sight that it made no sound.

"What in the...?"

There was a moment of self-doubt in the car's wake. She wasn't sure what she had just experienced. Maybe she just hadn't been paying attention.

She waited for another car to go by. One followed seconds later, and that one too passed in complete silence. No throaty exhaust notes. No tires slapping on concrete. No incoherent echo of a stereo played too loudly. The stifling night air suddenly felt dangerous. That was the first thought that came to her mind and it refused to leave. Something about all this was dangerous. She was in danger.

Rachel hurried back inside, closing the door behind her with a palpable sense of relief.

But the relief didn't last.

She thought of seeing Paul's mother and reaching into the pantry for the breaker switch and touching human skin instead. She asked herself why in the hell she was still here.

"Okay, right. Time to leave," she said. "Time to get in the truck and get the hell away from here."

She slid into a pair of jeans and put some clothes and her toothbrush into an overnight bag and headed for the backdoor.

Rachel got out onto the landing at the top of the wooden stairs that led down to the backyard and stopped.

Something was wrong.

She scanned the yard. On the other side of the carport was the familiar shed and concrete slab where the neighbors kept that miserable dog of theirs. It was standing up now on that concrete slab, facing her, its chain trailing out behind it and disappearing into the darkness on the other side of the shed. The dog was barking furiously, but there was no sound. And the yard was filled with shadows. More than the various objects along the fence line could account for. They looked intensely black against the green of the lawn.

Something was definitely wrong.

Rachel felt afraid. She had a sense that something was coming, the way one can smell the air and know a storm is on the way, and it paralyzed her. She tried to move her feet and just couldn't.

Then the dog was gone. She was watching it when it was sucked up into the darkness behind the shed. She blinked at the empty spot on the concrete slab. One moment the dog had been there, the next it wasn't. It was if some giant thing had grabbed the other end of the chain and yanked it back into the darkness with an almost cartoonlike suddenness.

"Oh my God."

She dropped the overnight bag next to her foot and clamped a hand over her mouth. There were naked men coming out of the shadows, moving like flowing water around the shed and across the lawn and over the fence into her yard.

One of the men in the front of the advancing crowd crossed into a yellow circle of lamplight and the sight of him took Rachel's breath away. He was a bent, gray-colored, skeletal thing. The face was grotesque and strangely protruded because of the way the body was bent forward. The skin seemed ill-fitting over the skull, almost like it had started to sag off the cheek bones. The eyes were vacant. The mouth seemed drawn-in, puckered like an old apple. But the most horrible thing about the man was his staggeringly advanced state of emaciation. His knees and elbows and knuckles seemed engorged. His thighs looked sickly. His biceps were so thin she could have probably encircled them by putting her thumb and forefinger together. His stomach had a sunken-in shape that made her wince.

She was thinking heroin addict until she saw the black Y-shaped stitching on his chest. It was only then that she thought of death.

She screamed.

There were more of them now.

Her eyes darted back and forth across the yard in blind panic. They were staggering across the yard in fits and jerks. They seemed so slow, and yet the distance between them and the house narrowed every second.

One of them hit the wall below her. She looked down at him, and he turned a dead face up at her.

"No," she said, barely able to make a sound for the painful beating of her heart. "No, you stay away!"

But the dead thing never hesitated. It slapped its hands against the wall and started to scale upwards, climbing with an insect-like motion that brought a fresh wave of screaming to Rachel's lips.

She ran inside and locked the door and scanned the room for something she could slide against the door to bar it. She saw the couch and got behind it and shoved it all the way across the floor to the door. It hit with a thud that was answered by a pounding from outside. She screamed, then screamed again as a hand punched through the top of the door and pushed it inwards. A man's gray, sunken face appeared in the hole, followed by his bare arms and shoulders.

She staggered backwards into the coffee table.

There was a crash to her left. Another one of those things was punching its way through the wall. Actually tearing its way *through* the Goddamned wall. Behind her, there were more of them breaking through the glass patio doors.

"No," she whimpered. "Stay away! Oh Jesus please, stay away!"

She was cut off, and they were getting closer. She tried to scream but couldn't. All she could make herself do was stumble backwards towards the bathroom and beg them not to come any closer.

She tripped over one of her boxes of books and when she looked up one of the dead things was almost on her.

She scrambled to her feet and picked up the box and threw it at the thing with everything she had. It hit the dead man in the shoulder and the box exploded open, spilling paperbacks everywhere, but the dead man didn't even flinch from it.

"No," she said. "Come on. No."

Her back hit the bathroom wall and her hand dropped to her side and the doorknob.

Right away she thought, *Get inside. Now!*

She slipped inside the bathroom, and right as she was about to slam the door saw Paul's Barber fifty cent piece and the cordless phone on the bedside table. She grabbed them both and closed and locked the door.

Rachel squeezed Paul's coin in her left hand and used the thumb of her right hand to punch in 911. She focused on the coin as the phone rang.

Please, Paul, help me. Oh Jesus, Paul. Please.

There was a crash on the other side of the door that made Rachel scream. The coin went flying out of her hand.

A woman's calm, almost bored voice came on the line. "9-1-1, do you need police, fire or EMS?"

Rachel screamed out something unintelligible about dead men tearing down the walls.

The dispatcher broke in and said, "Ma'am, I can't understand you. Ma'am, please. Ma'am, you need to—"

The bathroom door exploded open, and a moment later there were dead hands all over her.

Chapter 22

Paul was so exhausted when he arrived at the Eastside Substation that he didn't even notice Mike coming in right behind him from his jog.

Mike called out to him.

Paul stopped, turned around.

Mike looked Paul up and down and said, "Dude, what the hell happened to you? You sleep in that uniform?"

"Huh?"

Paul looked at himself. Only then did he realize he was still wearing his uniform pants and the black t-shirt with the worn-in sweat stain from where his body armor had been the night before. He was covered in dust and he smelled like rotted wood.

"What happened?" Mike asked. "Rachel kick you out?"

Paul didn't answer.

Mike laughed. "Holy shit. She did. She kicked you out."

"I don't want to talk about it, Mike."

"Man, you don't have to. One look at you and anybody could see it. It's written all over your face. Either she kicked your ass out, or you've been drinking for the last twelve hours."

"Mike, please..."

Mike threw up his hands. "Hey, it's cool, dude. You know what I always say—you're not a real policeman until you're on your third marriage."

Paul turned away, but Mike stopped him.

"Hey, Paul, come on. Wait. I'm just kidding." He said, "Look, you need to get changed out in a hurry. If Garwin sees you walking around in only part of the uniform like that, he'll write you up so fast you won't know if you're coming or going. And he won't care what kind of deal you got going at home. He isn't much on discipline, but the uniform is one of his pet peeves."

Paul just nodded and headed for the locker room. Mike followed him. He was still breathing hard from his run.

He said, "You've got an extra uniform, right?"

"Yeah," Paul answered. "All except the t-shirt. I guess I can just wear this one again."

"Like hell. Dude, you are not riding in the same car with me in that thing. You smell like goat piss. I got an extra you can borrow. I'm about as wide as you are tall, so it should fit you. What are you, a two XL?"

"Yeah," Paul said, then added, "Thanks."

"Still a man of few words, eh?"

Paul sighed. "It's been a bad day, Mike. You wouldn't understand."

"You'd be surprised," Mike said. "And we're gonna be spending the next eight hours together in the car. That's gonna feel like forever if you're gonna keep all this shit bottled up. You can talk to me about it. I mean, don't get the wrong idea or nothing. I ain't Barbara Walters. Your ass starts crying I'll throw you out on the pavement. But if you got some troubles, I don't mind listening."

Paul nodded.

"Seriously," Mike said. "No bullshit. I know more about wrecking a marriage than just about any man alive. You can listen to me, do the opposite of whatever advice I give you, and you should be golden."

That got a chuckle out of Paul.

"There you go," Mike said. "At least you're not gonna mope on me all night." He looked at Paul and said, "You're not, right?"

"No."

"Good. Listen, after you get dressed, you should call her. Tell her something nice. I mean, even if she yells at you. Don't make her beg you to come back. And you don't have to beg either. Just say something nice and leave it on that. Don't get into it. If she screams or yells or calls you names or whatever, just say something nice and then get off the phone. She'll be thinking about what you said all night, and when you come home—" he made a skating motion of one palm gliding over the other "—you'll be in like Flynn."

He accented it with a wink.

"I'll think about it," Paul said.

***

"44-70."

Mike was driving. Paul was looking out the window at the ruined shell of an apartment building. Mike waited for Paul to acknowledge the call, but he just went right on staring out the window, oblivious.

Mike keyed up and said, "44-70, go ahead, ma'am."

"44-70, make 360 Jaffrey. Complainant states she's pregnant and her husband just hit her in the stomach and threw her down the stairs. Sorry, Mike, I got no cover available. I'll start the next available your way."

"10-4, ma'am," Mike said. "We're on the way."

Paul swiveled the laptop around to his side and started to run the history on the address.

"Don't bother," Mike said.

301 |

"You know the address?"

"Yeah. The guy's name is Jimmy Schultz. Date of birth is 12-12-86. Last time I ran him he was on probation for methamphetamines. He's a burglar, too. If we catch up with him, you can pretty much count on him being high. First he'll run, then he'll want to fight."

Paul ran the guy's name on the MDT and got a felony warrant hit.

"Look at that," he said to Mike, and swiveled the laptop towards Mike.

They were southbound on Loop 410, the freeway almost empty ahead of them. Mike had gunned the Crown Victoria and now they were doing over ninety miles an hour. As the car rolled up and down over the uneven road, Mike glanced at the screen.

"Blue warrant from the State Parole Board," Mike said. "Sweet. Looks like Jimmy came up dirty on his last drug test. Man, I'd love to get a hold of him. You're gonna love this guy. He's a major sack of shit."

Paul closed the MDT's screen and leaned back in his seat, watching the freeway through the windshield.

"You're getting used to my driving, aren't you?" Mike said.

"Huh?"

"You don't look seasick."

"Yeah," Paul said, noticing that for himself now. "How about that?"

***

Paul's first thought when they entered the apartment was that somebody had been shot at close range with a shotgun. Everything in the room was white. From the carpet to the walls to the ceiling fan to the brand new leather furniture set, all of it was as white as a cloud on a summer day. Except now of course it was spattered all over with Louisiana Hot Sauce.

The smell was horrible. Paul picked up on it before he entered the room. It irritated his nose and his throat and his eyes with the same intensity that he had felt when Rachel tried to make homemade enchiladas and burned the sauce. It was the same peppery burn.

Their complainant was a skinny girl of nineteen with stringy black hair and tattoos down her right her arm and splotchy bruising all over her skin. Paul had come to recognize the look as one of the calling cards of the career junkie. The swell of pregnancy was just starting to show beneath the black tank top she wore.

She told them her boyfriend was high again on meth and that he had flipped out on her when a guy had called the apartment asking for her. He got so mad he took a giant one liter bottle of hot sauce and splashed it everywhere, all over her new furniture.

"All this furniture's brand new? How much did it cost?" Mike said.

"It cost me eighteen hundred dollars," she said. "That bastard ruined it. You see that? Look at that. That's felony criminal mischief right there. You gonna arrest him for that?"

She had her hands on her hips now, her lips pressed together so tightly they seemed to disappear entirely.

"Ma'am," Mike said, "when you called you said he hit you. You said he threw you down the stairs."

"Shit, he hits me all the time. You people don't do nothing about it."

"Have you ever filed charges on him?"

"No, that's your job."

Paul willed himself not to breathe in too deeply. He had become aware of an underlying stink in the place that not even the hot sauce could completely conceal. It was like set-in sweat and grime and rot. Meanwhile Mike was using as much patience as Paul had ever seen him use. He was trying to tell the girl that what she really needed was for EMS to take her to the hospital so that she and her unborn child could get checked out by a doctor.

"Bullshit," she roared. "I ain't got no money. I ain't got no job. I ain't got no insurance to pay no doctor with. I just wanna know what you're gonna do about my furniture. You gonna arrest him or what?"

Mike's patience did have limits, though.

"So you ain't got no job, and you ain't looking for no job, but you got brand new eighteen hundred dollar white leather furniture. You got a big screen TV over there, too. I bet you get about a thousand channels on thing. You got money enough for all that, but you ain't got money to get your unborn child checked out?" He made an exaggerated show of looking around the apartment. "I don't see no kid stuff around here. No crib, no toys, no books on childcare. That little baby of yours is off to a great start, huh?"

"Fuck you," she said.

Mike just shrugged. Then he called for EMS to check out the girl and an evidence technician to come out and take pictures of her injuries.

"I ain't gonna go with them," she said.

"Listen, girly. Personally, I don't give a shit about you. I can take one look at you and tell your life is going nowhere. You're an oxygen thief as far as I'm concerned. But that baby inside you is something else. I don't know what he did in a past life, but unless he was Jeffrey Dahlmer I know he doesn't deserve a momma like you. So this is what I'm gonna do. You don't merit the paperwork it's gonna take me, but I'm gonna handle your situation right down to the letter of the law. And when we're done, we'll see if we can't talk you into going to a doctor to check that kid out."

"Yeah?"

"Yeah."

"You gonna pay for that?"

"Nope. You sell enough drugs to buy this furniture and that TV over there, you should be able to divert some of your profits to your kid."

"Fuck you."

Mike smiled. "Well, that's one way to look at it. Another way would be to say that your failure as a parent is my job security."

"Asshole."

She sat down on a corner of her couch that wasn't covered in hot sauce and wouldn't look at them, and that pretty much ended the conversation until EMS arrived.

***

Two hours later, as they were walking down the stairs and out to the street to their patrol car, Mike said, "You know, Paul, I fucking hate the public. I mean, I used to love this job. I used to have so much fun. Nowadays though, I'm beginning to feel more and more like Collins. I just dread it, everyday."

"Yeah," Paul said. "She was a piece of work."

"It's not just her. She was human trash, yeah, but it's not just her. Have I ever told you my idea for solving San Antonio's crime problem?"

"No," Paul said. "This ought to be good."

"This is the way I see it. We take the whole eastside of San Antonio, divide them up into two teams, and stick them on opposite sides of the Alamodome. It'd be like dodge ball in school when we were kids. Remember that? Except, instead of balls, we put a whole pile of loaded weapons between the two teams. We let them shoot it out, and the last person left standing we file murder charges on. Problem solved."

But Paul had stopped listening midway through Mike's rant. They had made it down to the front lawn of the apartment building and he was watching the gap between two buildings across the street.

He said, "Hey, Mike, what was that guy's name again? The boyfriend who beat her up?"

"Jimmy Schultz."

"Look over there," Paul said, and pointed at a man slipping between some scraggly shrubs across the street. "Is that him?"

Mike broke into a smile.

***

"Hey Jimmy!" Mike shouted.

The man never even looked back. He balled his fists, hopped once on one foot, then broke off into a dead sprint between the buildings.

Paul and Mike went after him. Paul left Mike behind almost immediately. There was a sagging wire fence at the end of the alley, still shaking from where Jimmy had just climbed it, and Paul hit it at a run. He was already throwing himself over the top as Mike entered the alley behind him.

Paul landed in a graveyard of old appliances. Everywhere he looked he saw rusted refrigerators and stoves and washing machines and pile after pile of worthless junk. He scanned the darkness, aware of the sound of his own breathing, and listened.

He heard movement off to his right. Mike was climbing over the top of the fence behind him. Paul caught Mike's eye and pointed towards the noise.

Over there, his gesture said.

Mike nodded, then let himself drop to the ground in silence. The two of them pulled their guns and advanced on Jimmy.

Mike came up on him first. Paul saw Mike throw his back up against a refrigerator door and then shout, "Get down on the ground, Jimmy! Down!" Then, his voice suddenly shifting from commanding to scared shitless, Mike shouted, "Oh shit! Gun! Drop it, Jimmy. Drop it!"

There was a noise of somebody scrambling through the junk. Metal shelves and pipes and debris fell from their piles and clattered on the floor as Jimmy scrambled out from his hiding place and under the metal fence.

Paul ran forward.

Mike shouted, "Paul, no," but it was too late. Paul was already belly-crawling under the fence.

When Paul came up on the other side he was facing a vast expanse of undeveloped scrub land. Mesquite and oaks and cedar grew in wild effusion. Grasses and shrubs were neck high in the spaces between the trees. Paul caught sight of their man slipping between a pair of gnarled oaks and he took off running for him.

He could hear Mike behind him telling him to stay back, but he didn't listen. Paul reached out with his mind and locked in on Jimmy. He could feel the man's fear. He could feel Jimmy's blood pounding inside his ears, the heart thudding madly in his chest. The man was terrified, and Paul was feeding off that terror. It was making him stronger, and as he tore through the trees and the tall grass he sensed something powerful gathering itself together inside him.

By the time they cleared the thickest part of the trees Paul was almost on the man. He turned and saw Paul behind him and let out a terrified shriek. The gun was still in his hand, but he didn't try to use it. He seemed too scared to realize it was even there.

"Stay away," he screamed, and then turned sharply and ran for a black line in the ground about thirty yards off to their right.

Paul stayed with him, gaining on him. He was completely focused now, every nerve in his body alive with energy. The man reached the black line just ahead of Paul and suddenly fell away out of sight. Paul followed without hesitation. It was an embankment, and the man was tumbling down it, towards a black weed-choked pool of water at the bottom.

He tumbled all the way into the water, then scrambled to his feet. He turned on Paul and almost got the gun up in time.

"Drop it!" Paul said.

Jimmy obeyed immediately, tossing the gun into the weeds at Paul's feet. His eyes were wide with a fear. His whole body was shaking.

"Please don't kill me." He sank to his knees. "Jesus, please. Please don't."

"Get down," Paul said.

Jimmy obeyed that order, too. He flung himself face down into the water, his fingers laced together over the back of his head.

Paul waded into the pool and stood over Jimmy, who was just keeping his face above the water, but refused to look at Paul. He was shaking worse than ever now, and it sounded like he was crying. Paul heard him muttering over and over again, "Please don't hurt me. Please. Please don't hurt me."

Paul handcuffed him, then pulled him to his feet. He dragged Jimmy out of the water, and as he started up the embankment, still dragging Jimmy, who had gone as limp as a dead man, he heard Mike screaming over the radio for the helicopter.

Paul grabbed his radio with his free hand and said, "44-70, tell my partner I got our guy. I'm bringing him back now."

The relief in the dispatcher's voice was palpable. She said, "44-70, 10-4. Are you okay?"

"Yes, ma'am. I'm fine."

"Copy, 44-70 Alpha? He's okay."

"10-4, ma'am," Mike said. "Paul, where are you?"

"I'm coming back to your location, Mike. Just stand by. I'll be there in a sec."

Mike met up with them right where the trees started to get thick. He gave Paul a look that was part condemnation, part palliation. "Damn, Paul, you had me fucking worried, man."

Paul walked right by him.

"Hey, what the hell?" Mike said.

Jimmy started whimpering. He turned to Mike and said, "Please don't let him hurt me. Please, get him away from me."

"Be quiet," Paul said, and Jimmy instantly went still. "Come on. Move it."

They reached the fence and had to go single-file along it to skirt the buildings where the pursuit had started. Mike let Paul go first. Then he pushed Jimmy behind Paul.

"I got him," Mike said. "Go ahead."

He grabbed one of Jimmy's biceps and Paul let go of the other one.

306 | Joe McKinney

But as soon as Paul let go, Jimmy started to fight. He bucked away from Paul and tried to scramble past Mike with everything he had. Mike wasn't expecting the move and got pushed into a mesquite branch. He fell backwards and landed on his side, but was able to grab a hold of Jimmy's pant leg and hold him.

Jimmy fell face down in the grass and kicked at Mike's hand.

"Let me go," Jimmy shouted. "Jesus, please, let me go!"

Mike was still fighting with Jimmy when Paul calmly stepped over top of the handcuffed man and whispered in his ear. He instantly went still, like he had been running off electricity and Paul had just pulled the plug. When Paul hauled him to his feet again, the man's face had gone completely white, and there wasn't an ounce of fight left in him.

"Guess you ought to take him," Mike said.

Paul didn't say a word. He just calmly pushed Jimmy through the narrow path and out into the street.

They were almost at the car when the dispatcher came over the radio again.

"44-70, Officer Henninger."

"Damn," Paul muttered. He stopped Jimmy next to the back door of the car and keyed up his radio. "44-70, go ahead."

"44-70, switch over to three-lima."

Mike was coming up behind him. Paul gestured at him, asking him to take it so he could get Jimmy in the car.

Mike nodded. "44-70 Alpha. 44-70 Bravo has got his hands full at the moment. Can I switch for him?"

"10-4, Mike. Go to three-lima for Lieutenant Moss."

Paul opened the car door and pointed at the patrol car's backseat. "Get in," he said.

Jimmy did as he was told.

When he was inside, he looked up at Paul and said, "Please don't hurt me. I'll do anything, please."

Paul slammed the door on him in disgust. But as he did so he caught his reflection in the backdoor's window, and he saw, for just a second, what Jimmy had been seeing all along. He saw the wild, blood-crazy face of a demon etched into his own face like a palimpsest, and it was terrible.

Mike tapped him on the shoulder, and he jumped.

"What is it?"

"Paul," Mike said, his voice barely more than a whisper. He held up his radio for Paul to see. "Dude, you need to take this. It's about your wife."

***

An evidence technician was walking back towards the street as Paul ran up the gravel drive. She had a camera in her hand and a mystified look on her face. A Central Patrol officer was standing watch at the edge of the lawn, but he didn't try to stop Paul.

He wouldn't have been able to anyway.

Paul sprinted past a uniformed sergeant and two detectives in plain clothes, then hit the stairs and went up them three at a time. Inside, the apartment looked like a bomb had gone off. Most of the back wall had been punched in, rubble all over the floor. Broken glass crunched under Paul's boots as he stepped into the living room. He stopped right behind the couch and turned around in a slow circle, his mind simply unable to wrap around the destruction he was looking at.

"Rachel?" he said.

A hot breeze whistled through the holes in the wall. Red and blue emergency lights pierced through the shattered glass doors that faced the street. He stumbled through the wreckage like he was half dead. He felt dead inside. Behind him, he heard an unfamiliar voice call his name.

"Officer Henninger, I need to speak with you."

Paul didn't bother to turn around.

The man called his name again. Then he heard Mike say, "Bill, leave him be for a second.

"I need to get a statement from him."

"In a minute," Mike said.

Paul walked toward the bathroom. The door had been punched open. Part of it still hung from the top hinge. He saw the phone on the floor, and next to it, his Barber fifty cent piece.

He picked it up, closed his eyes, and squeezed the coin in his fist.

Somebody put a hand on his shoulder. He thought it was Mike, but when he turned around, he saw a lieutenant he didn't recognize.

"I'm Lieutenant Barry Moss," he said. "Has anyone talked to you yet, son?"

Paul shook his head as he rose to his feet.

"The detectives are going to want a statement from you."

Paul nodded.

"Do you have somewhere else you can go? I mean, after you give your statement?"

There was only one place in Paul's mind.

"Yes, sir," he said.

Moss said, "Good. When you're done with your statement, I want you to go there. Mike here will drive you. And don't worry about coming in tomorrow. I'll clear it with your Lieutenant. You just make sure you call him in a few days and let him know what's up."

Paul nodded again.

When Moss left, Paul stood in front of the bathroom mirror and looked at himself for a long moment. He could see more and more of his

father in his own features with each passing moment.
I'm coming for you, Daddy. We're gonna finish this.

Chapter 23

Two Sex Crimes detectives put Paul into an interview room at Police Headquarters and let him sit there for almost an hour. When they finally entered the room they explained that they had downloaded the GPS figures from his patrol car's MDT and compared it to the time stamp on Rachel's 9-1-1 call. They knew he was making an arrest on the eastside at the same time that Rachel was being abducted. "So we know you didn't do it," they told him. They just had a few other questions, they said. About mutual friends he and Rachel had. About Paul's enemies, if any.

Paul knew the routine.

He knew from his cadet training that more than eighty percent of violent crimes against women are committed by a man they know well, usually their husband or a boyfriend. "We'd be negligent," the detective who gave them their training on investigations explained, "if we didn't automatically start by looking at the husband or the boyfriend."

Paul knew the two detectives were working under the assumption that he was in some way involved with Rachel's disappearance. It wasn't enough that he was with Mike all night, or that six other witnesses could put him halfway across the city at the time of Rachel's abduction. A policeman who wanted to get rid of his wife would know from experience that attention would automatically fall on him simply because he was the husband. Any cop worth his salt would cover his tracks by being elsewhere during the actual attack. So the bit about them having just a few questions was a load of bull. They'd work on him as long as it took, and that was going to take too long.

He was seething inside, and he was maintaining his thin veneer of calm by will power alone. He had to get out of here, and he had to do it right away. They were going to consider him a suspect, he knew that. That much was unavoidable. But it was within his power to stop the interview short, and that's what he did.

One of the detectives asked him if he and Rachel had been having problems lately. He was a cop, right? A rocky marriage comes with the job, right?

He answered every question truthfully. He knew he had to. They would crosscheck everything. They'd talk to the next door neighbor who had seen him getting tossed out of his own house. So it would only hurt

310 | Joe McKinney

him later if he lied now. But as soon as they started to backtrack on questions, ask the same thing but from a different angle, Paul knew it was time to shut them down.

He focused.

Paul reached out with his mind and found their minds. He said, "That's everything I know about it. Will you call me please when you find something out?"

Both of the detectives went mentally slack.

One of the detectives, speaking very slowly, said, "Yeah, that's all the questions I have. We'll call you when we find something."

"Thanks," Paul said, and stood up and left the room.

**

"Take me to my truck," Paul said.

He and Mike were in the car now. Mike was driving, pulling out of one of the spots in the back lot of Headquarters reserved for patrol cars.

He said, "Paul, the lieutenant wanted me to take you home. Tomorrow morning, Collins and I can get your truck back to your house for you."

"Take me to my truck," Paul said.

"Okay," Mike said. "Okay, sure, Paul. Whatever you want."

They drove in silence back to the Eastside Substation, and Mike stopped the car next to Paul's truck. Paul got his gear out of the trunk and dropped it into the toolbox in the bed of his truck and waved once at Mike and climbed behind the wheel. He drove away and never looked back.

He never saw Mike again.

**

When the phone rang, the first thought that went through Keith Anderson's mind was that he had overslept. It would be Levy on the end of the line, calling to bitch him out for being late. Anderson was so miserably tired, and it was all he could do to focus on the glowing green display of his digital clock.

"Four o'clock," he grumbled. "Damn it."

Next to him, Margie said, "What? What is it?" She sounded like she wasn't really awake.

"I got it," he said, and swung his legs out from under the covers and ran a hand over his face as he tried to focus on the caller ID.

He didn't recognize the number.

"Hello?" he said.

Margie sat up next to him and said, "Who is it?"

He gave her a *hold on a second* wave of his hand and listened, and right away he was wide awake. "Paul," he said, "Paul, slow down. You're going too fast for me. Where are you?"

"I'm in a Stop-n-Go parking lot at the corner of Rosa Parks and Utley. You know the one?"

"I can find it," Anderson said. "Paul, what's going on?"

"When you get here," Paul said.

"No, Paul. Tell me. What the hell's going on?"

"I'll tell you everything when you get here. I'll tell you everything you want to know." There was a pause on Paul's end, then he said, "It's about Rachel, my wife. She's gone. He's got her."

That last part made no sense to Anderson. The air raid siren in his head that ordinarily would have been sounding the alarm was silent, and it never even occurred to him to wonder why. He looked down at his milky white old-man legs and sighed thoughtfully. Margie was sitting up beside him now, one hand on his shoulder.

"Who was that?"

"Officer Paul Henninger," he said.

"You mean, the one who—"

"Yeah."

"What did he want?"

"He wants me to meet him as soon as possible." Anderson turned so that he was facing her. "Margie, I think all this is almost over. For better or for worse, it's almost over."

He put one hand over hers and gave her a reassuring pat.

"There's so much I want to say, Margie. So many things I'm sorry for. It's like the world has been pulled out from under me and I'm standing here trying to figure out where it all went. I don't even know where to begin."

She gave his fingers a gentle squeeze.

He squeezed back.

"Did I tell you I've been seeing Bobby's face in every crowd I see? It's like...when John died. All over again."

If that worried her, she gave no sign of it. She knew him better than anybody else. Maybe she knew he had been seeing ghosts.

"We're both hurting. I'm sorry, too."

He nodded, and it amazed him how much they could say to one another without using any words. They were a team, the two of them. Two people, one love. He was, he realized, a very lucky man.

"I'll make you some coffee," she said.

He gave her a smile. "Thanks, Margie."

***

Paul watched Anderson's car pull into the parking lot. He crossed over to it and opened the passenger side door and climbed in. Anderson didn't speak. He sat there, waiting for Paul to make the first move.

Paul stared out the window for a moment. Then he looked at Anderson. He saw the picture of Anderson's dead son over the speedometer, and it made him think of the last time he and Anderson were together in the car.

"Turn off your voice recorder," Paul said.

Without saying a word, Anderson reached beneath his Mr. Rogers sweater and took a small, digital voice recorder from his shirt pocket. He showed it to Paul and pushed STOP. Then he put it on the dashboard.

"You're not gonna want a record of this anyway," Paul said.

"No," Anderson said, "you're probably right."

Paul told him everything. He started with his father, with the death of his father, and he told him about Mexico and Magdalena Chavarria and the murders at the Morgan Rollins Iron Works and the boy from the train yard and how the bodies disappeared from the morgue.

"But you know about that already," Paul said. "You saw your friend that night we went into the superstructure at Morgan Rollins."

"Yes," Anderson agreed. He appeared to think about that for a moment. "Is that what your father is? Is he some kind of ghost?"

"He practiced witchcraft. He tried to pass that on to me, but I killed him. And after that, he came back. So yeah, I guess you could call him a ghost. That word works as well as any. He's powerful. He used that power to come back, and he's using it now to control the dead from the morgue. Your friend at the Morgan Rollins factory, he was under my father's control. And seeing as I'm telling you this, you should probably know that I was, too."

Anderson looked up at him, suddenly nervous.

"I'm not now," Paul said, reading his look.

"How do I know that?"

"You don't, I guess. All I can tell you is that I mean to go after him. Maybe that will convince you. I mean to go after him, and I mean to stop this tonight. He's not going to turn me like he thinks he is. I'm going to stop him."

"He wants to turn you into some kind of witch? Is that what you said?"

"Of a sort, yes. That's probably the closest thing to what he has in mind that we would all know about. That's what I thought he meant. God, I was so naïve. I was thinking he intended me to be some kind of great unifier. I would bring peace to the world. I should have known right from the start that wasn't what he meant, but I let myself believe what I wanted the truth to be. I know now that he meant something much different."

"Different how?"

"A long time ago, when he was living with Magdalena Chavarria and her grandmother, my father learned how to control this power. But he's not a perfect conduit for it. It burns him up, like too much current going through too small of a battery."

"That's what the black stuff is."

"What black stuff?"

"We found this black, gritty resin at most of the scenes. It was inside some of the bodies, too. Bobby Cantrell had it in him. We had it tested and it came back as a mixture of human tissue and cedar resin."

Paul nodded. "I guess so. I've felt that stuff, too. I felt it at the train yard."

"So your father is burning himself up trying to get to you?"

"Trying to cross over, yes. He's not a perfect conduit, as I said, but he thinks I am. He thinks I can use that power to bring about an apocalypse."

"An apocalypse? You mean, like the end of days?"

"Something like that," Paul said. "But he would qualify that. He would say the end of these days, and the beginning of a new era. All things in balance. A beginning to every end, a death for every life."

"And you believe that?"

"That he's capable of bringing this about? That certain people can learn to use that power to change the world around them? Yes, I believe that."

"Do you believe you're one of those special people?"

Paul took a deep breath. He had hoped to avoid this.

"Hold up your hand," Paul said.

"What?"

"Like this," Paul said, and put up a hand, palm towards the windshield, like he was motioning for the traffic outside to stop.

Anderson held up his hand.

"Now what would you say if I told you your hand was on fire?"

Anderson smiled. "I'd say it feels fine."

"And if I made you believe that it was on fire."

"You couldn't."

But the last word came out in a gasp of pain. Paul had already found Anderson's mind, the tendrils of his own mind reaching through Anderson, taking hold of him. Sweat was popping out all over Anderson's skin now. He began to shake, thrashing from side to side against the steering wheel and door panel and the seat. His whole body was seizing up in pain and he couldn't control it. Paul let his mind drift back from Anderson's, but he didn't relinquish his control over it.

"How about now?" Paul said.

"I don't believe it."

Paul gave Anderson's mind another shove.

Anderson screamed.

"It's on fire! Jesus Christ, stop it!"

Paul was completely in Anderson's head now. He could see what Anderson saw. He could see himself through the man's eyes, enormous and horrible. He could feel the man bucking against the pain, and yet still resisting. He believed in the pain, but not in the source.

Anderson looked up at him then, his eyes full of tears, and begged for it to stop. He was whimpering like a dog hit by a car. He was ready to do anything to stop the pain.

Paul grabbed him by the wrist and said, "It's over."

Instantly, Anderson went still. He stared at Paul with demented, feral eyes. And then, by degrees, the wildness left him and his muscles went slack. His chest was still pounding, but he no longer felt the pain. He looked from Paul to his hand and seemed surprised that it wasn't black as charcoal from the fire.

"How?" he said, panting.

"A parlor trick," Paul said. "That's nothing. Every minute that goes by I can feel the power swelling inside me. I think, if I wanted to, I could make the ground split open beneath this car and swallow it whole."

Anderson was still pale. He said, "You're not going to do that, are you?"

"I wouldn't have called you here for that," Paul said. "But you've just seen two parts of my father's plan. You've experienced the pain. That much is easy to imagine. Consider every human being on the planet feeling that kind of pain all at once. Consider somebody who could turn that pain on and off whenever he needed to. You can see where that would lead."

"Yes," Anderson said.

"But there's more. You can beat a man until he's willing to say that up is down and one plus one makes three. Hell, you can terrorize his mind to the point where he'll probably even believe it. But you can never be sure that he's truly yours, body and soul. There's only one way to be absolutely sure. To make sure that power is absolute, and that is through death. I would show you, but I think you remember pretty well what it was like seeing your friend up on the superstructure. His old life is over, and now his new life has begun—completely under my father's control."

Anderson looked thoroughly unsettled, and Paul still had enough of a handle on his mind to know that the man was drifting, his thoughts forming only with the greatest difficulty.

Finally, he said, "Why did you call me?"

"My wife," Paul said. "My father has her. It's his way, I think, of forcing my hand. Of forcing me to come to him. When I do he will try to finish what he started six years ago. He'll try to turn me to his purpose."

"And you're going to fight him?"

"Yes. And when I do, I want you to get my wife out of here. Can you do that? Can you get her as far away from here as possible? As far away from me as possible."

Anderson flexed his hand, the memory of the pain was still fresh in his mind. Paul could feel the echo of it.

"Can you really fight him?" Anderson said. "How will you do that?"

"I don't know," Paul said.

"Well, what will you do? How can you possibly expect to fight somebody who's already dead?"

"I won't fight him in the way you mean," Paul said. "Not with my fists. Think of it like electricity. My father believes he can connect us. He believes by doing that he will make me stronger. I think I can turn that circuit back on him. I think I can blow the fuse."

Anderson let his hand fall back into his lap. "You're talking about suicide," he said. "You mean to kill yourself."

"If that's what it takes to stop this, then yeah, I guess I am."

"Paul, you can't."

"Keith, I'm not gonna argue with you. My mind's made up."

Anderson opened his mouth to speak, then stopped. He looked down at his hands in his lap.

"Are you ready to go?" Paul said.

Anderson sighed, then seemed to make up his mind about something. He looked at Paul then and said, "Son, you sound like you're in love with death. Like you've already made up your mind that that's where you're going. Listen to me, I have seen death. I've seen so much suffering. You have no idea. I've seen the dead rotting in the grass out in some abandoned field. I've smelled them cooking on the asphalt in the summer sun after a traffic accident. I've seen them on the autopsy table, all their dignity gone. You can't possibly want that for yourself. You have no idea what that would do to Rachel to live with that kind of knowledge. Paul, some wounds don't ever heal. Don't be that cruel to her."

Paul didn't hesitate with his answer. It all came out in a flood.

"Keith," he said, "I'm not at all sure who I am anymore. I used to know. I used to be so sure. I used to think I'd gotten a raw deal in the parents department. A psychopath for a dad. A mental vegetable for a mom. Then I became a husband. And then a policeman. All those things defined me in their own way. I knew where I came from, and I knew where I was headed. But now—Hell, I don't know. Everything I thought I knew about myself has turned out to be wrong. Can you possibly know what that's like, finding out that everything you know about yourself, about your past, is just wrong? Now I find out that I'm some kind of horror waiting to be loosed upon the world. I hate what I'm destined to become, Keith. Is it any wonder to you that I'm in love with the idea of dying? Wouldn't you feel the same way in my shoes?"

Anderson looked away.

"I don't know," he said, and it was the truth. "I really don't know."

Chapter 24

Anderson pulled his Ford Taurus into the south entrance of the Morgan Rollins Iron Works and turned off the lights. He turned to Paul and said, "So, what next? We walk from here?"

Paul looked up at the ruins. The place was dark, a twisted skeleton backlit by the distant, hazy orange glow of downtown. It cast long, intensely black shadows down the drive towards them. He cleared his mind and thought of Rachel. She was up there somewhere. He could feel her fear and her confusion as though they were his own.

"You're sure your father's up there?" Anderson said.

"I'm sure," Paul said.

"But how do you know? I still don't understand that. Is it some kind of telepathy?"

"I don't know what to call it. Maybe it is telepathy. All I can tell you is that I can feel Rachel's mind up there. She's scared and tired. But hearing her is like trying to pick a voice out from across the room with a loud party going on in between."

"And your father? You feel him, too?"

Paul nodded. "My father is different. With him, it's like stepping outside and seeing a tornado coming up the street. It feels like he's everywhere at once."

Paul turned back to study the superstructure. The Barber fifty cent piece was in his hands, glittering in the light from the dashboard as it rolled over the backs of the knuckles.

Anderson watched it fly back and forth, back and forth.

Finally he said, "Paul, why did your father choose this place?"

The coin stopped suddenly.

"This is where it all started for him," Paul said.

"I thought you said he learned this witchcraft stuff in Mexico."

"He did. But he was up in that superstructure when this vision of his first grabbed hold of him. This is where it all started to make sense to him. This is where he wants it to grab hold of me. I guess he sees in that a kind of balance."

Anderson looked up at the superstructure and frowned.

"You ready?" Paul said.

Anderson swallowed hard and said, "Yeah. Yeah, I guess I am."

***

There had once been an asphalt driveway that snaked its way up from the south entrance to the main parking lot in front of the iron works. After twenty years the asphalt had crumbled and grass had grown up through the cracks and squeezed in from the curb line, giving the edges of the drive a sort of beach-like shape. A tattered remnant of yellow crime scene tape fluttered in the air above the driveway. Metal fence posts leaned at odd angles along the western edge of the factory, and they cast long, intensely black shadows down the length of the drive.

Anderson was walking with his head down, shoulders stooped forward, like a tired man walking into a strong wind, and he was starting to breathe hard, even though the slope of the drive was not that steep.

"Wait up, please," Anderson said to Paul, his voice breathy and winded. "You're going too fast."

Anderson drew the Glock at his hip. As the detective came abreast of him, Paul watched a bead of sweat pop out of his forehead and roll down his cheek.

"You're not gonna need that," Paul said, nodding at the gun. "Bullets won't hurt him."

"It makes me feel better knowing I've got it."

Paul shrugged.

"When we get inside, I want you to go straight to the smokestacks. You'll find Rachel there. Get her and get her out of here."

"Okay," Anderson said. "Just don't walk so fast."

A wind moaned through the ruins above them, and it brought with it a fetid odor that was deeper than scorched vegetation and dust and rot.

Anderson groaned.

Paul turned and looked at him. He knew what was happening to the detective. His mind was being assaulted by despair and pain, his father's first line of defense. With his mind, Paul could feel the energy flowing around him like he was a rock in a fast-moving stream. But Anderson wasn't equipped to push that energy aside.

"Can you go on?" Paul asked.

Anderson closed his eyes and took a deep breath. When he opened his eyes again, the expression there was soul sick, but he nodded.

Good man, Paul thought. *Strong.*

They entered the superstructure and started climbing their way through the twisted, ruined mass of cables and pipes and collapsed metal walkways. "Up here," Paul said, and pulled himself onto an elevated catwalk. Then he knelt down and reached a hand through the bars for Anderson to grab and said, "Here, give me your hand."

Anderson reached up for Paul's hand, but then his gaze went over Paul's shoulder to the metal wall behind him, and his eyes went wide.

"Paul, oh my God!"

Paul was bent over through the bars. He looked back over his shoulder and up the three story high wall behind him. Ten naked dead men were spidering down it head first. Their hair hung down from their heads like dirty rags. Their ruined junkie bodies shone palely in the low light. A keening moan rose from the one closest to them, and it was answered by the others in a sickening chorus.

"How?" Anderson said.

Paul turned back to him. "Run!" he said. "Get going. Get to the smokestacks." He pointed to Anderson's right. "That way. Go!"

"What about you?"

"Go!"

Anderson backed away from Paul.

"Go!"

He turned his gaze up once more at the dead men coming down the wall and stumbled off in the direction Paul had told him to go. Then he disappeared into the dark.

Paul watched him go, then stood up, and waited for the dead men to come for him.

***

It was like slogging his way through a muddy field. Anderson tried to make himself move, tried to get his hands and legs to obey, but it was so hard. He just wanted to fall back on his butt and rest. There was a loud, droning noise at the edges of his mind that threatened to wash over him. He sensed it like the coming of sleep, so welcome, so warm, so easy to just give in and forget.

But he knew on some level that to give in was to die, and he wasn't ready to do that. Not by a long shot. He grabbed hold of the railing next to him and stumbled forward, climbing over rusted debris and closing his nose to the smell of the old blankets and rotting garbage that he passed along the way to the smokestacks.

He could see them off to his left. They were gray towers poking above a skeleton of pipes and machinery. What were they, two hundred yards away? He could make that.

Maybe.

But then a sound stopped him, a slight noise around the corner ahead of him.

It had to be the wind rustling the sheets of corrugated metal that hung from everywhere around here. There wasn't anything else up ahead.

He heard another noise, the straining of rusted bolts and hinges beneath a large weight. He stared into the dark ahead of him and shook his head. Footsteps sounded on the metal catwalk a few yards away. He could hear moaning, that same gut-turning moan he'd heard just moments before when Paul had tried to pull him up through the bars, and he knew what that dirty shape standing in silhouette ahead of him was.

Anderson felt the sweat on his lips. He could taste the dust in the air, and even before the dead man stumbled around the corner ahead of him, his arms raised towards him in a gesture of supplication, he knew it was Bobby Cantrell.

When Ram stepped into the light he almost seemed to be pleading with Anderson. Cantrell's jaw moved constantly. His hands, mottled with the purplish tinge of lividity, opened and closed as though he was begging for food. His words wouldn't come, though his face was twisted with the effort to make his wallowing tongue pronounce them.

Anderson pointed his gun at Cantrell. The weapon's molded grip wasn't any help. He was in such a state he could barely wrap his fingers around the receiver. The corpse shambling towards him obliterated every tenuous hold he had on sanity with each step. The rest of the world shrank away, and Anderson was left with an abomination moving towards him through the tunnel his vision had become.

Cantrell was barely recognizable. He had been in the South Texas heat for a week, the bacteria and the other microbes that fed on death eating him from the inside out, rotting him, creating a cloud of stench that moved with him. Anderson's lips curled up at the corner of his mouth in a sort of snarl, though it was a purely reflexive response to the smell. He brought up his gun and aimed it at his friend's chest.

"Stop, Bobby," he said, though he knew they were well past that point now.

Anderson could wait no longer.

He fired.

The first shot hit Bobby in the chest. He fired twice more in close succession. The bullets thudded into Bobby and shook him like a man shivering against a sudden chill.

But Bobby kept coming on.

Anderson's bowels almost let go. He raised the gun higher, took aim, and popped off another round.

The bullet hit right below the dead man's nostrils. It was a flawless take down shot, the sniper's sweet spot, designed to punch through the nasal cavity and turn the medulla oblongata behind it into a cloud of pink spray out the back of the head. And Anderson did see a wet chunk of something blow out the back of his friend's head. But it did nothing to stop the corpse. Bobby Cantrell continued forward, staggering on rotting legs, reaching for him with swollen, purple fingers, staring at him with dead eyes that felt nothing and contained no hint of memory, no recognition of a lifetime of friendship.

More dead men appeared behind Cantrell. They poured around the corner, nude and hideous with their thick black autopsy scars on their chests, the skin around the sutures puckered over by purplish skin that had swelled grotesquely by the action of expanding gas within their rotten husks.

Anderson turned and ran.

He bounded up a half flight of rusted stairs and swung himself up and over a railing beyond that. He ran down the length of the catwalk until he reached a section where part of the structure had given way. An open pit thirty feet deep yawned in front of him. He looked down and saw a mess of debris below him. Across the other side of the pit, a distance of maybe seven or eight feet, was the remainder of the catwalk. He could see it holding onto the metal wall to his right with frail looking mounts.

He turned and looked back. Cantrell and the dead men were coming. They weren't far away now. Where Anderson had been forced to stop and pull his soft, out-of-shape body up and over railings, or duck and belly crawl under loose sections of metal, the dead men advanced with the steadiness of ants.

He had to jump. There was no other alternative. They would be on him in another few seconds. He took a few steps back and muttered a quiet prayer. Then he ducked his head and sprinted for the edge of the busted catwalk and jumped for the far side. Anderson hung suspended in midair above the pit for a long moment, but even before his feet left the catwalk he knew he wasn't going to clear the pit. The instep of his right foot caught the jagged edge of the far side and he pitched over forward, landing hard face down on the other catwalk.

For a moment, everything went purple. His body, overloaded by pain and starving for the air that had been knocked from his lungs, refused to process the sensation. All at once feeling flooded back into him and he rolled over onto his back and screamed with pain. His foot felt like it had been sheared off, and he was surprised to see it still there when at last he could move his head enough to look at his own body.

Blood was pouring out of the wound, and there was a sharp, searing pain of pulled muscles along the backs of his legs and up and down his back, but that wasn't the worst of his problems. The metal catwalk was swaying like a tree in a stiff breeze. He could feel it moving beneath him, rocking against its mounts. There was a moment of dread that came from the foreknowledge of what was going to happen, and then his stomach rolled with nausea as the mounts gave way and the whole contraption upon which he lay went crashing over and down.

Anderson grabbed onto the railing. He felt the wreckage picking up speed, the collapsing metal groaning in protest. He imagined he could see the ground racing up to meet him, his body impaled upon tines of rebar sticking up from a debris pile.

And then he hit.

Everything rolled away beneath him and he hit, even harder than before, square on his right side. He tumbled downward on a tilted bit of catwalk and finally landed on his back. A wave of dirt rained down upon him and hit him in the face. Spluttering, he opened his eyes and saw metal. A large section of the catwalk had shifted downward and stopped just inches above his nose. Some sort of metal spar had speared into the ground less than a foot from his right ear.

But he was alive.

A thin groan escaped his lips. More dust sifted down from the debris above him and into his face. He shook his head and wiped it away with a bloody hand. Everything hurt, his whole body.

"Oh Jesus," he murmured against the pain. He could taste blood in his mouth.

Above him, the wreckage continued to shift and groan. He blinked the dust from his eyes and saw movement through the web of metal that had landed on top of him. Cantrell and the other dead men were moving through that web, and they were close by, maybe ten or twelve feet above him at the most.

Anderson closed his eyes and prayed.

***

Paul listened to the sound of gunfire echoing through the superstructure. Three quick shots in succession. Anderson was in trouble. And wasting his ammunition, too. These weren't Hollywood zombies. They didn't go down with a well-placed shot to the brain. They were extensions of his father's will, meat puppets at the end of a wire. As long as his father had need of them, they would continue to advance.

Several of the dead men dropped from the wall and onto the platform. They were in front of him now. Others had him cut off from behind.

But they didn't advance on him. They stayed back a good twenty feet. Paul stayed perfectly still. One of the dead men pulled a section of corrugated metal off the wall, exposing an empty space within. Paul looked into the blackness and knew it was a direct route into the center of the superstructure where the circular chamber, and his father, waited.

He scanned the faces of the dead men, and though their eyes were milky and vacant, he knew what they wanted of him. He was to go through there, and he was to do it of his own accord.

That was important. Somehow, in fact, it made all the difference. If he came willingly, it was his way of turning control over to his father, of surrendering his will. But to do that was to lose. Even if he fought, they would still subdue him and bring him to his father's feet—he knew that—

but he would do it with his will unbent. And that was the difference.

Yet it wasn't so easy to keep his chin up. The same power that had been growing exponentially within him over the last few days had now become something like a magnet. It wanted to cling to what was in that circular chamber. Even the simple act of standing still required a tremendous effort on his part. He wanted to go inside. Every cell in his body begged him to go. Only his will fought back.

He reached into his pocket and he took out the Barber fifty cent piece. He turned it over in his hand and it winked at him in the low light. He caressed the edges of the coin with his thumb, feeling the deep gouge at the top that had been worn smooth by countless hours of slipping through his fingers.

It felt heavier than normal. He closed his fingers around it and tried to focus on everything that had happened to him. When he told Anderson that he felt like everything he thought he knew about himself had turned out to be a lie, he wasn't being completely truthful. Yes, his childhood was a lie. He had been oblivious to his mother's suffering. He had lived in the same house as her for twelve years and never understood what his father was doing to her, how he was bleeding her dry, body and soul. And when his father had returned, he had almost gone over to him. He had almost believed in his father's vision. He knew now that was a lie, too.

But the one thing that had not changed was Rachel. That love remained, and it was not a lie. That part of his life was clear to the bottom of the glass, and when he held that Barber in his hand, he could touch the truth of that love.

When he opened his eyes again, he found it easier to hold his ground. One of the dead men held a withered arm out towards the blackness of the tunnel like he was leading a tour through an old Roman ruin. *This way to the other side, sir. Through here you'll see a lovely furnished colonnade that opens up to the public amphitheater. If you please, sir. Watch your step there...*

Paul shook his head.

The dead man dropped his arm. Two others advanced on him.

Paul slid his collapsible baton from his belt and snapped it open. He stood with it cocked back over his right shoulder, waiting for the lead dead man to walk into the sweet spot of his stroke.

"Come on," Paul said. "A little closer."

When the first dead man came into range, Paul stroked him upside the head with a blow so forceful it broke the man's neck and left a grotesque indentation just above the man's left ear. Paul drew the baton back over his shoulder and backpedaled. The dead man continued to advance, his head bent over to one side at an unnatural angle. His hands came up towards Paul and the fingers flexed. Paul stepped forward again and swung his baton. This time it was like hitting a rotten pumpkin. The skull gave way beneath the blow with a splat. Paul rained blows down on it again and again, reducing the man's head in seconds to something that looked like a deflated balloon.

And still it came on.

Paul swept its legs out from under it, then turned and tried to climb up the railing behind him. The dead were on him in moments. He fought with his fists and his knees and his elbows, slinging bodies off the side of the platform and down into the tangled wreckage beneath him, but there were just too many of them. They pulled him down to the floor and they twisted his arms behind his back and he felt the bite of his own handcuffs as they clamped down on his wrists.

Chapter 25

Rachel had crawled as far as she could go into a corner. Behind her, a pair of cement walls rose up twenty feet to the base of the smokestacks. The smokestacks towered up another hundred feet above the top of the walls. Gazing up at them made her dizzy. In front of her were huge piles of garbage laced through with skeins of heavy metal cables. Presumably, she was in some sort of abandoned factory, but what she was doing here, and what was to happen to her, she had no idea. The dead men who brought her here had evidently not wanted to kill her. They certainly could have if they'd wanted to. The way they'd punched into her apartment and pulled her from it like birds pulling a worm from the earth, she suspected they could have torn her to pieces.

Instead, they brought her here.

She really didn't even remember *how* she'd gotten here. One of them had slung her over his shoulder in a sort of fireman's carry and brought her into the backyard behind her apartment. They had stepped into thick vegetation that choked the alley beyond the fence. She'd felt weeds and branches tearing at her skin. And then they were through the vegetation and crawling over endless catwalks and piles of garbage. She had ended up here, tucked away in this corner.

Those things, those dead men, had been standing guard over her at first. But they were gone now. She was alone, scared and alone. There had been some strange noises, high, metallic popping noises that almost sounded like distant gunshots. After that, those dead men had scaled over the garbage and disappeared. They hadn't looked at each other. They hadn't spoken. They didn't seem to perk up like dogs to a whistle outside of the range of her hearing. They just climbed into the superstructure and vanished, like spiders into a sink full of dirty dishes.

They'd been gone for a while now. Slowly, almost as though she doubted that she could, she rose to her feet. She wiped her cheeks with the back of her hand and started walking through the wreckage, trying to be quiet, listening for anything, always expecting another of those dead men to suddenly step around a corner in front of her and tear her apart, until at last she came to a place where the superstructure had collapsed. The tangled mess before her seemed to be the remains of a catwalk and its supports. There was no way around it, and she couldn't climb over it.

It didn't look stable. And she certainly couldn't turn around and go back. Those dead men were back there.

Her only real choice was to try to go through it. She ducked down and found a small tunnel where a platform of some sort had collapsed over top of the catwalk itself. The metal lattice floor of the catwalk was tilted to one side, but if she held on to the railings and pulled herself along, she might be able to make it through. It looked like she'd have to crawl for about sixty feet, maybe less.

She grabbed the bottom rung of the railing and made her way into the tunnel with a hand over hand motion. Her toes provided a little grip on the lattice, but most of the weight was carried by the muscles in her arms, and after only a few feet of that, she was breathing hard and sweating. The metal bar became slippery in her hands, and though she was terrified, she knew she had to stop for just a second and catch her breath. She hooked one arm around a metal bar and stopped to rest. She closed her eyes and let her forehead rest against the metal lattice floor of the catwalk. When she opened her eyes again, she found herself staring through the metal lattice into another pair of open eyes.

She screamed.

***

"Be quiet! Goddamn it, shut up! Rachel, stop it. They'll hear you."

Hearing her own name seemed to calm her, and Anderson knew he'd guessed right. He made shushing noises after that, keeping his voice as low and as gentle as the pain up and down his right side would allow.

He said, "You're Rachel, right?"

"Yes," she said, her voice breathy. Her eyes were wide open, a deep, rich brown with flecks of green. She had dirt all over her face, and her features were twisted by fear, but Anderson could see, even beneath the fear and the dirt, that she was pretty. A little skinny for his tastes, but definitely a knockout.

"Who are you?" she said.

"I'm Keith Anderson. I'm here with Paul. He sent me to get—"

"Where is he?" she said. "Where's Paul? Is he okay?"

"I don't know," Anderson said, and he had to stop there. Speaking had sent a fresh wave of pain through him, and he closed his eyes and groaned. When he opened his eyes again, he was panting. "He wants to stop his father."

"His father?"

Anderson nodded. Her expression told him enough. She knew what was going on, or at least some of it. Enough to be scared as hell, anyway.

Slowly, he tried to move.

"He told me to find you and get you out of here."

"We have to find Paul first," she said.

"Rachel, those things...we can't fight them. I shot one of them in the head. We can't beat them."

"Then we have to get Paul out of here."

"He wasn't afraid of them, Rachel. I think he understands them."

"I won't leave here without him."

Anderson closed his eyes and tried to catch his breath. He couldn't see his right foot from where he was, but from the way the pain there was beginning to drown out everything else he knew that it was bad.

"Can you move?" she asked.

"I don't know," he said truthfully. "I think so."

"Try," she said. "You have to help me."

He reached up and grabbed hold of the edge of the catwalk, his left arm doing all the work.

"Can you help me get up there?" he asked.

"Yeah," she said. "Give me your hand."

***

A few minutes later, he had an arm over her shoulder and she was helping him away from the wreckage of the catwalk. They stopped in one of the walkways that led up to the superstructure, and Anderson sat down on a thick pipe and inspected the wound to his right foot. It wasn't as bad as he first thought. The cut was deep, and he would almost certainly need a tetanus shot, but they had been able to stop the worst of the bleeding with some tissues he had in his pocket.

His right side wasn't as bad it had first seemed either. He unbuttoned his shirt and looked at his ribs and saw the beginnings of a nasty bruise spreading down his flank, but at least none of the ribs were broken.

"Can you walk?"

"Yeah, I think so," he said. "But, Rachel, you know we can't fight those things. You have to know that."

"I don't want to fight anybody. I just want Paul."

"Rachel," he said, "you know he means to die doing this."

She looked at him like he had suddenly grown four extra heads. "What? No."

"He wanted you as far away from here as possible when that happened. He made me promise I would get you away from here."

"No, that's not right. Hurting himself wouldn't do any good."

"Rachel, he doesn't believe that. The way Paul told it to me, he thinks he can burn his father up by fighting him. Short circuit him."

"I won't let him hurt himself."

"Rachel, I don't think we have a choice. Even if I wasn't hurt like this, we wouldn't be able to fight what's out there. And we'll probably only slow Paul down. Come on, let me get you out of here. It's what Paul wanted."

Rachel shook her head. "I won't do that. I won't leave him here."

She got up to leave. He saw it on her face, and a sudden fear went through him. She was going to do this, with or without him. And if she did it without him, he'd probably die trying to get out of this place. He'd been a fool to come, he knew that now.

"Your mind's made up then?" he said to her back.

She turned to face him. "What would you do?" she said.

"I don't know," he said. "The same I guess. At least I hope I would. I just don't know. I got to tell you though, Rachel. I'm scared all the way down to my toes."

Moans echoed through the factory. Rachel lifted her head to the sound and her lips drew into an even tighter line. There was almost no color in her face now.

"I'm going," she said.

"All right," he said. He held up his hand to her. "Can you at least give me a hand up first."

She helped him to his feet, and a moment later, they were headed into the superstructure.

***

There was a dead man on either side of him, each one holding an arm. They dragged him into the circular chamber and dropped him unceremoniously at his father's feet.

Paul's eyes fluttered open and he found himself staring at a black pair of Red Wing boots with a high shine. His father was looking down at him. He looked the same as he had six years ago. His face was lean and deeply tanned, shoebox-shaped. The eyes were half-closed in a fierce squint beneath the brim of his black Stetson.

"We done with this foolishness?" his father said. "You gonna stop fighting me?"

Paul's mouth was full of blood. He spit it out, right at his father's feet. He missed by a good eight inches.

He looked at the blood and laughed and his tongue probed a loose tooth.

His father didn't even acknowledge the gesture of defiance. He stepped closer to Paul, walking right over the thick puddle of blood and spit Paul had just made, and knelt down in front of his son.

"It ain't gonna change nothing," his father said. He waited for Paul to say something. "Nothing, boy? Nothing to say to your old man?" Martin reached down and picked up some of the dirt in front of Paul's face and let it sift through his fingers thoughtfully. Paul watched the dirt catch the breeze and drift away, and he thought back to an early summer day when he was eight or nine and the two of them were in the peach orchard, his father testing the soil with his fingers and wondering out loud if there was going to be enough rain for a good harvest that year.

Paul pulled himself up to his knees. With his fingers he started digging for the handcuff key that was secured inside his waistband.

"Why are you fighting me, Paul? A few days ago, you were ready to accept this charge you've been given."

"You know what's changed," Paul said.

Martin Henninger almost smiled.

"Your mother didn't believe in none of this, Paul. To her, it was just craziness. She never really got it."

"She got it," Paul said. "I saw inside her mind. I know how scared she was."

A question flashed across his father's face. And something else, too. Was it alarm, something he hadn't anticipated?

"You know why she was so scared, Daddy? She was scared because you couldn't see the senselessness of what you're doing. That's the part she thought was crazy. All of this, your grand vision, none of it has to happen. There's no reason to make it happen. It doesn't serve any purpose other your own vanity."

His father shook his head. "That's not right, Paul. After all I've showed you, you don't know that? This isn't vanity, Paul. This is evolution. This is a better world."

"A better world? Daddy, you're insane."

"Your mother was the crazy one, Paul."

"You did a lot to make me believe that, Daddy. But I got to wonder why. That's the thing I don't understand. Why'd you think you had to kill her? I'd have followed you anywhere if you hadn't done that. If you'd have asked me to follow you, I'd have thrown down everything I own and gone with you."

"I know that, Paul. I knew that from the moment you first started walking and talking. Something told me even then that you were special."

Martin dusted off his hands and rested them on his thighs. They looked large and powerful. But his voice was delicate. It touched something vulnerable inside of Paul and coaxed it up to the surface, for his father's voice was resonating inside his head, too, lulling him into a quiet ease. The world around him turned to heat shimmers and grew dark. For a moment, nearly everything but the sound of his father's voice dropped away.

Paul's fingers had slipped off the handcuff key and his head rolled on his shoulders.

Would it be so bad to just stand up and let my father lead me into the new world? Would it really be that bad?

"The thing is, Paul, a boy's always gonna feel like he's grounded to this world while he's got his mother in it. You know what I mean? You tell me now that you would have followed me, and I'm sure you believe it, but I wonder if that's true. Don't you see? I couldn't take that chance with you. You got a different destiny laid out for you, son. You've been called upon to do a lot more than just fix a world that's dying. You've been called upon to tear it down and build a new one up in its place. That means you've got to kill this world before you can make it new again. Do you think you could kill a world that's got your mother in it? I had to create distance between you and her."

Something Magdalena said just before she died came back to him. *You need to center yourself in* this *world. Only your love in this world can do that. Find something worth holding on to, because the dead will take you over when you quit loving this world.*

The Barber fifty cent piece was still in his front pocket. It had helped him once already. It could help him again. He couldn't touch it with his fingers, but there were other ways to touch it. He reached out and closed his mind around it, thinking of Rachel, and he found he could shut out his father's voice almost completely. The man was still talking, but it was like he was standing on the other side of a glass now.

Paul took up the handcuff key again. He twisted his hand up and around the base of the handcuffs and probed with his finger until he found the keyhole. Careful to keep his mind clear and his movements slight, for he thought his father could still read his body language even if he couldn't penetrate into his mind, he worked the key first one way and then the other until he felt it catch and the ratchet arm release.

Martin Henninger stood up and looked down at his son. Did he sense his control over his son fading? Paul stared back at him from his knees and thought maybe he did. One cuff was off now and he was working on the other one. His father turned then and walked to the center of the chamber, where a large wooden pole rose ten feet into the air. His father motioned to a group of dead men standing in the shadows of the chamber wall and they brought forth a pair of huge Angora goats on leather leashes and tied them to the pole. Then the dead men slipped back into the shadows.

"Have you figured out yet what this ceremony means?" Martin said, turning to face Paul.

The other cuff came loose.

The Barber, Paul thought. *Focus on the Barber.*

"The goats are a symbol," Paul said, "of what happens to the world. One dies in sacrifice so that the other can be born anew."

"That's right. That's good, Paul."

Paul took the cuffs in his right hand, holding the connecting chain in his fist. The two ratchet arms swung loose from either side of his fist.

Don't ever let a bad guy get a hold of your cuffs, one of his tactics instructors at the Academy had said. *They start swinging those things around, with that ratchet arm swinging free, they can tear you to ribbons.*

At the base of the pole was a shallow brass bowl, and inside that a loose arrangement of oily wood chips, Lebanese Cedar. Martin struck a match with his thumbnail and dropped it into the bowl. The flame shrank away almost immediately and a thin, acrid-smelling column of smoke rose from the bowl, which Martin set down again at the base of the pole.

He put a hand on the head of each goat and spoke a few words over each. His voice was low, the words indistinct, but Paul knew what was being said. Even with his mind holding tightly to the Barber, his father's chanting was blaring inside his head like he was standing inside the throat of a ship's foghorn. And then his father grabbed one of the goats by the neck in his left hand and lifted it until the animal stood eye to eye with him, its back hooves kicking at the ground for purchase. With his right hand he removed his knife from his belt and quickly sliced the animal open from its throat to its anus.

He let the carcass fall to the ground.

The other goat he untied from the pole and turned it around to face Paul.

"Do you know why you must take the Scapegoat's heart as your own?"

Paul turned his gaze from the dead goat to his father. *The Barber. The Barber.*

"No clue," he said.

"You do, Paul. Think about it, boy. The world that's about to be born is symbolized by what's inside this animal. When you take its heart inside your body it beats beside your own. You become a bridge between what's gone and what's to be. You become the link that connects both of them. You become balance incarnate."

Martin brought the animal forward, so that it was standing right in front of Paul.

"You see it now? You see that by containing both worlds inside yourself, you inherit them both? That is important, boy. I want you to tell me you understand."

Paul's mind felt like it was stuck in mud. He struggled up towards consciousness, fighting against the noise his father was making in his head.

The Barber, the Barber, he thought.

He pictured the coin solidly in his mind, and gradually spokes of light formed from behind it, lighting a sort of corona around it. His father's voice grew quiet, less insistent, and the nightmare images of the world overrun by the dead shredded like tissue and scattered on the wind. The light behind the coin continued to grow stronger. It should have blinded

332 | Joe McKinney

him, Paul thought, but it didn't hurt to look at. In fact it seemed to spread a warmth through him, like something good was trying to reach for him. And then at once it came to him.

"Momma."

His father recoiled from him.

"Say the words, Paul. Tell me you see what this means."

Paul looked his father in the eye, and the faintest trace of a smile played at the corner of his mouth.

"Do you know what I see, Daddy?"

Martin waited.

"All I see is a dead man."

He sprang to his feet then and swung the cuffs at his father's face.

Paul's fist connected with his father's jaw and the contact sent a spike of pain up through the nerves of his right arm. It was like somebody had jammed an ice cold piece of metal up through the marrow cavity of his bone.

Paul fell backwards, holding back a scream, but only barely.

The cuffs had left a pair of jagged gouges in his father's cheeks. Black soot poured out of the wounds and drifted away on the breeze like windblown sand. But the wounds didn't stay open for long. As Paul watched, they healed over.

Martin's black Stetson had fallen to the ground. He picked it up and dusted off the brim and seated it back on his head. Then he turned his attention back to Paul.

"Boy," he said, "sometimes, you ain't got no smarts at all."

He stepped forward and grabbed Paul by the shoulders and shook him the way a dog does a stuffed rabbit.

Paul threw an upper cut that caught his father under the chin, but Martin's head barely moved. He took a step back and short punched Paul in the mouth. Paul's vision went black and he rocked back on his heels and teetered there for a moment before he started to fall backwards.

"Get over there," his father said, and grabbed him by the front of his uniform jersey and threw him into the pole.

Paul's head and back crashed into the pole at the same time and it knocked the air from his lungs. For a moment, his vision went purple. He let out a low, stuttering groan and started to slide down to the ground. His father caught him by the throat and hoisted him back to his feet. Paul's eyelids fluttered involuntarily. He tried to speak, but his father's fingers were wrapped too tightly around his throat. He managed a whistling gasp and that was all.

"Why do you think you have to fight me, boy?"

Paul couldn't answer.

His father removed his belt, and exactly as he had done six years before, wrapped the belt around Paul's throat so that he was lashed to the pole. Then he fed it through the buckle and yanked it tight and pushed the tine through the leather. The loose end he let fall against Paul's chest like a necktie.

"I told you once before, boy. It's gonna happen, one way or the other. Might as well come to me willingly."

"Go to hell," Paul gasped.

"I won't get to go there with you, Paul. I can open the doorway for you, but it'll be up to you to take this world there yourself. You'll see."

Then he grabbed the scapegoat just as he had done the first goat and raised it up with one hand. Paul heard it bleat with a small, scared voice. Its eyes were rolling wildly in its head, but its body was hanging limply from his father's fist.

Martin pulled the knife from his belt and held it so Paul could see.

"Make yourself ready, boy. This is where it starts."

***

They stepped into the circular chamber suddenly, unexpectedly. Anderson had been certain they were still several levels below the entrance, and he had been right about to say so when they rounded a corner and emerged into the starlit chamber.

They both gasped at the same time.

Paul was there, lashed to a wooden pole. The air smelled of death and blood and dust. That terrible sense of crushing defeat and pain he'd felt in the presence of the dead men was palpable here as well, and though he couldn't see them, he knew they were there.

As it was, all his attention was focused on the man in the black Stetson cowboy hat. He was standing a short distance in front of Paul, whose head was sagging to his chest and whose face was dark with blood, with a goat suspended in one hand. It took Anderson a moment to take all that in. The goat had to weigh two hundred and fifty pounds, and yet this man held it up one-handed as though it was an empty potato sack.

The man turned to face them. And Paul looked at them, but his face was too badly battered to show any emotion. Anderson stared from one to the other and he was immediately struck by the resemblance. They were obviously father and son. Anderson tried to raise a hand to touch Rachel on her shoulder, but his arm felt like it weighed a ton. He had seen movement in the shadows off to his right, and now that movement had turned into the dusky silhouettes of dead men shambling forward on broken legs, arms raised in a gesture that seemed like they were begging.

He took a step back. Rachel gasped beside him. More of the dead men were advancing on them from the left.

Everything he knew told him to turn around and run, and the impulse was so strong that he did turn around. But he didn't run. He couldn't have, even if his fear had gotten the better of him, for there were more of the dead men coming up behind them. They were cut off completely.

He and Rachel were back to back. He felt her grab his wrist, and for a moment he was certain she was as scared as he was. But then she relaxed her grip. Her hand moved down to his fingers and squeezed.

"Look," she said.

He turned, and what he saw, despite all his fear, made him stare in wonder. A woman had stepped out of the shadows behind Paul. She was small and thin, almost boney, and yet she radiated light. It filled her eyes and her skin was glowing.

She walked up behind Paul and stopped.

"Martin," she said.

***

Paul couldn't turn around, but he could feel the hand on his shoulder. He could sense his mother's presence as clearly as he could his father's. Light was pouring into the circular chamber, swirling around him, warming him, comforting him.

"Martin, I won't let you have him."

It was her voice. It was getting stronger, just as the light was getting stronger.

Paul's father turned around. He still held the goat in one hand, the knife in the other.

"Get away from here," he hissed.

"I won't let you have him," she said again. And then she stepped around Paul's right side and into his field of view. She was glowing. Golden gleaming light scattered from her hair.

Martin Henninger threw the goat to one side. It hit the ground heavily on one side and lay there, too stunned to move. He held the knife up, and the light from Carol Henninger glinted off it so brightly the blade seemed to turn molten in his hand. His father turned away from the light and the hand that had held the knife was up now in front of his eyes. Martin Henninger's face was twisted in rage, and he was still hissing at his wife, *Get out of here. Get out of here.* But he couldn't look at her. He couldn't even hold his head up now.

She crossed the remaining distance between them and folded him up in her arms. He struggled, but it did him no good. The more he fought, the brighter the rays of light between them became. It filled everything now, and from somewhere in the swirling brilliance, Paul could hear his father shrieking in rage and pain.

The dead men had been slowly closing in on them, but they too were stopped in their tracks. One of the men had stopped right in front of

Paul. A stray ray of light hit the dead man in the face and burned him away to ash within seconds.

There was an explosion of light and wind that hit Paul full on, filling up everything in his world at once. Yet there was no heat, and the light didn't hurt his eyes. There was only white, and the sense that, for a moment, something powerful beyond measure had passed through him and was pulling away, drifting off into nothingness.

When the light faded, and he was able to see again, he stared out across the barren floor of the chamber and saw ashes circling in the air. Rachel was there, standing next to Anderson, and she was coming towards him, closer, closer, her hands on his face.

Chapter 26

After the explosion, Anderson drifted in and out. His son John put an arm around him and asked him if he was all right, could he walk. "Sure," he said, and stumbled on his damaged right leg and fell to one knee. John picked him up again and led him away from the circular chamber. He was stronger than Anderson remembered. "Are those sirens I hear?" he said, and turned and smiled at his son. John was wearing a dusty, sweat-stained patrolman's utility uniform. His silver badge glittered in the starlight. His hair was cut to a regulation one and a half inches. Anderson was about to ask the boy when he'd cut it, how he'd found the time after he died, but he just closed his eyes instead. He had a hazy sense of things happening around him. They were climbing down stairs and over catwalks and through debris. When his vision cleared again John was handing him off to Bobby Cantrell, his face still bearing that frozen, surprised expression it had had on the autopsy table.

You're gonna be okay, Keith. Just take my hand. Come on now.

"Thanks, Bobby," he said.

"Huh?" Rachel said. She was down on the catwalk below him, looking up at him, one hand extended to take his.

Anderson blinked, and when he opened his eyes again, both Bobby and John were gone.

"Are you okay, Keith?" Rachel asked.

"Fine," he said. "I was talking to an old friend."

"Right," she said. "Okay, we're gonna get you an ambulance."

They made their way down to ground level. Rachel carried his right side, the hurt side, but Paul stood at his left and carried his weight. The world grew hazy again as they stepped onto the asphalt drive that led down to where their car was parked. There were bright lights down there, lots of them. Out of the flickering blaze Anderson saw a stream of dead men and women coming his way. He saw every murder victim, every suicide, every traffic fatality he had ever investigated, and they were coming up the hill towards him. Some were speaking his name.

They seemed so urgent, so concerned.

***

Anderson's eyelids fluttered open. Bobby Cantrell was looking down at him, then at the blood pressure cuff around his arm. Anderson was on his back, strapped down. The bed jostled under him, and for a moment he felt like he was on a boat. Bobby was swaying, too, but he seemed used to the movement.

"Why are we moving, Bobby?"

"Excuse me?" It was an EMS technician talking to him.

"Where's Bobby?"

"You lost a lot of blood there, partner. Just hang tight, okay? We're taking you to University Hospital. Is there somebody you want us to call?"

"Where's Bobby?" Anderson said again.

"Sorry, partner, I don't know who that is. How about your wife? You want me to call your wife for you?"

Anderson let his head sink back into the gurney. He stared up at the ceiling and thought, *Ambulance. Holy hell, I'm in an ambulance.*

"Yeah," he said. "Call my wife."

***

The next time he awoke, he was in a hospital bed. Margie was standing in the doorway, talking to John. They looked good together, mother and son. They turned and looked at him and he smiled.

"How are you feeling, Keith?"

"I'm good," he said to Margie. "I'm good." He reached over and took John's hand and squeezed it. He smiled at the boy. "It's been a long time since I've gotten to smile at you. It's nice."

John said something that Keith didn't catch, though that didn't seem important. All that mattered was that the boy was here. He had missed him so.

"Keith?"

Anderson's vision cleared, and John turned old and fat. Chuck Levy was standing where he had just been.

"I'm here, Chuck."

"Goddamn it, Keith. Why didn't you call me? Damn it. That was the stupidest thing I've ever seen you do."

Anderson let himself slip under again. It was so much nicer when the boy was talking.

***

Two weeks later, Anderson, red-eyed and bleary from the pain killers he was taking every two hours or so, sat across the desk from Deputy Chief Allen, waiting for him to finish reading his report on the Morgan Rollins incident. That's what they had started calling it around Headquarters, the

Morgan Rollins incident, though the final report Allen was reading now covered far more than that. It included Paul's in-custody death investigation originating from the train yard chase and the murders at the morgue and subsequent disappearance of the bodies and the final confrontation in which he was injured and Rachel Henninger was rescued from her kidnappers. Anderson had never written fiction in his life. And he took a special pride in the fact that he had never once lied, either directly or by omission, in a police report during his long career, though there had been plenty of opportunities, and even a few under the table, politically-motivated requests for him to do so. But the report Allen was reading now was a lie. From the cover sheet to the recommendation for case closure page, the entire thing was a fiction, a bold-faced lie.

He wanted to cross his legs but couldn't. The cut on his leg hadn't gone over to infection, though that had been close. But it still hurt like a son of a bitch. The ribs, too. Those were still tender, even after two weeks, and he felt a momentary wave of annoyance at not being able to heal as quickly as he once had.

Sitting still posed some unexpected problems. He found it was much easier when he sat down to keep the leg out straight and turn onto one side. Doing so made him look like he was slouching—or at best like one of those slapstick fools in the hemorrhoid commercials. But mostly he thought it just made him look lazy, and more than once he found himself gazing down at his body in that pose, the leg stretched out, the rest of him sunk deep into the chair, and thought of John. John had sat that way on the couch on Sunday mornings, his head still buzzing from the partying he'd done the night before. Anderson had been so furious with him back then, his rage never far from the surface. It had been a constant battle. He'd been thinking a lot about the bitterness of those days lately, and torturing himself with regrets.

He realized he had been staring out the window at nothing in particular, and he forced himself to come back to the present. Allen was still reading, stopping occasionally to go back twenty pages and read something a second or a third time. It all matched up. Anderson had been very careful about that. As far as fiction went, it was tightly plotted. Every lie made sense, every glaring lack of evidence was supported with a reasonable enough explanation.

And so what if it was a lie, he thought. There was no way he could have put what really happened in a police report. Nobody would believe it. They would think he was insane and that would have ended his career. They'd bring in some other detective and he would ask all sorts of questions that couldn't possibly be answered, at least not by anybody who knew the truth, and there was no sense in that. Better to let the dead be with the dead.

"You're still hurting," Allen said.

"Yes." He'd drifted off again, his mind staring off into nothingness outside the window. Anderson told himself to focus.

"Well I appreciate you finishing this up so quickly. You gonna take some time off?"

"I think so," Anderson said. He thought, *And refill my pain meds while I'm at it.* "Margie has some family in upstate New York. Might be nice to go someplace cool."

"You could visit the Baseball Hall of Fame."

Anderson smiled. "I was thinking the same thing."

A quiet filled the space between them. Allen was waiting for Anderson to speak, but Anderson just went right on smiling.

Allen sighed and pushed the report to the edge of the leather blotter on his desk.

"Three hundred and twenty pages," he said. "That's a lot of work in a very short time."

"Yes, sir," Anderson agreed.

"How's Jenny Cantrell?"

"Good. Margie's been with her a lot. You know that, of course. But I think she's good. I've told Margie about what happened, and she's talked to Jenny about it."

Anderson looked across the desk at Allen, an imposing man dressed in a dark charcoal gray suit, and in that moment he saw in the man's worn down eyes all the stress and sorrow and exhaustion that he too had been experiencing the past two weeks. It was almost behind them now. All Allen had to do was sign the report and they'd be done with it—the business end of it anyway. The emotional wake of this thing would go on a long time into the distance, and no amount of falsified reports would ever change that.

"I wish there were more answers than this," Allen said.

"I do, too."

"The Arson guys...they couldn't determine what caused the fire?"

Anderson shifted in his seat and hoped Allen would believe the groan he made was just because of the pain.

"No sir," he said, and waited.

This was the hard part. One of the hard parts, anyway. Anderson had created an Azazel cult and given them the mission of bringing Paul Henninger into the fold to replace his father. The cult was the cornerstone of Anderson's report, the scapegoat for all the unexplained events he described. But making up a cult meant he had to get rid of it, too. And that was where the fire in the circular chamber came in. They had all perished in the flames, and he and Paul Henninger and his wife Rachel had been lucky enough to escape just moments before the flames went out of control. It was the biggest lie in the whole report, but it beat the truth. If Allen could force himself to swallow this one last improbable detail, they could all move on with their lives.

Come on, Anderson muttered to himself. *Sign the damn thing. Just sign it.*

Allen swiveled his chair towards the window and looked out across the city. Anderson followed his gaze. The west side was shimmering in a whitish haze of dust and smog. It was indistinct and blurred, as if it too had died.

"We look like fools on national TV. You know that, right?"

Anderson said nothing.

"First Child Protective Services gets their faces rubbed in shit with those bigamists, and now it's our turn. You know I got a call from the president of ABC? They want to do a special on this for *Twenty-Twenty*."

Just sign it already. Please.

"No thoughts on that, Keith?" Allen said.

"No sir."

Allen nodded thoughtfully. Then he sat up straight and pulled the report in front of him again and turned to the recommendations page. His pen hovered over the bottom right corner, and Anderson realized he had been holding his breath.

Then he signed.

Anderson thought the noise the pen made scratching against the paper was the finest sound he'd ever heard.

***

Several days later he was standing in the parking lot of a Mexican restaurant down the street from Paul and Rachel's new apartment. Rachel and Paul were holding hands. He looked at them, at their youth, and thought he was pretty sure the two of them were going to make it. There was a certain resilience to the young, both physically and emotionally. What the two of them had was strong. He could see it in the way she curled her arm around his, in the way she smiled when he looked at her.

"I hear you haven't been back to work," Anderson said.

"I'm not going back."

Anderson nodded at that. The sun was shining down on them brightly. Oily spots on the road turned to pools of molten light, and for a moment, Anderson's heart quickened.

He had expected Paul to quit. Things would be too hard on him if he stayed. There were no criminal charges against him, and Anderson's report had cleared him of any other violations. There had been talk from a few civil rights attorneys on the east side about suing the Department over the death of the young man in the train yard, but even that had died down in the wake of the official findings. Anderson doubted the talk would ever move beyond the threat and posturing stage.

But even for all that, Paul couldn't stay. You make your reputation within the Department early on, and it stays with you forever. Paul's reputation would be set now, and his name would forever be attached to the Morgan Rollins incident.

"What will you do?" Anderson asked.

Paul looked at Rachel and smiled.

"We're going back to Comal County," she said. "They're hiring English teachers at Smithson Valley High School. I had my first interview on Monday and I got a call back this morning. If my next interview goes as well..."

"That's great," Anderson said. "How about you Paul? What are you gonna do?"

"I have a friend in the Comal County Public Works Office. He says he can get me a job."

"Excellent."

A police car pulled up and a sergeant and a lieutenant got out. Anderson shook hands with both of them as they walked by, two old gray heads like him.

"And, what about...?" He trailed off, not really knowing how to bring up the powers Paul had started to manifest before their encounter at the iron works. Anderson was pretty sure they hadn't gone away. In fact, he was pretty sure they were stronger than ever. He didn't know why that was, but he could feel it. Paul gave off a kind of mental heat. You could feel it when you looked him in the eyes.

Paul just smiled, but not smugly. Not at all. It was wan smile, one that spoke of lessons learned the hard way.

Anderson nodded again.

"Okay," he said. "Okay. It was good knowing you, Paul. You opened up my eyes."

They shook hands. He gave Rachel an awkward hug and she kissed his cheek.

"Thank you," she said.

Anderson turned away and walked off across the parking lot, and as he walked he whistled and thought of John and how lovely it was going to be when he saw him again.

Chapter 27

It was a Tuesday in late August, about two weeks after their breakfast meeting with Anderson, and Paul had been waiting around their new apartment for hours, hoping to hear from Rachel. From the kitchen window, he watched her truck pull into their parking space. He kept watching her as she walked up the stairs. She was carrying a manila folder full of papers and what looked like three or four textbooks. It was six o'clock now.

He turned to the table. He'd bought them a special meal to celebrate. In the center of the small table was a chicken he'd split in half and pan seared and garnished with fresh cilantro. It was steaming on a platter now, surrounded by two different colors of rice, brightly colored mounds of red skinned potatoes and corn and beans. Next to that was a loaf of warm, crusty bread and hot tortillas wrapped in a red and white checkered towel. Bowls of peppers and salsa and guacamole were strategically placed around a galvanized bucket of bottled beer on ice. He had sensed her getting close to home, so it wasn't hard to have dinner ready right as she walked into the apartment, but his powers weren't developed enough to know if she had good news or not. She hadn't called, and he wasn't sure what that meant.

She stepped inside, the sun behind her, shadowing her face.

"Well?" he said.

She came closer, and as the shadows left her face, he saw that she was smiling. She suddenly looked completely different, healthier than she had in weeks. He hadn't realized how worn she'd been, how tired. Now there was a golden radiance to her, like a tan, but more than that.

"You're looking at Smithson Valley High School's newest Eleventh Grade English teacher."

"All right!" He grabbed her and squeezed so tightly she gasped before breaking out in giggles.

"Paul, put me down."

He dropped her to her feet, but kept his arms wrapped around her. "I'm proud of you," he said.

"You better be." She gave him a peck on the lips and slid by him. She looked at the table, and her eyes went wide with delight. "Is that dinner? Since when do you know how to cook?"

He shrugged, still smiling.

She looked at the table he'd set. The smell of the bread had filled up the small apartment. He watched, satisfied with himself, as she closed her eyes and took a deep whiff. "A girl could get used to this," she said.

"When do you start?"

"Monday."

"Monday? Rachel, so soon?"

"Yeah, I know, right. I haven't even seen my classroom yet." She paused there, turned away from the table and the smell of the bread. Hesitantly, she said, "And I guess we can start thinking about that house?" Her inflection at the end made it a question.

Paul had gone with her to the school the week before, and they had seen a little place with some land not far from the school. There had been a tax foreclosure notice on it, and with the forty thousand dollars from the sale of his parents' farm that Paul had managed to stash in an IRA account, they could probably get it if they acted quickly.

"I think the timing might be right," he said.

Now she was really glowing.

She said, "But Paul, would you really want to have that much land again? I wouldn't know the first thing about how to work it."

"I can show you."

She put her manila folder down next to her dinner plate and eased into his arms, her hands on his chest.

"As long as you promise me something," she said.

"Like what?"

"Absolutely no goats."

And he laughed.

"No goats," he said.

***

From the street, the little four bedroom ranch house looked to be in pretty good shape. Living in it, though, was another story, and restoring it quickly became a labor of love for him. Paul worked during the day with his old high school buddy Steve Sullivan in the Comal County Public Works Office, but in the afternoons he'd come home and work on the roof and mend fences and clear cedar and burn the cuttings in sandy pits along the road that led down to their pasture. He hauled endless loads of rocks out of the fields and got the barn back into working order.

Sometimes, when she was done grading and the light was fading in the east, Rachel would come out to the back porch with a glass of iced tea. He would trudge in from whatever project he was working on, dust falling off him with every step, his t-shirt browned with sweat and dirt, and they would drink tea and watch the sun set.

And sometimes, after he'd showered and changed, they'd head back out to the patio and watch the fireflies skitter over the tops of the knee-high cheatgrass and tell each other about their day. Those were the evenings Paul liked best.

***

That April, an attorney with the City of San Antonio's Legal Advisor's Office called him and told him that the city had settled out of court with the family of Curtis Lowe III, the black kid from the train yard. As far as the City was concerned, the matter was now closed. Paul asked him if the family was going to try to come after him individually, and the attorney told him no, the matter was closed. Paul thanked him and hung up. He was relieved down to his toes. It surprised him, the depth of his relief. The final loose end of the whole mess was done, and even as he stood there staring at the phone on the counter, he could feel his worries leaving him.

***

Rachel taught summer school that year, and one day she came home with news that Randy Peyser, one of the senior assistant football coaches at the high school, had just been offered a head coach's spot at a school up in Austin. Brent Cobb, Paul's old coach, dropped a few hints that he was in the market for a new defensive coordinator. He hoped Paul was interested.

During his interview with Coach Cobb and Principal Mark Hardesty, the subject of his leaving the SAPD after working there less than a year had come up. Paul was pretty sure it would.

"Being a cop on the east side of San Antonio is sort of like being a zoo keeper," he told them. "There are shootings and fights and more drugs than you can imagine. It's no place to work if you're thinking of starting a family."

"You and Rachel are thinking of having a baby?" Hardesty asked, his eyes opening wide with delight. He had a full head of gray hair, but his eyebrows were solid black and bushy, like two bloated caterpillars about to tumble off his forehead.

"We've talked about it, yes sir."

"That's great," Hardesty said. The caterpillars teetered on the edge of falling.

Paul forced himself not to smile.

"Yes sir, I think so, too."

"I think the world of Rachel," he said. "Sharp as a tack, that one."

Paul nodded.

Hardesty turned to Cobb and a silent question passed from principal to head coach. *Well, what do you think?*

"I knew he was right for this even before he graduated," Cobb said. He gave Paul a wink.

"Outstanding," Hardesty said. "I couldn't agree more." He turned to Paul. "You understand, you'll need to complete a battery of teacher certification courses. And there is a time limit on those. You'll be in for some hard work."

"I can do that, sir."

"Call me Mark, please. This'll have to go before the board, of course. I don't want to promise ice cream before we milk the cow, but from where I'm sitting, I think we've found our first choice. There is one other thing though, Paul. May I call you Paul?" Paul nodded. "Good. There is one other thing, Paul. We are looking for a new Spanish teacher as well. It might help your chances with the board if you were fluent in Spanish. How about it, can you speak Spanish?"

Paul smiled. "*Sí, se puedo,*" he said.

***

Paul Jr. was born the next year, nine pounds, three ounces. Every checkup, the doctor would whistle and tell them he was off the charts for height and weight. He was going to be huge, just like his daddy. Rachel called him her little linebacker.

When Paul worked in the yard, Paul Jr. followed him everywhere, no shirt, his diaper sagging down to his thighs in the back. Sometimes Paul would sit on a chair in the yard and Paul Jr. would stand in front of him and watch in wide-eyed wonder as the Barber fifty cent piece flashed back and forth across the back of his daddy's hand. Then the coin would disappear, and Paul Jr. would gasp. And when Paul pulled it from behind the boy's ear, Rachel could hear him giggling all the way up at the porch

Those were Rachel's favorite evenings.

***

Three years later, Coach Cobb announced his retirement, and the head coaching spot fell to Paul. His first year, they made it all the way to the State quarter finals before losing to Odessa-Permian High School. Paul was thirty years old, a husband, a father, happier than he had ever been in his life.

***

On a cool evening in May, Paul and four year old Paul Jr. were in the backyard, looking out over a wide expanse of cedar forest that stretched off all the way to the horizon. Paul liked to stand here in the evenings and watch the cloud shadows pass over the land. There were six heifers down in the lower pasture now, and Paul could see them milling around near the dirt road that wound through the bottom ten acres of the property. A car pulled into the driveway and Paul Jr. jumped up and ran that way.

"Paul!" he said, running after the boy. "Stop. Wait!" He caught up with him and took him by the hand. "You don't ever run into the driveway when someone's pulling up," he said.

"Okay," the boy said. "Who is it, Daddy?"

Paul recognized the man behind the wheel right away. It was Keith Anderson. He had more gray hair and more paunch and he was even paler than he used to be. But he still wore his Mr. Rogers sweater over a white polo shirt and khaki slacks, and he still had the look of one who is forever overworked. Anderson closed his car door and waved at Paul. Paul caught a glint of sunlight off the silver badge on his belt and thought, *Still a detective, eh? Couldn't give it up.*

Anderson crossed to the other side of the car, still walking with a faint limp, and opened the door for a woman who might have been Anderson's age, or who might have been even older. It was hard to tell. She was skinny in a way that didn't seem quite healthy. She might have been pretty once. She wasn't now. Her eyes were rimmed with red and her skin had a washed out, almost gray pallor. To Paul, she looked bony and frail before her time, and there was an uneasy, dazed look about her that spoke of hard grief. Instinctively, Paul reached out to her mind with his, and found that he was right. He touched a grief so deep it took his breath away. Even before Anderson introduced them, he knew this was Jenny Cantrell.

"Why don't you take Mr. Anderson inside to see Momma," Paul said to the boy. "Mrs. Cantrell and I'll be in directly. Go on now."

"Okay, Daddy," Paul Jr. said. He turned to Anderson. "Come on, Mister." And then the boy was off to the house, Anderson chuckling under his breath at the boy's unbridled exuberance.

When Anderson and Paul Jr. were inside, Paul turned his attention on Jenny Cantrell. She'd been crying; he saw that now. Paul reached into her mind again and sensed how numb to the world she really was. It was like looking into a November sky and seeing nothing but a depthless gray.

"Why don't we take a walk," he said.

He went around the back of the house and out to the spot where he liked to stand and watch the cloud shadows pass over the land, and she followed him without a word.

***

"Hello?"

Anderson stood in the doorway and waited. The boy had almost flown into the house. He was out of sight now, but Anderson could hear him calling into the depths of the house for his mother.

He was standing in a comfortable sitting room lined with bookshelves. He scanned the titles for a moment then stopped. Nothing looked familiar, no Dan Brown or Clive Cussler. Sunlight filled the room through the windows on the wall to his right. There was a small desk sitting in a patch of sunlight off to one side, and on that were a laptop computer and a ceramic mug stuffed with pens that read *World's Greatest Teacher* and a framed photograph of Paul and Rachel and Paul Jr. smiling together in front of some kind of fountain. The room had a comfortable feel to it, a happy place, and that made him glad for Paul.

"Keith?"

Anderson looked up from the picture. He realized he had been lost in thought. Rachel was standing in the opposite doorway, Paul Jr. by her side.

"That's the man, Momma," he said.

"Thank you, baby," she said.

She ruffled the boy's shaggy brown hair and crossed the room to Anderson. There was an awkward moment where he wasn't sure if they were about to hug or shake hands, and in the end they came together for quick hug and then stepped back.

"You have a lovely home," he said. "A lot of books."

"Thank you," she said.

Motherhood had been good to her. Her figure had filled out a little, so that she didn't look as skinny as she had when he first met her, and there was a softness about her face that he liked. She had been cute before. She was beautiful now, more of a mature woman than just a girl.

"What are you doing here?" she asked.

He pointed out the window behind him with his thumb. Rachel stepped up next to him and they stood shoulder to shoulder, looking out across the yard. They could see Paul and Jenny Cantrell talking, facing one another, their heads bent together. He was holding her hands in his, and he was saying something to her.

"That's Jenny Cantrell," he said. "She's the widow of my friend Bobby Cantrell who..." The rest of the sentence clotted in his throat and he found he couldn't speak it.

She looked at him quizzically for a moment before it sank in. "Oh," she said. "Oh, I'm sorry, Keith. Is she...?"

"Not doing too hot, I'm afraid. These last few years, it's like she's just been going through the motions of life. Margie and I, we've been trying to help her, but she just keeps getting worse. Today the City dedicated a park to Bobby off of Evers Rd. She did okay during the ceremony, but afterwards, in the car, well...it wasn't good. She's hurting." He looked across the yard at the two figures standing there, framed in a window of oak trees. They still hadn't moved. "Anyway," he went on, "we were out this way, and I got to thinking about Paul. I remember how he helped me. I was wondering if maybe...well, you know."

She nodded. They both looked out the window. Anderson saw Paul reach into his pocket and then put something in Jenny's hands. Paul closed her fingers around whatever it was. Suddenly, light lanced out through Jenny's fingers. Anderson squinted, not sure what he had just seen. Maybe a trick of the light, the way sunlight dapples on water?

Jenny looked up into Paul's face then, and her mouth fell open. Even from across the yard, Anderson could see her expression change. There was light in her eyes, and finally, something other than grief. Was that relief he was seeing?

He wasn't sure.

***

Paul and Rachel and Paul Jr. stood at the head of the driveway and watched as Anderson helped Jenny Cantrell into the passenger seat of his car. Though a trace of the dazed uneasiness remained in her eyes, her face was glowing. Anderson closed her car door then went to his side, waved at them, and then drove away.

"What did you say to her?" Rachel asked. "She looks a lot better than when she came here."

"Yeah, I hope so."

"You gave her your Barber fifty cent piece." It wasn't a question. It wasn't an indictment either.

"Yes."

He had his arm around her waist. She moved it and turned and faced him. "Paul, are you okay? You look...I don't know. What happened over there?"

Paul told her that they'd talked about her husband. His body was never found. She had buried an empty coffin, thinking that that would be a hole deep enough for her grief. Anderson had known even then that it wouldn't be. An empty coffin had no meaning, he had told her. It was bottomless. You could never fill it. All that grief had to go someplace, somebody had to carry it. She had never wanted to believe that was true, but she had reached a point of absolute exhaustion. She had said she was too full of grief. That she had denied the truth of it long enough, and now that grief was crushing her.

"She told you all that?"

"Some of it," Paul said. "Some I sort of inferred."

"Inferred?"

"It was in her mind."

Rachel searched his eyes. She touched his cheek. "What did you tell her, Paul?"

"I told her that grief was a type of energy. Like all energy, it is what it is. It can't be created or destroyed, but it can be transferred."

Rachel shook her head.

"You know, after all these years, I still don't understand that kind of talk. I never would have pegged you for a mystic, Paul. Is your coin supposed to help her transfer that grief?"

"For her, the coin is just a prop," he said. "Something to help her focus. I guess you'd call it a placebo. For me, it had real value. Emotional weight. Giving it to her was my way of transferring positive energy to her."

"I'm confused. You said grief can't be created or destroyed. If you gave her your positive energy, what happened to her grief? Did it go someplace else?"

"She still has the memory of it," he said.

"But not the pain?"

"But not the pain."

Paul's powers were still growing, but he was a long ways from being able to explain them to Rachel. He had thought the call from the City's Legal Advisor's Office four years earlier was the end of the destruction his father had wrought upon their lives. He knew that wasn't the case now. There was still a lot of work to be done.

But none of that mattered right now. What mattered right now was that Jenny Cantrell's grief was where it belonged.

It had come home.

THE END

"Apocalyptic in the truest sense of the word, Jon Michael Kelley's *Seraphim* is a stunning thriller with the very fate of the world at stake. Beautifully written, with prose as lush as it is chilling, Kelley is part poet, part prophet, but a true master of fear, through and through. This is top notch stuff of highest caliber!"

—Joe McKinney, Bram Stoker Award-winning author of *Flesh Eaters* and *Inheritance*

SERAPHIM

A Novel by Jon Michael Kelley

Duncan McNeil is staring mistrustfully at a photograph of his daughter, Amy. She appears to be at or near her present age of ten, but the studio's dated stamp on the back indicates that the photo was taken nearly a year before her birth. More alarming, however, is the beautiful woman standing beside Amy, a woman with whom he had an affair in the periphery of his new marriage, during the time when Amy was conceived. And the fact that this photograph has been in his wife's possession for more than a decade is perhaps the most disturbing element of all.

Duncan's wife Rachel doesn't know about his affair with this woman, but he will soon tell her. And upon that revelation they will begin a journey that will take them clear across the continent, from California to Massachusetts, then ultimately into the boundless, uncharted territory of the human collective. There, a devil is waiting; the penultimate personification of evil. And he goes by the name of Mr. Gamble.

Trade Paperback | 334 pages | $16.95 | ISBN: 978-0615672953

Kindle eBook | $4.99 | ASIN: B008MU4O5C

Other books from Evil Jester Press

Help! Wanted: Tales of On-the-Job Terror
Edited by Peter Giglio

Featuring stories by Stephen Volk, Joe McKinney, Zak Jarvis, Lisa Morton, Jeff
Strand, Vince A. Liaguno, Gary Brandner, Amy Wallace, Mark Allan Gunnells,
Eric Shapiro, and many more!

Trade Paperback | 272 pages | $14.95 | ISBN: 978-0615536354
Kindle eBook | $4.99 | ASIN: B005Q1BMDM

The Quarry
Mark Allan Gunnells

Trade Paperback | 226 pages | $13.95 | ISBN: 978-0615598437
Kindle eBook | $4.99 | ASIN: B0073PMCY2

Attic Toys
Edited by Jeremy C. Shipp

Featuring stories by Jeff Strand, Joe McKinney, Cate Gardner, Lisa Morton, Piers
Anthony, Gary McMahon, Jeremy C. Shipp, Aric Sundquist, Kate Jonez, Amelia
Mangan, Phil Hickes, Nancy Rosenberg England, and many more!

Trade Paperback | 174 pages | $9.95 | ISBN: 978-0615614144
Kindle eBook | $3.99 | ASIN: B007ILCVQ0

Cameron's Closet: 25th Anniversary Edition
Gary Brandner
Introduction by Joe McKinney

Trade Paperback | 252 pages | $13.95 | ISBN: 978-0615641416
Kindle eBook | $3.99 | ASIN: B008190F4I

The Call of Lovecraft
Edited by Gregory L. Norris

Featuring stories by Ramsey Campbell, William Meikle, John F.D. Taff, Jacqueline
Seewald, R.E. Dent, Karen Dent, Scott Goudsward, and many more!

Trade Paperback | 346 pages | $15.95 | ISBN: 978-0615643397
Kindle eBook | $4.99 | ASIN: B00889O8DK

Evil Jester Digest Volume One
Edited by Peter Giglio

Featuring stories by Rick Hautala, Gary Brandner, David Dunwoody, Tracy L. Carbone, Aric Sundquist, and many more!

Trade Paperback | 162 pages | $9.95 | ISBN: 978-0615613246
Kindle eBook | $3.99 | ASIN: B007HPGA00

Short of a Picnic
A collection by Eric Shapiro

Trade Paperback | 148 pages | $9.95 | ISBN: 978-0615614595
Kindle eBook | $2.99 | ASIN: B007H33MDU

The Love of the Dead
Craig Saunders

Trade Paperback | 262 pages | $14.95 | ISBN: 978-0615668109
Kindle eBook | $4.29 | ASIN: B008IWWX48

The Fierce and Unforgiving Muse
Twenty-six Tales from the Terrifying Mind of Gregory L. Norris

Trade Paperback | 408 pages | $19.95 | ISBN: 978-0615614137
Kindle eBook | $4.99 | ASIN: B007IISM0W

Moondeath
Rick Hautala
Introduction by Christopher Golden
Cover art by Glenn Chadbourne

Trade Paperback | 314 pages | $17.95 | ISBN: 978-0615581026
Kindle eBook | $3.99 | ASIN: B006XZZOSE

Balance
A zombie novella by Peter Giglio

Trade Paperback | 138 pages | $9.95 | ISBN: 978-0615584287
eBook through Museitup Publishing | All formats | $3.50

Coming Soon...

Carnival of the Damned, edited by Henry Snider & David C. Hayes
Tears of No Return by David Bernstein
Windwalkers by R. Michael Burns
High Stakes, edited by Gabrielle Faust
The Summer of Winters by Mark Allan Gunnells
The Oblivion Room: Stories of Violation by Christopher Conlon
Candy House by Kate Jonez
The Corpse Also Rises by Lisa Olick
Evil Jester Digest Volume Two, edited by Peter Giglio
Deep Cuts, edited by Angel Leigh McCoy, E.S. Magill,
and Chris Marrs

Evil Jester Press

CPSIA information can be obtained at www.ICGtesting.com
Printed in the USA
BVOW08s1242181015

422988BV00003B/196/P

9 780615 690896